MUSES OF ROMA

Codex Antonius | Book I

Rob Steiner

Quarkfolio Books

Copyright © 2013 by Rob Steiner.

All rights reserved.

This book is a work of fiction. Names, characters, places and incidents are either products of the author's imagination or used fictitiously. Any resemblance to actual events, locales, or persons, living or dead is entirely coincidental. No part of this publication can be reproduced or transmitted in any form or by any means, electronic or mechanical, without permission in writing from Rob Steiner.

December 2013. Published by Quarkfolio Books.

Cover by 100covers.com.

For Sarah and Amelia, always.

PROLOGUE

Third year of the reign of Imperator Octavian Caesar Augustus

Marcus Antonius sat atop his horse outside Roma watching the smoke rise into the twilight sky above the Forum and the docks along the Tiber. Musket fire echoed throughout the city; fire engulfed the Senate House and the Temple of Jupiter Optimus Maximus on the Capitoline Hill. His new senses brought him the screams of citizens as his legions entered the city. The equestrian villas on the Aventine Hill lay in blackened ruins, pillaged by his men for every valuable they contained—artwork, gold, jewels, slaves.

The gods gave him the ability to take it *all* in, to sear it into his memory. To be sure, he knew he was allowing a blasphemy on the Eternal City. But that was the old order. Antonius would bring a new order, and he would rebuild Roma.

A rider charged out the Porta Capena less than a half-mile away, swerving around the crush of refugees exiting the gate. When he reached Antonius, he pulled in his reigns and reported to General Lucius at Antonius's side.

"We have him, sir," the rider said, breathless. "We captured him in his residence. He offered no resistance."

Lucius sighed, then looked to Antonius with a smile. "It's over, my lord."

"Very good," Antonius said, staring at Roma. "I want to enter my city now. I want to see Octavian."

Lucius hesitated. "My lord, we may have Octavian, but the city is far from secure. Octavian's men may still hide in pockets throughout Roma. We could have him brought out."

"Lucius, old friend," Antonius said, "you forget who I am now." He turned to Lucius. "The gods have made me their Vessel. They have great plans for me and for Roma. They will not allow any harm to come to me."

Lucius nodded slowly. "Of course, my lord."

Antonius spurred his horse forward before Lucius could order his men to follow. The mounted protective cohort rushed up to Antonius and surrounded him, each with one hand on his reins and the other on the stock of his musket holstered on the side of his horse.

Refugees flooded the Via Appia on the city's southeast corner. Some pulled carts while most carried nothing but their children and a sack thrown over their shoulders. Women, children, and the elderly—the younger men had mounted a futile defense of Roma's walls during the attack—gave him hollow stares, each one too exhausted to cry out to him. Such a crowd suggested Antonius's surprise attack had worked better than even he imagined.

Not my *plans*, he thought humbly. *This is the work of the gods.*

While Antonius's cohort eyed the refugees, Antonius looked on them with pity. He could not explain to them now why they should stay, that they should watch him make Roma greater than any king or dictator could.

Especially that whelp Octavian. *Excuse me*, he thought, *they call him* Augustus *now*. He glanced at the rubble of the great Roman walls blasted to gravel by his cannons. *I wonder how august they think their tyrant is now?*

The gods whispered to him, calmed his thoughts, and told him to focus on the tasks ahead. The citizens who fled today would return once they saw the first fruits of his plans, how he rebuilt the city with methods and materials with which the brilliant architects of Roma or Greece never dreamed. He would build monuments to shame the Great Pyramids of Egypt. The gods would show him how to create indestructible roads and magical carts able to run by themselves. And one day, when humanity was worthy, machines that flew faster than an eagle would take Romans to the firmament above, where they could bow before the gods themselves.

These were the plans the gods showed him every day since they blessed him in that crumbling Egyptian temple ten years ago.

Antonius and his cohort passed through the Porta Capena. The refugees still poured from the city, most too shocked to give him more than a glance. The further Antonius rode into Roma, however, the fewer refugees he saw. The areas nearer the gates were packed with plebian tenements that Antonius's legions looted first. Bodies lay crumpled on the ground, some shot, but most run through with the *gladius* Antonius's men still insisted on carrying. Antonius smiled at his men's preference for traditional tools over a superior weapon like the musket. They even insisted on wearing their armor, though the enemy had barely touched them since they started using the cannons and muskets.

On his left, the merchant class shops and tenements on the Aventine Hill were quiet. But on his right, the Caelian Hill was awash in screams, musket fire, and the crackle of burning buildings. Many of the city's richest patricians had villas on the Caelian. Antonius felt no mercy for the patrician nobles who lived there, for most had denounced him in the Forum and Senate, questioning his "moral character" for living in Alexandria with Cleopatra. Culling Roma's patrician class would be a bloody task, but a necessity for Antonius to establish his new order. By the time Antonius's men were through with them, the Caelian would look on the Suburba's slums with envy.

Six city defenders burst from an alley in front of Antonius. Three held swords, and all bore wounds and blood on their tunics, limbs, and faces. They stared at Antonius and his cohort, stunned to see him. Antonius's cohort was prepared. They raised their muskets as one and fired at the six men. Two defender heads exploded. Two more defenders took shots to the chests and fell to the cobblestones, while the other two escaped harm. With nothing left to lose, the two men screamed defiance and jumped toward Antonius.

Having fired their single shots, the cohort dropped their muskets to reach for their swords. But they would not intercept the enraged men before they reached Antonius. Antonius pulled his sword, ready to meet the two defenders, his heart quickening. He would *finally* join the battle. The gods could not hold him back now.

Shots rang out from the alley, and the two defenders fell before they could reach Antonius. Seven of Antonius's men emerged from the alley, looked at the fallen defenders, then up at him.

Antonius glared at the squad's centurion. "Well done, Servius Minicius."

Antonius knew every man's name in his legions. He met them all during the year-long march to Roma. His memory was another ability that made his men believe Antonius himself was a god.

Minicius stepped forward and bowed his head. "Thank you, sir. Sorry they surprised you, sir."

Antonius frowned a moment longer, then sighed and re-sheathed his sword. "Not your fault. Although you did deny me the chance to bloody my sword. Haven't had to pull it since Actium. Damned shame."

Minicius grinned. "My apologies, sir."

"Carry on." Antonius spurred his horse forward. "I expect you to clear the city of this sort by nightfall tomorrow."

"Yes, sir," Minicius called out.

As Antonius advanced further into the city, the scent of blood and smoke increased. He passed the Circus Maximus on his left; its large walls were pockmarked with musket shots. Antonius marveled at the marble columns and arches Octavian had recently installed along the walls of the huge rectangular racetrack. It had been years since Antonius last rode through Roma, and the new construction on the Circus was inspiring.

But the Circus was no more than a cheap bauble compared to what the gods had planned for Roma.

Several companies of Greek draftees formed battle lines outside the Circus, their muskets on their shoulders. When the Roman commander saw Antonius, he rushed over and saluted. "My lord, we weren't expecting you so—"

"What is happening here, Leget Durmius? I assume there are no chariot races today?"

"Hah, no, my lord. We got some defenders holed up in there. They barricaded the entrances, but they won't hold once we storm them. We're about to start if you want to watch, my lord."

"I have pressing matters with the city's former rulers," Antonius said. "I have every confidence you will accomplish your task, Leget."

Durmius saluted again as Antonius rode on.

Octavian lived in a modest two-story villa on the Palatine Hill overlooking the Circus Maximus. New walls surrounded the home. Antonius chuckled when he noticed a partially constructed corridor connecting the villa to the Circus Maximus. *The great Augustus is too much like a god to walk among the citizens of Roma, eh?* Antonius could not wait to show Octavian what real gods could do.

When Antonius approached Octavian's open gates, he spurred his horse into a trot and charged into the courtyard, surprising the centurions and soldiers who stood about inside. He stepped down from his saddle, and a centurion—Numerius Albius—ran over and saluted.

"My lord, we weren't expecting—"

"I know. Is he here?"

"Yes, my lord. He's in the atrium with his wife and daughter. Some Senators and the Pontifex Maximus are with them."

"Good," Antonius said, striding past the centurion.

He entered the house through the remains of the double wooden doors, which had been shot up and then battered with a ram. In the entryway, several wax busts of Octavian's ancestors stared at Antonius. He stopped at the last bust, Gaius Julius Caesar remarkably well rendered. It was the Caesar that Antonius remembered in Gaul, when he had watched the Gallic king Vercingetorix throw down his axe in surrender at Caesar's feet. Forty-nine years old, yet youthful, full of confidence and ready to conquer Roma.

Things didn't turn out like you expected, did they, you old dog? It could have been you in my place. Fortunate for me the gods and your "friend" Brutus felt otherwise.

Antonius made his way through the entryway and into the villa's atrium. Six soldiers stood nearby, and they snapped to attention when Antonius entered the room. Antonius ignored them, focused instead on the seven figures huddled on benches in front of the *impluvium* pool at the atrium's center. Ruddy sunlight fell through the open atrium, illuminating the figures with a bloody tint. Antonius had no trouble recognizing them.

Octavian stood up, his purple toga arranged precisely. Octavian's wife Livia and his fifteen-year-old daughter Julia sat behind him. Three of Octavian's most loyal Senators sat on either side of him. The Pontifex Maximus sat on a bench by himself, his black robes torn. The Pontifex whirled around and stared at Antonius with panicked eyes. A large bruise had spread across his mostly bald head, and his long gray beard hung in strings.

Antonius turned his gaze back to Octavian. The boy—Antonius would always consider Octavian a boy despite his forty-one years—stared at Antonius with the same arrogance he had the whole time they shared power as Triumvirs four years ago. Antonius glanced at the painted walls.

"I love the frescoes," Antonius said. "Perhaps I will make this house my own." He strolled past the walls, hands behind his back.

He stopped before a painting of Gaius Julius Caesar standing at the right hand of Jupiter. "I hear they call you Augustus now, 'son of a god.'"

"It is true," Octavian said, voice steady. "The Senate declared Caesar divine. Caesar adopted me as his son, therefore I am also divine."

"'Divine.'" Antonius grunted. "You know nothing of the divine."

"I suppose you do. How else could you create these wondrous weapons? Wooden sticks that spit fire, smoke, and metal. Iron tubes that destroy stone walls. What did your Egyptian whore's priests teach you?"

Antonius smiled. "*They* did not teach me anything. They showed me a temple where I found...well, it's a long story. Suffice it to say the gods have blessed me with knowledge you cannot imagine. These weapons, they are only the beginning. I will remake Roma. Conquering the known world is nothing. I will conquer lands no Roman has ever seen. I will bring Roma's light to every barbarian that toils and dies in meaningless darkness."

Octavian laughed. "Come now, Marcus, this is me. The Marcus Antonius I knew was happiest carousing in the whorehouses and drinking with his soldiers until he passed out. That man was no philosopher. He was no ruler. Now here you are claiming the divine legacy of Caesar? You will never be a Caesar. We both know it."

Antonius rushed forward, grabbed Octavian's throat, and slammed him against a wood pillar. The boy's eyes bulged at the move's speed and violence.

"You're right," Antonius whispered into Octavian's ear, "I will never be a Caesar. I will be so much *more*."

Antonius clenched his fist, crushing Octavian's throat and the vertebrae in his neck. He let Octavian fall to the floor. Roma's former ruler gasped for air, face as purple as his toga. Then his struggles stopped and he stared with lifeless eyes up at the red sky through the open atrium.

Livia and Julia cried out and went to Octavian, wailing over his body. Antonius ignored them and then motioned to the centurion nearby.

"Your squad can have the women for your entertainment," Antonius said, "but only after you do a few things first."

When he told the centurion his task, the three Senators sobbed in outrage and fear. The centurion nodded grimly, gave Livia and

Julia an appraising glance, then told his men to take the Senators outside.

Antonius turned to the Pontifex Maximus. The portly old man stared at Antonius with wide eyes and a gray face. Antonius put his hands on the quivering Pontifex's head and drew him close. "I am willing to overlook your support for Octavian. You were in a delicate position. You had no choice but to give his illegitimate rule the gods' blessing—"

"You're right, my lord," the man cried. "I had no choice. He would have killed my family if I had not gone along with—"

Antonius gave the man's head a gentle squeeze. He gasped, and his lips quivered.

"Do not interrupt me again."

The Pontifex nodded. Antonius smelled urine pooling around the man's feet.

"Now then. You had no choice but to give Octavian's illegitimacy your blessing. You could not have known it was wrong because the gods have never talked to you."

The Pontifex stared at him. "I am the Pontifex Maxi—"

"I know what you are. I know you *think* you heard the gods and could decipher their will by inspecting dog entrails. But you never really did, did you?"

The Pontifex's mouth opened and closed.

"It's all right," Antonius said soothingly. He watched two *flamens* dressed as Egyptian priests enter the room. One held a bronze bowl and the other a large bronze knife.

He looked back to the Pontifex. "Soon you will hear the true gods."

Antonius stood on the balcony on the second floor of Octavian's house, the racing fields of the Circus Maximus spread before him. Over three hundred crosses lined the field in neat rows, each holding the body of a Senator, patrician, or state official who had vocally opposed him. Antonius's spies in Roma had spent years keeping track of those who spread vicious lies about him. Those people now hung on crosses below and screamed for the mercy of a single spear thrust to the heart. He would not give them such mercy. The crows would take them first.

The Pontifex Maximus stood beside him, regarding the Circus in the morning light. Antonius looked at the man, noticed the gods had remade him. The sniveling coward he'd been three days ago was gone. The Pontifex looked on the Circus with the eyes of someone who *knew* why Antonius had ordered this.

The Pontifex turned to Antonius. "Brother," he said, "this world is ours."

Antonius smiled. "Why stop at this world?"

1,000 YEARS LATER

Chapter One

Marcia Licinius Ocella pulled the boy through the teeming Forum Romanum. She squeezed through the crowds and merchants as she scanned those same crowds for the men chasing them.

She ducked beneath a red and gold banner hanging from a street lamp. It proclaimed the coming millennial celebrations for the Antonii Ascension. In a month, Roma would be filled with dignitaries and citizens from Terra and every other Republic world. Even kings, consuls, and princes from many Lost Worlds and the Zhonguo Sphere would attend.

All to celebrate a lie.

"You are hurting my arm," the boy said.

Ocella stopped and looked at him. She'd been squeezing him tight enough to leave red marks on his bare forearm. She eased her grip but did not let go.

"Sorry. You have to keep up with me." Ocella scanned the crowds behind them again.

"I am trying," he said, moving closer to her side.

The boy wore a common sleeveless shirt. Though the day was hot and humid, he wore the shirt's cowl over his head, a trend among plebian children. Ocella was glad Roman fashion allowed for a way to hide the boy's face.

"How much further?" he asked.

"It's on the Aventine. A ways yet."

"How far is the Aventine?"

"We're in the Forum, it's just—"

She glanced down at him. He had spent his life in a single house on a single hill, so he would not know the streets and landmarks most normal Romans knew from birth. She would have to be patient with him. The boy was not a normal Roman.

"We'll be there soon," she finished.

Her Umbra training made her hyper-aware of how to spot a tail, but the Forum crowds strained even her skills. Plainclothes agents needed minimal competence to hide among this human crush. She gave up on mentally recording every face, and concentrated on just getting through the Forum without losing the boy. They would never make it out if she kept running into merchant stalls or tripping over garbage on the ground.

Once they emerged from the Forum, they had to contend with crossing the Appian Highway. Ground carts zipped by at dangerous speeds on the city's main north-south highway, and there were no crosswalks or pedestrian bridges nearby. Ocella glanced up the street, saw a bus idling a dozen paces away.

When she turned to the boy, a glint caught her eye. Two lictors approached from behind, their silver helmets shining in the setting sun.

"Come on." She grabbed the boy's arm and pulled him toward the bus. She tried to act as if she was late for the bus rather than fleeing the lictors. She didn't know if the lictors were walking their beat or looking for her. She didn't want to take the chance.

Ocella pushed the boy on to the bus, deposited her sesterces in the coin box, and moved the boy to the back. They sat in an empty seat, and she glanced outside at the lictors. They continued to walk past the bus, locked in conversation.

They may not want to scare us, she thought. *They've already commed in a report and a Praetorian squad is waiting at the next stop—*

She took a deep breath. Her heart had been racing for the last hour. She had to calm down. *Remember your training,* she thought. *Panic kills.*

"Is it much farther, nanny?" the boy asked. "I'm hungry." He had the expression of any twelve-year-old boy running errands with his caretaker. Bored and hungry.

He raised an eyebrow, and she almost laughed. She was the experienced Umbra Ancile, yet he did a better job maintaining their cover than her nervous actions thus far. Nearby passengers read paper copies of the *Daily Acts* or stared out the windows. The bus was not as crowded as the Forum, but anyone could be a Praetorian. She had to play the part: an ethnically Indian nanny slave taking her Roman *dominar's* child on an outing.

"Not far, Lucius," she said with an affectionate smile. "I'm sure your Uncle Titus will have a large dinner ready for us when we get there."

"You think he'll have that *garum* from Pompeii he always talks about? I want to try it."

"He said he would. Your Uncle Titus doesn't make idle promises."

They bantered for the ten minutes it took to reach their stop on the Aventine. Partly to throw off eavesdroppers, but mostly to calm their own nerves. While the boy's speech tended to slip into a noble accent at times, he impressed Ocella with his knowledge of plebeian slang.

On the Aventine Hill, they exited the bus and walked through a run-down neighborhood. All apartment tenements and homes on the Aventine were no more than four stories. The Collegia Pontificis forbade any Roman building to rise above the Temple of Jupiter Optimus Maximus on the Capitoline. Trash heaped in alleys and alcoves. Obscene graffiti on the walls depicted the local aediles and quaestors having sex with various farm animals. No graffiti showed Senators, the Collegia Pontificis, or the Consular family. No one would dare.

Ocella found the house on a quiet street in the Aventine's southeast corner. She tapped on the door politely with her foot, waited a few seconds, then tapped again.

"Maybe he is not home," the boy said.

"He's here. He better be..."

She raised her knuckles to rap on the door, but then it opened. The grizzled face of Numerius Aurelius Scaurus peered at her from the entry's shadows.

"You weren't followed?"

"Doubtful."

He sighed, then noticed the boy standing behind her. His eyes widened.

"Blessed Juno, you got him out. Get in before someone sees you. Hurry!"

Ocella and the boy entered the house. Scaurus slammed the door and barred it. He punched in a code on the pad beside the door, and it emitted a chirp as more locks slid into place.

Like most Roman patricians, Scaurus displayed wax busts on the shelves next to the door. Ocella was surprised to see only two: Gaius Julius Caesar and Marcus Tullius Cicero. As far as Ocella knew, Scaurus was related to neither man.

"I have no notable ancestors," Scaurus said, standing next to Ocella. "So I choose to display dead Romans I admire. The Julii, though social outcasts these days, have long been friends of my family." Scaurus stared at her meaningfully. "Caesar reminds me of Roma's excess. Cicero reminds me to laugh."

Ocella wondered at such a strange statement. Before she could comment, Scaurus asked, "How did you do it?"

Ocella opened her mouth, but he cut her off. "Wait, we need to get rid of your Umbra implant."

"How?"

"Gifts from more friends of the family. Come with me."

Light from the setting sun shone through the skylight above the atrium garden in the house's center. Small trees and plants cast shadows on the frescoes and paintings on the walls. The shadows seemed to grasp at Ocella with clawed fingers.

Scaurus took them through the kitchen, where a single house slave prepared dinner. The dark-haired young man ignored them. Ocella was somewhat startled that the slave was a real human and not a golem. Most Romans used golems these days since they were cheap to maintain. She didn't think Scaurus was wealthy enough to own a human slave.

One more thing you never knew about Scaurus, she thought. *Are you surprised?*

The boy stared at the olives and breads sitting on the counter, and the lamprey strips sizzling on the grill-stove. Ocella's own stomach rumbled as she realized she had not eaten in almost twelve hours.

Scaurus opened the pantry and waved his hand before the light pad. A warm glow from the ceiling lit the shelves filled with dry foods. He reached behind some pickled herring jars, his whole arm extended.

"This house has been in my family for almost two hundred years," he said while reaching to the back wall. "My Saturnist ancestors recognized the need to accommodate *guests* such as yourselves."

Ocella heard a click, then stone moving against stone as the shelved wall pushed back four feet. There was little room to squeeze through the opening, but Scaurus managed it and motioned them to follow.

"Cleon," Scaurus called, "shut the pantry behind us?"

"Yes, master," the slave said from the kitchen.

Ocella and the boy entered the space behind the pantry. They stood at the top of a staircase descending into darkness. Scaurus waved his hand before a light pad, and small globe lights on the ceiling revealed the stairs and the landing at the bottom. Scaurus hurried down.

The boy looked up at Ocella, and she said, "It's all right. He's going to help us."

The boy was still uncertain, but turned and followed the retired Praetorian Guardsman down to the cellar. The pantry door scraped shut behind them. Ocella flinched.

At the bottom, Scaurus turned on more lights. Ocella blinked at the suddenly illuminated room. It matched the dimensions of the house above. Four rows of bookshelves stood to her right, each filled with old-fashioned scrolls and bound books. To her left, sat a desk with a tabulari projecting a holographic spinning Terra above the keyboard. At the room's far end, four single-sized beds, a dining area with couches, and a visum globe in the center.

"If you have to hide," Scaurus said, "there's no use hiding like barbarians."

Ocella glanced back up the stairs. "Is that the only way out?"

"Of course not. Wouldn't do to have a safe house without an escape hatch."

"Where is it?"

"I'll tell you after the procedure."

Ocella nodded. "How did you get a Liberti tabulari?"

"It wasn't easy," Scaurus said. He went to the tabulari desk and searched through the drawers. "Even the former Praefectus of the Praetorian Guard has trouble getting the, er, finer things from our friends on Libertus. The embargo on Liberti items hasn't removed them from Roman homes. Just made them more expensive."

"Are these from the Ascension?" the boy asked, studying the scrolls on the shelves.

"Yes, sire," Scaurus said. "Birth records for everyone in the Antonii family after the Ascension. Your lineage."

The boy looked at him. "They would kill you if they found these."

Scaurus grunted. "Better than crucifixion. Now you know why my ancestors built that pantry door."

Scaurus found what he wanted in the drawers. He unraveled a hairnet with small clear beads, similar to what fashionable Roman women wore over their long braided hair.

"The Praetorians will dissect your former associates down to the atom," Scaurus said, walking to Ocella. "Once they figure out how the implants work, they will detect the signals. When that happens..."

"They will find me," Ocella said. "And him." She watched the boy search the scrolls and books. Now and then his mouth formed a wondrous 'O' when he found something interesting. "I can't hide him forever."

"Bah! I thought you Umbra Ancilia were invincible, immortal, or whatever the superstitions say you are. You haven't left Terra yet and you're already despairing. If you were still a Praetorian I'd clap you in the ears right now for such talk. Now let me put this on you."

Ocella asked, "You sure it's safe? The Umbra implant works with my higher brain functions. I can't protect Cordus if I'm brain dead."

Scaurus put the net over Ocella's head, adjusting it so it fit over her scalp and ears. "Well, granted, it's never been used this way. We've only used it on retired Umbra Ancilia whose implants were already deactivated. But it should work on your live implant...in theory."

"What?"

"How *could* we test it? One, a live Ancile would never submit to it. Two, there's never been anyone like Cordus in human history who could use it this way." Scaurus gazed at the boy. "A new age for humanity begins with him, a new hope for—"

"I know, Scaurus, but like I said, I can't protect him if I'm brain dead."

"If you don't neutralize this implant, you'll be dead anyway."

Once again, no choices. Only the single, dark path filled with anguished screams.

"Let's get this over with."

Scaurus nodded. "Sire, a moment please."

Cordus put down the book he'd been studying and walked over.

"Ocella, sit in this chair. Sire, if you would stand in front of Ocella."

Once Scaurus positioned them correctly, he said, "Do you know what you need to do, sire?"

Cordus shook his head. "I have never done this before."

"I know. But have the "gods" done it?"

Cordus's eyes went blank. He stared past Ocella as if looking through the walls and at the horizon. He blinked, then nodded.

"They have ideas on how to disable it." He frowned. "They need to test some things first. It may hurt a bit."

Ocella swallowed. "Go ahead, Cordus. I trust you."

He smiled weakly, then his gaze turned blank again.

Ocella's scalp tickled as the device activated whatever energy Cordus's "gods" used. Someone whispered in her right ear. She half turned, but Scaurus stood on her left. The whispers grew louder, though not in a language she understood.

Cordus's brow furrowed, and he blinked again.

"That was not the right path," he said. "They need to try another."

Ocella inhaled and nodded. Cordus stared at her head with that blank gaze.

White light exploded before her eyes. She gasped and heaved backward in the chair.

"It's all right, it's all right," Scaurus said as he grabbed her arms.

"I can't see anything," Ocella yelled.

"I think I have it," Cordus said.

The light exploded into millions of flashing images—her past sins and sins she had yet to commit.

Ocella screamed.

Chapter Two

"Dariya," Kaeso Aemilius said into his collar com, "why's there no gravity on the command deck?"

"We are in space, sir," Dariya's voice squawked from the com.

"Dariya—"

"We are fixing it, sir."

"Vallutus will be here in a half hour."

"I could be fixing it now if you stopped hounding me, sir."

"Just get it done."

Kaeso floated to the command couch in the ship's cockpit and strapped himself in. He had been standing behind the couch checking the navigation systems when the gravity cut out. He was glad he finished his hot Arabian *kaffa* a few minutes before. He would've had to replace the systems in the entire command deck instead of his First Engineer.

He glanced out the command deck window. His old freighter *Caduceus* was docked to a hollowed-out asteroid way station above the Lost World Reantium. Like most way stations, this one sat in geosynchronous orbit above a world the gods had blessed with an interstellar way line. Reantium was an impoverished world in an impoverished star system, populated with less than a hundred thousand Roman and Zhonguo political dissidents who were simply happy to be out of prison.

The one valuable commodity Reantium did have was its single way line jump to Roman territory and the world that might hold Kaeso's next job.

"What happened to the gravity?"

Lucia Marius Calida floated up through the ladder well in the command deck's rear. Kaeso's pilot was dressed in the white uniform of a Liberti merchant officer. While Kaeso did not force his crew to wear the merchant uniforms, he did ask they put on their best jumpsuits when a client came aboard. He appreciated Lucia's attempts to bring some semblance of military discipline to the crew. She would never stop being a Legionnaire, despite the unpleasant circumstances of her departure.

"Dariya's working on it," Kaeso said. "And by that I mean Daryush is working on it."

Lucia scowled. "Bet Dariya kicked a switch, or something."

"Let's hope it's that simple. Gravity's gone on the command deck only, right?"

"And Bay One. And the forward quarters."

Kaeso closed his eyes again. *The* Caduceus *is an old ship*, he reminded himself. *Old ships have old problems.*

"Centuriae, it's the third time this month Dariya has screwed up," Lucia said, pulling herself into the pilot's couch next to Kaeso. "If she's the reason we lose this contract—"

"We don't know what happened," Kaeso said. "Reserve judgment until you know the facts."

"I know. All I'm saying—"

"I'm not having this discussion again."

"Centuriae, they're escaped slaves. We can never enter Roman space, much less get a Roman contract, with them on board. Daryush doesn't have a tongue, and Dariya may as well not have one either; her Persian accent, at best, marks her as suspicious. Why should we eliminate half of humanity from our client scrolls just to keep two Persian twins from—?"

"Enough," Kaeso said, his headache worsening. "Everybody on this damned ship is fleeing from something. Right, *Legionarie*?"

Lucia set her jaw and turned to her pilot's console. Kaeso knew he wounded Lucia every time he brought up her past, but he knew it was the surest way to stop her screeds against Dariya.

"Dariya may be a pain in the ass sometimes, but she—and especially her brother—are valuable members of this crew. Just like you."

Lucia said, "Gravity's out in Bay Two. And it just went out in the crew quarters."

Kaeso groaned. Right on cue, the panicked voice of Gaius Octavious Blaesus thundered from the com.

"Centuriae? Centuriae! The gravity's out in my quarters. My maps and books are all over my cabin. I think I'm going to be sick. You know I can't take zero gravity!"

"Calm down, Blaesus," Kaeso said into his collar com. "Go to the corridor, it's still on there."

"For now," Lucia muttered. Kaeso pretended to ignore her.

"All right...all right...yes, good," Blaesus said. "But all of my research has turned into a cloud of papers. I just organized the landing site maps. Vallutus will be here in a half hour and it will take me at least that long to—"

"Dariya and Daryush are working on the grav now," Kaeso said. "In the meantime just grab as much as you can."

"I can't go back in there, Centuriae! Not unless you want to show Vallutus maps and proposals flecked with vomit."

"We can call up the maps and proposal from *Caduceus's* network."

"Maybe the maps, but not the proposal. I wrote it long-hand on scrolls and now they're floating around with all my clothes."

"You were a Roman Senator, for Jupiter's sake. You can make up a speech in your sleep."

"Yes, I am a brilliant orator. But that's only after I've studied my material, practiced counter arguments—"

"*Cac.*" Kaeso unbuckled himself from the pilot's chair. "I'll be right there." He floated to the hatch, then said over his shoulder to Lucia, "Don't pester Dariya. I don't want another hissing match between you two while she fixes the gravity."

"I'm your trierarch," Lucia said. "First officers are supposed to pester the crew."

"And stop pouting. Ping me when Vallutus is at the hatch."

Kaeso floated down the ladder well, pulling himself hand over hand down the rungs. As he neared the bottom, he felt the second level gravity tug at him, so he swung his body around and climbed down feet first. The full single gravity held him when he hopped down onto the corridor floor.

Now in a normal grav corridor, Kaeso's head did not pound as much as it had in the command deck's zero grav. It did not improve his mood though. His ship was breaking down minutes before he met with the biggest client he ever had. He needed that client's job to pay for docking fees at Reantium's way station. And fuel, air, food, water...

Nestor Samaras ducked his head through the pressure hatch just as Kaeso entered.

"Blaesus just said the gravity is off."

"Dariya's working on it."

Nestor was about to speak, but closed his mouth and stepped back to allow Kaeso to move past. The quiet Greek medicus was good at reading Kaeso's moods, for which Kaeso was grateful at the moment. But he didn't want the medicus keeping a potential surprise to himself just to avoid Kaeso's ire.

"What is it, Medicus?"

"I wanted to request a line of credit to buy more raptor gizzards for the way line jump rituals."

"We're out?"

Nestor nodded. "We used up the last one for our jump here."

Kaeso sighed. "How much?"

Nestor pulled on his short, black beard and licked his lips. "Five hundred sesterces for a ten-canister case."

"Five hundred—!"

"Centuriae, raptors are not native to this star system so they are hard to come by on the waystation. They must be imported from a Roman aviary, or a Lost World. The closest Lost World aviary is four way line jumps away."

Kaeso rubbed a hand over the coarse stubble on his head. "Can't we just this once skip the ritual?"

Nestor paled. "We cannot jump without the gods approval or protection, Centuriae. We could get stuck between realities, thrown off course into unknown space or a star or a planet—"

"Fine," Kaeso said. "Talk to Lucia and she'll send the funds to your tabulari. But only buy enough for this jump. We'll need the rest of the money in the ship's purse for bribes when we get to Menota." *If Vallutus still hires us once he's seen the ship.*

"Yes, Centuriae. Thank you."

Kaeso walked on, then turned. "Don't go into Bay Two. Gravity's out there."

Nestor stopped. "Do you know when it will be fixed? I need to get a new delta generator battery."

"Why not recharge the one already in the machine?"

"It's not taking a charge anymore. I just checked."

"The one in Bay Two is our last battery."

"Do you want me to buy a new one when I get the raptor gizzards?"

Kaeso thought a second, then shook his head. "We'll just have to take our chances for this job. We can't afford it until we get paid. Maybe luck will be with us for a change."

Nestor smiled. "There is no such thing as luck, Centuriae. Only the will of the gods."

"Right."

Kaeso squeezed around a corner and arrived at the crew compartments. Blaesus stood outside his quarters staring inside.

The former Senator wore the usual outfit he wore for potential clients—a ceremonial white toga over his white Liberti merchant jump suit. Kaeso thought he looked dressed for a funeral.

"You almost got it, boy," Blaesus said.

"This one?" a voice responded from inside.

"No, the one next to your left foot. Yes, that one. There you go."

A scroll flew out of the room, hit the wall behind Blaesus, and then dropped as it encountered the corridor's gravity field. Blaesus picked it up, unrolled it, and sighed.

"I knew that boy was good for something," Blaesus muttered to Kaeso, "besides the arena."

Kaeso stopped next to Blaesus. Flamma Africanus floated in the zero grav inside Blaesus's hatch, reaching for the maps and scrolls bumping around the room. The tall, lanky Egyptian cursed every time he knocked his head on the walls or ceiling.

"At least there's more room in the arena," Flamma grumbled.

"You never set foot in an arena, my boy. Your golems did."

"I saw through their eyes. I felt their pain— *Cac!*" Flamma rubbed his head where he'd slammed it against the bulkhead. "Need anything else? I'm more beat up grabbing your scraps than I ever got in the arena."

Kaeso grinned. "You boys have things under control here. I'll check on that gravity fix."

"Please do, Centuriae," Blaesus said. "I'd like to sleep in my quarters tonight."

"Oh, and Blaesus, don't wear the toga around Vallutus. Romans make him nervous. Especially politicians."

"Centuriae, the toga is who I am. You might as well ask me to cut off an arm."

"I'll do it," Flamma said, landing in the corridor. "Ax or saw?"

Blaesus frowned. "Your bloodlust knows no bounds, gladiator. Centuriae, a toga shows I respect a client enough to wear the best clothing I have. Lucia is wearing her old Legionnaire uniform, am I right? Now *that* would make any barbarian nervous."

"She's wearing her Liberti merchant whites," Kaeso said. "Quite different from Legion red."

"Still too militaristic for my taste," Blaesus said.

"Stow the toga, Blaesus."

The old Senator heaved a great sigh. "Very well, Centuriae. But only if you get the gravity back on in my quarters. I won't go in there again until I can walk in."

"Working on it," Kaeso said. He brushed past Blaesus and headed to the back of the crew deck.

"Because I will not store it in anything other than the sacred box it came in when I was voted into the Senate," Blaesus called after Kaeso. "It would be blasphemy to do otherwise."

Kaeso waved a hand over his shoulder as he reached the end of the crew deck, and then climbed down the ladder well to the engineering deck. He was greeted with metallic clanking and Persian curses. While Kaeso's Persian was limited to simple greetings and requests for directions, he had no trouble understanding Dariya's shouts.

In the engine room, Daryush worked at a tabulari, his large hands deftly moving windows and components around the interface. Behind him, Dariya swung a large wrench at a compartment door. The clang upon impact was deafening even in the noisy engine room.

"What are you doing?" Kaeso yelled over the humming engines and Dariya's swings.

Dariya looked up, annoyance plain on her dirty face. He almost wanted to back up and leave the room before she came at him with the wrench.

"I told you we have it under control, sir," she said.

"Looks like it. Why are you beating up my ship?"

"This son of a whore compartment door is corroded from the leaking grav fluid behind it. I cannot open it to fix the leak. Thus, the beating."

She took another swing at the door and the clang was even louder. Daryush didn't flinch, and kept moving windows on the tabulari interface.

"Use the torch," Kaeso said. "Grav fluid won't catch fire."

"Your ignorance would amuse me if it would not kill us all. Sir."

"Then educate me."

"The fluid is not flammable, but the torch could damage the generator itself. I do not recall any spare grav generators laying around," Dariya said. "Or spare anything."

Daryush grunted from the tabulari, then raised both arms in triumph. The white teeth in his big smile contrasted with his dirty face. His grunts and gestures told Kaeso he'd done something for which he was proud.

Dariya went and checked his readout. "'Ush, you are amazing. We have gravity, sir."

"What did he do?" Kaeso asked.

"He shut down the grav generator and redirected the inertia cancellers to simulate gravity. We should be fine as long as we don't make any sudden accelerations."

"Shouldn't be a problem while we're docked at the way station." Daryush turned to Kaeso with a proud smile.

Kaeso clapped him on the back. "Very good." He turned to Dariya. "When can you get the grav generator leak fixed? We'll need the inertia cancellers once we undock."

"As soon as I can open this son of a whore compartment."

"Fine. Just make sure Daryush's fix doesn't short out any other systems."

Dariya looked at Kaeso as if he just said he could breath in space. The fraternal Persian twins had been aboard *Caduceus* little over a year, and Daryush's fixes had never made things worse. They had made an old, broken-down star freighter run well past its expiration date. Despite Dariya's gruff attitude and Daryush's lack of a tongue, Kaeso thought they were the best engineering team in the Lost Worlds.

Especially for their price, which was virtually nil compared to other engineering teams he'd interviewed when he first bought *Caduceus*. Kaeso hated paying the twins a tick higher than indentured wages, but he had to pay his entire crew the same. It was a condition of working on a ship that specialized in smuggling services amidst tight competition from criminal syndicates in both Roman and Liberti space.

Kaeso's com chimed. "Centuriae?" Lucia asked.

Dariya's lips curled in disgust, and she turned back to the compartment she'd been beating. Kaeso ducked out of the engine room before she could start the earsplitting "repairs."

"What?"

"Vallutus is at the entry hatch."

Early...

"Tell him I'll be right there," Kaeso said. "Have Blaesus report to the galley with his maps and proposal. Make sure he's not wearing that toga. Tell Flamma to heat up some spiced wine. And it wouldn't hurt for you to—"

"I'll take care of it, Centuriae. Now go meet him before he walks away."

Kaeso stayed on the engineering deck and made his way through the cramped corridor to the main entry air lock at the ship's nose. He passed the two cargo bays, Bay One on the left and Bay Two on the right, both depressingly empty. At the airlock between the bays, the external monitors showed Vallutus in the way station connector. He was a short man, bald, with a paunch hanging over his jump suit's belt. His gaze furtively swept up and down the waystation corridor. Kaeso supposed his nervousness was natural considering the job he had for *Caduceus*.

"Salve, Vallutus," Kaeso said into the speaker. "I'll have this door open in a moment."

"Salve, Centuriae Aemilius. Thank you."

Kaeso pointed at a few buttons on the tabulari interface. Red warning lights flashed near the door, and a buzzer sounded as air pressure equalized in the connector. Kaeso then moved a slider on the tabulari, and the *Caduceus's* entry hatch slid open. The way station hatch at the other end of the connector also opened. Vallutus hurried in, and Kaeso went to meet him.

"Welcome aboard *Caduceus*," Kaeso said, extending his arm.

Vallutus took his arm in a firm grasp. "I cannot stay long, Centuriae, but I thought I should tell you in person. Honor demands it."

Kaeso did not like the sound of that.

"We can talk in the galley."

"No, I cannot stay long. I'm breaking the contract. You will get your cancellation fee, as we agreed."

Kaeso stared at Vallutus. "I don't understand."

"Centuriae," Vallutus said in a hushed tone, "I was foolish to hire you to go to Menota to begin with, no matter how many marques are still there. It is a dead planet with a violent, tragic history. If radiation from the Roman diraenium bombs doesn't kill you, the Cariosus plague will. Now Libertus has its no-landing treaty with Roma."

"What? When did this happen?"

"Newscriers announced it over the system bands two hours ago."

Kaeso shook his head. "That doesn't change anything. Landings have always been illegal. Roma patrols the entire system."

"I have no problem crossing Roma. But Liberti *numina*..."

"My friend, Liberti *numina* do not exist."

Vallutus's eyes widened. "You should not say such things! Of course they exist. They are what has kept Libertus free since its founding. How else do you explain the Roman fear of conquering Libertus, the one world that has made so much trouble for them for centuries? It's the Liberti *numina*. Everyone knows that. You would do well to respect them yourself—you're Liberti."

"Yes, but—"

Kaeso didn't know what to say. How could he explain to Vallutus the "Liberti *numina*" were not what he thought? That they were not god-like spirits protecting Libertus from the Romans or the Zhonguo Sphere or the other tyrannical empires and governments that coveted its prosperity? How could he explain it to Vallutus in a way that would not kill Kaeso on the spot?

"Vallutus," Kaeso said slowly, "the Liberti *numina* are a myth. They do not exist. They are just a story concocted to scare off anyone who would threaten Libertus."

Vallutus scoffed. "Do you think the Romans are afraid of a story? My friend Aemilius, I have personally seen how those who cross the Liberti end up. I have seen ships explode carrying men or cargo wanted by the Liberti authorities. Some of my less savory associates were assassinated in places protected by trusted men and solid security systems. The *numina* are real, my friend."

"Vallutus, the *numina* are not real. They're—"

Light and pain exploded in Kaeso's eyes and behind his right ear. He shut his eyes and leaned against the connector wall until the pain subsided. When he opened his eyes again, Vallutus stared at Kaeso fearfully.

"Centuriae, are you well?"

"Fine," Kaeso grunted. "We need this contract, Vallutus. I promise you, with your resources we can bribe the Roman patrols to let us land on Menota. We can get into the vaults. My crew has the skills. We can handle the radiation and any Cariosus. The money is just sitting there, Vallutus, waiting for someone who's not afraid of shadows to take it."

"No, you proved it just now, Centuriae. You insulted the *numina* with your denial, and from a son of Libertus. They tried to strike you down."

"No they didn't. It was just a headache."

"I'm sorry, Centuriae," Vallutus said. "I will deposit the cancellation fee into your ship's account within the hour. Good day to you."

Vallutus turned and hurried out of the connector. Kaeso watched him leave with anger, sadness, and a little bit of fear.

"Centuriae," chimed Lucia's voice from Kaeso's collar. "Why did I just see Vallutus leave?"

Kaeso swallowed. "Have the crew meet in the galley."

"Blaesus and Flamma are already there. I'll call Nestor."

"And the twins."

Lucia paused. "I doubt Dariya will listen to me if she's got a leak to fix."

"Then tell her it's an order from me," Kaeso said. "You're my damned Trierarch, Lucia, the second-in-command. You shouldn't need the threat of me to back you up. This feud between you and Dariya is wearing on me."

Lucia paused again. "Centuriae, what just happened?"

"We lost our contract with Vallutus. We have some decisions to make."

Chapter Three

"So that's it," Kaeso told his crew in the galley. "Vallutus is out. Our funds for the way station docking will run out in three days. We need a contract now."

The crew's grim faces reflected Kaeso's mood. Blaesus sat at the table drinking the warm spiced wine Flamma had set out for Vallutus. Flamma and Nestor sat on either side of Blaesus, staring at their cups. Dariya and Daryush leaned against the far wall of the cramped galley with their hands in the pockets of their greasy jumpsuits. Lucia stood beside Kaeso, her arms folded over her Liberti merchant uniform, now unbuttoned at the collar.

Blaesus responded first. "I for one never believed in the Liberti *numina*. Whole lot of rubbish meant to scare Roman kiddies before bedtime. You were in the Legions, Lucia. I suppose you told a good *numen* ghost story around the campfire, eh?"

Kaeso glanced at Lucia, who shifted on her feet uncomfortably.

"Sure, stories," she said. The set of her jaw told Kaeso she knew more than just stories.

"I am not so sure they are stories," Nestor said, his quiet Greek accent ominous. "My previous employer once told me he had a partner who killed a Liberti lictor when they raided his slavery stable. He bragged about it, and scoffed at the Liberti *numen* tales. One night, in a tavern filled with over sixty loyal men, he went to the latrine...and never came out."

Flamma leaned close. "He died on the *cac* pot?"

"No, he just never came out. He disappeared. Many saw him go in, my employer included, but no one ever saw him leave. When my employer went to check on him, all he found was a single drop of blood on the floor."

Blaesus downed his spiced wine. "Perhaps he crawled down the *cac* pipes."

"You mock," Nestor said, "but these things happen to people who cross Libertus. The Liberti have powerful patron gods."

"Latin myths do not scare me," Dariya said. She pulled a pendant with a winged disc from beneath her collar. "Ahura Mazda, Lord of Wisdom, protects me and all who acknowledge him."

"Ah," Blaesus said, pouring more wine into his cup, "your gods can beat up our gods, eh?"

"All right," Kaeso said, "before we get into a religious fight, let's talk about our options. We need money to keep flying. Otherwise, I can't afford to run this ship, much less pay you."

Lucia asked, "What about the cancellation fee from Vallutus?"

"It'll cover the cost of raptor gizzards, but not way station docking fees."

Blaesus took a sip of wine. "Vallutus can't be the only 'collector' wanting to pilfer Menota."

"He's not," Kaeso said, "but we don't have time to find another one. It took weeks to build enough trust with Vallutus so he was satisfied we weren't undercover Roman agents. It'll take that much longer now that Libertus is watching Menota."

The crew thought quietly for almost a minute.

Flamma broke the silence. "The patrician lady who introduced us to Vallutus. Maybe she's a collector?"

Blaesus snorted. "Old Barbata may be a collector, but she doesn't have the money to pay for our services. She gambled and drank away her family's fortune and had to flee Roma in disgrace. All she has now are contacts with people who'd rather not hear from her."

Flamma grinned. "Sounds familiar, eh, Senator?"

Blaesus slammed his wine cup on the table, some of it sloshing over the top. He glared at Flamma, nostrils flaring. "Just what are you implying, *gladiator*?"

Flamma's grin faded. "Calm down, I was just joking."

"Well your wit is as flaccid as your sword arm. Or other parts of your anatomy, if the gossip columnists were right."

Flamma jumped up, his lanky frame towering over Blaesus.

"Flamma, sit down," Kaeso said. "Blaesus, stop drinking."

Flamma eased back into his seat, eying Blaesus venomously. Blaesus smiled at Flamma, then gave Kaeso an exaggerated salute, a fist to the chest and then a straight arm. "As you wish, Centuriae."

"Is there anyone else who could finance a landing on Menota?" Kaeso asked.

Blaesus gave a lopsided grin. "The only ones I know won't return my calls." He eyed Flamma again, and then took a drink.

"Fine," Kaeso said. "Then if nobody else has a better idea, I say we go to Menota anyway. Without a patron."

Now the crew stared at him, shocked. Kaeso didn't look at Lucia, but he knew her officer's reserve struggled to keep her face calm.

As Kaeso expected, Blaesus spoke first. "I applaud you, Centuriae. Your oratory skills are improving. You give us a picture of our dire situation and led us to consider ideas that would never work. Once we realize how neck-deep in *cac* we are, you throw out the plan you wanted all along. Now that we're good and desperate, you think we'll jump at it. Well done, Centuriae."

"Thank you."

"Just one question: how does the Centuriae propose we land on Menota? Keep in mind we don't have a patron to loan us the money to bribe the Roman sentries."

"We use what's left in the *Caduceus's* reserves, along with Vallutus's cancellation fee."

Nestor cleared his throat. "Centuriae, we still need the raptor gizzards for—"

"We'll get those when we come back."

Nestor paled. "Centuriae, we cannot—!"

"Nestor, Zhonguo ships and ships from a dozen other agnostic worlds zip around the universe without raptor gizzards, and they don't get lost. I think the gods will forgive us for this one trip. If it makes you feel any better, we'll sacrifice some extra gizzards on our next voyage."

"No, sir, it does not make me feel better. All it takes is one unholy way line jump into oblivion and there will not be a 'next voyage.'"

Lucia said, "And there won't be a 'next voyage' if we don't get the money for these bribes."

"Granted," Blaesus said, "the raptor sacrifice is, um, a tradition we can do without—"

"It is more than tradition," Nestor said. "It is our petition to the gods for—"

"—But we don't have the coordinates Vallutus was going to give us. I know the vaults' approximate location on Menota, but not precisely. Menota has a lot of landmass on which we could get lost."

"Make an educated guess," Kaeso said.

"Ha, an educated guess, he says. If I'm wrong, we could wander the radioactive ruins for days. The Roman sentries will not give us days, even if they are well-bribed."

"When are you ever wrong, Blaesus?" Kaeso asked.

Blaesus laughed. "Centuriae, you're making me look bad. If I wasn't so drunk, I'd easily avoid all your oratory traps. Very well, before you humiliate me again, I accept your challenge and will endeavor to make an 'educated guess' regarding the vaults' location. May the gods have mercy on us all."

Kaeso looked at the rest of the crew. "This is a dangerous job. We'll be dodging Roman sentries and the Cariosus plague. Possibly Liberti security of the *human* variety." He eyed Nestor.

"So I'm going with or without you," Kaeso said. "Because I've nowhere else to go. I've never asked for a vote on jobs, and I'm not starting now. But you're not slaves or indentured servants. Only freedmen on this ship. So if this job isn't for you, you're welcome to sit it out. No hard feelings."

Kaeso paused, giving them a chance to get up and leave, or give him better ideas. No one moved or spoke.

"What say you?"

After a silent moment, Lucia said, "I will go, Centuriae."

Kaeso turned and nodded to her, though she kept her arms folded with an uncertain air.

"Of course I'm going," Blaesus said. "The promise of riches and adventure is what lured me to this crew in the first place. Flamma, stop giving me that sour face and put your lot in with us. I couldn't bear a voyage with no one to debate the merits of empire versus republic."

Flamma stared at Blaesus and then shrugged. "Fine, old man."

Dariya said, "We will go, too. We are not afraid, eh, 'Ush?"

Daryush nodded his shaved head vigorously.

Kaeso looked at Nestor. "We need a medicus. We can operate the delta sleep and figure out the clean suits on our own, but if something goes wrong..."

Nestor sighed. "Centuriae, once again, we cannot perform a way line jump without the proper rituals." Then he winced. "But I suppose the frozen chickens in the freezers would perhaps appease the gods. Just this once."

Kaeso grinned. "Good. Dariya, how's the grav generator?"

"I opened the compartment without too much damage," she said. Glancing at Daryush, she added, "We should have it done within the hour."

"Then we leave in six hours as scheduled. Thank you all."

Lucia waited until the crew filed out, shut the galley hatch, and then turned to Kaeso. "Centuriae, I think this job is a bad idea."

"Of course it is, but it's the only choice we have. The money on Menota will keep us flying for years. All we have to do is go down and take it."

"Sir, I understand that, but there are acceptable risks and insane risks. In my opinion, this falls under the latter."

"Opinion noted. Anything else?"

She frowned. "The Liberti *numina* are real."

Kaeso closed his eyes. "Lucia, I've told you—"

"I saw one."

Impossible, Kaeso thought. "What did you see?"

Her gaze dropped to the floor, as if embarrassed at what she was about to say. "Before the Kaldethi Rebellion blew up, my century was ordered to surround the Libertus embassy on Kaldeth to prevent any dissidents from defecting. One night a Kaldethi mob tried to get a dissident *flamen* into the embassy. My century formed ranks to stop them. The mob threw rocks and firebombs at us. We returned fire. We killed many."

She stopped, gathering her thoughts. "Then the centurion next to me grabbed my arm. His...his back was arched in a strange angle. Then a red line opened on his throat, as if by an invisible blade. His blood sprayed on me. Some other soldiers behind him suffered the same fate. Their throats just opened up. The mob saw my men fall and pushed forward. Our pulse rifles couldn't stop them. They stampeded over us and got the dissidents past the Libertus gates."

Lucia put her hands in the pockets of her uniform. "Once the mob passed us, I saw...a figure. It shimmered like a black road on a hot day. I could only see its arms. They were covered in blood. I fired at it, but it ducked behind a building. I never saw it again."

Kaeso knew he'd have to be careful with what he said next. The pain behind his right ear had started and would make him pay for revealing too much.

"I don't know what you saw," he said. "It could have been anything. You said yourself it was a dark, chaotic night. Lucia, I promise you; there are no *numina*."

Lucia gave a mirthless laugh. "You always say that, yet you never give me proof. How do you *know*, Centuriae? Please tell me, because I want you to convince me they're not real."

A quick stab of pain came from the implant. A warning. Kaeso had no intention of saying anything, but the implant never missed an opportunity to remind him of his vows.

"You're right," he said. "I'll never convince you with my words alone. Do you trust me?"

She gave a noncommittal nod.

"Lucia," he asked again, "do you trust me?"

She looked up at him. "I do."

"Menota has Cariosus and Roman sentries. That's it. Look to those two problems. They're big enough, so don't add mythical creatures to your worry list."

He knew she wasn't convinced, but she nodded anyway. "Yes, Centuriae."

She turned and left the galley without another word. Kaeso stared after her. His entire crew had a secret past from which they ran, him included. But at least they could choose whether or not to reveal their secrets. Kaeso had no such luxury. If he revealed what he knew of the "Liberti *numina,*" his implant would kill him on the spot and the "*numina*" would track down his crew and silence them to keep Liberti's centuries-old secret.

Because that's what he did when he was a "*numen.*"

Chapter Four

Nestor raised the knife above his head, then brought the serrated point down into the breast of the partially thawed chicken on his sacrificial cutting board.

"Oh, Jupiter Optimus Maximus," Nestor chanted from his post on the command deck, "we ask your permission to travel through your realm."

Nestor split open the chicken's ribcage with a quick, expert motion. He removed the gray, semi-frozen heart and held it above his head.

"Accept this offering," he said with a wince, "from a beast of flight. If it pleases you, grant us a safe journey through your way lines so we may arrive at Menota."

Nestor put the heart into a clay bowl and mashed it with a mallet until it was a gray paste. He then sprinkled some powder over it, touched the mixture with a small fire torch, and the sacrifice sparked into flames.

Kaeso suddenly remembered the fire alarm on the command deck, and lunged for the off switch before the noxious smoke could trigger the alarm. Avoiding the shrill warning siren was not his goal. He just didn't want Nestor to waste another good chicken if his ritual was interrupted.

Once the sacrifice had burned away, Nestor nodded to Kaeso and then strapped himself into the delta operator's couch behind Kaeso and Lucia.

"All hands," Kaeso said into his collar, "perform undocking check." He turned to Lucia. "Environmental?"

"Connector tube is retracted and entry hatch is secure," she said, moving her fingers across her tabulari sliders. "Atmospheric and power cables disconnected."

"Engineering."

"Grav and inertial cancelers are stable," Dariya's voice said from his com. "Thrusters active. Ion drive powering up. Way line drive ready for coordinates."

"Navigation."

Lucia said, "Way line coordinates entered, Centuriae. Awaiting way line bearing from Way Station Control."

"Delta."

Nestor said, "Delta wave powered up and ready for way line jump."

"Good," Kaeso said. "Way Station Control, this is *Caduceus* requesting permission to undock."

"*Caduceus*, Way Station Control," a voice crackled. "Permission granted. Proceed according to your flight plan to way line jump point."

"Thank you, Control," Kaeso said. "Lucia, undock us."

"Undocking."

A small shudder rippled through the ship. The Reantium waystation's docking port shifted and turned sideways outside the command deck window. *Caduceus's* thrusters backed the ship away from the way station, then Lucia pointed the ship's nose down 90 degrees from their original position.

"Hope Dariya's repairs worked," Lucia muttered and then tapped the ion drive slider on her tabulari. The ship blasted forward beneath the waystation's gray, rocky surface.

"She did something right," Kaeso said. "We're not stains on the wall."

Lucia grunted as she moved a slider farther up to increase the ship's speed.

Kaeso watched out the window. This was his favorite part. Most space travel was spent in unimaginable emptiness. But this moment, when *Caduceus* left a way station, he could see a star ship's fantastic speeds with his eyes. The gauges told him the ship's velocity, but to see the twelve-mile wide way station literally disappear from view...well, it amazed Kaeso every time.

"Wayline jump point in seven minutes, sir," Lucia said.

Kaeso tapped his collar com. "All crew, prepare for way line jump."

Outside the window, Kaeso saw other starships lined up at the way line jump point. He counted six ships ahead of them. They all varied in size and shape, depending on the world or nation from which they originated. One ship had the shape of a gliding eagle, the classic Roman design. While the eagle-like wingspan was of little use in the vacuum of space, Romans liked the design's symbolism. *Caduceus*, on the other hand, was a Mercury-class gray ovoid with four engine cones protruding from the rear. About as ugly as ships came, but made of solid Liberti engineering. She was old before Kaeso was born, but she'd be flying longer than the "throwaway" Roman bird in the way line queue.

A large freighter, perhaps two miles long, floated at the column's head. It was not a design Kaeso recognized. It seemed patched together from pieces of other ships. Its engines flared; the whole ship *stretched* forward and then vanished, on to one of three possible terminus points: the Lost Worlds of Acestes, Quiritis, or the dead Roman world Menota.

Kaeso guessed the Lost Worlds, since only fools would defy a Roman and Liberti quarantine.

When he saw a ship ride the way line, sometimes he really thought humanity was traveling through the realm of the gods. Less than a thousand years ago, the fastest mode of transport was either horse or trireme. Now men jumped between stars. If the gods had not given humanity this gift, then perhaps humanity was close to godhood itself? Both options worried Kaeso.

"Way line jump in thirty seconds, sir," Lucia said.

Kaeso blinked away his musings. "Nestor, engage the delta sleep."

"Delta sleep engaged."

Beside Kaeso, Lucia's eyes closed and she settled back into her couch. A small snore escaped her open mouth. He glanced at the delta monitor on his tabulari and saw that only he and Nestor were still awake.

"All crew under delta sleep," Nestor confirmed. "You now have delta control, Centuriae."

"Thank you, Nestor," Kaeso said. "See you in the Menota system."

Nestor's silence told Kaeso he was either under delta now or still nervous about jumping. Kaeso checked Nestor's delta readouts. He was safely unconscious.

Kaeso watched the way line countdown. Rather than let the delta systems put him to sleep, he preferred to engage his delta sleep at the last possible moment. While the ship was programmed to enter the jump point on its own—something he could not change without an extreme emergency shutdown—he hated giving up control over his consciousness to the ship.

When the clock ticked down to two seconds, Kaeso engaged his delta sleep. He closed his eyes...

...and then found himself facing the command deck ceiling. His head had fallen back in the delta couch. He looked out the command window and saw black space and stars. Beside him, Lucia snorted once, then opened her eyes. She blinked several times, then checked her tabulari.

"Way line jump confirmed, Centuriae."

Nestor exhaled loudly.

"Coming about," Lucia said.

The stars outside the command window moved to the left, and then Menota's gray-white outline appeared from the right, filling the window. The planet had once looked like any other settled planet in human space—blue water, brown-green landmasses, and swirling white clouds. Now thick, gray clouds covered the entire world, courtesy of Roman mass drivers. A ring of rocks and metals surrounded the planet, remnants of an ancient moon destroyed by Menota's gravity millions of years ago.

"Roman patrols?" Kaeso asked Lucia.

"No ships on scope, sir, but two drones hold a position a hundred miles from the way line. And they just shot a courier missile into the way line."

Kaeso nodded. "No doubt they saw us. The Romans will be here soon enough."

Nestor asked Lucia, "Any Liberti ships?"

"None. The pact was just announced yesterday, though. Doubt Libertus had time to get ships out here that fast."

Kaeso said, "The Liberti Defense Force wouldn't be able to muster enough ships in less than a day. I don't think they're here yet."

Liberti Umbra ships, on the other hand...

A twitch of pain behind his right ear reminded him not to think such things.

Kaeso unstrapped himself from the delta couch and stood. "Lucia, yell if you see *any* ships. Nestor, let's go get the clean suits ready."

"Two Roman Eagles just left the way line from behind us," Lucia said. "Beacons identify them as *Corus* and *Virtus*."

Kaeso went back to his command couch. "Here we go."

No sooner had he sat down than a voice came over the ship's com. "*Caduceus*, this is Roman Eagle *Corus*," said a Roman with a Terran accent. "You are in restricted space. You will turn your vessel around and proceed to the way line jump point. Any change in your course and you will be fired upon. Acknowledge."

"Not much room for negotiation," Nestor mumbled.

Time to see if Vallutus was right, Kaeso thought. Along with the cancellation fee, Vallutus had given Kaeso the code phrases he planned to use when he bribed the Roman sentries. Kaeso tapped the com on his tabulari.

"*Corus*, this is *Caduceus*. We have authorization from Menota's Agricultural Praetor to land on the planet and conduct soil tests."

"We have no record of any scheduled landings today. Turn your ship around now or you will be fired upon."

Kaeso bit his lip. Damned bad luck to have a junior officer challenge him on the com rather than the ship's centuriae. "It was Praetor *Gurges*, my lord. Please tell your centuriae it was *Praetor Gurges* who authorized this landing. Your centuriae will have the records." *Fortuna grant it be so...*

There was a long pause, a minute which felt like an hour to Kaeso. Sweat trickled down his back. Why the wait? Was he unlucky enough to run into the most honest centuriae in the Roman fleet? Kaeso never heard of a Roman centuriae who would ignore a bribe.

"*Caduceus*," the com said. "Power down your ion drive and prepare for boarding."

"Damn," Lucia cursed.

"Confine your crew to quarters," the com continued. "You alone, Centuriae, will meet the boarding party. Do you have any weapons onboard?"

Kaeso sighed. Better to be honest and avoid any surprises. "We have seven pulse pistols."

"You will place all seven pistols in your galley. Any crewman seen with a pistol—even if it is holstered—will be shot. Acknowledge."

"Acknowledged."

"Come about to bearing 271. *Corus* out."

"You heard the man, Lucia. Power down the ions."

"They'll take us back to Roma for sure," Lucia murmured.

"Not if they take the bribes." Kaeso said into his collar, "All crew return to quarters and lock your doors. They're going to board us. Lucia?"

"Sir."

"Stow the pulse pistols in the galley and get to your quarters."

"Maybe we should keep—"

"I don't want anyone shot by mistake. Stow the pistols."

"Then I should at least be with you when they board."

"Again, no. They ordered everyone but me to their quarters. We're in no position to disobey them. Besides, I don't think you want Roman Legionaries seeing you."

She sighed. "No, sir, but it's too dangerous for you."

"Why are we still talking about this? Follow my orders, Trierarch."

Her eyes narrowed, then she said, "Yes, Centuriae."

Kaeso turned to Nestor. "You, too, Medicus."

The Greek nodded, then unstrapped himself from his delta couch and exited the command deck, leaving Kaeso to watch the two Roman Eagles grow larger in the window.

Chapter Five

At *Caduceus's* entry hatch, Kaeso moved the sliders on the tabulari to equalize the pressure in the air lock. At the other end, several helmed heads peered through the Eagle's airlock window.

"Docking secure, *Caduceus*," the *Corus* officer said over Kaeso's collar com. "Open your hatch."

Kaeso moved a tabulari slider, and the airlock hatch opened. The first thing he saw were red Roman boots. *Caduceus's* nose was docked with the *Corus's* underbelly like a suckling wolf, so the Romans had to climb "down" through their connector and then reorient themselves ninety degrees when they met *Caduceus's* gravity field.

As soon as the helmeted soldiers could stand, they stormed through the hatch with their pulse rifles pointed at Kaeso's head. He noticed the charge indicator near each rifle's trigger showed 'maximum', and their projectile clips were likely full as well. Their faces were hidden behind gold visors.

"Hands on your head," the lead soldier ordered. He was a centurion, judging from his shoulder stripes. Kaeso backed away from the controls and placed his hands on his head.

"Face the wall."

Kaeso turned. The centurion shoved Kaeso's back and pressed him into the wall. Gloved hands patted him down, removed his collar com, and then put bindings on his wrists.

"Is this necessary?"

"You the ship's centuriae?"

"Yes."

"Where's your crew?"

"In their quarters, like you asked. The pistols are in the galley. Like you asked."

"Where's the galley?"

"Down the corridor, up one level, first hatch on the right."

"Rullus, Silo, secure the galley and the pistols. Centuriae, you said you had seven pistols, right?"

"That's right."

"There better be."

Two Roman soldiers in dark-red uniforms proceeded down the corridor, their pulse rifles raised in a firing position. Kaeso made sure his crew were in their quarters before he docked with the *Corus*, but he prayed they wouldn't be stupid enough to use the latrine right now.

The soldiers yanked Kaeso away from the wall and turned him toward the airlock hatch. The Romans stood at attention as the Centuriae of the *Corus* stepped through. She was like most Roman Eagle Centuriae Kaeso met in his time with Umbra: short, gray-haired, and with an imperious bearing that would impress the Consul. She sniffed the air and scowled.

"Let's get this over with, centuriae," she said, as if addressing a dog on a *cac* run. "I have no desire to be here any longer than I have to. Your ship smells of rotten cabbage."

Kaeso bowed his head. "I can assure my lady we've never transported rotten cabbage."

She looked at him, gauging whether or not he was being insolent.

Kaeso said, "I didn't catch my lady's name."

"No, you didn't. Why does the good Praetor Gurges want a Liberti ship to study a planet the gods have declared a blasphemy on humanity?"

"The Praetor believes soil samples can—"

The Centuriae snorted. "Soil samples? The planet is irradiated. It will be thousands of years before moss grows there, if ever. What does he want with dead soil?"

Kaeso paused and then smiled his most charming smile. "My Lady Centuriae, we both know why I'm here. We both know why you're here. So to limit the Lady Centuriae's olfactory exposure to my ship, I suggest we discuss our arrangement."

The Centuriae upturned her lips in a quick smile Kaeso almost missed. "Very well, centuriae. Let us discuss terms then. I will permit you to land on the planet for twenty-four hours after you transfer a port entry fee to the *Corus's* purse."

The Centuriae sounded so official when she explained the bribe's terms that Kaeso thought he was talking to an actual way station customs officer.

"How much is the, um, port entry fee, Lady Centuriae?"

"How much do you have in your ship's purse?"

"We can contribute 500 sesterces."

The Centuriae laughed, then turned toward the airlock. "Centurion, confiscate the ship and arrest the crew."

"I meant 1,200 sesterces, Lady Centuriae," Kaeso said.

She paused, then turned her head. "A good start, but it's still not enough. The Collegia Pontificis have released a Missive of the Gods saying any ship landing on Menota will be damned for all eternity. The gods don't issue such strong proclamations too often."

"We have 1,500 in the ship's purse."

The Centuriae sighed. "You're making this hard for me. Fifteen hundred may satisfy me, but I have the centuriae of the *Virtus* to consider, and he has more expensive tastes than I."

"You can check the tabulari yourself," Kaeso said. "It's all we have."

She stared at Kaeso, once again evaluating him. "I will grant you this concession: we will take the 1,500 sesterces in your ship's purse. Also, once you return from the planet, we will board your ship again and confiscate 70% of what you find on the planet. I'm willing to 'overlook' the remaining thirty percent."

"Thirty..."

"Come now, Centuriae, let's not be greedy," she said with a straight face. "If what the stories say is true, thirty percent of what is down there is more than enough to buy yourself a new ship. From the look and stench of this one, you could use an upgrade."

"Lady Centuriae, my crew and I will be risking our lives. Shouldn't we deserve at least half?"

"I happen to believe the vaults are a myth," she said. "The Roman fleet is thorough when it comes to its duties. Anything valuable was certainly evacuated or destroyed. From where I stand, I'm only getting 1,500 sesterces out of this deal."

"Yes, but thirty percent is—"

"Thirty percent or I destroy your ship. Decide now."

Kaeso shook his head. "I suppose I have no choice, do I, Lady Centuriae?"

She raised an eyebrow.

"I accept your ladyship's most generous offer."

The Centuriae turned and entered the airlock. "Transfer your ship's purse to *Corus* as soon as we leave. If you try to run after you leave the planet, I will destroy you whether or not your 'soil collection' was successful. You have twenty-four hours."

Once the Roman centuriae left *Caduceus*, the centurion unbound Kaeso's hands. He rubbed his wrists. "Is she always so generous?"

Kaeso could not see the man's expression behind the gold visor, but the centurion faced Kaeso a moment and then gave him a slight nod.

After the Romans left the connector tube, Kaeso sealed the outer airlock door. He reattached his collar com and said, "All crew, the Romans have left *Caduceus*, so you can leave your quarters. They have graciously allowed us to land."

Lucia's voice came back, "What did we have to give up, sir?"

"Everything in the ship's purse," Kaeso said, climbing up to the command deck, "and seventy percent of what we take from the planet."

"So we keep thirty percent?" Lucia asked.

"Uh-huh."

After a long silence, Blaesus laughed. "Vallutus was giving us twenty-five. Well done, Centuriae! I had no idea you were such a vicious haggler."

Kaeso entered the command deck and strapped himself into his delta couch. "No haggling, we just got lucky. The catch is we have twenty-four hours on the planet. Vallutus said he could get us three days, which means we'll be grabbing fewer marques."

"Indeed," Blaesus said. "But I'm happy to work a little harder for five percent more."

Lucia entered the command deck and strapped herself into her pilot's couch. Kaeso said into his com, "All crew prepare for landing. We enter atmosphere in fifteen minutes."

Chapter Six

Caduceus fell through Menota's atmosphere. Kaeso's tabulari readouts told him Lucia was doing a fine job "steering the pulse pellet" that was *Caduceus*. All any pilot could do during re-entry was aim the ship at a certain point on the planet, then let the atmosphere slow the ship enough to where the engines could take over the descent. It was the most dangerous part of space travel due to the frictional, gravitational, and inertial forces pushing and pulling the ship. At least *Caduceus's* grav and inertial cancelers kept the ride somewhat smooth.

"Re-entry burn complete," Lucia said. "Switching to thrusters and grav propulsion."

A small drop in his stomach told Keaso the grav propulsion kicked in, making the ship "ignore" the planet's gravity and float in the atmosphere. Out the window Kaeso saw billowy gray and brown clouds a mile below *Caduceus*. It was beautiful and peaceful from this high up, but he knew the planet's surface was quite different.

"I don't see any beacons from the old cities," Lucia said. "We'll have to make visual confirmation of our landing site." She glanced out the command deck window. "Don't know how we'll see anything in this soup."

"That's what you pay me for," Blaesus said, entering the command deck with his rolled maps and scrolls. "My encyclopedic wisdom and sharp wit."

Kaeso stood up from his command couch. "Well sit that wisdom and wit in the couch and find our landing site. We should be through the clouds in a few minutes."

"The honor is mine, Centuriae," Blaesus said as he sat in the couch. "And thank you for keeping the couch warm for my old bones."

Kaeso gave him a sideways look. "You seem extra gracious. You weren't in the wine again, were you?"

"Centuriae," Blaesus said, looking over his scrolls, "the only thing I'm drunk with is excitement at exploring a new world."

Kaeso nodded, satisfied with Blaesus' response and the absence of wine on his breath.

"Entering lower cloud cover," Lucia announced.

The ship dove toward the gray clouds at a thirty-degree angle. When *Caduceus* entered the clouds, the view outside turned gray and black. Condensation gathered on the window and on the camera lenses outside the ship.

"Let us see what we can see," Blaesus said, moving some sliders on the tabulari. "Starting terrain scans."

The view on the tabulari monitors turned from the gray clouds to color-coded terrain. Red outlines indicated mountains, greens for valleys, and blues for the small bodies of water left on the planet. Kaeso did not see any cities or other human ruins.

"How far are we from the site?" Kaeso asked.

When the former Senator didn't say anything, Kaeso asked again.

"I'll tell you when I find it," Blaesus said. "Remember what I said about not having Vallutus's coordinates? Patience, Centuriae."

The thing Kaeso found hardest about command was allowing his crew to do their jobs without hovering over their shoulders. Once the mission started, there was little for Kaeso to do besides stand back and watch his crew perform. When they did well, all he could do was feel useless. Lucia piloted the ship, Blaesus looked for the vaults, and Kaeso stood behind them both with hands in his pockets. It was a feeling he still hated after three years as Centuriae of *Caduceus*.

Lucia turned to Blaesus. "We're above the sector Barbata gave us. See anything yet?"

"Not...yet..." Blaesus said, going from the tabulari monitors to his scrolls. "Can you bring the ship below these clouds?"

Lucia frowned. "The clouds are a thousand feet above the ground."

"I need visual input. These damned color-coded readouts don't have the same flavor as sight. I need sight to feel my way to the location."

"You'll feel it if we crash into a mountain," Lucia said.

"I thought you were a better pilot than that?"

"I'm already getting proximity alerts from the mountains, and we're two thousand feet above the nearest peaks."

While Blaesus and Lucia bantered, Kaeso stared at the open map scroll on the former Senator's lap. It was an old satellite print from the days before the Roman bombardment, when Menota was a lush world with a thriving Roman colony. Before the Cariosus plague threatened to escape this one world and spread throughout human space. Blaesus had circled certain valleys and mountains with a red wax pencil.

"Blaesus, the locations you circled are nowhere near Pomona," Kaeso said, searching for the colonial capital on the map. "Weren't the vaults in the city?"

"My good Centuriae," Blaesus said, "the bits of information Barbata gave us indicated the vaults were hidden in the mountains."

"No, she said they were in 'the canyons of sector 2109 beneath a white tholus tree.'"

"I circled sector 2109 on the map, but I doubt we'll find any living tholus trees down there."

A twinge of pain shot from behind Kaeso's right ear, and he grimaced. Kaeso had assumed Blaesus would know Pomona's landmarks. Kaeso recognized the term 'canyons of sector 2109' from an Umbra mission he'd once performed on Menota. How to explain to Blaesus without revealing how he knew?

"In Pomona there was a street with a colosseum on one side and a theater on the other. The locals sometimes called it the Canyon since both buildings were so large."

"I never heard that. But then again I've never been to Menota." Blaesus looked at Kaeso. "Have you?"

A warning burst from the implant, but Kaeso masked his wince. "No," he lied, "but I knew someone who visited years before the Cariosus struck."

Lucia shook her head. "The Legion slagged every city on the planet. Even if the vaults are in Pomona, there's no way we could dig through six feet of glassed rock."

"Ah," Blaesus said, "but the Legion did *not* slag Pomona. They irradiated it with diraenium bombs. Killed two million citizens and every organism there so they would not have to destroy the planet's only temple consecrated to Jupiter Optimus Maximus. The gods would not look kindly on such a desecration."

Blaesus then turned to his map. "Pomona *is* in sector 2109. And it would make more sense for the vaults to be in a city where they'd be easier to access. What was the street's name, Centuriae?"

"I don't know," Kaeso lied again. "Look it up in the tabulari. We now have less than twenty-three hours to find the vaults and get the money, so let's start with the location that makes the most sense."

"As you wish, Centuriae. You hear that, dear Lucia? No flying through cloud-covered mountains. You get to fly through a cloud-covered city."

"Praise Juno," Lucia muttered. "The Pomona beacon is no longer transmitting, or Menota's nav satellites. We'll have to do this the old-fashioned way. What are the longitude and latitude coordinates for Pomona?"

Blaesus turned his map over and then relayed a series of numbers. Lucia tapped them into her tabulari. The view out the command window tilted right and down. Kaeso glimpsed land through the gray clouds, and then the ship dropped beneath the cover. A blackened landscape spread out below them. Kaeso had been to dead moons and planets, but they'd all evolved that way. Menota was a murdered world, killed by Roman mass drivers and diraenium bombs. With the little light filtering through the thick clouds, Kaeso could see barren hills and mountains, empty lake and riverbeds, and glossy black craters from mass driver impacts.

Wind buffeted *Caduceus*. Kaeso grabbed the command couch to steady himself. Not for the first time, he wished the ship's inertial cancelers compensated for impacts like it did for acceleration and deceleration. Maybe he could buy a new inertia system with the money they might find in Pomona.

Would find, he corrected himself. *Thinking failure breeds failure*, his old Umbra mentor had hammered into his psyche.

"There's Pomona," Lucia said.

The ship's nose cameras showed a city with buildings just as gray with ash as the surrounding hills. Where once a thriving, growing city had flourished, now the empty husks of markets, temples, and homes remained. The Romans may not have slagged the city, but their diraenium bombs were just as effective.

"Blaesus, where is this Canyon street?" Lucia asked.

"According to the tabulari, it's in the city's northeast sector." He looked up from his map to the monitors. "There," he said, pointing to two large elliptical buildings across the street from each other.

"Where should we land, sir?" Lucia asked Kaeso.

"Right between them, if you can."

Lucia clenched her teeth. *Caduceus* was not a large ship, and would easily fit between the colosseum and the theater, but landing there would be a challenge in the violent winds running through the valley at sixty miles per hour. Nobody said anything as Lucia guided the ship into the "Canyon." She hovered over the road separating the two structures, the winds buffeting the ship, pushing it backwards, but she held the sliders on her controls and allowed the ship to descend. There was a small bump as the ship settled on its pads, and then all was still.

"Grav and inertial fields off-line," Lucia said. "Thrusters powering down. We're here."

"Lucia," Blaesus said, "your skills are unmatched."

"I wouldn't have needed them if we had a landing system from this century." She glanced at Kaeso.

"Your landing system is in those vaults," Kaeso said. "Let's go get it."

Chapter Seven

"See the new display on your visor?" Nestor asked the crew once they were suited up in Bay One. Kaeso noticed the new red box in his helmet visor's corner display. There were two bars labeled 'Radiation' and 'Contagion.'

When everyone said they did, Nestor continued, "Watch that display. I programmed it just for this job. The suit will protect you from the bulk of any radiation."

"'Bulk?'" Dariya asked as she checked Daryush's suit. The big man grunted, and gave her an upturned thumb. Dariya smiled, nodded, and then patted him on the shoulder.

Nestor said, "You will not get any more radiation than you would standing outside on a sunny day. However, if some should leak into the suit, that display will tell you how much."

"How's it different than the normal rad display?" Lucia asked. Her eyes darted across the interior display only she could see. Like Kaeso's helmet, Lucia's followed her eye motions and responded to blinks that told it which displays to show on the visor.

"Normal rad displays won't pick up the diraenium Romans use in their irradiation bombs," Nestor said. "This new display will."

Kaeso focused on the display and blinked twice to bring it to full size on his visor. "I suppose the 'Contagion' would be our friend the Cariosus."

"Yes, Centuriae," Nestor said. "It monitors your suit's interior for contamination. If that alarm goes off...well, we are leaving you behind."

Flamma adjusted his helmet latches, then asked, "I thought the diraenium bombs killed off everything?"

"They were supposed to," Nestor said, "but the vaults are underground. There might be pockets of virus the bombs did not reach."

Flamma nodded, and the crew was quiet.

"Well," Blaesus said, rubbing his gloves together, "I cannot wait to get started."

Kaeso went to the cargo bay's door controls and moved a slider. Red lights flashed within the bay. Kaeso said into his com, "Verify your suits are secure."

One by one the crew gave their affirmative. Kaeso checked the fittings on his suit one last time and then checked his visor to ensure it was sealed.

"Opening outer doors," Kaeso said, then moved the slider to the open position.

The cargo ramp lowered with a grinding Kaeso heard in his helmet. Dust and ash blew into Bay One from outside. When the ramp touched the ground, he saw swirling eddies of fine debris moving on the street. The light was gray, even though it was near noon at this longitude. Kaeso picked up his tool bag, slung it over his shoulder, and led the crew onto Pomona's dead streets.

The howling wind pushed Kaeso left; he had to lean into the wind to avoid falling over. He looked at the colosseum and the amphitheater ahead. The hazy sun barely penetrated the cloud cover, but it illuminated both structures just enough to see their dark, massive outlines through the polluted air. Kaeso blinked at his visor and his helmet lights came on. They lit up the air particles around him, making it even more difficult to see, so he switched them off.

He turned and watched his crew lumber down the *Caduceus's* ramp in their EVA suits. They all carried a tool bag over their shoulders. Lucia's Legionnaire training helped her move gracefully in her suit, while the others fought simply to stand straight in the wind.

Kaeso frowned. Once again, guilt surged through him. *They are not trained for this. We should be smuggling Arabian* kaffa. *A job you know they can do. They're not Umbra Ancilia. They're not even Legionaries.*

"They're competent enough," Kaeso muttered to himself.

"You say something, sir?" Lucia asked, approaching him. "Your lips moved, but I didn't hear you on the com."

"Nothing. Blaesus, where's your map?"

Blaesus lumbered up to Kaeso, then stumbled forward as a wind gust almost sent him into Kaeso's arms.

"A bit breezy today," he said. "I scanned the maps onto the ship's shared network. You can find it in my folder. Here are the scrolls Vallutus was kind enough *not* to ask for when he backed out."

Kaeso took the scrolls and then blinked at his visor to bring up the ship's network. He found the maps in Blaesus's folder, ignored the ones of the local hills and mountains, and opened the file showing the vaults' layout.

"Everyone open the vault schematic," Kaeso ordered.

Dariya approached with Daryush shuffling behind. "Should we not find the vaults first?" she asked.

"The schematics will tell us where the vaults are," Kaeso said. "Look for vents, power generators, anything that would need connecting to the outside. Private citizens built these vaults. I'm betting the vaults won't be self-contained like a military bunker."

The crew studied the layouts for a minute, then Dariya said, "Ah..."

When she didn't say more, Lucia demanded, "What?"

Dariya ignored Lucia.

Kaeso said, "Dariya?"

"Sir, I believe our Roman friends used an Iris for their com systems. If you check the schematics around the access room just outside the vaults, you will see switch boxes with the Iris symbol."

"So?" Lucia asked. "Many banks use Iris."

Kaeso grinned. "Yes, and they need a nice, big antenna array to bypass the way station relays and send their signals into their own store of com drones next to the way line. Look for an Iris array on the colosseum or amphitheater. It should be someplace high up."

Peering into the ashy gloom, Kaeso realized his order would be harder to follow than it sounded. Kaeso told the crew to split up. Kaeso, Dariya, Daryush, and Flamma walked around the colosseum, while Lucia took Blaesus and Nestor around the amphitheater's exterior.

Kaeso had seen the many colosseums on Terra, even the Colosseum Maximus in Roma. While the Pomona colosseum was not as large as the Maximus, it was still big enough to make it difficult for Kaeso to search for a rooftop Iris antenna in the seething atmosphere.

"Where are all the bodies?" Flamma asked, staring at the colosseum.

"I thought Romans burn golem bodies after gladiatorial matches," Dariya said.

"I'm not talking about gladiators. Where are all the citizen bodies? If the city was irradiated without warning, shouldn't we see some bodies?"

Kaeso scanned the street and realized Flamma was right. It had been two years since the planet was destroyed. If the diraenium bombs killed all living organisms as advertised, there would be no bacteria around to decompose any bodies left in the open, nor would there be any animals to feast on the remains. There should be thousands of people laying in the streets, sitting in the crashed cars and buses, lying in the doors of buildings. Besides the dust and ash, the whole street looked as if it was deserted when the bombs fell.

"Maybe they took shelter?" Dariya said.

"They wouldn't have had time," Kaeso said. "The Eagles jumped through the way line and bombed the planet within minutes."

As Kaeso pondered the riddle, Lucia's voice came over his com. "Centuriae, I think we found the Iris."

"Acknowledged. We'll be right there."

When Kaeso's team reached Lucia's location in the back of the amphitheater, she pointed to a wide circular shadow on the theater's roof.

"Is that your Iris antenna?" she asked Dariya.

Dariya peered into the gloom. "I cannot tell for sure in this muck, but it seems the right dimensions. Well done, centurion."

Kaeso could almost hear Lucia's teeth grind at Dariya's intentional misidentification of her former rank. Before Lucia could respond, Blaesus said, "I spotted it. Apparently my eyes are used to seeing through cloudy cataracts."

Kaeso grinned. He appreciated the old Senator's knack for defusing tense situations. Even if he sometimes created them.

Kaeso pointed to a door at the back of the amphitheater. He tried the handle, but it was locked so they proceeded around the side to the front of the building to find the main doors open.

"Ah," Blaesus said once he entered the lobby. "Now I can stand up straight like a civilized man and not fight that infernal wind."

"Which way now?" Flamma asked.

The theater's main lobby would have been as opulent and beautiful as any Roman theater, if it was not covered in gray ash. Beneath the grime, colorful frescoes graced the walls behind smooth marble statues of the gods standing on pedestals. Darkened chandeliers hung from the ceiling far above them. A wide, red-carpeted staircase with marble handrails wound its way up to the theater's second level.

The wind moaned through the theater.

Kaeso brought up the vault schematics on his visor. They showed that the only entrance was from an elevator. Kaeso scanned the lobby for an elevator and found one at the far end near the base of the staircase. He walked to the elevator and pressed a button. Nothing happened.

Dariya grunted. "I am surprised you even tried, sir." She pulled a crowbar from her tool bag. "I have the key."

She inserted the crowbar into the space where the doors met and pulled back on the bar. The doors groaned open an inch or two.

She motioned to her brother. "You take a pull, big man."

Daryush nodded, then put his gloved hands on the crowbar and grunted as he pulled the doors open another foot. Kaeso grabbed one side of the door, Daryush the other, and they both pulled again, opening the doors to shoulder width. Kaeso turned on his helmet lamps and peered down into the blackness. The elevator car rested at the floor below them, its top a foot below the entrance. Kaeso squeezed between the open doors, taking care not to snag his oxygen backpack, and stepped onto the car's roof. He found a rooftop access hatch and gave it a good stomp. It fell into the elevator with a soft thump on the carpeted floor.

Dariya peeked through the doors. "No way we can fit through that little hatch. Not with these suits."

Kaeso checked the vault schematics on his visor again. "You're right. Good thing this isn't the elevator we want." He stepped back into the lobby.

"Of course," Dariya said, checking her visor. "This shaft is too narrow. It's got to be a freight elevator."

"Let's try the loading docks."

The crew walked through the lobby and onto the theater floor. Ash-covered busts sat in alcoves along the walls. More frescoes covered the walls with scenes from bawdy comedies to tragic dramas. Above them hung a spectacular chandelier with hundreds of tiny, dangling crystals. It looked like an upside down tholus tree.

Kaeso grunted, then pointed up at the chandelier. "Our white tholus tree."

"So Barbata knew what she was talking about after all," Blaesus said. "Should we start digging up the seats beneath it?"

The crew ignored Blaesus and continued walking down the aisle.

A colorful set graced the stage, as if awaiting the next performance. It was a scene from ancient Greece, with Greek gods and

Greek lettering painted on marble columns. Kaeso's Greek was limited, but he could make out "Thebes" on a column.

"Seneca," Blaesus said wistfully. "It's a scene from the first act of *Oedipus*, I believe. It's been years since I saw a play by him. The Seneca troupes in the Lost Worlds don't compare to a true Roman company."

Flamma chuckled. "Give me a good Atellan farce any day. Seneca depresses me."

"Atellan farces are vulgar," Blaesus scoffed. "Just the sort of taste I'd expect from a gladiator. Lucia, please tell me you are not a vulgar plebe like our gladiator comrade? Seneca or Atellan?"

"I've never been to the theater," she said.

"You've never... But why? You call yourself a Roman and you've never been to the theater?"

"Why spend a dozens sesterces and two hours to sit in a crowded theater when I can watch dramas on my own visum?"

"Oh, my dear, it's the experience you pay for, not the story. We'll remedy that once we're all rich. Then you won't have any excuse to avoid live plays. I'll take you to a good Seneca play, perhaps *Oedipus* in memory of this adventure. I think you'd like it. I suppose we could find a decent enough company outside Roma. Perhaps Libertus has one. What say you, Centuriae? Are the Liberti uncultured barbarians like all good Romans are taught to believe, or do they have good playhouses with quality actors?"

"I wouldn't know," Kaeso said. "I'm more of a reader. I'd rather read the worst book ever written than see the best play ever made."

Blaesus laughed. "Centuriae, I'm not sure if you're joking or serious. To be honest, it doesn't matter. A clever response nonetheless."

Kaeso climbed the six stairs up to the stage and then weaved around the set pieces to the curtains behind them. He parted the curtains and stepped into the tight corridor. His headlamps illuminated the dusty air ten feet in every direction.

"Lucia, take your group left and I'll go right. Call if you find the elevator."

"Yes, sir."

Kaeso led Dariya, Daryush, and Flamma to the right. Collapsed rigging lay scattered on the floor. He stepped around it, warning the others as he did so.

Kaeso saw the first body backstage. It was a man, naked, lying on his back, his empty eye sockets staring at the ceiling. The irradiated city and dry climate had preserved the body well. Though the skin was leathery, the man's facial features were clear. He had no hair that Kaeso could see, and his neck was swollen as wide as his head. A Cariosus victim.

Kaeso took a deep breath and stepped over the man.

Dariya said, "There's your body, Flamma. Happy?"

Flamma exhaled, but said nothing.

Kaeso turned another corner and saw the freight elevator doors. Five more bodies lay before them. He shined is helmet lights on the bodies and saw they were also Cariosus victims. Men and women, all naked, with swollen necks and no hair. Kaeso noticed the elevator had dents and scratches in it. As Kaeso approached, he saw the shredded fingernails on each body, the tips a pulpy mush.

Daryush began to moan. Dariya took his hand in hers. "It's all right, 'Ush, I'm here. Just don't look at them."

"He's not gonna get sick, is he?" Flamma asked. "'Cause that would be nasty if he got sick in a—"

"Shut up, Flamma," Dariya said. "He is not sick." Dariya led Daryush away from the bodies to the other side of the backstage.

Kaeso activated his com. "Lucia, we found the freight elevator."

"We're on our way, sir."

"Be aware there's debris and...bodies on the way."

She paused. "Acknowledged."

When Lucia, Blaesus, and Nestor arrived, Daryush still stood in a corner with his back to the bodies, Dariya trying to soothe him.

"Yes," Blaesus grumbled, "they would have to block the door."

Nestor walked over to the bodies and inspected them. He looked up at Kaeso with grim eyes.

Kaeso turned to Flamma and Lucia. "Let's move them."

When both paused, he said, "They're dead. They're no longer contagious. The diraenium bombs killed off any virus long ago."

They both nodded reluctantly, then each grabbed a body's ankles and pulled it off to the side.

Kaeso couldn't blame them for hesitating. All the Umbra training left in him screamed to get as far away from these bodies as fast as he could. He ignored the screams, grabbed the ankles of a body, and pulled it away from the elevator.

"Um," Blaesus said, "am I the only one wondering why they scratched the elevator door hard enough to destroy their fingers?"

Lucia grunted as she moved another body. "To escape the diraenium bombs would be my guess."

"They were in the Cariosa's final stages," Blaesus said. "They'd have no concept of the danger. My guess is they knew someone was alive beyond those doors. Someone to satisfy their hunger."

"Blaesus," Kaeso said, "please give us a hand."

He sighed. "I'm an old man, but I will do my best."

Once they cleared the bodies from the elevator door, Kaeso asked Dariya for her crowbar. She whispered something in Persian to Daryush, then went and handed Kaeso the bar.

"Is he with us?" Kaeso asked.

Dariya glared at him. "He will be fine. It just takes him longer to get used to...terrible things. Not everyone can look on a dead body without flinching."

Kaeso took the crowbar from Dariya, and wondered when dead bodies stopped bothering him. *After your first assassination*, he reminded himself. *After that, they all became just another slaughtered animal.* Kaeso thrust the crowbar's edge into the elevator doors and yanked back harder than he intended. The crowbar came out and he stumbled backward. He slammed the crowbar on the floor.

"Easy, sir," Lucia said, rushing over to him. "Are you all right"

"Fine," he said. "I'm fine."

He grabbed the crowbar, went back to the door, and inserted it again. This time he opened the door three inches. Kaeso and Lucia pulled it open with their hands. When the opening was shoulder width, he aimed his headlamps down the shaft. There was only blackness beyond his lamps' range. He could not see the elevator car below, or when he looked up. He pulled his head out and studied the dark control pad on the wall to the right.

"Flamma," he said, "think you can handle it?"

Flamma snorted and unslung his tool bag. "I built my own gladiator golems, so I think I can hook a battery up to a wall pad."

As Flamma worked, Dariya brought Daryush back to the group. His brow was sweaty and furrowed, and he kept his wide gaze on the elevator.

"How are you, big man?" Kaeso asked.

Daryush shrugged.

"We'll be out of here soon," Kaeso said. "We'll be rich enough to install a brand new engine on *Caduceus*. You'll spend months tinkering with it."

The big Persian brightened a little. Kaeso glanced at Dariya, and she gave him a grateful nod.

The elevator began to hum. Kaeso turned to see the wall pad aglow and running through a start-up routine.

"Got it," Flamma said.

Once the pad's controls came on, Flamma pushed a button on the display, and the elevator cables began moving. The car rose above the floor, its interior light pouring from its partially opened doors. It stopped when it was parallel to the floor, and then the doors opened all the way.

"How long will the battery last?" Kaeso asked Flamma.

"An hour. I got another one, in case this takes longer."

Kaeso turned to the crew. "Ready?"

They all nodded in their helmets, their eyes wide. Even Blaesus seemed a little nervous now that it was time to go underground.

"Remember," Kaeso said. "All we have to do is grab the paper in those vaults and we're rich. We won't have to work another day for at least...a month."

Each one grinned. Except for Daryush who still looked ill.

Kaeso stepped into the elevator and the crew followed. Once everyone boarded, Flamma brought up the car's control pad and checked a few readouts.

"I think we got the right place," he said. "The display above the door says there's one level below ground, but the pad says differently. Just a few hacks here...and there..."

The door slammed shut, and Daryush jumped. The elevator began to descend.

"We're on our way," Flamma said.

The control pad dinged when the elevator reached the basement level, but the elevator continued to descend. The crew remained quiet.

"Schematics say the vaults are a hundred feet below ground," Kaeso said, more to break the nervous silence than to provide information the crew could see on their own visors.

"Check your 'Contagion' and 'Radiation' levels," Nestor said.

"Medicus," Blaesus said, "if any were in the red, I think you'd have heard screaming by now."

The elevator stopped with a thud, and the entire crew flinched. Then the door opened to darkness.

Chapter Eight

Kaeso stepped out of the elevator. His helmet lights illuminated the hallway fifteen feet ahead. A layer of dust coated the cream-colored floor, and billowed up when Kaeso walked on it. He swept the hall with his lights, illuminating the smooth walls. There were no decorations or patterns, and Kaeso saw through the dust and grime that the walls were the same cream color as the floor. Light domes ran down the center of the ceiling, but none were lit.

Kaeso passed several doors on each side of the hall and followed the schematics to the vault room door. It was red, metal, with a hand-shaped identipad on the right side.

"Flamma," Kaeso said.

"Got it, Centuriae." The young Egyptian pulled out his tools and went to work on the pad.

"Sir," Lucia said, facing the black hallway.

"What?"

She shined her helmet light down the hall at two doorways. One was half-open and the other closed, its handle broken off.

"We're bound to find open doors down here," Kaeso said.

"I mean the floor."

Kaeso looked at the floor between the two doors. Foot prints and scuff marks in the dust allowed him to see the cream tiles. The marks were recent judging from how the tiled floor shined in his lights.

Lucia glanced at Kaeso, then drew her pulse pistol. Kaeso did the same.

"What is it, Centuriae?" Nestor asked from behind.

"Everyone stay here," Kaeso ordered. "Lucia and I'll be right back."

Kaeso and Lucia approached the opposite doors cautiously, Kaeso in the lead with Lucia a step behind him.

"Watch the closed door," he told Lucia when they arrived. "I'll check the open one first."

"Yes, sir."

His heart thumping, Kaeso held the pistol in a firing position with his right hand, and pushed open the door with his left. His lights showed a small room with metal shelves. Empty boxes and canisters littered the shelves and floor, some ripped apart. Or chewed apart. Cans with vegetable and meat labels, ripped boxes of dried rice and noodles, and *garum* bottles all lay empty on the floor. There wasn't a morsel of food left, as if everything had been licked clean. Kaeso searched the small room, but could not find any other boxes or cans with food.

"Anything, sir?" Lucia asked.

"It's a pantry. Or used to be. Been cleaned out. We're not alone down here. Flamma, how're you coming with that pad?"

"Almost there, Centuriae."

"Hurry up. Lucia, let's check the other door."

Kaeso left the pantry, passed Lucia, and stood to the left of the closed door. Lucia went to the other side. Kaeso did a countdown with his fingers from three. When he reached zero, he pushed open the door.

A kitchen. On the right was a flat top stove in one corner. To the right of the stove was a sink and more counter space. There was a door to a walk-in freezer on the left side of the room, next to an external refrigerator. A square table with no chairs stood in the center of the room.

"Why is there a pantry and kitchen in a vault meant to store bank marques?" Lucia asked.

"Probably a bomb shelter as well," Kaeso said. "When they founded this colony, the Menota system was on the edge of Zhonguo space."

Lucia nodded. Sixty years ago Roma and Zhonguo fought repeated border skirmishes, which blew up into the Nox War. That little conflict went badly for the Zhonguo and moved the border six way line jumps into Zhonguo territory. Menota was now well within Roman space, and the threat of indiscriminate bombing from the Zhonguo had ceased. Ironically, it would not be the Zhonguo that bombed Menota.

Kaeso walked over to the stove, where two pots sat on the cold burners. Both pots had a black residue at the bottom, as if left on the burner after most of the contents were scooped out. Black stains covered the entire stove, along with the counter space beside it.

Lucia opened the freezer door and sucked in a breath. Kaeso looked past her to see dozens of bones piled inside the dark freezer. Skulls stared back at him with yawning jaws. Dried flesh still clung to many of the bones. A flash of insight told him how it went down here for the survivors. First they cleaned out the pantry. After they ate all the food, they ate their dead. When the dead were gone...they created more.

He thought back to the footprints outside the doors. Could they have survived this long, though?

"Go back to the door and keep watch," Kaeso told Lucia.

Lucia nodded, went back to the door and stood in the hallway. Kaeso shut the freezer door and then opened the refrigerator. Four desiccated heads stared back at him. They were hairless, with brown leathery skin pulled tight around their skulls. Kaeso shut the door and left the room.

"Flamma."

"Another minute."

Nestor approached Kaeso, glancing at the doors. "What did you find, Centuriae?"

"Heads, bones, dirty pots."

"How old?"

"A few months, no more."

Blaesus cleared his throat. "The planet was bombed two years ago..."

Kaeso scanned the dark hallway beyond. He saw no other doors, but his visor told him there were two more rooms ahead, and then the hallway ended at a T-shaped intersection. If people had survived down here since the bombing, they were that way. And they would be infected with the Cariosus. Kaeso fought his implant's warnings to flee this tomb as fast as possible. *Not yet, not yet, not yet*, he repeated to himself. He had to keep the demons at bay just long enough to get—

"I'm in, Centuriae," Flamma said. The door clicked, and Flamma pushed it open.

"Finally," Dariya said. "Let's get the marques and leave this dungeon."

Daryush grunted his agreement.

"Articulate as always, my Persian friend," Blaesus said and followed them inside.

Kaeso turned to Lucia. "Watch down that hall. Let me know if--"

"You'll know, sir."

Kaeso entered the vault room to find his crew staring at the shelves. Stacks of paper sealed in clear plastic sat on each shelf. Blaesus walked over to one shelf and sighed.

"There must be 30 million sesterces worth of marques in this room," he said.

"Gods be praised," Nestor breathed.

"We're on a timer, people," Kaeso said, walking to a shelf and unslinging the bag from his shoulder. "Blaesus and I will load the bags. Dariya, Daryush, and Nestor will take the bags up to the ship. And bring back the cargo carts. We're going to need them."

Almost seven million sesterces for us, if the Romans keep their word, Kaeso thought as he stuffed marques into the large bags. *A million each.* He didn't know the interest rates on Liberti accounts, but he knew they'd be enough for his crew to avoid work for the rest of their lives. Kaeso could sell the ship to Lucia and quit the smuggling business without worrying about his people. He wouldn't have to solve their problems or keep them fed and clothed. He wouldn't even have to worry about the Roman authorities finding them. He wouldn't have to worry about them *at all*. They would have the means to do whatever they wanted, and he would...well, he would do something else.

After fifteen minutes of packing and loading the bags onto the ship's cargo cart, the mood in the vault room had gone from tense anxiety to jovial banter on how they would spend their loot.

Blaesus described the villa he would buy on a lake on Capri, a resort moon in the Libertus system. He would spend his days reading, writing, and eating the richest, fattiest food he could buy.

"Maybe even a dally with a rich patrician widow," he said with a wink at Kaeso.

Flamma said, "I've always wanted to open a gladiator training school."

Blaesus laughed. "I would've thought your, um, misunderstanding with the Collegia Pontificis had soured you on the arena."

Flamma shrugged as he zipped up the bag he just filled. "I still love the arena. I just never liked the fame or the...taboos associated with it."

"Like falling in love with your golems?" Blaesus asked.

Kaeso prepared for an angry outburst from Flamma, but the young Egyptian just shrugged. Perhaps the new money eased his sensitivity over the subject.

"Yes, " Flamma said in a quiet tone. "Like that."

Kaeso had never asked Flamma the whole story behind his flight from Roma, since he figured that was Flamma's business. But like anyone who knew anything about the Roman gladiator sport, Kaeso knew Flamma had committed the religiously unacceptable act of declaring Arial, his female gladiator golem, a 'human.' Though Romans used human genes to build golems in large vats, the Roman Collegia Pontificis had decreed that golems were not human, thus making it morally easier to use them as gladiators and sex toys.

If Flamma had stuck to just sleeping with his golem, there wouldn't have been an issue. Though the Collegia frowned on sex with golems, they tolerated it so long as it was discrete. With Roman patricians paying top sesterces for the best sex golems, there was no real way to stop it anyway.

However, for Flamma to declare Arial human...that was high order blasphemy. The Collegia banned Flamma from the arena for life and forced him into exile.

"I loved programming new golems," Flamma said, "giving them life, and testing them against the best in the Republic. I'll have enough money for a new identity, so that won't be a problem. It'll be like when I first started. When I did it because I loved it, not because people expected me to do it. How about you, Nestor?"

Nestor had just walked into the vault room pushing an empty cargo cart after unloading the first marques on the ship.

"I will continue to travel," Nestor said. "The gods have created a wondrous universe, and humanity has not seen a fraction of it. I want to see what is out there. Perhaps I will find other races. Humanity cannot be the only mortal intelligence the gods created."

Kaeso listened to his crew's dreams with satisfaction. They all had their own ideas that did not involve him or *Caduceus*. It made him feel better about his own plans.

That is, until Dariya spoke up. She and Daryush were still unloading bags on the ship, but her voice was clear over the com.

"How can you people abandon the Centuriae?" she asked. "He has given you so much, and the first chance you get you run? Daryush and I will stay with *Caduceus*. We go where Centuriae Kaeso goes."

Kaeso sighed. He appreciated Dariya's loyalty, but he wanted—

"Something's coming!" Lucia screamed.

She fired six rounds from her pulse pistol, then dove into the room. Kaeso went to slam the door, but came face to face with an inhuman visage. It was emaciated and pale, with a bulging neck and hairless body. It snarled at Kaeso, its lips the color of iodine, its teeth yellow. The creature grabbed Kaeso's suit with bony fingers. Kaeso slammed the door on the thin arm with all his strength. The crew rushed over and pushed the door closed against the creatures pushing from the other side. The door latched shut, and a sickening crack filled the room as the creature's arm sheared off and splattered to the floor. Flamma hit the door controls with a gloved hand to lock the door.

The infectees pounded on the door, growling and screaming their hunger. But Kaeso knew it was not growling or screaming. It was a language, one that everyone outside Umbra thought was animalistic shrieks by people who had lost their humanity to the Cariosus. Kaeso didn't need his Umbra implant to know what the infected people on the other side wanted.

Chapter Nine

"Mavor's balls! How can anyone still be alive in here?" Blaesus shouted over the pounding and screaming at the door. He stared wide-eyed at the severed arm on the floor. Nestor bent down to inspect the arm.

"Careful, Medicus," Kaeso said.

"I won't touch it." Nestor used a screwdriver from his tool bag to turn the arm over. "They are starving."

"Obviously," Blaesus said, "and we're the juiciest morsels they've seen in two years."

Lucia holstered her pistol. "I bet they came down for shelter from the diraenium bombs. They must have brought the Cariosus with them."

"I know Cariosa are tough," Blaesus said, "but two years in this vault? How did they breathe? Where did they get their water?"

"There must be something here we haven't seen yet," Kaeso said, watching the door and listening to the screams.

"You mean air tanks?" Blaesus said. "An underground cistern not on the schematics? Maybe they've watched dramas on their tabulari this whole time? And we were so close to becoming richer than—"

Kaeso rounded on Blaesus, but Flamma beat him to it.

"Hey, old man," Flamma said, grabbing Blaesus's arm. "We're not dead yet."

"Centuriae," Dariya's voice crackled over the com. "What's happening?"

"Stay on the ship, Dariya," Kaeso ordered. "Don't come down here. Survivors with the Cariosus attacked us."

"Is everyone all right?"

"Yes, we're safe in the vault room."

"Safe?" Blaesus said.

"Maybe they'll give up," Flamma said. "Sooner or later they'll figure they can't beat the door down."

Blaesus turned to him. "Didn't you see reports on the Cariosus, or the bodies upstairs? They won't give up until they've turned their hands to pulp scratching and beating that door."

Dariya said, "We're coming down, Centuriae."

"Negative, Dariya. You and Daryush stay up there. I don't know how many Cariosa are out there, but it's more than one. All they have to do is rip your suit and you'd be dead...or joining them."

"I have a plan, sir. We will be there in fifteen minutes."

"Dariya, you will obey my orders and stay on the ship. Dariya? Dariya!"

Kaeso ground his teeth. Dariya and Daryush were brilliant engineers, but he had no idea how they'd react in a fight. Dariya might be willing, but was she able? And Daryush, despite his size, fled to his bunk whenever two of the crew had a mild disagreement. Could he fend off several mad, inhuman Cariosa?

The Cariosa continued pounding on the door and screaming in their nonsensical tongue. Blaesus was right; they would not give up, even when their fists were bloody mash. When that happened, they'd start kicking the door until they collapsed on their broken bones. Then they'd start smashing their heads against the door. Kaeso knew what the virus drove its hosts to do. It would use their bodies until their muscles or bones no longer worked.

He knew the Persian twins were his crew's only hope, but his mind railed at his own greed and stupidity for getting them in this fix to begin with. He knew this had been a possibility, but he also knew this was his best chance to escape the chains of responsibility without abandoning his crew.

"Centuriae," Lucia said, interrupting his thoughts. "I have twelve rounds in my gun. You haven't fired yours yet, so you have sixteen."

"How many did you see out there?" Kaeso asked.

Lucia paused. "Three came at me at first, but I saw four more behind them. More shadows behind those four, I think. I don't know how many."

"So even if we hit them with every last round, do you think we could stop them all? They won't stop."

Pain exploded behind his right ear, and this time Kaeso couldn't stop the gasp that came with it.

"Sir?" Lucia put her hands on Kaeso's arms to steady him.

He took a ragged breath. "I'll be fine. Just a headache."

"That was no headache, sir."

Nestor stooped next to him. "What's wrong, Centuriae?"

"I'm fine," Kaeso growled. "Let's think up a plan before Dariya and Daryush do something stupid."

Lucia eyed him with worry, and he knew he'd have to give her an explanation later.

Later. He wanted to laugh aloud at his worries over "later." *Always the optimist*, he thought.

"As I was about to say, sir," Lucia said, "we may not have a choice. We can't stay down here in these suits to wait those things out. We have six hours of air left."

"Wonderful," Blaesus said. "I won't hold my bladder the next six minutes."

"Not to mention," Lucia continued, "we'll get thirsty."

"Noted," Kaeso said, staring at the door.

Dariya's voice crackled over the com. "Do not do anything just yet, my friends. And Lucia. We have a little surprise for your Cariosa."

"What are you going to do?" Kaeso asked.

"You would rather not know, sir. I would advise you all to stay there until I tell you to come out."

"Dariya, what are you going to do?"

"Stand by."

The floor hummed, and a faint murmur came from behind the wall on his left. The wall closest to the elevator.

"Hey, Cap," Flamma said, "I think they're coming down."

Fortuna grant them your luck, Kaeso prayed.

Kaeso could feel the elevator more than hear it over the Cariosa shrieks. When its rumbling strengthened, the pounding on the door stopped, along with the screaming. All was quiet outside except for the elevator's motors.

"Dariya," Kaeso called, "they know you're coming. They'll be right outside the door when it opens."

"That is what I'm hoping for, sir."

Lucia shook her head. "She's going to kill us all."

"I am going to save your ass, Trierarch. I suggest you all move to the back of the vault room. I do not know how hot this will get."

Once the crew huddled in the far corner behind three rows of shelves, Kaeso said, "We're away from the door."

"Good," Dariya said over the com. "Open it, 'Ush."

Kaeso heard Cariosa shrieks, Dariya's Persian curses, and pistol shots. Daryush screamed once, and then an explosion made the shelves tremble. Then silence.

"Dariya!"

"We are fine, sir," she said, her breathing labored. "I think we got them all."

"Got them with what?"

"The last of the way line plasma."

Kaeso was too stunned to speak, but not Lucia.

"You fool!" she yelled. "Now we can't leave the system!"

"We can buy some from the Romans," Dariya said.

"Why would they sell it to us? They'll leave us stranded first. They'll probably take all the marques anyway."

Blaesus said, "Trierarch, I for one am glad Dariya did what she did. At least now we'll be alive to haggle."

A knock came from the vault door. "Are you coming out or what?" Dariya asked over the com.

Flamma hurried over, punched some keys on the control pad, and the lock clicked. He opened the door to find Dariya standing there with her hands on her hips. Daryush was behind her, staring back at the elevator door. Kaeso nodded to Dariya, then entered the blackened, steaming corridor and looked back at the elevator. The lights from the car illuminated seven charred forms in front of the door. None moved, but he didn't count them dead. Not at all. He'd seen Cariosa come back from much worse injuries.

"All right," he said. "Everyone grab the last bags. We're leaving."

Lucia looked at him. "There are still millions of marques left."

"Really?" Kaeso said. "Don't you think we've had enough of these vaults? We're getting out now before we're ambushed again."

"Centuriae," Blaesus said, "there's only one load left. I'm willing to risk it if everyone else is."

Kaeso stared at him. "You're the one who wanted out the most."

Blaesus shrugged, then glanced back at the last marques. "I'd say Dariya took care of the problem. Would be a shame to leave these for the Romans to pick up."

Flamma nodded. "Let's get it all, sir."

Kaeso glanced at Nestor, who shrugged. He sighed. He wanted every last sesterce just as much as they did. But they had no idea what they were dealing with, and there was no way to explain it without the implant liquefying his brain.

The longer you stand here, the longer you stand here, he thought to himself.

"One more load," he said. "Let's move."

The crew sprang into action, while Lucia stood guard in the hallway again. Kaeso walked back to the elevator. The scorched bodies had curled into a fetal position when they roasted in Dariya's plasma conflagration. Kaeso was glad he couldn't smell them.

Who were they? Did they have families and people who loved them? How *had* they survived down here for two years? Even a Cariosus-infested body needed water, air, and food. They had eaten the food in the pantry and then eventually turned on each other. Could that alone have sustained them?

The missing bodies.

Of course, Kaeso thought. Somehow the Cariosa had reached the surface and dragged away all the irradiated bodies. That was how they survived. But how did they endure the radiation up top?

"Be careful, Centuriae," Nestor said from behind him.

"I know."

He drew his pulse pistol and fired into the head of the nearest body. The red and black head exploded. He shot each head and then walked back to the crew.

Lucia stared at him. "Paranoid?"

"Yes," he said, holstering his pistol.

A Cariosa jumped at Lucia from the darkness before Kaeso could warn her. The emaciated, bald madman hit her with the force of a large gladiator golem, knocking her onto her back. Kaeso drew his pistol, aimed at the madman's head, but the Cariosa ducked. Lucia pushed the Cariosa up and then rolled over. Before Kaeso could shoot, he saw movement down the hall. Three more forms ran at them. Kaeso shot two in the head, but the third sped toward Lucia. Before it reached her, Dariya charged out of the vault room and slammed her shoulder into the madman's flank, hurtling him into the blackened hall. The Cariosa bounced off the wall and back into Dariya, screaming its guttural language. Both tumbled into the vault room.

By this time, Lucia had turned over and pinned her attacker to the floor. She brought her pistol against the thing's head and fired. The head blew apart, and the Cariosa stopped struggling. It still twitched as Lucia jumped up. She turned and aimed her pistol down the hall at any other attackers.

Dariya's curses blasted over the com as she struggled with the Cariosa. Kaeso ran into the vault room to see Daryush, Flamma, and Nestor trying to pull the thing off her. It took all three to pry its arms off Dariya's neck and then throw the Cariosa into the corner. As soon as it was clear, Kaeso shot the attacker in the head and it crumpled to the floor.

"Dariya?" Kaeso said, turning to the door, his pistol raised. He stood next to Lucia, facing the dark hall again.

"I'm fine, sir," she said, breathing heavy. "I'm fine...I think I..."

A dire alarm toned in Kaeso's helmet, and he checked his visor to see a contamination warning from Dariya's suit. Kaeso looked back in the vault room, found Nestor's eyes.

"Her suit's torn," he said, helping her up. "We need to get her back to the ship now."

"Was she bit?" Kaeso asked.

When Nestor didn't respond, Dariya did.

"Yes, Centuriae, it bit me."

Chapter Ten

Quintus Atius Lepidus stood with folded arms in his Ostia villa's atrium. He watched his fifteen-year-old son, Silus, practice sword forms against the Zhonguo slave Lepidus had bought for just this purpose. The boy's two-handed katana was a speeding blur against the slave's attempted defense with his own katana. The slave held his own, however, so Lepidus was pleased the boasts of the herder from whom he bought the Zhonguo were accurate.

"Move your feet," Lepidus said to his son. "Don't stand in one place."

Silus moved his feet to his father's satisfaction, then brought his two-handed katana around and severed the slave's right leg. The slave screamed and fell to the ground, blood pumping from the new stump. Silus stood over the slave, his breath heavy, sweat glistening his forehead. He eyed Lepidus.

"Don't look at me," Lepidus yelled. "Finish your enemy."

Silus raised his sword, ignored the slave's pleas for mercy, and drove the sword into the slave's heart. The slave gasped. Blood spurted from his mouth; he twitched a few seconds, and then his eyes went vacant. Silus pulled the katana from the Zhonguo's chest, the tip dripping blood.

Lepidus rushed over and grabbed his son's arm. "Never take your eyes off your enemy until you finish him. He can still kill you as long as he draws breath. Do you understand?"

Silus nodded, his eyes lowered. "Yes, father. I'm sorry, I don't know what I was thinking."

Lepidus sighed, then embraced the boy. "You did well today. You killed him in less than five minutes, a vast improvement. Your progress makes me proud."

Lepidus nodded to the slaves standing nearby. Two slaves hurried into the atrium, put down a body bag, and rolled the dead Zhonguo into it. Once they zipped the bag, they hauled it away while two female slaves rushed in and scrubbed away the Zhonguo's blood with sponges.

Silus grabbed a towel from a nearby table and wiped the blood from his sword. He then returned the sword to the scabbard on his back in a fluid motion.

"Father, why must I practice with this Nippon weapon? Why not a good Roman *gladius*?"

Lepidus smiled. "I wish a Roman *gladius* was superior to other swords. But it's not. The gods gave us wisdom to use the best tools available. It would be blasphemous to ignore the wisdom of using the best tool simply because a barbarian made it. That wisdom has enabled Roma to guide humanity's evolution. You see, *we* are open minded—the rest of humanity is not."

The boy stared absently at a potted tree in the atrium, which he tended to do when Lepidus spoke of Roman virtues. Lepidus could not blame him: He did the same thing when *his* father lectured *him*. It was the nature of youth to gain wisdom through hard experience rather than listen to wisdom explained.

Lepidus noticed his master slave, Kalan, approach. He stopped several paces away, head bowed and waiting for Lepidus to notice him.

"What is it, Kalan?"

His eyes to the floor, Kalan said, "My Lord, a courier from the Collegia Pontificis is at the door. He says he has an urgent summons for you."

Lepidus and Silus were supposed to attend the gladiatorial championship tonight between Herculaneum and Alexandria. He had box seats two rows up from the glass wall, seats that would make Senators envious. But an "urgent summons" from the Collegia meant he had to leave immediately for a mission that would end in the death of an enemy of the Republic. His duty to the State and to the gods required his presence, even if it meant disappointing his only son.

"Have the courier wait for me in the library," Lepidus told Kalan. The slave bowed, then hurried off.

Lepidus turned to Silus. "I may not be back tonight. I want you to use the tickets. Take a friend from the gymnasium."

"*We* were supposed to go."

"I have a duty to Roma."

"I know your duty," Silus said, and turned to go. "I'll call Titus. Maybe he doesn't have more important things to do." He walked away to his room.

Lepidus watched his son leave, choosing to ignore Silus's disrespect to his *paterfamilias*. Most house leaders would never allow their children such liberal license, but Lepidus knew the boy was honorable and respected his father. The gods had taken the boy's mother at an early age, so Lepidus gave Silus more leeway than his father had given him. Children weren't complete unless they had both their fathers and mothers to guide them. If a child lost one or the other, he would never have the same advantages as other children with a proper family. But despite the handicap of one parent, Silus had grown into an honorable young man. He just had moments where he allowed his temper to take control. It was a handicap Lepidus constantly worked with Silus to overcome.

Unable to coach his son now, Lepidus strode through the atrium and to the other side of the house. He opened the library door, and a courier golem dressed in a gray suit and white toga stood at attention.

"I thought you were from the Collegia?" Lepidus said, entering the library. "Where is your finery?" Courier golems from the Collegia wore ceremonial gold armor over a black cloak, and a gold helmet with red plume.

"The Collegia wished this meeting to be discreet, Evocatus Quintus Atius Lepidus," the courier said in the clipped monotone of a golem.

Lepidus raised an eyebrow. His meetings with Collegia couriers were always "discreet" affairs, but that never stopped them from sending an adorned messenger to his house.

"Well out with it, golem."

"Not here, Evocatus," it said, glancing at the open door behind Lepidus. "I am to escort you to the Temple of Jupiter Optimus Maximus. The Pontifex Maximus wants to give you your new assignment personally."

Lepidus studied the golem. He'd never had to go to the Temple to receive mission details. Every mission Lepidus took was sensitive, from assassinations to the negotiations of deals the Collegia could not be known to negotiate. And every assignment came from a courier golem, the most secure way to pass sensitive information Roma had ever developed. Electronic messages could be intercepted and decrypted. Courier golems never gave up their information, and were programmed to "die" if they fell into the wrong hands.

What could be so important that the Collegia did not trust a courier golem?

"I've been instructed to tell you, Evocatus, that you should not expect to return home until after this assignment is complete," the golem continued. "You are ordered to come with me after you've acknowledged receipt of this summons."

Lepidus nodded. He was a servant of the gods and the State. Obedience was his duty.

And the mystery only enhanced his curiosity over the mission. It had been weeks since his last one. He was restless.

"I will be ready in an hour," Lepidus told the golem. He left the courier and went to get his mission pack. He always kept it ready for these occasions, so he could leave within minutes.

He wanted the hour to break the news to his son.

Lepidus threw his pack into the back seat of the courier's aero-flyer and then sat in the front. The courier climbed into the pilot's seat on the right and sealed the doors. He tapped some keys on his controls, and the flyer rose smoothly above Lepidus's Ostia villa without a sound or a bump of turbulence. Lepidus shaded his eyes from the sun's glare off the Mare Mediterranean to the west. The courier rotated the flyer so it pointed east, and then it shot over the Tiber River toward Roma.

Within two minutes, the flyer sped into Roma's air space. Lepidus's awe never lessened each time he flew above the Eternal City. He made out all Seven Hills, the homes of wealthy patricians covering them all. Most prominent among the Hills was the Capitoline, where the Temple of Jupiter Optimus Maximus towered above all other buildings in Roma. Its columns gleamed white in the sun, and its bas-reliefs along the top displayed colorful images of the god who had made Roma capitol of Terra and most of human space. The Senate House stood nearby. Though smaller than the Temple, it was no less grand with its circular structure, columned arches, and twenty-foot high statues of Roma's greatest politicians.

In the Suburba valleys between the Seven Hills rose the plebeian tenements and commercial towers. Most had classical Roman facades: lots of columns, arches, orange tiled roofs, with bas-reliefs on the larger banks and merchant offices. Though not as beautiful as the historic and grand structures of the Seven Hills, the plebeian buildings had their own simple beauty that showed the practicality of Roman citizens.

The courier circled above a rooftop landing pad adjacent to the Temple. "When we land, Evocatus, I will escort you to the private office of the Pontifex Maximus. He will give you further instructions."

"What is my mission?" Lepidus asked mostly to himself as he watched the city.

"I do not have the information you request. The Pontifex Maximus will explain the mission."

Lepidus nodded, expecting nothing more from the golem.

Once the courier landed the flyer, he unsealed the doors and stepped out. Lepidus slung his pack over his shoulder and followed the courier off the windy pad toward the guard station. Two Capitoline Triad Custudae, dressed in black jumpsuits and with pulse rifles slung over the shoulders, stood at attention on either side of the guard station door. They wore round Capitoline Triad patches on their arms—the white faces of Jupiter, Juno, and Minerva on a dark blue field with gold trim—rather than the black togas and red-plumed, gold helmets the Custudae wore at the Temple's public doors.

The guards did not move as the courier walked past them into the station. Inside, another Custudae at a console desk handed an identicard to Lepidus.

"Sir, please press your thumb here," the Custudae said, holding a thumb pad out to him. Lepidus did so, and then looked at the indenticard. The small card blinked, and then his picture and name displayed. Lepidus frowned, uncomfortable with having his arrival recorded. At least the card didn't show his name, only his Evocatus rank. His name had been classified years ago.

The courier led Lepidus to an elevator, and they took it down to the sixth floor. They walked down an ornate hallway with frescoes, statues, and portraits of the gods lining the walls on either side. Red curtains hung next to the multiple windows on the left and right, golden sunlight illuminating the hall. At the end of the corridor, the courier guided Lepidus onto a balcony above the Temple's main floor. Below were hundreds of worshipers on their knees surrounding two *flamens* standing on a raised dais. The *flamens* wore white tunics with blue togas and waved incense burners over a chained pig in the dais' sacrificial pit. The *flamens* chanted an old Latin hymn asking Minerva for a bountiful harvest in the coming autumn months. Lepidus paused, then bowed his head and clasped his hands in front of him.

The courier walked back to him. "The Pontifex is waiting."

"He can wait two more minutes."

"Evocatus, he asked—"

"You are a soulless golem, so I don't expect you to understand, but human beings respect the gods."

The golem closed its mouth and then waited next to Lepidus.

Lepidus knew how to affect a certain tone and a glare that made most people give him what he wanted. Courier golems, however, could not be intimidated. It likely realized Lepidus wouldn't leave until the ritual ended. Lepidus didn't care, so long as the golem left him in peace to give his respects to Minerva.

Once the hymns and the squeals of the dying pig stopped, Lepidus raised his head. "Lead on, golem."

The courier turned and took Lepidus to the right, along the balcony that encircled the Temple's vast hall. They approached the entry to another corridor guarded by two Triad Custudae on either side. While they wore the ceremonial fluff of the Custudae, Lepidus knew they were trained as well as the Custudae on the rooftop. Lepidus and the courier walked past them, and they did not blink. He knew sensors along the way scanned his identicard. If he wasn't authorized to be here, he never would have made it into the Temple.

The hall they entered was more opulent than the one connecting the Temple to the administrative building. Though Lepidus had never been here, he knew the offices of the Collegia Pontificis were close. He frowned at the statues within the alcoves along the hall. Unlike the Temple hallway, these statues were of previous Pontiffs. Lepidus thought it unseemly for statues of mere humans to have such a prominent place in the Temple of Jupiter Optimus Maximus. He understood they were not in the worship hall proper, but at least a token acknowledgement to the gods should be displayed.

Lepidus calmed his annoyance. The Collegia had been the voice of the gods for a thousand years. The gods spoke to the Collegia and Consul, who gave the wisdom and technology of the gods to the people through divinely inspired Missives. He had to trust in the Collegia, for they would do nothing to anger the gods. He had faith the Collegia knew best.

The courier stopped before a large, polished oak door.

"When you enter, Evocatus, please kneel and—"

"I know how to address the Pontifex, golem."

The courier nodded, then put his hand on a control pad next to the doors. The lock in the doors clicked, and the courier turned the handle on the right door.

Lepidus entered an office that could have been used by the first Pontifex. Marble shelves filled with scrolls, leather-bound books, and parchments lined three entire walls of the large, rectangular room. The shelves rose from the polished, white marble floor to the ceiling twenty feet above. Ceiling frescoes depicted the gods granting wisdom to the Pontiffs, and then the Pontiffs announcing that wisdom to the Roman people by reading from Missive parchments. On the office's far end, a large oak desk covered in scrolls stood before the bookshelves. Three cats, a large gray and two whites, lounged on the desk at different corners, their tails swaying back and forth languorously. All three stared at Lepidus through squinted eyes.

Besides the light domes on the ceiling, there was no technology in the room that wasn't used when Marcus Antonius became Consul.

At the door to an open balcony stood the Pontifex Maximus Decimus Atius Avitus. He surveyed Roma's skyline, his hands clasped behind his back. The Pontifex wore the dark blue tunic and matching trousers all *flamens* wore when not performing rituals or speaking to the people. The only physical difference between Avitus and a *flamen* was the Ring of the Pontifex on his left hand, and the rings of his House on his right.

Lepidus and the golem sank to one knee, bowed their heads, and waited for the Pontifex to notice them.

"You may leave us, courier," the Pontifex said, his back to them still. The courier stood, retreated out the door, and then closed and locked it.

Though Lepidus continued bowing, he sensed the Pontifex turn around and approach, his soft-soled sandals whispering on the smooth floor. When the Pontifex stood in front of him, he said, "You told the courier one hour, brother. You're three minutes late."

"Am I excused to look at Your Grace?"

The Pontifex sighed. "Get up," he said and then walked back to his desk.

Lepidus grinned and stood. He rarely spoke to his older brother Avitus since his election to Pontifex Maximus three years ago.

Such was the nature of a sacred position—not to mention Lepidus's frequent missions across the Republic—that kept the once close brothers apart. When he did talk to Avitus, he never resisted the chance to give his brother the same teasing he'd given when they were children. Avitus may be a Vessel of the gods now, but he was still an Atii.

"What is so urgent that it makes you send a courier in a grav flyer to bring me here?" Lepidus asked. "You've always used golem messengers."

Avitus eased into the high-backed chair behind his desk. The large gray cat stood up and then hopped into Avitus's lap. Avitus stroked the cat's back, his vacant gaze locked on a point beyond Lepidus's left shoulder. It made him feel like Avitus was talking with the gods. Maybe he was. That gaze was one of many things that changed when Avitus was elected to the Collegia Pontificis.

Along with his sudden love for cats.

After a few moments, Avitus focused on Lepidus. "Brother, a matter has come up that requires your talents to remedy."

Lepidus put his hands on the desk's polished wood, eyeing Avitus. The two white cats regarded him without moving. There were no chairs before the desk. The Pontifex Maximus accepted guests who either knelt before him or stood at attention.

Lepidus was neither a supplicant nor a lackey.

"Just which one of my many talents do you require, Your Grace?"

Avitus stared at Lepidus, and then his face sagged. Lepidus saw the fear and fatigue Avitus hid so well. It shocked Lepidus, and he blinked. But within that blink, his brother's face returned to that of a stern Pontifex Maximus.

"What I'm going to tell you is sensitive," the Pontifex said. "You have an apprentice, yes?"

"Gnaeus Hortensius Appius."

"You trust him?"

"I wouldn't have made him my apprentice. Brother, your drama act is wearing on my patience."

Avitus rose to his full height, the gray cat jumping off his lap. "I don't care about your patience, Praetorian," he snarled. "You will hear the mission in good time."

Lepidus stood straight and then bowed his head. "Forgive me, Your Grace."

"I want your oath that you will not reveal the mission details to anyone but your apprentice. You may use any resources you deem necessary, but they are not to know *all* of the details."

"What details?"

"You will know when I tell you the mission," Avitus said. "I want your oath upon the soul of Triaria."

Lepidus snapped his head up, glaring at Avitus before he could stop himself. The pain and anger in his eyes must have been startling for Avitus blinked uncertainly.

"I swear," Lepidus said in a low growl, "upon the soul of my wife Triaria that I will not reveal the mission details to anyone but my apprentice." Then with a sneer, he added, "And I will know which details when I hear the mission."

Avitus nodded, satisfied with the oath Lepidus just swore. He sat in his high-backed chair again, putting his ringed hands on the chair's arm rests.

"Three days ago, Marcus Antonius Cordus went missing from the Consular residence."

Lepidus shrugged. "The boy has been known to wander Roma in disguise. He's a curious lad. So what?"

"We think this is more than exploring. When he 'wandered' in the past, he always took a trusted slave with him as a protector and guide. He was never alone. This time he took no slave."

"So he wanted to be alone."

"On the second day he was missing, a slave found a tabulari pad in Cordus's rooms that no one in the Family gave him. The Family limits his access to external information, and a non-secure tabulari is forbidden. Cordus had one. The tabulari was encrypted, but our technicians opened it."

Avitus paused, and gazed over Lepidus's shoulder again. His right eye twitched and his lips moved as if whispering something to...someone. Lepidus waited until Avitus refocused on him. "The encrypted files held a diary written by Cordus expressing his desire to defect to Libertus."

Lepidus scoffed. "Brother, a member of the Consular Family, touched by the gods, cannot have a 'desire to defect to Libertus.' The gods would never have allowed such a blasphemy to be born into the Consular Family, much less as the Heir."

"No, the gods would not allow such a beast to wear the Purple. That is why the boy's corruption is not natural. It was instigated by a Liberti agent."

"How could a Liberti agent get close to the Consular Family? The minds of anyone who enter the Consular residence are scanned for nefarious thoughts. I've seen the screenings. They do not miss anything."

"Perhaps not on a normal agent. A Liberti *Umbra Ancile* is a different matter. They have ways around our security that we do not understand."

"Don't tell me you believe in the Liberti *numina*, brother," Lepidus said. "That would not do for the Pontifex Maximus."

"Umbra Ancilia are real, but they are not *numina*. They are as human as you or any other Praetorian. They simply have technology we do not understand. Yet."

Lepidus frowned. Talk like this disturbed him, especially from the Pontifex Maximus. How could the godless Liberti have technology greater than Roma's? For that matter, why would the Pontifex Maximus admit this to Lepidus, even if they were brothers?

"According to Cordus's diaries," Avitus continued, "he wanted to see Libertus, but without a Pontiff's guidance or Praetorian security. In other words, he wanted to go alone."

Lepidus shook his head. "More circumstantial evidence. Just because the boy wants to visit a foreign country does not make him corrupt."

Avitus sighed. "I do not expect you to understand how the gods interact with the Consular Family, nor do I wish to explain it to you. Suffice it to say the gods do not allow such desires to exist in the Consular Family or the Collegia."

"You just said he might have been corrupted. How could he be corrupted into defecting to Libertus if the gods do not allow such desires to exist in him? If he is missing, then it is obviously a kidnapping, as improbable as it seems."

Lepidus still found it hard to believe any kidnapper could get into the Consular residence, even a fabled Liberti Umbra Ancile. But that thought was preferable to the idea that a boy one step below deity could be 'corrupted.' Such a thought chilled and sickened him.

Avitus studied Lepidus, as if considering what else to tell him. Lepidus knew his brother. Despite the years apart, and his connection to the gods, Lepidus could still tell when Avitus held something back.

"Kidnapping is possible. So is the unthinkable case that Umbra somehow severed Cordus's link with the gods. That is where you come in, brother."

Avitus stood up, reached into his toga, and pulled out a data chit. "I want you to go over the boy's diary entries. Find any clues as to his current whereabouts. If he was kidnapped, you will rescue him from the Liberti barbarians. If he was corrupted, you will terminate him."

Lepidus glared at Avitus, who did not look away.

"I know what I am asking, brother," Avitus said quietly. "I know I have asked you to do hard things in the past. This is the hardest, which is why I came to you. If the boy is corrupted, he is no longer touched by the gods and he is no longer the Heir. He cannot be allowed to live. His defection would sow doubt among the people regarding the infallibility of the Consular Family. I don't have to explain how disastrous that would be for the Republic."

Avitus walked from around the desk and put his hands on Lepidus's shoulders. "It is the will of the gods," he said. "And the will of the Consul."

Lepidus nodded. "I will do my duty, Your Grace. As I always have."

He took the data chit from Avitus and placed it in a pocket within his toga. "I will either rescue the boy or I will kill him. Anything else, Your Grace?"

Avitus shook his head. "You may go."

Lepidus bowed and then hurried from the office without another word. He feared if he opened his mouth he would vomit on the Pontifex's clean marble floor.

Chapter Eleven

Daryush wailed and pounded on the glass outside *Caduceus's* Cargo One. Dariya put her hands on the glass from inside. She spoke into her collar com, which transmitted her voice to the crew.

"'Ush, you have to calm down," she soothed. "I will be fine."

She looked at Kaeso standing with folded arms behind Daryush. Kaeso returned her look, but he knew his eyes held no confirmation she told Daryush the truth. While massive anti-radiation serums eliminated any diraenium in her, the wounds from the Plague-ridden attackers were another matter. Nestor had examined Dariya's bite wound, and it had broken through her EVA suit *and* her skin. More tests confirmed she had a small fever, which would get worse in the coming hours. Kaeso noticed a slight puffiness around her neck already. If she followed the typical pattern of the Cariosus, she would lose consciousness within six hours, stay unconscious for another twelve, and then wake up a violent, inhuman creature. She would no longer be Dariya, the brave and intelligent Persian Kaeso had hired. She would be an animal. The only cure Kaeso could give her at that point was a pulse bullet to the head.

"Listen to me, 'Ush," Dariya said, her voice preternaturally calm given what she knew would happen to her. "I need you to do something for me. Can you go to the engine room and re-tune the ion drive's coils? I never had a chance to tune them when we landed, and it has to be done before we take off. Can you do that for me, 'Ush?"

Daryush stopped wailing, but his chest still heaved and tears streamed from his eyes. He thought about what she asked with the far-off gaze he got while lost in an engineering problem. He nodded, then turned and walked past Kaeso toward the engine room.

Dariya watched him go through glistening eyes. She sat down hard on a plastic crate and put her face in her hands.

Lucia came down the ladder from the command deck and stood next to Kaeso, watching Dariya. She clenched her teeth. "Do we need to keep her in there like an animal?" she asked. "The Cariosus is not airborne."

"If I go mad," Dariya said in her hands, "I will attack you all, and then I will have your deaths on my soul. Even yours would bother me, Trierarch."

"Nestor said you won't be symptomatic for another six hours," Lucia said. "Don't you want to, I don't know, hug your brother one last time?"

Dariya looked up at Lucia. "More than you know, Roman."

"Then how can you be so callous?" Lucia asked. "Daryush is—"

"Enough!" Dariya screamed. She jumped up and slammed both palms on the Cargo One window. Then slammed them again and again. Her palms turned red, leaving bloody prints on the glass. She snarled and yelled in the same nonsensical gibberish as the other Cariosa in the vaults. The language of the Cariosus.

"Dariya!" Kaeso shouted.

She didn't listen. He rushed to open the cargo door to restrain her, but she stopped abruptly. She gaped at them as if she'd just woken up. She looked at the glass and then her hands. Kaeso watched helplessly as she sat down and cried.

"Please, just go," she whispered.

Kaeso motioned Lucia toward the ladder. Once they were on the command deck, Kaeso saw through the windows that night had fallen over the dead city. Even with the command deck's overhead lights off, and the only light coming from the control panels, the view out the window was blacker than any deep space he'd ever seen.

Lucia turned to him, her face alit with the reds, blues, and whites from the display panels. "We can't let her become one of those things."

"I know," Kaeso said, sitting in the pilot's couch. He thumbed his collar com and said, "Nestor, report to the command deck."

He turned to Lucia. "I have an idea, but we have to go to Libertus."

Lucia hesitated. "Why Libertus? Do they have a cure they're holding out on Roma?"

A sharp pain from Kaeso's implant reminded him of his Umbra oaths. "Something like that," he muttered.

"Even if the Liberti can help us, we still can't leave this system. Dariya used our last way line plasma, and you know the Romans won't sell us any. They're my people; I know how they think."

"I know how they think, too," Kaeso said. He activated his tabulari and searched his personal folders on *Caduceus's* network.

Lucia stood over his shoulder. "Equipment manifests for Roman Eagles? Centuriae, that data is classified. How did you get it?"

"Please don't ask."

Kaeso felt her stare on his back.

Nestor entered the command deck. "Yes, Centuriae?"

"Dariya has six hours until she's symptomatic, right?"

"Yes, although it is an estimate. It could be more or less."

"How much more or less?"

Nestor shrugged. "Four minimum, eight maximum. Why?"

Kaeso told Nestor his idea.

"Centuriae, I am not aware of any tests proving that works."

Lucia snorted. "Of course not. The Collegia Pontificis weren't interested in curing the Cariosus, only wiping it out, victims and all."

"Could it work?" Kaeso asked.

Nestor shrugged again. "In theory."

"Good enough," Kaeso said, "because unless you have a better idea, it's the only way we keep Dariya alive until we reach Libertus."

Nestor and Lucia were both silent.

"Have Flamma, Blaesus, and Daryush report to Cargo Two," Kaeso said. "We've got a lot of work to do before we see the good Lady Centuriae of the *Corus*."

They completed phase one of Kaeso's plan and then took off from Pomona. *Corus's* Lady Centuriae called within moments of them leaving Menota's atmosphere.

"I assume congratulations are in order, Centuriae Aemilius," she said when her head displayed above Kaeso's tabulari. "The only reason you'd leave so early is that you found your mythical vaults and are ready for boarding."

Kaeso smiled. "We found the vaults, my Lady Centuriae."

She cocked her head. "How much?"

"Over thirty million sesterces."

"Thirty million," she breathed, her glazed eyes telling Kaeso she was dreaming of how she'd spend her share. "You got it all?"

"Every last sesterce."

She nodded. "Well done indeed."

"We're ready to transfer your port entry fee to you."

"Yes, about the port entry fee," she said. "It is no longer required."

Kaeso raised an eyebrow. "Well that is most generous of you, my lady. Thank you."

"We are confiscating everything in your cargo hold," she said with a grandmotherly smile. "Under the Menota Treaty, which Libertus just signed, we are authorized to stop, board, and impound contraband on ships entering or leaving Menota space. Even Liberti flagged ships. My pilot is sending you coordinates now. You will bring your ship to those coordinates so *Corus* can begin boarding. Any attempt to run and you will be fired upon. Are my orders clear?"

Kaeso sighed. "Yes, my lady. Although I should mention the sesterces are not on my ship."

The Lady Centuriae sighed. "Oh?"

Kaeso tapped a key on his console. "I'm sending you a visual feed right now. You should have it on this channel."

She looked at her screen, and her eyes narrowed.

"What you see, my Lady Centuriae, is a stack of Menota marques—over thirty million sesterces worth—surrounded by way line plasma canisters. The marques are still on the planet in the Pomona vaults."

Hopefully she's never seen the backstage of a theater, he thought.

She smirked. "I can blow you out of the sky right now and then go retrieve the marques myself."

"Maybe. If you can get past the tripwires we set up. You probably can, which is why I programmed this little device." Kaeso held up his personal tabulari. "It's transmitting a stop signal to the receiver next to those canisters. If this tabulari is destroyed, or if I turn it off, then the canisters will incinerate those marques."

Her lip curled. "I don't believe you."

"Are you willing to take that chance? Are you willing to bet your comfortable retirement in that Mediterranean villa?"

She stared at Kaeso, her jaw clenching and unclenching.

"Look, you can have the marques," Kaeso said. "I have two, simple requests that I have no doubt you will think a fair exchange."

Her stare was colder than space. "What are your...requests?"

"Four canisters of way line plasma and one sleeper crib."

The Lady Centuriae laughed. "So you mortgaged all of your way line plasma to hold the marques hostage while you negotiate for a single sleeper crib? If I'm not mistaken, you have seven crew, including yourself. What need do you have for a single sleeper crib?"

"That's my business, my lady. I think it's a fair exchange. Thirty million sesterces for one sleeper crib and four way line plasma canisters. Your Eagles have more than enough of each. Fortuna has smiled on you this day, my lady."

Kaeso waited for a stab of pain from his implant, but to his surprise, none came. He fought the urge to search the ship proximity displays on his console.

"Spare me your fake piety," she said. "How can I be sure all thirty million sesterces are in that pile you're showing me? The view is awfully dark."

"I suppose you're going to have to trust me. And Fortuna."

This time Kaeso did glance at his proximity displays. *Where are they? Perhaps Menota's rings...?*

She grunted. "I will discuss this with my colleague on *Virtus*," she said, and then her head disappeared.

Lucia said, "That's a good sign. If she wasn't considering it, she'd have destroyed us by now."

Kaeso searched the empty space outside the command window. Menota was behind them, so all he could see were stars and the running lights of the two Roman Eagles miles above them. He studied his proximity display. Only the Eagles registered.

"Yes," he muttered, "a good sign."

Minutes passed without a response from *Corus*. Lucia tapped her fingers on her console. "Come on," she said. "It's thirty million sesterces."

"They'll take the money," Kaeso said, still searching the stars outside the window. "They're arguing over what to do with us once they have it."

"We'll be long gone by the time they get the money," Lucia said. When Kaeso didn't say anything, she asked, "Won't we?"

Kaeso remained quiet. Even if the Romans did what they said they'd do, it would take Kaeso's crew at least an hour to get the way line plasma canisters hooked up to the way line drive, and at least fifteen minutes for the plasma to spool through the drive. Then there were the two Eagles blocking the way line jump point through which *Caduceus* could escape....

Kaeso hated plans that relied on luck and the gods, and this plan was all luck and gods.

The com chimed, and the head of the Lady Centuriae materialized above his tabulari once again.

"We accept your proposal," she announced. "Proceed to the coordinates my pilot sent you earlier. We will meet you there in one hour. You will transmit the exact location of the marques to us and disable the plasma canisters around them. Once my men have the marques, we will send over the sleeper crib and way line plasma."

"I'm sorry, my lady," Kaeso said. "We get the sleeper crib and way line plasma first, then we send you the marques' location. You know it will take us an hour to install the canisters. More than enough time for you to blow us out of the sky if you do not find all thirty million sesterces."

She stared at him. "Very well. Be at those coordinates in one hour." She ended the transmission.

Lucia sighed. "Why did you have to give her that idea, sir?"

"She's a Roman. It already crossed her mind," Kaeso said, receiving the coordinates from *Corus*. "I'm sending the coordinates to you. Take us out."

Lucia moved some sliders on her pilot's console. The stars outside the command deck window shifted as the ship came about and shot toward the rendezvous point.

"How can it take them an hour to gather one sleeper crib and four canisters of way line plasma?" Lucia asked.

When Kaeso didn't say anything, she continued, "It won't take them an hour. They're using that time to search for the marques in Pomona. When they find them, they'll destroy us."

"Possibly."

Lucia sighed. "So we're dead no matter what we do."

Kaeso looked at her. "I'm sorry I brought us here."

Lucia had a sudden warmth in her eyes. It surprised Kaeso, especially after he all but admitted they were going to die.

"Centuriae, you did what you thought was best. You had no choice. I admit I had my doubts; I also knew it was either this job or we sat on our hands waiting for the ship to fall apart."

"At least you'd all live to serve on another ship."

"What other ship?" she asked. "It's only a matter of time before Libertus and Roma negotiate an extradition treaty. When that happens, none of us would find legal work anywhere. We'd either have to turn ourselves in or serve on pirate ships."

Kaeso grinned. "We're not pirates?"

She gave him a rare smile. "We may do things that are less than legal, but at least we don't attack unarmed vessels. There's no honor in that."

They spent the rest of the journey to the rendezvous point in silence. *Caduceus* arrived within twenty minutes, but the Eagles were not there. Kaeso expected that.

Still searching for the marques, he thought. *They'll be here when they find them. Then we see if this is the last gamble I ever make.*

Kaeso turned to his console and activated the camera in Cargo One. Dariya sat on a box talking to Daryush through the Cargo One window. Daryush no longer cried, but his head was down and he nodded periodically. Kaeso did not turn on the audio, but he watched them for a long time.

The com chimed. "Here we go," he said as he activated the com. The head of a stern-faced Roman officer materialized.

"Centuriae Aemilius, you will power down your engines and prepare for docking with *Corus*. Once again, your crew is confined to quarters and only you will open the connector hatch. We will transfer your sleeper crib and way line plasma to you once your ship is secure. Acknowledge."

"Acknowledged," Kaeso said. The proximity display showed two Roman Eagles approaching *Caduceus* fast. Too fast.

"Centuriae..." Lucia said, staring at her display.

"I know. They found the marques." *I was never a good gambler. Now my crew will pay my debt with me.*

"We should make for the rings," Lucia said.

"We'd never make it."

Kaeso looked out the command window, waiting for the flash of launching missiles from the two Eagles. The ships grew from white moving dots to—

Brilliant light enveloped the two Eagles, and for a moment Kaeso thought they had launched. But the flashes were too bright.

Lucia saw it too. "What happened? They're not on my display."

Kaeso released a long breath. *You* were *out there. Let's see if my implant will kill me.*

"Centuriae, there's another ship near where the Eagles were," Lucia said. She squinted at her display. "Impossible..."

"What?"

"It has no beacon."

To Lucia's Roman experience, a ship couldn't fly without a beacon. By international treaty and long-standing religious custom—often more powerful than law—all starships had an identifier beacon built into their hulls. The engines activated the beacon and the beacon activated the way line plasma, thus making interstellar travel along the universal way lines possible. Even pirate ships had a beacon that transmitted their identification, false though it may be.

But Liberti Umbra ships did not operate by normal rules. They did not use the same engines every other human starship used.

As Kaeso expected, his com console chimed. He activated it, but no holographic head materialized.

"*Caduceus*," said a voice with a Liberti accent, "either Fortuna is your patron god, or you knew we were here."

Lucia frowned in confusion, but Kaeso smiled. He thought he recognized the voice, though he couldn't be sure. The voice was masked, and it had been three years since he last heard it.

"I wasn't sure you heard me the first two times."

"We did," the voice said. "We just didn't want to get involved."

"Why did you?"

There was a pause. "You have an infectee aboard?"

Kaeso figured if Umbra was out there, his 'emergency code' references to Fortuna would get them involved. He knew his odd request for a single sleeper crib would start them thinking, especially considering the planet he just left. Umbra never got its hands on a Cariosa before the Romans destroyed the planet, and that was a treasure over which he gambled they'd "get involved."

"We do," Kaeso said, "but unless you have a sleeper crib, she won't last another three hours. You destroyed the one I was negotiating for."

"They weren't going to give it to you, and you know it," the voice said. "Prepare for docking."

When the com light turned off, Kaeso saw through the window an Umbra ship blink into existence right above the *Caduceus*. It was slightly smaller than *Caduceus*, and resembled a black teardrop with no running lights. It was hard to see due to its black matte hull. The only way he could discern the ship visually was how it blocked the stars behind it.

Lucia cried, "Gods below, where did that ship come from? Did they destroy the Eagles? Who are they?"

To Kaeso's surprise, his implant issued no warning pain. However, he didn't want to tempt Fortuna. "They're going to help Dariya, and they're going to help us get to Libertus."

"Centuriae, I need more than that."

Kaeso stood up from his command couch. "That's all I can tell you right now. You'll just have to trust me."

He left the command deck before she could laugh at him.

Chapter Twelve

Kaeso stood before the docking hatch console waiting for the connection indicator to flash. A small shudder announced *Caduceus* had docked with the Umbra ship. Once connected, he looked through the docking hatch window for someone on the other side to traverse the connector tube between the two ships.

"You do realize what you've done, right?" said a voice from behind him.

Kaeso turned to see a tall thin man with gray, cropped hair leaning with folded arms against the bulkhead. He wore the plain gray jumpsuit of a common merchant starship crewman.

"They improved the projectors since I left," Kaeso said. "Nice. If I didn't know this came from my implant, I'd think you were standing on my ship. Galeo?"

"My disguises never fooled you, did they, Kaeso?"

Kaeso smiled when Galeo's clean-shaven face shimmered. The man also wore an Umbra cloak. The "cloak" was a mesh suit that covered the wearer's entire body. It projected whatever identity the wearer's implant could make up. Most Ancilia wore an Umbra cloak while on missions to hide their true faces. Or to make themselves invisible.

"The cloak may disguise your face, but it never hid your condescending voice."

Galeo laughed, then strode forward and gave Kaeso a tight embrace, which Kaeso returned. *He even feels real*, Kaeso thought with wonder. If his deactivated implant could make it seem like Galeo was really here, he wondered what an activated implant could do now.

"I've missed you, old friend," Galeo said. "The Ancilia these days are all business-first types. Don't know how to have fun like we used to."

"Is that what we had? Fun?"

Galeo's smile melted, replaced by a sad gaze Kaeso thought the suit rendered well. *They* have *made improvements since I left. I mean, since I was "relieved."*

"Well," Galeo said, "let's just say they were interesting times." His eyes scanned the corridor. "So this is your ship."

"Don't let her looks fool you. She has a good heart."

"And her crew?"

"Scoundrels, one and all."

"Just like their Centuriae."

Kaeso shrugged.

"And one Cariosa," Galeo said. "What were you thinking, going down to Menota? You knew the danger."

Kaeso clenched his teeth. "My centuriae couch doesn't have the resources of the most prosperous planet in Human Space to back it up. Until you sit in that couch, you won't understand our situation, so I don't want a lecture."

"You want me to stick my neck out for a disgraced former Ancile. I think I've earned the right to give you a lecture."

"If you bring in a Cariosa, your bosses won't care if she came out of Hades' ass, much less from a disgraced former Ancile. You'll be a hero."

Galeo snorted. "You don't know my current bosses."

"Come on, Galeo. She's one of my crew and she's going to die—or worse—if she doesn't get into a sleeper crib now."

Galeo hesitated. "I don't know who Fortuna has smiled on more today: me or you."

"If you bring in a Cariosa, it'll be you."

"Not what I meant." Galeo sighed. "You think we were patrolling Menota, don't you?"

"Why else were you here?"

"We were following you."

Kaeso looked at him. "I haven't told my crew anything they shouldn't—"

"That's not why we're here. An incident has occurred that requires your expertise."

Kaeso blinked. "What incident could make the Umbra Magisterium want my help? I'm disgraced, remember?"

"You should know the gods work in strange ways."

"What incident, Galeo?"

Galeo unfolded his arms and walked over to the Cargo One window. Kaeso had closed the metal shutters before Galeo boarded so Umbra wouldn't see Dariya until they agreed to help. Galeo put his hands on the glass, though, as if he knew she was there.

"What I'm about to tell you falls under your implant's concealment protocols."

Pain sparked from Kaeso's implant as it received the signal from Galeo's implant. Now Kaeso could not reveal the conversation he was about to have with Galeo. *One more thing I need to hide from my crew.*

"Two months ago we learned that a high-ranking member of the Roman government wanted to defect to Libertus."

"How high?"

"Consular Family."

Kaeso felt his mouth hang open. "Is that possible?"

"We don't know."

"It's a trick," Kaeso said. "A Consular doesn't up and defect to Libertus. They just want our Ancilia to make contact, flush them out."

"It occurred to us. Either way, we had to be sure, so we sent an extraction Ancile to find out."

When Galeo paused, Kaeso asked, "Well?"

"According to the extraction Ancile, the Consular did want to defect. No tricks."

Kaeso shook his head. "I still don't buy it. I worked in Roma almost my entire service with Umbra. You know the missions I took. The Consulars are worshiped like gods, which they think they are. Never heard of one that didn't. How did your Ancile verify this wasn't all *cac*?"

"Operational secret."

Kaeso laughed. "How am I supposed to help you if you won't tell me anything?"

"Let's just say it was good enough for the Magisterium to order the Ancile to extract the Consular."

"So what happened?"

Galeo turned back to the glass. "Something went wrong. Last month our Ancilia in Roma, and all across Terra, were rolled up. At first we lost communication. Then their implants went nil."

Kaeso gritted his teeth. Nil implants meant death, for only Umbra Vessels infected with the sentient Muses could disable active implants without causing death to the implanted.

"How many?" Kaeso asked.

"All of them."

All of them. There were over two hundred Ancilia in Roma when he was in Umbra ten years ago. If every Ancile was rolled, Umbra and Libertus were blind to Roman activities and plans. Libertus didn't have hosts of Legions or fleets of warships like Roma. It relied on Umbra Corps' ultra-clandestine tools to neutralize any threats. Those threats were dealt with subtly, using everything from the fear of Liberti *"numina"* to political sabotage by well-placed Ancilia in the Roman government and targeted assassinations. The small military of Libertus kept the larger empires from seeing it as a threat. With its economic and cultural growth over the last fifty years, however, Libertus was now *de facto* leader of the Lost Worlds and a gem for expansionist empires. Only two things kept the empires from invading: fear of angering the other empires, and fear of the legendary—and Umbra-invented—Liberti *numina*.

But if all the Umbra Ancilia on Terra had been killed, Libertus was defenseless against the Romans.

A young girl's face danced through his memories, a face he tried hard to forget every day lest the pain destroy him.

"All of them," Galeo continued, "except one. The extraction Ancile. Her last transmission said she had contacted the Consular who wanted to defect. She said he had a secret that could bring down the Roman Republic."

Kaeso gave a weary chuckle. "How many times have we heard a Roman defector promise that?"

"She also said the Romans know what the Muses are, and this defector has information about a cure Roma is developing against them."

Kaeso wanted to laugh again, but then it made sense. How else could the Romans have captured every Ancile on Terra without knowing the Muses exist? The technology the Muses gave Libertus was in many cases decades, if not centuries, ahead of any other world or empire in human space.

If the Romans knew the greatest ally of Libertus was a sentient alien virus Umbra called the Muses, and Roma developed a weapon against them, then Libertus would lose its only means to defend itself.

"These are extraordinary claims," Kaeso said. "Starting with the defection of a Consular and ending with the fact this extraction Ancile seems to be the only Umbra Ancile to survive the roll-up. How convenient for her."

"Not necessarily. Last week we lost all communication with her implant."

"She went nil?"

"No nil transmission. Silence."

One impossibility piled on top of the other. Implants were virtually indestructible. Even if the Ancile fell into a star, the implant would *still* transmit a nil signal before it went off-line. Only a Muse-infected Umbra Vessel could disable an Ancile's implant.

What happened to the universe since I left Umbra?

"I know what I've told you so far is hard to believe," Galeo said, "but there's more."

"Of course there is."

"The extraction Ancile is the last Ancile in Roma. First, we need to find out if she betrayed us. Second, we need to know if her claims of a Consular defector are true. That's where you come in, my friend."

"Why me? Again, I'm a *former* Ancile. I'm sure you have plenty of young bulls itching to get into Roma."

"Of course we do. In fact, we sent some in the day after we last heard from our extraction Ancile. Their implants went nil as soon as they landed on Roma."

"So the Magisterium wants to kill me, too? I may not have a glamorous life, but I prefer to keep it."

Galeo smiled. "We have a theory. Since Roma can now detect active implants, it would be unwise to send more Umbra Ancilia until we've figured out how their new tech works. So we need to send someone who doesn't have an active implant, yet knows his way around Roma and is acquainted with Umbra protocols."

"Ah, and my name was at the top of the list?"

"More like the bottom. Every other retiree above you was either too old or turned us down."

"Yeah."

"There's another reason we want you to go. The extraction Ancile is Marcia Licinius Ocella."

Kaeso shrugged. "Should I know that name?"

"Probably not. It's the name Umbra gave her when she entered the Corps." Galeo paused. "You'd remember her as 'Spuria.'"

Spuria.

My dead wife's sis—?

Kaeso's deactivated implant could not have driven the wind out of him as much as that name. Memories unbidden exploded in his mind, memories of a life before Umbra. His relationship with Spuria, their break-up, and then falling in love with Petra. His beloved Petra, and their beautiful daughter Claudia. Their happiness.

Then Petra's violent death. Kaeso's near madness over the loss. His emotional neglect of his own daughter. His failure as a father.

Kaeso didn't realize he was on his knees until Galeo helped him up.

"I'm sorry, old friend," Galeo said. "I knew this would be hard for you. It always is with us."

Kaeso waved him away. "I'm fine," he grunted. "I'll be fine."

But Kaeso knew he would not be fine. The implant, even when dormant, protected him from the memories before Umbra. It enabled him to adjust to his new life outside Umbra, made it easier for all Umbra retirees to avoid contacting former friends and family. All Umbra Ancilia had to "die" to every person in their former lives when they joined the Corps. The Corps even arranged funerals with golem bodies to give family and friends closure. Such was the price to join an ultra-secret agency unknown to everyone save the Liberti Consul and select members of the Liberti Defense Force. Not even the Liberti Senate knew Umbra existed.

His family thought he was dead, and dead men do not show up on their family's doorstep without drawing attention. That was why the implants clouded the memories of former lives. For the Ancile's own protection. It worked well.

Until a name or place triggered the memories, and brought them back full force. The concealment protocols in Kaeso's implant prevented him from contacting his family, but now, remembering Spuria's name—*Ocella!*—all the memories and guilt from before Umbra were now a crushing weight he struggled to hold up.

"For what it's worth," Galeo said, "I argued against bringing you in for exactly this reason, but the Magisterium decided this mission was too important."

"What is the mission?" Kaeso asked. *Need something else in my head besides my daughter's face from the last time I saw her. When she told me she hated me.*

Galeo eyed him, as if waiting to see if he would crack under rediscovered memories. Kaeso stood straight, his chin level.

Galeo sighed. "You were among the best Umbra had, you know Roma, and you know Ocella. The Magisterium wants you to infiltrate Roma and find Ocella. Bring her out, along with this Consular defector, if he exists."

"If she's turned?"

"Terminate her."

Kaeso nodded, expecting as much. "I accept the mission."

Galeo raised an eyebrow. "That was quick. Your price?"

Kaeso managed a weak smile through the memories assaulting him. "Three things. One, cure my infected crewman."

"You know we don't have a cure for the Cariosus. It's a Muse strain, and *they're* sure as Hades not going to tell us if one exists. Even if we wanted to develop a cure from your crewman's blood, it could take months, if at all."

"We could keep her in a sleeper crib until you develop one."

"Kaeso, the Muses would never allow Umbra to work on a cure. They would sooner let the Romans wipe us out than help us find a way to kill them. Your only hope for your crewman is the Consular defector, because a Muse-strain cure will never come from Umbra."

Kaeso nodded, assuming that would be the answer. Still, he had to try. He did not like that Dariya's life hung on the word of a Roman traitor.

"Two, I want Liberti citizenship for my crew."

"Your crew is made up of Roman fugitives. Escaped slaves, Legion deserters, extortionists...shall I continue?"

"Liberti citizenship will protect them from extradition and keep them from being arrested if they wander back into Roman territory. You know you can make this happen."

"Fine," Galeo said. "Next?"

"I want back into Umbra."

Galeo smiled. "I think a cure for the Cariosus would be easier."

"If I can bring back Ocella *and* this defector, then that's got to be worth something to the Magisterium. At least enough for them to ignore me making a corrupt senior Ancile nervous."

Galeo winced. Kaeso never found out who had him "relieved" of his duties, but Galeo, his handler, must have known. Kaeso had been investigating a slave trafficking network from the Lost Worlds to Roma, and was close to learning the name of the Ancile who ran the network. Then he was suddenly accused of the crime he was investigating. All the evidence he had passed along to Umbra somehow pointed to him, and he was dishonorably discharged from Umbra. Those in Umbra who knew him well, like Galeo, knew he'd been framed, but their implants prevented them from helping Kaeso. Which confirmed to Kaeso the framer was a senior Ancile.

"You will never get back into Umbra," Galeo said. "For argument's sake, let's say what you believe is true, that a senior Ancile set you up. Do you think that Ancile will allow you back in, only to have you discover his name?"

Kaeso didn't think Galeo would agree to Umbra reinstatement. He would've been suspicious if Galeo had, but Kaeso had planted a seed that Galeo would take back to his superiors. If Kaeso completed this mission, the Magisterium might see what they lost when they let him go. Maybe his reinstatement would be more valuable to them than the senior Ancile they protected. Particularly since it sounded like the entire Umbra presence on Roma needed rebuilding from the ground up.

"Fine, at least citizenship for my crew. Deal?"

Galeo nodded. "It can be arranged."

"And suggest the reinstatement, would you?"

"I will, but it's never going to happen. Besides, why do you want back in? I would've thought you'd be a little bitter."

"I suppose I'm a patriot and a fool."

"Nobody's that foolish, or patriotic. Tell me why and I'll consider passing along your request."

Kaeso glanced around the corridor, noticed a hairline crack in a ventilation pipe that ran into the cargo bays. *One more repair to add to the list.*

"I'm not a good centuriae," Kaeso said, "but I was a good Ancile."

Galeo nodded, understanding in his cloak-rendered eyes. *Yes, the cloaks are much better than when I was in. The things I could do with these new tools.*

"I'll ask some questions," Galeo said, "but I wouldn't sell your ship just yet. So if by the grace of Juno you do get back in, what will you tell your crew?"

"Not your concern."

It was true, but he didn't explain it to Galeo because he had no idea what he'd tell his crew if Umbra reinstated him. Whatever he told them, he knew they deserved a better centuriae than him. One who wouldn't risk their lives with dangerous jobs just to keep flying.

Galeo nodded. "Very well, we'll bring over a sleeper crib for your crewman and way line plasma for your ship. We will escort you back to Libertus where your ship will go through some minor upgrades."

"'Minor upgrades?'"

Galeo smiled. "Well, not so minor, but I think you'll enjoy them. They'll get you into and out of Roma a lot easier."

"Wait, you want me to take *Caduceus* to Roma?"

"And your crew. You will infiltrate Roma as a licensed courier from Libertus."

"No way. I just told you, my crew are wanted in Roman space."

"We'll give them credentials and gene coatings to match. The gene coatings won't fake a blood test, but they will fool any skin scan they'll get at customs."

"I said no. I can't ask them to do that. I'll go in alone like I always did."

"How will you extract Marcia Licinius or the defector? With what ship? Every Ancile on Roma is gone. You'll have no contacts there to arrange transport. You'll need a ship, and you'll need one with the upgrades we'll give yours."

A cold weight formed in Kaeso's stomach as he realized Galeo was right. He'd never done an extraction. Umbra had always sent him in to make sure certain Romans never left.

But he could not put his crew in such danger. Not again.

"I still have non-Umbra contacts there," Kaeso said. "I can work something out."

"How do you know they're still alive? If Roma killed our Ancilia, what makes you think they missed your contacts?"

"Why them?" Kaeso asked "Why not Liberti security forces? I'm sure they have undercover agents they could loan us."

"None who are ready to go in time, or who know your ship's systems. Gods, *Caduceus* is 80 years old. Your crew knows the ship and works well together. You cannot fake that kind of familiarity or teamwork, especially in front of a curious Roman customs official."

Kaeso clenched his teeth. "Don't patronize me. You can just tell me we're expendable."

Galeo frowned, but didn't say anything.

"I don't know if I can get them to go," Kaeso said.

"You'll think of something. Or you won't get what you want." Galeo paused. "It was good seeing you again, old friend. I'm sorry for opening old wounds."

Kaeso was silent. It was all he could do to keep those old wounds from tearing him apart.

Galeo nodded to him one more time and then disappeared.

Kaeso peered through the docking hatch window. An Ancile in a pressure suit, with a gold faceplate masking the Ancile's identity, pushed a motorized lift with a sleeper crib and several way line plasma canisters. Kaeso tapped a button on his console, and the docking hatch opened with a hiss. The Ancile pushed the lift through the hatch and then turned back to the Umbra ship.

"We can keep the lift?" Kaeso called out.

The Ancile didn't acknowledge him. Kaeso shrugged, then tapped his collar com. "Attention all crew, meet in cargo hold corridor."

Chapter Thirteen

Kaeso's crew stood in the corridor between the cargo bays. Except for Dariya, who stood next to the glass in Cargo One, listening over the com. Kaeso's implant allowed him to tell his crew Libertus wanted them to go to Roma to extract a noble defector who knew how to cure the Cariosus. The reward would be Liberti citizenship and a possible cure for Dariya. He could not say the noble was a Consular with an alleged secret that could "bring down the Roman Republic," and he certainly could not reveal the facts about Umbra or Ocella.

They took the news better than he thought they would—they didn't mutiny and throw him out the airlock. Instead, they all stared at him as if he said he saw Mercury streak past the command deck window.

Blaesus said, "I would rather kiss Bacchus's soggy ass than return to Roman space."

"It is Liberti citizenship," Nestor said. "That is quite valuable."

"Not if I'm crucified before I get it, which will happen to us all if we're caught in Roman territory. Except you, Flamma. You'll be tackled down and married to the first noble adolescent whose father used to be a fan."

Flamma grimaced.

"Why us?" Lucia asked Kaeso. "Doesn't Libertus have its own security forces for this?"

"Exactly," Blaesus said. "I don't doubt the bravery of you all, but none of us are trained for this."

"He's right, sir," Lucia said. "We'll be caught for sure."

"I agree," Kaeso said, "you're not trained for this. That's why you're not going."

Lucia narrowed her eyes. "You're going alone?"

"Yes."

"You're joking," Lucia said. "You can't even pilot this ship on your own, much less go to Roma by yourself."

"Once we reach Libertus, they will add automated system controls to *Caduceus*. I will run the ship just fine from the command deck. And thanks for your confidence in my piloting skills, Trierarch."

"But *you're* not even trained for this," Lucia protested. "Commanding a shuttle in the Liberti Defense Force doesn't make you a spy."

Kaeso clenched his teeth against the warning pains from his implant.

Thankfully, Dariya interrupted Lucia. "Will it not seem odd if you dock at a Terran way station without a crew?"

"My credentials will show I just bought the ship, and I'm going to Terra to hire a new crew."

Lucia laughed. "Your credentials? I suppose our Liberti friends will give you those as well?"

"Yes."

Blaesus cleared his throat. "Your paperwork may be in order, but out of curiosity, Centuriae, how will you get through the gene identity scans at customs? We Romans love our Terran security."

"Libertus will give me a gene coat," Kaeso said.

"Gene coat?" Nestor asked.

"A layer of fake skin that masks genes from external scans. They'll get me past any gene scanner in a Roman port."

Gene coats were Umbra technology, but they were no longer under Umbra concealment protocols. They were still classified since the "mainstream" Liberti security forces used them, but Kaeso found he could speak of them without his implant driving a spike through his brain.

"Interesting," Nestor said. "Liberti magic always amazes me."

Kaeso grinned inwardly at the Greek medicus, wondering what he'd think of Umbra's other Muse-revealed tools.

Lucia scoffed. "Sir, you would need our help even if you had the skills for this mission. Besides, leaving us behind would be an insult to our honor. We've pledged ourselves to you."

"We're not military," Kaeso said, his voice hard. "We're merchants. My first responsibility as your merchant centuriae is to ensure you don't get killed following my orders."

"Like going to Menota?" Lucia asked, glancing at Dariya behind the glass. Kaeso also looked at Dariya, but her eyes did not meet his.

"Yes," Kaeso said quietly. "Like going to Menota. I won't make that mistake again. So *un-pledge* yourselves. You will wait on Libertus until I come back. After that, you will have Liberti citizenship and then you can find a more respectable job."

Kaeso hated pushing his crew away. His guilt over the anger and hurt he saw on their faces was almost enough to compete with the pain brought on by his memories of Spuria (*Ocella!*). But he would not risk their lives and freedoms by taking them to Roma, especially for a mission he wanted for his own reasons. They could rage against him all they wanted, Umbra could threaten to cancel the mission for not bringing them, but he would not budge. Even if he risked losing their friendship. At least they'd be alive to hate him.

"Well," Lucia said, her face twitching, "if the Centuriae is so eager to be rid of us, I suggest we not to waste another moment. Everyone prepare for way line jump in twenty minutes."

She turned around without being dismissed, strode down the corridor, and climbed the ladder up to the command deck. Daryush gave Dariya a plaintive look, but she nodded at him to follow Lucia's orders. He went to the loaded lift with sad eyes and pushed it toward the engine room. Blaesus and Flamma glanced at each other, at Kaeso, and then left the corridor.

Nestor said, "Centuriae, I will help Dariya with the sleeper crib."

"Give us a minute first."

Nestor nodded, then walked down the corridor. Once he had climbed the ladder to the upper levels, Kaeso said to Dariya, "You ever been in one of these?"

"Once," she said, eying the sleeper crib. "As punishment."

Sleeper cribs were only used in extreme emergencies these days, like when a starship was out of way line plasma in a system without a way station. Almost every world required its space merchants to undergo sleeper crib training to obtain a commercial space license.

But Kaeso knew she referred to her time as a Roman slave. Kaeso had watched sadistic Roman masters throw a slave into a vat, seal the top, and then pump in sleeper fluid. The slave thought it was water. After the vat was full, the slave would try to hold his breath as long as he could, but then his body would betray him and he'd take a breath, thinking he was about to drown...and breathe the oxygenated sleeper fluid. Kaeso had watched Roman masters bet hundreds of sesterces on whose slave would hold their breath the longest.

"Centuriae, your plan is crazy."

"I'm going alone, Dariya."

"I hate to admit this, but I agree with Lucia. Your time with the Liberti Defense Force does not qualify you for a spy mission in Roma."

"The decision is final," he said in a tone that told Dariya he was finished discussing the matter. She closed her mouth. Her eyes were red-rimmed and thin blue veins crawled in delicate patterns around her neck.

"When we get to Libertus," Kaeso said slowly, "they will take you to their medical facilities."

"What will they do to me?"

"They're going to help you."

Dariya smiled sadly. "Of course they will."

"I need you to do something for me first," Kaeso said. When he told her, Dariya nodded.

"If I can get in that coffin, I can take a blood sample from my arm," she said. "Centuriae, I need you to do something for me as well."

"Of course."

"Take care of Daryush."

"You can take care of him yourself."

"Please, Centuriae, I see it in your eyes. I am going to die. I do not believe in this miracle cure for a minute, but I want Daryush to have his freedom. I want him to—" Her voice caught, and then she paused to collect herself. "I want him to be happy and free. Can you promise me that, sir?"

Kaeso didn't know what to say to Dariya. She had never made such an emotional plea before, and he knew how it grated on her to do it now, even to her centuriae. Knowing that made it all the more powerful. How could he not give a dying woman such a promise? Yet how could he make a promise he knew he couldn't keep if he went back to Umbra?

"When we get back," Kaeso said, "I will make sure Daryush is free. But his happiness depends on you surviving. I can't promise you this cure exists, because it's all a rumor. If it *does* exist, you will have it."

Dariya nodded. "I suppose that is the best I can get from you, Centuriae."

"You'll need to get in the crib now," Kaeso said, "but I need that sample before you do."

She nodded, went to the medical kit strapped to the wall and pulled it down. She went through the contents until she found the syringe. She plunged the needle into her arm and withdrew enough blood to fill the container. She did it without flinching, and Kaeso was never more proud to be on the same crew with her.

After she finished, she put the blood-filled syringe on the box next to her. Kaeso said, "We don't want to waste any time. Can you get in the crib on your own?"

She stood and started taking off her clothes. "I can do it. I have no choice."

Kaeso thumbed his collar com. "Nestor, she's ready."

"Should we tell Daryush first?" Nestor asked over the com. "Not to be fatalistic, but he may want to say goodbye?"

Kaeso glanced at Dariya, her naked back to him. "No," she said. "We have already said what we need to say to each other. I do not want to talk to him again until I am healed."

Nestor climbed down the corridor ladder and approached Kaeso.

"She's ready," Kaeso said.

"Centuriae, our jump sacrifice—"

"We don't have any more chickens," Kaeso said, striding down the corridor. "Besides, there's not much more the gods could do to us."

Nestor groaned.

Chapter Fourteen

"Does Libertus put on games?" the boy asked.

"Games?" Ocella said absently. She continued studying the tabulari, where she searched for transportation routes out of Roma that the Praetorian Guard had not yet secured. So far, Fortuna had not been with her. Even the ground car merchants required gene scans before they would rent vehicles. While the sudden security restrictions—without official explanation—puzzled average Romans, it was something they had grown used to over the years, especially since the Kaldethian Rebellion.

"Yes, games," Cordus said. He pointed to the visum where two gladiator golem teams sliced at each other with swords, spears, and spiked clubs. The coliseum spectators cheered and whistled insults and praise at the combatants. An unseen moderator described every swing and strike with as much passion as the mob in the stands.

"Not exactly," Ocella said, frowning at the spectacle and turning back to the tabulari. "Liberti prefer 'games' with no killing."

The boy looked at her, curious. "There is no killing in Roman games either."

"Not even golems."

"Really? Why not? They're not human. They're controlled by drivers on the sidelines. See?"

He pointed to the "driver" teams wearing goggles, black gloves, and black boots. The drivers made the same hacks and swings as the golems they controlled on the battlefield. The camera zoomed in on a large, muscled golem as he was decapitated by an equally massive golem. A gout of blood erupted from the dead golem's neck. On the sidelines, the dead golem's driver threw up his hands, then ripped off his goggles and slammed them to the ground.

"We still don't like it," Ocella said, turning back to the tabulari.

"Strange. What sort of games do Liberti watch?"

Ocella sighed. When Cordus was in a curious mood, it was better for her to answer his questions than work and have him constantly interrupt her. She'd learned much about the boy's personality in the two weeks they'd been trapped in Scaurus's basement. She tried to put herself in the boy's place. He'd led as isolated a life as anyone save a prisoner. He was educated in Roman culture, and maybe a sprinkling of other Terran cultures that still retained a non-Roman identity, but any planet beyond Roman space would be a mystery to him. Though Liberti culture, entertainment, and goods found their way to Roma despite the embargoes, the Consular Family chose not to be "tainted" by such barbarian garbage. So naturally the boy wanted to learn everything he could about Libertus.

"We like almost any kind of racing you can imagine," she said. "Humans, horses, ground-cars, aero-flyers, space sails. We even have leagues for dog racing."

"Dog racing? But they're so filthy."

Ocella smiled, knowing the Roman nobles' aversion to dogs. If a Roman noble had a pet, it would be a cat. Long ago they adopted the ancient Egyptian veneration of felines as vessels through which to communicate with the gods.

"Dogs are quite intelligent actually," she said. "Many Liberti keep them as pets."

Talking about dogs suddenly made Ocella homesick. She had a dog when she was a child, a Laconian hound named Horace that loved nothing more than to chase her through her parents' vast maize fields on Libertus. She had loved him more than her siblings at times. She thought of purchasing a dog when she got home, but quickly dismissed the idea. Her life as an Umbra Ancile kept her from forming any attachments. Dogs, cats, fish, husbands, children...

The boy wrinkled his nose. "Yes, I heard people in the Lost Worlds keep dogs as pets. How do you keep them from getting *cac* all over themselves?"

"They usually don't, but they do require more maintenance than cats."

The boy shook his head. "I do not think I would like a dog when I get to Libertus. I prefer cats. Although I suppose I *would* like to see a dog race." He drifted into his own thoughts, watching the last gladiator golems stab at each other with tridents.

Ocella turned back to the tabulari, wondering not for the first time what the boy's life would be like after he left Roma. He had no idea how to care for himself. Would he adjust to a new life in the real world, or would he want to return to the comfort and security of his old life? Ocella prayed his "talents" would enable him to adjust. So much depended on those talents...

Ocella flinched when the grinding of stone on stone came from the top of the stairway. She jumped up and drew the pulse pistol from her hip holster. She stood to the side of the stairs, hearing boots on the steps. When Scaurus came down, he eyed her drawn pistol.

"Your wariness is commendable," he said, "but I thought you'd recognize my footsteps by now."

Ocella holstered her pistol. "Steps can be faked."

"Indeed."

Ocella glanced at the boy. He had not even noticed her get up, or Scaurus come down the stairs. He watched the gladiator games with that faraway expression.

Scaurus chuckled. "He hasn't moved since I left this morning."

"He's bored."

"He's done exploring my texts?"

Ocella nodded. "Finished them last week."

"Well you two may not be here much longer if my source is correct."

Cordus sat up and looked at Scaurus as if seeing him for the first time. "Salve, Scaurus. You found us passage off world?"

"It's not guaranteed. My source still has a bureaucratic hurdle to overcome." Scaurus smiled. "But I'm rather confident he will come through."

"Where?" Ocella asked.

"Linthius."

"Linthius," Cordus said. "A good choice. On the edge of Roman space, one way line in and out. A dead end."

"Which means minimal security," Ocella said. "It doesn't border any other power. Nothing beyond Linthius but empty space." She looked at Cordus. "Sooner or later you'll have to tell me about the planet you seek. The one with the proof."

Cordus shook his head. "Not until we reach Linthius. If you are captured..."

"Right," Ocella said. The Praetorians broke everyone eventually.

Scaurus broke the uncomfortable silence. "We still need to get you two to the spaceport without—"

A low chime sounded from the stairwell. Scaurus's eyes narrowed. "I'm not expecting anyone at this hour."

He hurried up the stairs, and Ocella went to the tabulari. She accessed the security cameras from the front door. A tall, thin man with gray-blond hair cut short to his scalp stood at the door. He had a hard, angular face, but his lips had a friendly turn. He was dressed well in a dark blue coat with gold embroidery along the sleeves.

Ocella drew her pistol again and hurried over to Cordus.

Chapter Fifteen

Lepidus tapped the chime again. He grew impatient from the wait, but he did not let it show in front of the small camera embedded in the frieze above the door. It was well concealed, though not to Lepidus's professional eye. Let them see a courier or a Zoroaster evangelist. Just not a Praetorian.

The door opened, and a dark-haired slave squinted at him. "Yes?"

"I'm here to see Numerius Aurelius Scaurus," Lepidus said. "Is your master home?"

"I'm sorry, my master is away. May I take a message?"

Lepidus nodded. "Tell your master my employer has secured the travel papers he requested. I have strict orders to deliver them only to him. I will come back tomorrow." Lepidus turned and walked back down the street.

He had barely walked past the home when he heard the door open further.

"Wait," a voice said from behind.

Lepidus allowed himself a brief smile, then he affected the surprise of a courier who did not expect to see the house master chasing him.

"*Dominus*," Lepidus said, bowing his head, "your slave said you were out."

"I was occupied. Who sent you?"

"Your man at the travel *officiorum*. He wanted me to tell you the travel papers you requested are ready."

"I requested no travel papers."

"I...I'm confused, *dominus*. My magister said—"

"Who are you?" Scaurus asked, his eyes narrow.

Lepidus smiled, then stood straight and walked to Scaurus. "I'm glad we can dispense with this fiction, Scaurus. I don't think I could have kept it up much longer."

"Who are you?" Scaurus repeated.

"Someone trying to save your hands and feet from crucifixion."

"What?"

"May I come in?"

"Not until you tell me who you are."

Lepidus pulled a small scroll from his cloak and handed it to Scaurus. He took the scroll, unfurled it and read it. "Office of the Pontifex Maximus?"

"We have questions concerning your associations. May I come in, or do I need to call the lictors and bring you before the magistrate tonight?"

Scaurus smirked and then handed the scroll back to Lepidus. "I fail to see what the Pontifex Maximus needs with an old Praetorian like me, but you are welcome to come in."

Scaurus turned on his heel and strode back into his home, leaving the door open for Lepidus. He smiled at the old man's back and then followed him inside.

Upon entering the home, Lepidus noticed two curious wax busts displayed in a prominent position reserved for the family's ancestors.

"Gaius Julius Caesar and Marcus Tullius Cicero," Lepidus said, studying the busts. "Interesting. Were you related to either?"

Scaurus glanced at the busts. "Not to Gaius Julius, but a distant relation to Cicero. Though I doubt you're here to discuss my lineage."

"If not for Gaius Julius, I'd almost think you were a democrat."

When Scaurus shrugged, Lepidus laughed. "How does an old Praetorian who served the Consular Family his whole life end up an advocate for mob rule?"

Scaurus raised an eyebrow. "I'm sorry, sir, you know my name but I do not know yours."

Lepidus bowed. "Quintus Atius Lepidus."

"Well, Quintus Atius, I have always been a 'democrat,' even while I served the Consular Family. I never saw a contradiction then, nor do I now."

Lepidus folded his arms. "How can you believe mob rule is preferable to decrees that come directly from the gods? Do you believe the Senate can give the Consul and the Collegia better advice than the gods?"

Scaurus's slave brought a pot of *kaffa* from the kitchen and set it on a table next to two couches. Scaurus walked over to the pot and poured two cups, handed Lepidus a cup, and then motioned him to a couch. Lepidus sat down, but set the cup of *kaffa* on the table next to the pot.

"The gods are all knowing, obviously," Scaurus said, sipping his *kaffa*. "But surely they have better things to do than set tax policy or direct sewer repairs or even provide for public safety. That's something a freely elected Senate can do."

"The Consul's bureaucrats do that quite well. If they didn't, the Roman race would never have conquered Terra much less the stars."

"Ah, but *have* we conquered Terra? Rebellions flare up around the world every few years. Have we conquered the stars? Humanity is more fractured now in space than it ever was on Terra. I believe that if our people have a voice in public affairs, then other races would be more willing to accept Roman rule."

"The people only need to obey the will of the gods expressed through the Consul and the Collegia. That will bring them happiness and prosperity. It has made Roma strong for a thousand years. Why change?"

"Because the gods gave human beings free will and an intellect. Why would they order us *not* to use either gift? To obey them without thought? Why they might as well have made us all ants. All I say is let human beings use their free will and intellect to handle the minutia of the Republic."

Lepidus nodded, considering. "So you think the Consul and Collegia are lying to the people regarding the gods' demands for complete obedience?"

"Not lying," Scaurus said carefully. "Just misinterpreting."

"Interesting ideas, Scaurus. I've heard them before like any student of discredited theories, and I'd love to debate governing philosophy with you all night. I mean that, but I'm afraid I have other business with you. Do you know a Praetorian named Marcia Licinius Ocella?"

"Of course. How can you be a Praetorian and not know who she is. It was I who sponsored her. Why?"

Lepidus was impressed with Scaurus's poise and the way he put pride into his response, as if he didn't know the woman had kidnapped the Consular Heir of Roma.

"Well, it appears she spread some rather dangerous ideas around the Consular household."

"I only sponsor the most honorable and loyal Romans to the Praetorian Guard," Scaurus said, acting insulted. "Ocella is a patriot from a proud family. If you are in the know as much as you seem, then her recent actions should prove that. So what if she reveres tradition, including Roma's democratic past?"

Lepidus smiled. *The man is a good actor indeed.*

"Her recent actions were a boon to the Republic's security. Liberti agents will no longer infiltrate Roma as they used to. But I was not referring to democracy."

Scaurus looked at him. "Then what, Quintus Atius? Stop wasting my time and get to your point."

Lepidus leaned forward. "Your woman convinced the Consular Heir to defect to Libertus."

Scaurus stared at Lepidus. And then he laughed. Lepidus joined in the laughter. They were like old friends sharing stories of their younger, wilder days.

Scaurus wiped a tear from the corner of his eye. "Ah, Quintus Atius, for a moment I thought you were serious."

"My dear Scaurus, I am serious."

Lepidus drew his pulse pistol from his cloak, turned, and shot Scaurus's slave in the heart. The slave stumbled backward, dead before he fell to the ground, a pulse pistol tumbling from his right hand. Lepidus then aimed the pistol at Scaurus, whose own pistol was halfway out his sleeve. Scaurus froze.

"You disappoint me," Lepidus said, snatching the pistol out of Scaurus's hand. "How can an old professional like you lose his skills so quickly? You've only been out of the service, what, five years?"

Scaurus stared at him, his jaw clenched. Lepidus produced wire bindings from his cloak and tossed them in Scaurus's lap. He examined the couch.

"This seems sturdy enough," Lepidus said.

Scaurus didn't move. "What do you want?"

"Bind yourself to the couch and I will tell you."

"I'm not shackling myself to—"

Lepidus fired into Scaurus's left foot, obliterating the big toe and the two next to it. Scaurus screamed.

"Shh, Scaurus, calm down. Surgeons do wonderful things with prosthetics these days. More gifts from the gods you want our Consul to ignore. Now bind yourself to the couch or I'll shoot your other foot."

With shaking hands Scaurus weaved the bindings around his hands and then through the couch's metal armrest. Lepidus tapped the com on his collar and said, "Appius, you may come in now."

"I have rights," Scaurus growled as he finished wrapping the wire around the armrest. "I am a Citizen of Roma. I'm a patrician from a noble family. The Consul has named me Friend. You will suffer for this."

Lepidus leaned over and engaged the lock on the wire, then sat down on the couch facing Scaurus. He holstered his pistol and stared at Scaurus. The old man stared back defiantly several moments, then looked away.

"I thought so," Lepidus said. "Where is Marcia Licinius Ocella?"

"I have no idea," Scaurus said through a clenched jaw. His eyes were red from the pain in his foot. "I'm not her *paterfamilias*. Go talk to him. I need a medicus now."

The front door opened behind Lepidus, and he turned to see his apprentice, Gnaeus Hortensius Appius, enter the house. The young man was dressed in a black cloak and had the blond hair and angular face of his Nordic ancestry.

"Sit down, Appius," Lepidus said, "and watch a master liar spin his tales. He was Praefectus of the Praetorian Guard for twenty years, and the Consuls never suspected he was a traitor."

Appius sat down without a word, staring at Scaurus like he was a rat under the dissection knife.

Scaurus trembled. With pain, fury, or fear, Lepidus couldn't tell.

"You have no right to do this to me," Scaurus said. "If you have charges, bring them."

Lepidus took a small knife from his cloak and placed it on the table next to Scaurus. "There will be no charges, no tribunals, no pleas for mercy to the Consul. No one will save you."

Lepidus leaned forward, inches from Scaurus. "You will tell me what I want to know, and then I will kill you. It is up to you whether your death is quiet, or your agonized screams echo throughout the Aventine."

Scaurus stared at Lepidus, anger and pain contorting his face ...and then his features sagged. He looked like a man resigned to his fate. Lepidus was a little disappointed.

"You would break me," Scaurus said.

"I'm glad you see reason. I don't have time to play with you. Where is Marcia Licinius Ocella? Where did she take the Consular

Heir? The gods will receive you quickly if you confess your crimes now."

"The gods. Yes, they will take me. But what of you, Quintus Atius Lepidus? Do you serve them or the Consul?"

"There is no difference. They are both divine."

Scaurus shook his head sadly. "If you only knew your true masters."

Then he bit down hard. White foam gushed from his mouth and he began convulsing. Appius leaped off the couch, grabbed Scaurus's head, and stuck his fingers town the man's throat to get him to gag up the poison. Scaurus choked, heaved once, and then was still, his eyes staring vacantly at Lepidus. Appius continued digging his fingers around in Scaurus's mouth.

"Enough," Lepidus said. He grabbed the knife from the table and sheathed it in his cloak. "He's gone."

Appius shoved Scaurus down onto the couch. "Gods damn him," Appius growled. "He knew the boy's location." Then he turned to Lepidus. "How did *you* know it was him, sir? There was no evidence to suspect him."

Lepidus regarded Scaurus's body. "I followed a guess inspired by the gods, no matter how improbable that guess may have seemed. Licinius earned the Consul's trust by rooting out the Liberti agents in Roma. But she is also the only Praetorian not to report after the boy's disappearance. Scaurus was the one who recommended Licinius to the Guard. Therefore I concluded he might know her best."

Appius shook his head. "I never would have had the courage to interrogate a man as powerful man as Scaurus based on a guess."

Lepidus smiled. "Sometimes you need to listen to the gods when they whisper guidance to you."

"He was a legend, a hero of the State. To think he was a traitor."

"Only the Consul and the Collegia are infallible," Lepidus said. He glanced around the house. "Call in your team. All evidence of tonight's events must be removed. The public will be saddened to hear Numerius Aurelius Scaurus died of a heart attack. He will be remembered as a legend, a hero of the State."

Appius scowled, then nodded. As he stood to leave, Lepidus said, "Ensure your men search this house from the weather vane to the foundations."

Ocella and Cordus huddled on the couch in pitch-blackness. When Ocella heard Scaurus's screams, she immediately powered down everything in the underground sanctuary—the tabulari, the visum, the lights, the ventilation unit. Anything that might give off a power signature the agents upstairs might detect once they began their search. Scaurus had said the sanctuary was shielded from power leakage, but it was best not to test its effectiveness with their lives at stake.

"Will they find us?" Cordus whispered, huddled next to her. She could not see him, couldn't see her own nose, but she heard the tremor in his voice.

"I don't know," she whispered back.

"What will we do if they come down?"

She could barely hear him speak over her heart pounding in her ears. "We'll fight them."

"I cannot go back," Cordus said. "They will tear my mind apart looking for—" Ocella felt him shudder. "Will you make sure they do not take me?"

Ocella clenched the pulse pistol in her right hand. "They will not take either of us."

The boy tucked his head into her shoulder and was silent. They both sat in the dark, waiting for the sound of stone grinding on stone.

Chapter Sixteen

Kaeso had barely awakened from his delta sleep after *Caduceus* left the way line, when a stern voice came over the ship's com.

"*Caduceus*, this is Libertus Way Station Control. Proceed to cargo docking port 1201. Any deviation from your course and you will be fired upon. Acknowledge."

"Acknowledged, Control," Kaeso said. "Setting course for cargo docking port 1201."

The stars shifted in the command window as Lucia reset *Caduceus'* heading. She growled from the pilot seat, "I'm tired of hearing we're going to be fired upon."

Kaeso shared her feelings, but said nothing. The Centuriae was always in control, always knew what to do. Especially when he was *not* in control and did *not* know what to do.

One more mission and I may be back in Umbra working alone. And not responsible for seven other lives.

It had been a long time since Kaeso last visited Libertus. He gazed at the familiar sunlit northern continent with longing and dread. He grew up in the continent's center, in a province called Fabricium near the provincial capital Alexandria Novus. As a young man he'd made his home there with Petra and Claudia. At least until Petra's death, and the day he abandoned his daughter.

"Sir?" Lucia said.

Kaeso blinked at her.

"I asked for your orders after we dock. They're going to board us, right?" Her tone was all business. *She's still mad.*

"We do what they say."

Lucia nodded slowly. "Yes, sir."

Kaeso went back to watching Libertus grow larger in the command window.

It had been ten years, Kaeso decided. Yes, ten years since he last walked on Libertus. His last day on the planet had been the day he joined Umbra. The day he died to his family, friends, and his old life. After that day, Umbra had secreted him away to the moon of a gas giant in the Liberti system. He still didn't know—or remember—the moon's name till this day. His implant made the details hazy, but he remembered the moon was a cold, barren rock with no atmosphere. Most of his training was underground in air-filled caverns. During surface drills, he remembered staring through his EVA helmet past the red gas giant above toward the bright blue light of Libertus. And he would wonder what his daughter was doing.

Kaeso squeezed his eyes shut, then quickly opened them. The pain had not abated since Galeo mentioned Spur— Ocella. He welcomed the chance to return to Umbra, to clear his name. But now he saw his daughter every time he closed his eyes. It was always that last image of her, with a red face and tear-streaked cheeks, cursing him. And he knew he deserved it.

"Approaching way station, sir," Lucia said.

Kaeso tore his gaze from the planet and watched the approaching Libertus Way Station. It started as a speck of blinking light, turned into several specks, and then tiny starships flitting to and from the wheel-shaped way station. Unlike the hollowed-out asteroids of Roman way stations, the Libertus Way Station was entirely artificial, like a silver, rotating wagon wheel. It was built from the abundant ores mined from the lifeless moons and asteroids in the Libertus system. It had been a monumental effort often criticized in the Liberti Senate for its cost and scope, a project taking over twenty years to complete. Its saving grace, though, was the rotation it used to simulate gravity rather than expensive gravity generators that required fuel Libertus had to import from other star systems. The way station made Libertus the crown jewel of the Lost Worlds, and the center of commerce and culture for worlds that refused Roman rule.

While all eighteen Lost Worlds were different in culture, religion, and language, they were all united in their desire to be left alone, to live their lives without interference from Roma or any other human empire. It was a Roman Consul that first called the Lost Worlds "lost"—since they refused the benefits of Roman rule—but they kept the name over the centuries as a proud display of independence. Libertus became their *de facto* capital. While there were no official political ties, the Lost Worlds were a trading bloc that gave them the economic openness of a nation without the entanglements of a unified government.

A ripe fruit such as Libertus would have fallen long ago to Roman or Zhonguo dominance but for one thing: Umbra Corps, an organization few Liberti knew existed. Oh, there were rumors and conspiracy theories among the Liberti—most invented by Umbra—of a secret army keeping Libertus free. How could there *not* be such an army? Though Roma grew weaker each year, its Naves Astrum far outnumbered all the warships in the Lost Worlds combined. In a one-on-one fight, Libertus and the Lost Worlds would never stand a chance. It was a common assumption that *something* protected Libertus from Roma and the Zhonguo Sphere.

That *something* was what kept conspiracy theories clogging up the tabulari bands. Kaeso smiled inwardly at the theories, anything from the gods' intervention to economic blackmail. Some theories even suggested the Zhonguo secretly protected Libertus, since Libertus was a lucrative market for their goods.

Kaeso wondered how the Liberti would react if they knew the only thing standing between them and Roman slavery was a thousand patriots allied with a sentient alien virus Umbra called the Muses.

Not even Kaeso had believed it when he was first recruited. A thousand Umbra Ancilia against humanity's greatest empires? All with the help of an ancient alien virus that infected the first Liberti settlers when they colonized the planet? Kaeso had never been a religious man, but he had found it easier to believe in the entire Roman Pantheon than an *intelligent* alien virus. A virus had helped Libertus not only gain the prosperity and technological superiority she now enjoyed, but ensured her safety through means that made "clandestine" a description too laughably mild.

The proximity alarm startled Kaeso. He glanced out the window, saw the way station's docking port a quarter-mile away.

Lucia reached out to a control pad between them and tapped a button. The wailing stopped. "Sorry, sir. Forgot the alarm."

He noticed her set jaw and furrowed brow.

"You need to smile more."

Her eyes widened, and Kaeso saw the reddening skin around her neck. "Yes, sir," she said.

Kaeso hadn't meant to make her feel uncomfortable, so he added, "The whole crew needs to smile more."

She nodded and then hurriedly said, "Ion drives disengaged. Docking thrusters online."

Lucia completed the docking procedure flawlessly, as usual. The moment the ship switched over to the way station's power and air, a stern voice came over the com.

"Centuriae Aemilius, you and your crew will proceed to the cargo hold with your infected crewman. You will remove all clothing and await decontamination teams. Acknowledge."

Kaeso gritted his teeth. "Cargo One is not a private or warm place for decontamination."

"This is not a negotiation, Centuriae. If you and your crew are not there when the decontamination teams board, they will forcibly move you there. Acknowledge."

"Who do they think—?" Lucia growled.

"Acknowledged," Kaeso said. "*Caduceus* out." He thumbed his collar com. "All crew report to Cargo One and remove your clothes for decontamination. Let's go, Lucia."

Still grumbling, Lucia unlatched her couch belts and followed Kaeso off the command deck.

When he and Lucia reached Cargo One, Daryush was the only one there. He stood naked, his hands on the sleeper crib containing Dariya. Kaeso stood next to Daryush, and looked at Dariya through the frosted window. Her eyes were closed, her mouth slightly open, and her short black hair floated around her head. A single bubble escaped her nostril and floated to the sleeper fluid surface.

Daryush turned to him with pleading, teary eyes.

"We're going to help her," Kaeso told him. "I swear it."

Daryush turned back to the crib, sighed, and continued to stare at his sister.

Behind Kaeso, Blaesus and Flamma entered the bay.

"Not that I'm opposed to displaying my prominent manhood," Blaesus declared, "but isn't there a better place for this? It's freezing in here."

"It's not up to me," Kaeso said, walking to the connector hatch.

Nestor followed behind Blaesus and Flamma. "It makes sense," the Greek medicus said. "The cargo bays have the most room for their decon equipment."

Blaesus grunted. "I'm not removing one article of clothing until they get here. Otherwise they'll find a frozen old man with a huge—"

"Get undressed," Kaeso ordered. "They're here."

Kaeso watched on the external cam as seven decon crewmen filed into the docking tube. All were dressed in white decon suits with helmets and faceplates covering their heads. Five carried metal cases, and two held each end of a metal trunk. Kaeso unlocked *Caduceus's* connector hatch, which opened with a hiss. The two men in front dropped their cases and aimed pistols at Kaeso.

"Into the cargo bay, Centuriae," a man said from behind the two gunmen.

Kaeso turned and walked back to Cargo One. His crew stared at the decon unit as they stormed onto the ship.

"Your whole crew here?" the leader asked. He and the others—besides the men with guns—set down their cases and opened them. Each contained expanding trays of electronic instruments, syringes, tubes, bandages, and other medical supplies. The two carrying the large trunk set it down, opened it, and began removing what looked like a portable shower.

"Yes," Kaeso said, standing between the decon unit and his crew.

Six more decon members came through the portal carrying instruments they waved in the air. One went into Cargo Two across the hall, while the others proceeded down the corridor.

"You will all remove your clothes and step into the shower," the leader said.

"Hold on," Kaeso said. "We've done everything you asked, now we—"

"I'm not asking, Centuriae," the leader said. The two men with pistols raised them at Kaeso.

"Neither am I, Medicus," Kaeso said, staring past the gunman at the leader. "We are not your enemies. So you will treat my crew with some godsdamned dignity. Understand?"

"I don't have time for this," the leader said. "Get them in the showers."

A gunman tried seizing Kaeso. Instinct made Kaeso grab the gunman's wrist with one hand, disarm him with the other, and twist his arm behind his back. Kaeso put the gun to his head. The other gunman stumbled backward in shock, but kept his gun aimed at Kaeso. He half-turned to the leader as if wondering what to do.

"Jupiter's cock!" the leader yelled. "We're trying to save your lives!"

"We both know there's no cure for the Cariosus," Kaeso said. Behind him, Daryush gasped. "What's in the 'showers'?"

The man Kaeso held struggled, but Kaeso wrenched his arm up further. The man grunted, then went still.

"It's just a shower! It'll wash off any virus on your skin."

"The virus can't survive outside the body. It's blood-borne."

The leader blinked, his mouth opening and closing. "Of course it can. It's like any other virus, it can survive up to—"

"This isn't 'any other virus.' What is in the shower?"

A voice came from the connector hatch. "Centuriae Aemelius. Is there a problem?"

Kaeso kept his focus on the decon leader. He knew the tall man in the decon suit stepping through the hatch was Galeo.

"Not unless I get some simple answers," Kaeso said. "You his boss?"

"I am," Galeo said. "I'm Medicus Pullo. What answers will make you put down that pulse pistol?"

"To start, why do you have gunmen in here, *Medicus* Pullo?"

Galeo entered the Cargo One and stood next to the decon leader. Galeo still wore the same face he'd worn when he last talked to Kaeso.

"For our protection," Galeo said. "Cariosa are quite violent. Which you're demonstrating right now. If you or your crew were infected, we would need to stop you if you attacked us."

"If I was infected, I'd be chewing on this man's neck right now," Kaeso said. "What's in the shower?"

"Hot water. Soap. An anti-viral agent that'll remove the dead skin from your entire body."

"Sounds painful."

Galeo shrugged. "It itches."

"Where did the other men go? The ones with the instruments?"

"They're checking your ship for contagion. They should be done with their sweep in a half hour. This is not a big ship."

"Dariya?"

"We're preparing a facility, but it'll take a few days before it's ready. In the meantime, she'll be quarantined here, in her sleeper crib. Any other questions?"

Kaeso shook his head. He pushed the gunman he held toward his partner. The gunman turned around, as if to attack Kaeso, but Kaeso kept the pistol pointed at him. The gunman's partner grabbed his arm.

"Tell your thugs to leave," Kaeso said. "And bring us some privacy curtains for our showers."

Galeo nodded. "Of course. You men, go find some curtains for your patients."

Both gunmen turned to the decon leader.

"Now," Galeo said quietly. Both men hurried out of Cargo One and back into the connector tube.

The lead medicus turned to Galeo. "Sir, you told me this was an emergency. If these people are Cariosa—"

"The only carrier is in that sleeper crib," Galeo said. "The rest are clean. If they weren't, we'd know."

"You can't be sure."

"There's no such thing as sure. That's why you and your men are here. You are a precaution, not the solution."

The medicus leader's mouth became a thin line, then he turned and began organizing the instruments in his case.

Kaeso lowered the pistol, flipped its butt to Galeo, and handed it to him.

"Can I speak to you alone, Centuriae Aemilius?" Galeo asked.

"Of course, *Medicus Pullo*."

"Sir, what should we do?" Lucia asked from behind him.

Kaeso turned around to the shocked stares of his crew. He realized they'd never seen him disarm someone like he'd just done. He frowned, for it was one more piece of his history they'd ask him about. One more piece he couldn't reveal.

"When they come back with the curtains, you can shower," Kaeso said. "And do what the medicus tells you." He glanced at the decon leader, and added, "Within reason."

The medicus leader's nostrils flared, but he said nothing.

When Kaeso and Galeo were in the corridor between the cargo bays, Galeo asked, "What was that?"

"We're not criminals."

"The Romans would disagree."

"Stop playing with me, Galeo. What's happening in Umbra right now?"

"Those men are not Umbra."

"Obviously. They're civilians, so why are they here? I'd have thought a Cariosa would've been grounds for high-level concealment protocols. Umbra handlers only. Not these outsiders."

Galeo's lips thinned. "Umbra is in a crisis. Our resources are spread thin containing the damage your old friend has inflicted."

"She may be innocent. You said we don't have all the information."

"Perhaps, but we're in a crisis that's stretching Umbra's resources farther than they've ever been, thus the civilians. Now will you please play nice and do what they tell you? The showers and other procedures will protect you and your crew."

"I know."

Galeo gave an exasperated laugh. "Then why the theater?"

Kaeso stared at his crew through the Cargo One windows. All five were huddled together and whispering as they watched the medicus team set up privacy curtains for their showers. Lucia caught Kaeso's eyes through the window, and she nodded.

"Because I'm tired of hearing I'm going to be fired upon," Kaeso said. "And that medicus was an ass."

"Well you'll need to control your pride and follow orders if you want back into Umbra."

Kaeso looked at him. "I'm back in?"

Galeo held his hands up. "I didn't say that. They didn't dismiss the idea, but neither were they warm to it. Right now I'm sure you're the subject of heated debate in the Magisterium. If you do the mission and don't create more problems than you solve, then you might have a chance."

"Right. Oh, and my crew is not coming with me."

"You see, that's what I meant by creating problems," Galeo said and sighed. "We've been over this, Kaeso. We don't have time to train a new crew."

"I'm going alone. Just like I've always done."

Galeo clenched his teeth, shook his head. "Kaeso, if you don't do as you're ordered, the Magisterium will arrest your crew and extradite them to Roma. Not to mention you'd forever burn any chance you have at getting reinstated. Do you want that?"

"They won't arrest my crew because they know I'd never go on this mission. Judging by the help these days, they need *me* to go to Roma. Are they going to screw that up just to punish me for bending a few rules?"

Galeo stared at Kaeso. "Why are you doing this? This just proves you can't follow orders."

"Once I'm back in, I will follow orders just fine." Kaeso regarded his former mentor and friend. "Galeo, I *want* back in. I'm committed to this mission, but my crew did not sign up for this. They have no idea what can happen to them in Roma. What the Praetorian Guard would do to them if they were caught working for us. They actually think crucifixion is the worst that can happen. On my honor as a centuriae, I can't put them in that kind of danger. Honor is still an Umbra prerequisite, isn't it?"

"Honor?" Galeo snorted. "Honor is a luxury for the military and civilians."

"I won't take them. If the Magisterium can't accept that, then the mission is off."

Galeo frowned.

"They'll just have to trust me," Kaeso pressed. "They know my record. *You* know my record. I've always been a loyal patriot. Still am. The reasons for my discharge were administrative *cac*. I can do this mission, but they have to let me do it my way. Like they did when I was an Ancile."

"What happens if they call your bluff?"

Kaeso shrugged. "Then my crew goes back to Roma in chains. Which is what will happen anyway if they go on this mission."

Kaeso turned to his crew in Cargo One. He saw their shadows behind the shower curtains as they rubbed the scalding water and antiviral soap over themselves.

"Do they know you want to abandon them?" Galeo asked. "That you don't want to be the centuriae of a smuggling freighter?"

Kaeso scowled. "You ask too many questions. Will you pass on my conditions or what?"

"I will, and there will likely be howling, spitting, and gnashing of teeth before they realize you have them by the balls and accept your demands. And you wonder why you were kicked out."

"Jealousy?"

"Go take your shower."

Kaeso went back to Cargo One while Galeo walked through the connector tube to the way station. As soon as Kaeso returned, Blaesus emerged from behind the shower curtain, drying his body with a large white towel.

"Centuriae, the shower was exhilarating. My first hot one in weeks. I don't know why you were complaining before."

Kaeso began removing his clothes. "Wait until the anti-viral agent kicks in. You'll be itching your body red before the hour is out."

The old Senator's eyes widened as Kaeso entered his own shower. When the hot water fell over him, he smiled. He was going to miss playing with Blaesus.

Chapter Seventeen

"I found it," Cordus called out.

Ocella scrambled from the ductwork in the ceiling, dropped to the floor, and hurried to where Cordus shouted. He stood before a low hole behind one of Scaurus's massive bookshelves, which was swung outward like a door. The hole was maybe four feet by four feet, barely enough room for an adult to crawl through.

"How did you find it?"

"I wanted that book," he said, pointing to a bound copy of Cicero's *De Republica*. "It would not come out, so I pulled harder and the bookshelf moved."

Ocella smiled, but she felt only sadness. She should have expected the old man would make Cicero his means of escape. She was confident he was dead, for he had not returned since the Praetorians arrived. Ocella and Cordus had spent a harrowing two days in the basement since the Praetorians had torn the house apart upstairs. She was sure they'd find the basement, kill her, and return Cordus to his prison.

But they had not. Scaurus had likely gone to his death without giving up Ocella and Cordus. She shuddered to think what he had to endure before the end.

Even though the Praetorians had left, she did not want to leave the basement in case the house was still under surveillance. So for the last two days, Ocella and Cordus had kept themselves busy by searching for this secret escape hole. With each passing hour, however, she grew more fearful that Scaurus lied, that she'd have to lead Cordus out a back window upstairs, which the Praetorians surely monitored.

Now the boy may have saved them.

"Does this mean we can leave?" Cordus asked.

"*I* will meet with Scaurus's contact. *You* will stay here."

Ocella rushed over to the locker with coats, togas, and clothing Scaurus had given them. She selected a long black coat with a hood. She found an Umbra-built voice mimicker on the top shelf, and smiled. She shouldn't have been surprised at Scaurus's resourcefulness—he was the head of the Praetorian Guard for twenty years and would know how to get what he wanted. She placed the mimicker in her coat's inner pocket and then shut the locker doors.

"I can handle myself on the streets of Roma," Cordus said indignantly.

"When have you ever been 'on the streets of Roma'?"

"I snuck out of the palace many times."

"With loyal slaves," she countered. "Never with Praetorians waiting to kill you. Look, I just need to find Scaurus's contact. I can't skulk in the shadows if I have to make sure you're with me all the time. I won't be gone long. Once I get the passes, I'll come back. Then you can show me these street skills you learned from your slaves when we go to the ship."

Cordus regarded her a moment, then sighed. "Fine."

He turned around, sat down at the tabulari, and called up a game of *latrunculi*. The holographic squared board auto-populated with pieces.

"That better not be over the bands," she said.

"No, it is against the tabulari. Go, you are disturbing my concentration."

Ocella remembered again why she'd never wanted children.

Ocella went back to the tunnel behind the bookshelf and peered into the darkness. She couldn't see more than six feet ahead, so she went back to Scaurus's desk—enduring Cordus's silent frowns at the interruption—and took the small pen torch she'd found the other day. Back at the tunnel, she got on her hands and knees and crawled with the pen torch in her teeth lighting the way ahead.

She came to the end of the tunnel thirty feet from the basement. She pointed her pen torch up and saw the tunnel became a shaft. Metal rungs stuck out from the wall, but she could not see the top within her torch's limited range. She put the torch back in her mouth and started climbing.

She reached the top twenty feet up and found a metal hatch with a wheel. Balancing precariously on the ladder rungs, the pen torch in her mouth, she tried turning the wheel. It stuck at first, but moved after much grunting and pulling on her part. The hatch issued a series of clicks, and then she pushed up. The hatch only moved a fraction, so she pushed harder. An avalanche of dirt fell through the opening onto her head, and she struggled to keep her balance on the rungs. When the falling dirt stopped, she pushed the hatch again. More dirt trickled over her as she opened the hatch all the way. It made surprisingly little noise after years of disuse.

The sky was dark, and cool air rushed down to dry the sweat beads on her forehead. She shook the dirt from her hair and tried to wipe it from her face with her coat sleeve. Once she had blinked away most of the dirt in her eyes, she poked her head above the ground.

At first she thought she was in Scaurus's garden, towards the back of his property. To her right was a large stone wall, and an olive tree towering above her. To her left was a red-painted house. She realized it was the house next to Scaurus's, and that she was in their garden. Lights blazed from inside, and she saw the neighbors were hosting a dinner party. Guests walked back and forth in front of the windows, and a man and woman stood on the patio sipping from wine goblets. They held each other closely, laughing quietly. They seemed more interested in each other, for they did not seem to notice Ocella's head peeking out of the ground. She thought she was well hidden, since the olive tree and three large bushes cast a large shadow around her.

The question now was how to leave the garden. Her first thought was to mingle with the guests, but she dismissed that idea. A sweat-streaked, dirty face was not worn to Roman dinner parties. No, if she did not want to be seen, she would have to wait for the man and woman to leave the patio before she scrambled over the wall. Patience was the most useful thing Umbra had taught her.

But after almost fifteen minutes watching the two lovers exchange kisses, she was quickly losing her patience. The painful spasms in her calves and back from balancing on the ladder rungs made her all the more willing to kill the lovers and be done with them.

Two young men in white togas and wine stains burst from the patio doors, singing "What Lies Between My Lady's Thighs." Ocella was never gladder to hear that vulgar song. The two lovers exchanged annoyed looks, then went back inside.

To Ocella's horror, the two young men stumbled straight toward her, swinging their wine goblets and singing as loud as their voices could muster. There was no time to pull the hatch over her, so she ducked down inside the shaft. The men went to the stone wall six feet to Ocella's right, then she heard them relieving themselves on the wall. She held her breath, praying they were too drunk to notice the deep hole six feet away. It was dark, so her chances of remaining undetected were good.

But she would not underestimate the serendipitous luck of a stumbling drunk. She slowly reached for the pistol in her coat.

"Rufus, Ahala," a male voice shouted from the patio. "Get in here, the dancers are starting."

The two men made a triumphant howl, then staggered back to the house, still screaming the vulgar song. Ocella made sure they went inside, then jumped up from the hatch, and crouching low, quietly closed it. She moved some dirt on it and covered it with dead leaves. Once again ensuring nobody from the party was outside, she leaped to the top of the wall a few feet above her, pulled herself over, and dropped to the alley on the other side.

She scanned the alley to her left and right. Besides stray dogs fighting over garbage, the alley was deserted. She searched the surrounding buildings, but saw no sign of Praetorian surveillance. Either they were well hidden, or they had abandoned all hope of finding clues at Scaurus's home. Until she was sure, however, she would assume the former. She hurried to another dark alley, walked fast for several dozen yards, past more garbage-eating dogs, then down another alley. She stopped to listen for footsteps behind her. Nothing.

Ocella took her coat off and shook out the remainder of the dirt, then rapidly ran her fingers through her hair. She was glad she had cut her once long black hair short to better fit into the Praetorian Guard, for the dirt would never have left her hair without a good washing. She used the coat's interior to wipe more dirt from her face, then put it back on. She paused to get her bearings, then headed right, toward what she assumed was the Via Ostiensis.

Scaurus mentioned his contact was a Zhongguo with a merchant ship in the Mars Trading Fields. It wasn't much to go on, but since the Zhongguo were rare in Roma—and Terra—since their diaspora 300 years ago, she thought Fortuna might be with her if she asked around. It was not that late, so the contact might still be at his ship.

She put the hood over her head and merged into the crowds packing the Via Ostiensis. This part of the Aventine was renowned for its taverns, gambling dens, and brothels. Ocella figured she would have no problem fitting into the plebeian revelers filling the streets. Young men wearing their finest togas, their arms around each other or a prostitute, shuffled down the street singing songs just as vulgar as the two in the garden. She passed a small ceremony honoring Bacchus, seven men and women standing before a priest holding a wine cup to a ten-foot idol of the god. Their chanting was as boisterous as she'd expect to find in a prayer to the wine god. To her right was a small park where a dozen old men played *latrunculi* on stone tables. She even passed a street fair where a small comedy troupe performed. Ocella did not stop to watch, but judging from the half-naked performers and the positions they mimicked, it was a play well suited to the street's clientele.

Ocella found a taxi zone and stood on the sensor pad. A small electric taxi pulled in front of her and then opened its door. Ocella got in the back seat, and the door closed.

The friendly male voice came from a hidden speaker. "Destination?"

"Mars Trading Fields," she said.

After a pause, the taxi said, "Five sesterces, please. Account number?"

One of the first tricks Umbra taught her before coming to Roma was how to hack an electric taxi. You never knew when you'd need to get somewhere fast, and you didn't want to leave an electric trail by using a traceable account number. Electric taxis did not have an interface, relying on voice for commands and identification. If a passenger's account number did not match with the voice pattern on record, there would be no transaction and the taxi would not run. It would have been easier with an active implant—she could have used it to send an override command directly to the taxi—but that was why she brought another tool.

She took out the voice mimicker she got from Scaurus's locker, a tool built by Umbra for this purpose. She thumbed the record button and said, "Maintenance override."

She rewound the recording, adjusted the treble and bass settings, and then played the recording into the taxi microphone. "Maintenance override," her adjusted voice said from the mimicker.

"Destination?" the taxi asked again.

Ocella adjusted the mimicker settings again and then played her altered voice. "Maintenance override."

The taxi paused, then said, "Override accepted."

"Take me to the Mars Trading Fields."

"Of course. Estimated time to destination...seven minutes."

The taxi zipped into traffic and headed down the Aventine toward the Tiber. Ocella kept her hood up. She wasn't worried about people outside the taxi noticing her, but rather the dome light camera above her head inside the taxi. Sooner or later the taxi company would discover her unauthorized "maintenance override," and they would search the camera footage to find out who had done it. Hopefully she and Cordus were long gone from Roma by then. If not, a taxi company tracking her down for a five-sesterce fare would be the least of her worries.

The taxi pulled up next to the marble-columned entry to the Mars Trading Fields exactly seven minutes after its estimate on the Aventine. The Trading Fields were a vast market of merchants from across the Republic, along with some Lost World merchants lucky enough to obtain a selling license from Roma. Almost anything could be found in the Fields, from exotic produce and meats to clothing, media, and slaves (human and golem). Most vendors sold their wares right from the back of their cargo ships. Though the hour was late, Ocella noticed the gates to the Fields were still open and customers trickled in and out.

"Mars Trading Fields," the taxi said.

Ocella said, "Find a place to park and wait for me."

"Of course."

Ocella opened the door and stepped onto the street before the Trading Fields entry. The taxi zipped away from the gate and parked itself in a spot along the street less than a block away.

Ocella spared a look at the Trading Fields' entry as she hurried through the gates. A dozen two-story marble columns built over six hundred years ago supported a classical roof structure over the entry. Bas-reliefs along the roof showed images from the Fields' past: its beginning as a herding field for sheep, a training field for ancient Roman militia, a gathering for elections, and its current use as a market for commodities from across the Republic. The customers were sparse near closing time, but Ocella had no trouble imagining the throngs streaming through the columns during the Trading Fields' prime hours.

Once inside, Ocella passed dropships with their wares displayed beside them or from their open cargo doors. Exotic scents filled the air: fruits, vegetables, and spices from every corner of Terra and the Republic. Strange art from distant worlds were arrayed on shelves and tables and on the ground. Vases, sculptures, paintings, holographic comedies and tragedies, synthesized music from non-Republic nations. Ocella passed caged animals from off-world—reptiles with feathery wings, dog-like creatures with furry tentacles sprouting from their sides, insects the size of Ocella's hand mimicking the voices of passersby. Even an experienced Umbra Ancile like her struggled to keep her focus on the crowd rather than the vendors calling her attention to their wares.

The Zhonguo contact—if he existed—would be at the back of the Fields. Roman merchants always populated the sections near the gates. The foreign merchants, however, were put in a section downhill from the main Fields and next to the Tiber riverfront. The stench of dead fish, excrement, and chemical pollution was the price foreigners paid to do business in the largest market in Roma.

It took Ocella longer to get to the foreign section than the taxi ride to the Fields. Along the way she had to avoid aggressive merchants trying to make their final sale of the day, side-step blood in the street from the butcher merchants cleaning their stalls, and twice hide between stalls to avoid silver-helmed lictors on foot patrol.

She reached the entrance to the foreign section, descended cracked stone steps down a steep gravel hill, and started searching the parked ships for a Zhonguo merchant. Though the foreign section was far smaller than the Roman section, there were still dozens of stalls and parked dropships lining the riverfront. It could take hours to search every one.

She found a merchant from Aqalax, a small Lost World one way line jump from Roman space. His ancestors were from Terra's Atlantium continent, for his skin was dark bronze and his long black hair was decorated with beads. He was packing up his goods when Ocella approached.

"Can you tell me where the Zhonguo district is?"

He stared at her, and Ocella was about to try the dominant language on Aqalax when he replied in accented Latin, "There are no Zhonguo here." He waved toward the riverfront. "Maybe farther down."

Ocella thanked him and proceeded down the dirt road.

She passed stalls and ships from all over Terra and the Roman Republic. Egyptian, Ethiopian, Indian, Palestinian, Greek, and more merchants from Atlantium. Some smaller Lost Worlds were represented as well, like Roma Nova which was close enough in culture to Roma, yet not a vassal world and thus considered "foreign." She asked several merchants about the Zhonguo district, and she got the same response as the Aqalax merchant. She continued on.

She reached the end of the riverfront and still had not found a Zhonguo merchant. She cursed under her breath, realizing she should have known this was a futile search among the hundreds of stalls and ships on the Fields. She sighed and then made her way back along the riverfront toward the Roman sections. Perhaps the Zhonguo contact worked for one of the Roman merchants. She tried not to despair at the thought of searching the entire Trading Fields for a Zhonguo face.

As she passed the Aqalax merchant again, he smiled at her. "My lady, a hot drink of fresh ground *xocolatl*? The *xocolatl* on my world is far sweeter than from my honored ancestors in Atlantium. One sip and you will agree, my lady."

The merchant tried handing her a cup of dark liquid, but Ocella declined and kept walking. "Are you sure, my lady? Your family would bless you for bringing home such a sweet and filling treat. Especially your son."

Ocella stopped. She turned back to the merchant. He held a cup to her, but he also held a small canister with an elaborate logo painted on the front emblazoned with the word "*xocolatl*."

"A free sample for my lady," the merchant said. "All I ask is that if the sample agrees with you, perhaps you'd be so kind as to come back and buy a generous portion for you and your family."

Ocella walked back to the merchant and cautiously took the canister. "Thank you."

"Instructions are inside the canister. Be sure to follow them explicitly or else the drink will not satisfy."

Ocella nodded.

"Very good," the merchant said, his smile widening. "Is the lady interested in any other produce? I'm packing up for the night, but I would be happy to unpack anything of interest to my lady."

"I believe I have what I came for."

"Of course. Good night to you, then."

Ocella turned and started back up the stone stairs to the Roman section, holding the small canister in her left palm. She made her way through the Fields, avoiding lictors and passing merchants shutting down for the night.

When she emerged from the gates, she walked straight to the taxi and got in. Before ordering the taxi to leave, she opened the canister and searched the contents. It contained a dark brown powder that smelled both sweet and bitter. On the canister lid were instructions on how much *xocolatl* to mix with hot water or milk. She poked her finger through the dark powder but found nothing in it. She ground her teeth, hoping she hadn't mistaken a simple merchant trying to make a sale as Scaurus's contact. She dumped the dark *xocolatl* on the taxi floor and searched the canister bottom. Scrawled on the bottom was a date and time.

Noon. Two days from now.

Ocella screwed the canister lid back on, put it in her pocket, and then told the taxi to go back to the Aventine. Two blocks from Scaurus's house, she ordered the taxi to stop.

"Delete recent destination logs," Ocella ordered the taxi.

"Logs deleted."

"Go to the intersection of Via Ferinum and Via Hollae in the Suburba, wait for three hours, and then discontinue maintenance override."

Ocella hoped an electric taxi sitting near the high-crime corner of Ferinum and Hollae would make a tempting target for thieves. Three hours was enough time for thieves to strip the taxi of all its valuable parts. It would take days for the taxi company to dissect the taxi's electronic brain to figure out what happened.

She got out of the taxi and made her way through the revelers, passed the vulgar play still going strong, and then ducked into the alley behind Scaurus's house. She arrived at the wall to the yard with the hatch and listened a few seconds. Hearing silence on the patio, she jumped to the top of the wall and peeked into the garden. Nobody outside. She pulled herself over and jumped down onto soft grass. She hurried over to the hatch and pushed away the dirt and leaves she'd put over it. She opened the hatch, stepped down onto the ladder rungs, and then tried as best she could to pull some fallen branches next to the hatch as she quietly closed it. The neighbors would notice the hatch the next time they decided to pick olives from their tree. Ocella hoped it was after she and Cordus were gone.

She climbed down the rungs and scurried back through the tunnel to the dim basement sanctuary. She stood up and closed the bookshelf over the tunnel.

"Cordus?" she called as the bookshelf clicked shut. She peered around the free-standing bookshelves, but did not see him at the tabulari.

"Cordus."

He was not on the couch watching the holo either. The bathroom door was ajar, but it was dark inside. She pushed open the door and turned on the light. He wasn't there.

"Cordus, you're being a baby. Where are you? I have some good news."

After a fruitless search, she yelled, "Cordus, this isn't funny."

Ocella's annoyance began turning to panic. *He actually left.* She tried thinking like the boy. He burned to leave the basement, she knew that, and he had an elevated opinion of his street sense. Whether or not he had ancient knowledge in his brain, he was still a twelve-year-old boy who would not stand a chance against common street toughs. He could be lying in a gutter right now, his body violated, his throat slit—

Ocella stopped. She could not let herself think what might have happened. She had to concentrate on her situation as she knew it. *Think like the boy.* Where would he go? He had no money or a voice account, so he could not have hired a taxi or taken a bus. He had to have walked. This was the first time he'd ever been on his own. He would want to see as much as he could. Even the most mundane, plebeian pastimes would fascinate him. She had been gone less than two hours, and given his curiosity, he could not have walked farther than the Aventine.

She searched her memories for anything he might have said, any hint as to what he wanted to see on his own. Games? The nearest coliseum was by the Forum, a two-hour walk if the boy took his time. She didn't think he would go near the Forum because even he knew how dangerous it was to stray too far. He didn't want to get caught any more than Ocella. What Aventine "sights" would interest a young noble out for the first time?

Or maybe someone had seen her leave the tunnel, then came through to take Cordus. She felt blood drain from her face as she realized the Praetorians could be watching the house right now, waiting for her to come out again, waiting to take her back to their headquarters and make her talk.

She hurried up the basement stairs to the house and saw the secret pantry door was cracked open. Cursing, she opened the door wider so she could slip through. She pulled out her pistol, and stepped quietly into the dark kitchen.

The lights were on in the rest of the house, making Ocella hesitate. The Praetorians likely did that so they could see anyone moving around. She stayed in the kitchen's shadows and did a brief visual search of the room, but did not find Cordus. She did see a large blood stain near the couches next to the door, and she said a silent prayer for Scaurus's soul to find rest in Elysium. She also noticed the front door panel said it was locked. Cordus didn't know the key code, so he couldn't have left that way. She didn't think the boy was so colossally stupid as to climb through a window, though the fact he'd not only gone upstairs but left the house made her doubt that assumption.

She went back through the secret pantry door, taking care to close the door this time, and down the stairs. She stood at the foot of the stairs, trying to calm her shaking hands, trying to ignore the nausea rising from her gut and the cold sweat tricking down her warm back. She pounded her fists on a bookshelf. She had completed dangerous missions for Umbra and had never felt this panicked. She had to stop, to breathe.

Then she noticed a sheet of paper on the floor next to the tabulari. She bent down and picked it up, turned it over, and read Cordus's elegant penmanship.

"I have gone for a look around. No fear, I shall be careful and return presently."

Cordus must have put the paper on the tabulari, but it had fallen to the floor.

Ocella crumpled up the paper and threw it at the tabulari. She grabbed a fresh coat from the locker, then hurried over to the wall bookshelf and opened the tunnel. As she crawled through, she decided if street toughs hadn't killed the boy, she would.

Chapter Eighteen

The party guests were inside, so Ocella jumped from the hatch and scurried up the wall before anyone could come out and delay her from strangling Cordus.

She hurried down the alley and onto the Via Ostiensis. If anything, the crowds were larger this time. It was less than an hour before midnight, the prime of the Aventine's revelry. Ocella kept her hood up, and scanned the crowds for Cordus and obvious tails.

She passed the taverns and brothels, knowing Cordus would be curious, but not comfortable there by himself. She walked by the old men playing board games, searching the gray and bald heads for a head of black hair. She didn't see anyone under sixty.

She stopped at the street play, which had switched from a vulgar sex show to a vulgar puppet show. The crowd roared with laughter as a puppet with a Zhonguo's creased eyes tried making love to a squirming dark-skinned Kaldethian.

Ocella searched the audience and found the boy sitting in the center. She took a deep breath, relaxed her clenched fists, and sat down just behind him. Cordus laughed right along with the crowd. No one paid attention to him despite the fact he wore no hood and had on the same high-quality tunic and coat he'd worn when they'd escaped the Consular Palace. Once again she thanked the gods that pictures of the Consular Family were forbidden in Roman media—the Praetorians' own security protocols were the only thing keeping Cordus from being recognized on the streets.

Ocella leaned forward and whispered in his ear, "Cordus, what do you think you're doing?"

The boy jumped and turned around. When he saw her, his face went from terrified to annoyed. He turned back to the stage.

"I am enjoying this play. Watch with me."

"We're leaving," Ocella said. "Now."

"I am staying until the play is finished."

Ocella ground her teeth. Umbra had taught her many ways to incapacitate a human being, but never how to quietly drag an insolent child out of a public place. She didn't know if Cordus would fight if she grabbed him by the scruff of his neck. Considering his recent behavior, she wouldn't put it past him. So her only choice was to endure the puppet show until *His Majesty* was ready to go.

After another fifteen minutes of sophomoric jokes and unrealistic puppet sex, the show thankfully ended and the audience stood to leave. Cordus turned to her with a grin.

"You have to admit that was funny," he said. "They never had shows like that in the Palace."

"Let's go," Ocella said, then grabbed the boy's arm and pulled him down the street.

They had gone several dozen steps before the boy yanked his arm from her grip. "I do not know why you are so angry." He straightened his coat, but continued walking beside her. "I was only gone for an hour. Praetorians do not congregate on the Aventine."

Ocella pushed Cordus into a shadowy alley. She wanted to wait until they got back to Scaurus's house before she screamed at him, but she couldn't hold her anger that long. She grabbed the boy's shoulders and used all her will to avoid slapping him.

"You heard what happened to Scaurus less than three blocks away! The Praetorians are watching the house, you fool, so what makes you so sure they aren't watching the surrounding streets? They have face-recognition cameras scouring the city for you! Every godsdamned camera on every godsdamned utility pole, taxi, or whorehouse peepshow can do that!"

Cordus's eyes grew darker as she railed on him. *Let him get mad.* The boy had to know how much danger he'd put himself in by leaving the safe house.

"Do not call me a fool," Cordus said sullenly once Ocella had paused her rant to catch her breath. "I would have slit my own wrists if I had to endure another moment in that basement."

Ocella's mouth opened for another tirade, but she stopped. She had felt the same way. It was why she had worked so hard to find Scaurus's secret exit. Not only had she wanted to escape and find Scaurus's contact, but she had also needed to get out of that stuffy, constricting basement where she'd spent the last two weeks. Even if it meant risking capture.

She sighed. "You scared me, Cordus."
"Because you did not want to get caught."
"No," she said, "because I was worried about *you*."
He looked up at her. "Me?" It seemed like the most foreign concept he'd ever heard. It made her more angry at the Consular Family for how they had treated this boy his whole life.
"Yes," she said.
She surprised herself as she said it, because she meant it. She had been more worried about the boy's safety than her own fate. It stunned her, and she knew she had to stamp out that feeling. The boy was a mission, and her mission was to get him off Terra. She could not afford an emotional attachment to this child. It would compromise some hard choices she might have to make before this was over.
Cordus studied his feet and tucked his hands in his toga. Then he lifted his chin. "I am sorry I worried you. That was not my intent. I...I should not have left the basement. You are right, I put us in danger."
Ocella realized she still held his shoulders, so she released him. "Just don't do it again. We'll only be there two more days."
Cordus nodded, then brightened. "You found the contact?"
"I think so. He wants us to meet him at in the Mars Trading Fields in two days. I think we can both survive the basement that long. And that means no more trips upstairs."
"Upstairs?"
"In Scaurus's house," she said. "No more exploring, understand?"
Cordus's brow creased. "I did not go upstairs."
"But the pantry door was open."
"I only went through the tunnel and the hatch in the garden."
"Then why was the pantry door...?"
Ocella's palms moistened. She pulled Cordus further into the alley's shadows.
"What is it?" he asked.
"I think someone was in the basement."
She scanned the crowds, searching for anyone who would stand out as a Praetorian or a hired lictor. *Was that a Praetorian?* She decided against the young man across the street. He guided his aged mother through the crowds, and Praetorians would not use old women for props. They might get in the way.
"What do we do?" Cordus asked.
"We can't go back to the house."

Two men burst into the alley from around the corner, one bumping into her. She pushed the man away, drew her pistol, and aimed at both. They stopped, their eyes wide. Then the man who bumped her vomited on his shirt and shoes. The other man burst into drunken laughter.

"Easy, lass," said the older man in a drunken slur, "we ain't trying to rob you. My nephew here's just making more room."

He laughed again. The sick nephew, straightened, his legs wobbly. "That ought to do it. Let's go back before they run out of wine."

They both staggered from the alley and around the corner.

Ocella holstered her pistol, then grabbed Cordus's hand and hurried down the alley.

"What are we going to do?" Cordus asked again.

She didn't answer him. Because she had no idea.

Lepidus watched the woman and the boy run.

"Should we follow them, sir?" Appius asked.

"No. The tracker will do that now."

Lepidus glanced at his apprentice, who pulled off his vomit-stained tunic and tossed it in the trash. He fit right in with the rest of the Aventine's half-dressed plebeian mob. Some of the passing women—and a few men—gave Appius appraising stares.

"Well done, Appius. I didn't believe you could vomit on command. Interesting talent."

"Been able to do it since I was a child, sir. Got me out of many meals I didn't want to eat."

Lepidus smiled. "Just as long as the tracker is secure."

"I placed it behind her neck. She won't find it unless she's looking for it."

Lepidus nodded. The tracker was a recent gift from the gods to the Collegia Pontificis. A clear bit of adhesive no bigger than a fingerprint, enabling Lepidus to track the woman so long as she stayed on Terra.

"Congratulations to you, too, sir," Appius said. "I didn't think they'd run after seeing the pantry door ajar."

"Subtlety is far more powerful with people such as Marcia Licinius Ocella," Lepidus said, watching the woman and boy leave the alley at the far end. "She is not only a trained Praetorian, but a skilled foreign agent. She'd only leave the safe house if she knew it was too dangerous to stay. Let her believe we're sloppy. It will be to our advantage in the long run."

"Now we follow her."

"Yes. She will lead us to her contacts, and then we will cleanse Roma of all foreign terrorists and assassins." He frowned at Appius. "Find a shirt, will you? People are staring."

Chapter Nineteen

The Umbra Navigator ducked through *Caduceus's* connector hatch and smiled at Kaeso. He was a young man, maybe mid-twenties, with the blond hair and freckles of Germanic ancestry. Though his face did not shimmer, Kaeso knew he wore an Umbra cloak. All Ancile did while working.

"Kaeso Aemilius," the Navigator said, holding out his hand. "I am so honored to meet you. You're a legend. Your missions are still studied in the Academy."

Kaeso glanced around, making sure his crew wasn't nearby. "Galeo, are you trying to kill me? Talk like that will turn my brain into *garum*."

Galeo's eyes focused behind Kaeso. "This must be your engineer?"

Kaeso turned, saw Daryush peeking from the engine room hatch. As soon as Kaeso saw him, Daryush withdrew.

"Looking forward to meeting you," Galeo called out.

Kaeso scowled, then said in a quiet voice, "What's with the new disguise?"

"I couldn't come as Dr. Pullo, could I? Your crew would suspect something odd about a medicus who also happens to be an engineer who can install these 'magical' upgrades to your engines."

Kaeso looked past Galeo and toward the empty corridor behind him. "Where's your equipment?"

"I'm on a scouting mission. I want to see what modifications you need to get the upgrades to talk nicely with your ship."

Kaeso nodded, then motioned Galeo to follow him. "Some advice. You look like you're two months out of the Academy."

"That green, eh?" Galeo's eyes lost their focus, and then his face began to age. Slight creases appeared around his eyes and mouth, and his skin grew a bit looser around his cheeks. His hair went from bright blond to a duller tone with a stray white hair here and there. Galeo now looked to be in his lower forties.

"Good?" he asked.

"Good," Kaeso admitted. "I couldn't do that with my cloak when I was in. Not without shutting it down first."

"Many things have changed since then, old friend."

"Right," Kaeso said, then turned to Galeo, blocking his entrance to the engine room. "Like you becoming an infectee?"

Galeo stopped and narrowed his eyes. "Nothing gets past you does it?" he said in a low voice.

"Even my semi-active implant can feel a Vessel in the room. I felt it when you were 'Dr. Pullo,' but there were other men in the cargo bay, so I wasn't sure if it was one of them. Now you're the only stranger on my ship."

"Interesting," Galeo said. "Well to start, you know we don't like being called 'infectees.' Implies we have a disease, and that is not true. I know you said it to watch my reaction. Please don't test me again."

Kaeso nodded. "My apologies. Calling you 'Vessels' always seemed too religious."

"You're not a religious man? You were once very pious. Before Umbra, you attended all the rituals with your family."

"Get to your point."

"Easy, Kaeso. I'm just saying one man's faith is another man's nonsense. The Muses bless Vessels with their wisdom. And make no mistake; I consider it a blessing. You would too if you became a Vessel when you had the chance."

Kaeso frowned, remembering the offer just before he was blacklisted. To this day he was still unsure why he turned them down. It was what most Ancilia worked toward throughout their career.

Except Kaeso had never been comfortable with it. He knew the ancient Muses gave Vessels the 'secrets of history,' but he never liked the idea that he'd...change if he accepted the offer. And not just his personality, but rumor had it the change was also physical. Vessels never left their private residence without their Umbra cloaks, so only other Vessels knew for sure what the physical change was. It never sat well with Kaeso, even when he was at his most loyal to Umbra.

"What do you want to do to my engines?" Kaeso asked.

Galeo smiled. "Not much. Just make them outrace the gods."

Before Kaeso could comment, Lucia dropped down from the upper level. "Centuriae," she said, then stared at Galeo.

He gave her a warm smile. "You must be Lucia Marius Calida, the trierarch. It is an honor to meet you, my lady." He bowed to her like a Roman nobleman to a patrician matron. Kaeso stifled a smile as Lucia's lips curled in abject contempt.

When Galeo straightened, he also saw the look and frowned. He turned to Kaeso. "Is your entire crew as cynical as you?"

"Who are you?" Lucia asked.

"Call me Navigator," he said. "I'm here to upgrade your engines." Kaeso knew 'Galeo' wasn't even Galeo's real name, but it was his Umbra name, and not to be revealed outside Umbra.

"What kind of upgrades?" Lucia asked.

Galeo seemed confused. "Did your centuriae not mention it?"

She kept her focus on Galeo. "My centuriae doesn't confide much in his crew anymore."

"Well," Galeo said. "I can't go into the details, because they're classified, but I can tell you there are few ships in existence that can do what *Caduceus* will do when I'm done with her."

"Wonderful," she said. "Too bad the crew won't experience this."

"What do you want, Lucia?" Kaeso asked.

"I wanted to see what our *friend* is going to do to our engines. Someone needs to know how to work them when you bring the ship back from Terra." She looked at Kaeso. "You were coming back, right?"

"If I may," Galeo interrupted, "there will be no difference in how you run the ship from the command deck. So it's not necessary for you to waste your valuable time watching me make modifications you won't even notice."

"Lucia," Kaeso said, "I'll watch him. You still trust me, right?"

She stared at him several moments, then turned and climbed the ladder back up to the command deck. Galeo was about to say something, but Kaeso raised his hand. Kaeso called into the engine room, "Daryush?"

The large Persian peeked around the corner.

"Give us the room, please," Kaeso said. Daryush nodded, then squeezed between Kaeso and Galeo, and climbed the ladder. Kaeso turned and motioned Galeo into the engine room.

Galeo studied the tabulari console and shook his head. "I never thought I'd see a Falcon 2.1.1 again. You have given me quite the challenge, Centuriae."

"It's old, I know."

Galeo laughed. "Falcon 4's are old. *This* has been around since Marcus Antonius Primus took Roma."

"Can you modify it?"

"We'll see," Galeo said, opening the ship's engine specs.

"What did you mean saying *Caduceus* will 'outrace the gods'?"

Galeo scrolled through the virtual pages on the tabulari with inhuman speed. "For one thing, the ship won't need to follow a way line for interstellar travel."

Kaeso blinked. "How will it travel if not by way line?"

"Let me back up. It will still use way lines, but not the kind you and every other human being use. Without wading too deep into way line physics, the way lines you know are rare and powerful. That's why planets with way lines are so coveted and fought over for centuries. Terra happens to be lucky enough to have a way line in its solar system, as does Libertus."

"I *am* a starship Centuriae."

Galeo smiled as he reviewed the ship's engine logs. "To put it simply, every speck of mass in the universe has a quantum level way line connecting it to every other speck of mass in the universe. Umbra has learned how to build an interstellar engine that can ride those quantum way lines. In other words, *Caduceus* will not have to ride known way lines to get from one system to another. It will ride the *quantum* way lines and go anywhere in the universe it wants to go."

"Delta sleep?"

"You still need delta sleep during a quantum way line jump," Galeo said. "We still haven't figured out way line madness."

Kaeso had assumed *Caduceus's* Roman infiltration would involve more fake identities and bribes. None of which would fool a competent Roman way station customs agent in the midst of a crisis. It was the main reason Kaeso didn't want his crew coming along.

But the quantum way line drives changed everything. Umbra had discovered the magical interstellar drive that humanity had sought since going to the stars. If this drive became public, it would make obsolete almost 800 years of colonial settlement and military strategies. It would open up for colonization whole new planets and systems without major way lines. Libertus—and Terra—were 'protected' by a buffer of way line jumps, with each jump guarded by heavily armed way stations that could send warning drones to the next waystation. These new engines meant any hostile fleet could appear above a planet at any moment without traveling the known way lines.

Kaeso now understood why Galeo didn't want anyone watching over his shoulder while he installed the new systems.

"When will you tell them?"

Kaeso blinked out of his reverie. "What?"

"Your crew," Galeo said. "When will you tell them you want to rejoin your *old* crew."

"I'd rather not have this conversation with you."

"Let me give you some advice, from one 'old' Ancile to another. It is better to be up front about these things. Your little stunt with my medicus yesterday showed you care about your crew. Don't dishonor them by lying to them."

Kaeso wanted to laugh. "Don't lie to them, you say. How can I *not* lie to them? How can I *not* keep things from them, when if I tell them who I was or what you are, their lives would be forfeit? I've done nothing but lie to them since I first met them."

Galeo looked at him, understanding on his Umbra-cloaked face. "Our vocation demands we keep terrible secrets. Do terrible things. Because if we don't, if we drop our guard for a second, the Romans would do to us what they did to Kaldeth and other nations throughout history. Libertus would become just another jewel for them to store in their Tarpian Vaults. A breeding ground for slaves and soldiers and drafted colonists. I know you're still a patriot, Kaeso Aemilius. I know you would give your life to keep that from happening to your countrymen. To your daughter."

A wave of grief hit Kaeso again. He swallowed hard and kept himself steady. The waves were weaker as his semi-active implant adjusted to emotions he had not felt since before he joined Umbra. He hoped the damned implant would keep the emotions in check while he was in Roma. The last thing he needed were the distracting memories of how he abandoned his own daughter.

Once the grief subsided, a burning anger filled Kaeso at Galeo's cheap ploy. "Stop," he snarled. "You know what it does to me when you mention my—my daughter."

"I'm sorry, old friend, but I want you to remember what you're fighting for."

I remember, Kaeso thought. *That's the problem.*

Kaeso glanced at the tabulari. "Are you done?"

"Yes, I believe I have what I came for. The modifications should work even on this old girl." With a grin, he said, "Let's make her dance, eh?"

Chapter Twenty

Lepidus and Appius sat in a ground car made to look like a common electric taxi. The Praetorians had modified this "taxi" so a person could drive it, giving its passengers a subtle disguise in the busy Roman streets.

It also had the tracker controls built into its console.

Lepidus watched Marcia Licinius Ocella and the boy walk up to the Temple of Empanda, both wearing dirty cloaks with their hoods up. They blended with all the other stinking beggars waiting for their daily ration of soup and bread.

Appius shifted again, which annoyed Lepidus. "What is it, Appius?"

"Nothing, sir."

"Speak, boy. Apprentices learn by asking questions."

"I'd never question your wisdom, sir, but..."

Lepidus glared at the young man. "If I wanted a slave who took orders without thinking, I would have brought one. What is your question?"

"Well, sir, it's been two days and all they've done is go from one beggar's temple to another. Perhaps we should just arrest them now and rescue the boy before the woman hands him over to the Liberti."

Lepidus grunted. "Have you no fear of the gods? That's a Temple of Empanda. They have sanctuary as long as they are within its walls. Yes we have the power to storm in there, but it would not be proper."

Appius nodded, but Lepidus could tell he still wanted to enter the temple nonetheless.

"Patience, Appius. They won't go from one beggar's temple to another for the rest of their lives. They're wasting time until they find a way out of the city. Once their contact has made all the necessary arrangements, they will attempt to leave. In the meantime, they need to eat."

Appius frowned. "It just seems like an awful risk, sir. She could hurt the boy any time. I won't lie, sir, but my first instinct is to save the boy."

"Your instincts are honorable," Lepidus said, watching the woman and boy enter the temple. "But what makes you think the boy *wants* to be saved?"

"You still think he wants to defect?"

Lepidus shrugged. "It's a theory I won't ignore out of religious piety. The Consular Family may be touched by the gods, but they are still human. If the boy wants to defect to Libertus, than that means the gods have abandoned him, for whatever reason. Which means he is just another boy."

"And if he does wish to defect? Will you be able to...?"

Lepidus turned to Appius. "Your hesitation is admirable. He is the Consular Heir. This *should* be hard for you. I would doubt your faith in the gods if it weren't."

"It's just that—with respect, sir—the thought does not seem so difficult for you, yet you are the most righteous I know. Will you kill the boy if necessary?"

Lepidus sighed, and looked back at the Temple of Empanda just as the boy and the woman entered its open doors and disappeared among the other beggars.

"Did I ever tell you I fought at the Battle of Caan?" Lepidus asked. He turned back to Appius, who'd gone pale. The young man shook his head once.

"It was as bad as the stories and holos say," Lepidus said. "Never mind the disaster occurred because incompetent generals decided to land our dropships right in the middle of the Kaldethian strongholds. Wanted to end the war in one blow, they told us. Surprise the Kaldethians. We just had to show them the might of the Roman Legions, and they'd drop their guns and flee into the hills, they said."

Lepidus remembered the pompous General Aulus Pontius, his fat face glistening with sweat in the cold Roman flagship as it orbited Kaldeth. The staff officers had cheered his naive little speech, sure of victory over the Kaldethians. There wasn't a *soldier* among them. If there were, they wouldn't have cheered.

Lepidus, a tribune at the time, had clapped politely, but doubt grew in his belly. He had exchanged a glance with his wife, Triaria, a centurion in the cohort Lepidus commanded. She had the same wariness in her eyes. He remembered the conversation they'd shared the night before as they lay naked in each other's arms, the sweat from their love still cooling. Why not bombard the strongholds first, Triaria had asked. Reduce them to rubble and let the Legions mop up the survivors. Lepidus said that was not an option, for it would destroy most of Kaldeth's wealthy cities. That was the real reason Roma wanted Kaldeth. Roma needed her in one piece. Triaria had still doubted, despite Lepidus's assurances the gods and numbers were on Roma's side.

"Needless to say," Lepidus continued, "it did not turn out that way. This race of soft, Lost World merchants were waiting for us, and they were prepared. I lost a third of my cohort in less than fifteen minutes after our dropships landed. The other centuries in my legion fared the same. So it was *we* who dropped our guns and fled into the hills."

Lepidus regarded the tracker console. Ocella moved slowly, perhaps in the bread line.

"Once we regrouped and reorganized, General Pontius gathered all the tribunes and railed against the cowardice of our cohorts; how they had not only humiliated Roma but had dishonored the gods. He told us the Consul and the Collegia Pontificis had ordered a punishment. Or rather, received a Missive of the Gods, to be exact."

"Decimation," Appius said.

Lepidus stared at the console without seeing it, remembering that day. "A Missive of the Gods only comes when the gods make new technology and wisdom available to the Consul and the Collegia. They are rare these past generations. The gods were truly displeased.

"I had everyone in my cohort line up in formation, officers included, as the cohorts from the legions who had *not* dishonored themselves leveled their guns at us. I counted out each soldier, one to ten. I shot the tenth soldier in the head. Most cried and begged when I got to them. They were the easy ones, for they were the cause of the order. It was the honorable ones that were hard, the ones that stood their ground, their eyes forward as I put the gun to their head and pulled the trigger. I couldn't have been more proud of *them*."

Lepidus sighed. "My wife accepted her fate that way."

Appius was quiet, then said, "Sir...?"

"My wife's number turned out to be ten." Lepidus chuckled. "I'll bet Fortuna got a laugh out of that, eh? I admit I hesitated when

I got to her. But she looked at me, her chin raised, and she gave me a quick nod. She knew what I had to do. She was a soldier and a patriot. I loved her more in that moment than I had in the five years we'd been married. I pulled the trigger and sent her to her honorable reward in Elysium."

"Evocatus...I don't know what to say."

Lepidus turned to Appius. "Why the pity, Appius? The decimation worked. The gods were pleased. We took Kaldeth. Granted, we did not take it in the pristine condition we had hoped. The Kaldethians had to pay *some* price for Caan. I have no doubt my wife's sacrifice, her honorable death and her advocacy for our cause in the afterlife, is what brought the gods back to our favor."

Lepidus turned back to the console. Ocella was stationary in a different part of the Temple now. Likely eating her meager dinner.

"I am a pious man," Lepidus said, "but the gods have revealed to the Pontifex Maximus that Marcus Antonius Cordus may be a traitor. If he is, my duty is to kill the traitor. Even if he is the Consul's son."

Chapter Twenty-One

The Temple of Empanda had the stench of a hundred years worth of beggars. Ocella resisted the urge to cover her mouth with a cloth as she and Cordus stood in the entrance. Their growling stomachs, however, kept them from fleeing to the fresh air outside. She made sure Cordus's hood was over his head and then, with clenched teeth, motioned him inside.

They had not eaten in over twenty-four hours, not since the night they left Scaurus's house. They had found another Temple of Empanda near the Aventine, but there were too many lictors about for Ocella's comfort, so they had walked on. They returned several hours later, but Ocella had noticed a single lictor standing across the street from the Temple, his arms folded, leaning against a wall under a discount holo merchant's awning. Despite their hunger, Ocella and Cordus did not enter the Temple. They found this Temple of Empanda in the Suburba, in the shadow of the Temple of Jupiter Optimus Maximus on the Capitoline Hill. Ocella had observed it for an hour from an alley before she was satisfied there were no lictors or Praetorians watching.

Judging from the signs near the Temple door, the cafeteria was fifty feet ahead and around the corner to the right. In the entryway to the left, a stout marble statue of the goddess Empanda stood with her arms open, welcoming all into her sanctuary.

They found the food queue twenty feet past the entrance and joined the shuffling crowd. Most were single, homeless men who looked as if they'd just awoken from a bed filled with their own vomit. Some were hollow-eyed women toting small, emaciated children.

Ocella glanced at Cordus, who held his head high as he waited in line. She wanted to tell him not to act so...regal. He was supposed to be a beggar. His shoulders should have been slumped, his head down, his eyes defeated. Instead he looked as if he stood in a receiving line next to his father, awaiting foreign ambassadors paying him homage. There was nothing she could do now, considering all the people around them. They were so caught up in their own troubles that she doubted they'd notice a child with a noble posture. But if she noticed, a Praetorian would.

Ocella and Cordus did not speak to each other—at Ocella's orders—while waiting. When they got to the cafeteria, the smell of cooked fish and porridge made Ocella's mouth water. Cordus's eyes glittered at the brown-robed Empanda priests handing out plates with slabs of cooked white fish, a bowl of porridge, and a chunk of dark bread. Once they reached the front of the line, a tired priest with a long beard and long brown hair handed them each a plate with food.

"Go with the goddess," he intoned as he handed them a plate. He gave the same blessing over and over again to the people behind Ocella and Cordus.

They made their way through the crowd toward empty benches in the main worship hall. Baskets of bread and corn sat upon the altar, with another statue of the goddess looking on. Candelabras with lit candles lined both sides of the altar, and a bronze bowl smoked with sweet incense. Two brown-robed priestesses knelt before the altar swaying left and right, the backs of their shaved heads to the worship hall. Ocella could barely make out their monotone incantations asking for Empanda's blessing on the temple, the offering, and the people within its sanctuary.

As soon as they sat down, Cordus began shoving food into his mouth, not bothering to use the spoon in the porridge bowl. Ocella dug into her food with equal fervor. While the meal was not what she'd grown used to as a Praetorian in the Consular residence, right now it was the most divine meal she'd ever eaten. Cordus apparently thought the same; he was done eating before Ocella finished half her plate.

Cordus put his empty bowl aside and sat quietly next to her, watching the priestesses pray. After they finished and had refilled the incense bowl, they both walked away, their mouths moving with silent prayers as they returned to the vestibule behind the altar.

Cordus watched them shut the door to the vestibule, and then he turned to her. "What training do you need to be an Umbra Ancile?"

He said it in a quiet voice, but Ocella still glanced around to ensure nobody was listening. Besides the priestesses, no one was within thirty feet. She chewed her food and then said, "A lot."

Cordus raised an eyebrow. "Well, yes," he said, "but what *skills* do you need."

Ocella stirred her porridge with her spoon. "It's not so much skills as personalities that are important. You can learn any skill you want so long as you want to learn it. But try teaching an impatient man patience, or a pessimistic woman optimism. Someone who gives up on a task after a little resistance won't even attempt the impossible tasks Umbra requires of its Ancilia. Umbra looks for people who *want* to do the impossible."

"That sounds vague," Cordus said.

Ocella smiled. "I know," she said and then took another bite from the bread she dipped into the porridge. "Like I said, anyone can be trained to do a task. But people either have persistence and courage, or they don't. Both are given by the gods, and no amount of training will instill them."

"I imagine it was hard betraying them."

Ocella felt her smile melt and a cold shadow fall over her spirit. The boy noticed her change in demeanor, and quickly said, "I have a talent."

Ocella tried to shake off her sorrow, forcing the smile back on her lips. "Obviously, or we wouldn't be here."

"Something more mundane than *that* talent."

"Alright, what can you do?"

"I can hold my breath for three minutes."

Ocella almost choked on her porridge when she started laughing. It was such a normal boast from a child in a situation that was anything but normal. She sat in a Temple of Empanda, listening to the Consular Heir of the Roman Republic brag that he could hold his breath for three minutes. All the stress and worry and fear that had built up over the past few weeks burst from her in uncontrollable laughter.

Through the tears in her eyes, she could see Cordus looked insulted. She calmed herself, and said, "I'm not mocking you. It's just that it was the last thing I expected to hear from you right now."

Cordus nodded. "Do you want to see me try?"

"No, that's fine."

"You do not believe me. How about a wager?"

Ocella hadn't seen Cordus this animated since before they fled Scaurus's house. It was amazing how fast a full belly can lift one's spirits.

She narrowed her eyes in mock doubt. "If you can hold your breath for three minutes, I'll give you my bread."

Cordus greedily eyed the bread sitting on Ocella's plate.

"If you can't," Ocella said, "you have to do what I say *without complaining* until all this is over. Deal?"

"I never complain."

Ocella stared at Cordus until he said, "Very well."

Ocella found a wall clock near the back of the worship hall above the door to the hallway and cafeteria.

"Okay, I'll time you. Ready?"

He nodded.

"Go!"

He took a deep breath, his cheeks puffing out, and held it. He folded his hands in his lap and stared at her with an arched eyebrow, as if bored with the whole contest already.

Ocella poked him in the ribs with her finger. His eyes bulged and he squirmed away from her, but he kept the breath in. She grinned and poked him again. He released his breath in an explosive burst.

"That is not fair," he cried, a smile brightening his face. "You cannot tickle me."

"I don't recall a 'no tickling' rule."

"No tickling, then! No touching me at all. In fact, do not even look at me."

"How will I know you're holding your breath?"

"Fine, you can look at me, but do not make me laugh, or the wager is off."

"I promise. Go!"

He sucked in another breath and held it. He watched her warily this time, and she tried her best not to smile or make him laugh. She glanced from Cordus to the clock on the back wall.

"One minute," she said.

Cordus continued holding his breath, his face flushed from the exertion.

"Two minutes," she said, nodding. "Impressive."

He nodded back, a proud smile tugging at his puckered lips. His cheeks now turned pink, and Ocella was tempted to call off the bet for fear Cordus would pass out, but he did not seem to waver nor were his eyes glassy.

"Thirty more sec—"

"Sire?"

A young man with unkempt hair and a shaggy beard stood before them. He swayed on his feet and the stench of sour wine hung heavy around him. He wore the tattered red tunic of a Legionnaire, the golden eagle emblazoned on the breast now brown with grime and wine stains. His right arm ended in a ragged pink stump just above where his elbow should have been.

Cordus expelled his breath.

"Sire, it is you!" the man said, then prostrated himself in front of Cordus. "I saw you last year in Atlantium Auster after we put down the rebellion there. You toured our legion with your blessed father. I knew it was you, sire. I exist to serve."

Ocella jumped up and yanked the man to his feet before anyone around them could hear him.

"I don't know who you think the boy is," Ocella whispered into his ear, "but we do not want to be bothered. Go on your way and leave us be."

"I am not who you think I am," Cordus said quietly. "But as a *citizen*, I thank you for your service to the Republic."

The man brought himself up as tall as he could, still swaying, then slapped his hand to his chest and extended it in a military salute. "Thank you, sire. I understand you don't want to be bothered," he said with a slur and then a wink. "Good of you to tour the beggars rows; see the poorest of your people. You're a kind one, sire. My friends won't believe—"

Ocella grabbed the man's arm and pulled him toward the vestibule hallway behind the altar.

"Hey!" the man protested, barely able to walk.

"I've got more wine," Ocella said, "for one of Roma's finest soldiers."

"You do?" He stopped struggling and let her drag him toward the hall. Once they were in shadows and around a corner, Ocella looked up and down the corridor. Seeing nobody, she slammed the soldier against the wall.

"Hey, why so rough?" he said. "Where's the wine?"

"I'm sorry, friend. You were in the wrong place at the wrong time."

She put a hand over his mouth and plunged her knife into his heart. His eyes widened with fear and pain, and he grunted through her hand. He struggled a few seconds, and then his eyes glazed as he slumped to the floor. Ocella pulled her knife free, wiped the blood off on his clothes, and then put it back in her cloak. Her shirt was soaked with the man's blood, so she wrapped her cloak around herself. She hurried out of the hallway, grabbed Cordus's arm, and pulled the wide-eyed boy toward the temple doors.

"Put on your hood," she told him, as she did the same.

He complied, his face ashen. "What did you do to him?"

She didn't respond.

She hurried Cordus out of the Temple, past the beggar line, which had grown larger since they'd been inside. She searched the street for anything out of the ordinary. The usual beggars shuffled toward the Temple, taxis zoomed past while some were parked along the street waiting for fares. There were few merchants in this neighborhood, mostly discount emporiums, money lenders, and shady taverns. She took this all in as she pulled Cordus down the street, expecting an outcry at any moment from the Temple behind them. She did not exhale until they had rounded the corner and were out of sight of the Temple.

"Did you kill that man?" Cordus asked. When she didn't respond, he asked, "Why did you kill him?"

"Nobody can know who you are," Ocella said, scanning the streets. "Even drunk fools."

Cordus's voice quivered. "He was not a fool. He was a Roman soldier. He did not deserve to die in some stinking temple."

Ocella pulled the boy into an alley, grabbed his arms and made him face her. "Listen to me. What else needs to happen before you realize this isn't some play or adventure holo? You have no idea the danger we're in. You think you do, but you don't. How can you? You've spent your life in a palace being coddled and told how great is your destiny. In the real world people die and are killed for stupid, godsdamned reasons."

He stared at her, his eyes glistening. For the first time since this all began, Cordus finally looked like a scared little boy, and not the arrogant Consular Heir.

Good. He needs to be scared.

"You didn't have to kill him," he whispered, and shrugged away from her. "I remembered him. I remember that day with my father when we reviewed the legions. His name was Gaius Vibius. The remains of his arm were bandaged, but he stood at attention as any whole soldier. He looked down at me as I passed and winked. I remember thinking, what courage. This man had lost most of his arm, yet his spirits were high enough to show me he thought nothing of his injury. I thought he was a true Roman."

The tears flowed down Cordus's cheeks, but he didn't sob. "I do not know how he came to such a lowly state, but he did not deserve to die like that."

"Nobody deserves to die like that," Ocella said. "That man—however honorable he might have been—would have bragged about seeing you to his cohorts, who could have told the nearest lictor or Praetorian. He had to be silenced. It's as simple as that."

Cordus stared at the ground, tears flowing.

"You have a good heart, Cordus," she said. "That's why you should let me worry about these things."

He shook his head, and then stalked from the alley. Ocella had no choice but to follow him. "Where are you going?" she asked.

"To the Mars Trading Fields," he said. "We meet your contact tonight. I do not want to be late."

Hidden in his comment was the message that he wanted to be rid of her company as soon as possible. She was not surprised. She did not like her own company either.

Chapter Twenty-Two

Kaeso finished reading the same paragraph in the Umbra intelligence report a third time when Lucia entered the command deck. He flicked off his tabulari display and turned to his first officer.

"The Navigator is ready to disembark," she reported. "He wants to speak with you before he leaves."

Her tone was icy. She was never good at hiding her emotions. Over the last two days she had gone from overt hostility to quiet seething. He considered it progress.

The clock on his console said it was just after midnight way station time. He rubbed his eyes, stood up and stretched. "Why didn't you call me down with your com?"

"It's broke and I'm too tired to fix it," she said, turning toward the ladder. "I'm going to my bunk, unless the Centuriae needs anything else."

"No," Kaeso said as Lucia disappeared down the ladder. "That'll do for tonight."

He wasn't sure if she heard him, and he doubted she'd return if he called her back. The whole crew did their jobs admirably, though without their usual spirit considering they wouldn't see their hard work in action. Blaesus suggested they install cameras so they could see how the ship performed on the mission.

"I want to ensure my tedious hours of reprogramming way line functions is put to good use," he said before he retired to his bunk earlier. "And if the Centuriae breaks this ship, we'll have a record for when we sue him for ruining our livelihoods."

Nestor and Flamma were more easygoing, completing without question the tasks Galeo ordered. Kaeso assumed they were not as upset with staying on Libertus as the other crew.

But Kaeso knew they were worried about him and Dariya.

Nestor had gone over the delta sleep procedures so many times that Kaeso wondered if the Greek medicus thought he was an idiot. Nestor had documented every step for each procedure—down to the color of the buttons he had to push—and had fastened a paper note to Kaeso's console on the command deck telling him where to find the procedures in the tabulari.

Flamma placed three large boxes of his latest hardware innovations in Kaeso's already cramped bunk. Kaeso had no idea what most of the gadgets did, but Flamma insisted they could someday save his life. Kaeso assured Flamma that he would make good use of the gadgets if he ever fought arena golems. The young Egyptian scowled at Kaeso's attempted humor and then proceeded to go over how each device worked.

Even Daryush had given Kaeso a ragged little doll, the wear and stains making it difficult to determine if it was a boy or a girl. In Daryush's broken Latin and hand gestures, he explained it was a good luck charm his parents gave him when he was a child, just before he and Dariya were sold to the Roman patrician they served most of their lives. Kaeso was honored by the gift since it was obviously valuable to Daryush, but he couldn't promise he'd wear it around his neck at all times like the large Persian wanted.

Kaeso descended the ladder to the cargo deck. Galeo waited near the connector hatch, and nodded to Kaeso.

"All finished," he said. "We'll test the drive tomorrow. I have no doubt you'll be impressed."

"No doubt."

"Your crew were more than competent. You could use their help on Terra."

Kaeso rubbed his eyes. "I'm not going to—"

"Yes, yes, you don't want to put them in any more danger than you already have. But I get the impression they're used to danger. Kaeso, they would follow you to Hades if you asked them. A centuriae should never discount that kind of loyalty. Or abandon it."

"If this mission goes well—and I get what I want—I won't be a centuriae anymore."

Galeo regarded him, and acted as if he wanted to say something.

"What?" Kaeso asked.

"I heard from the Magisterium a few hours ago. They won't let you back into Umbra."

Kaeso looked at him. "Just like that?"

"You knew your reinstatement would be a hard sell. If it's any consolation, the decision was split."

"Who voted against me?"

Galeo gave him a sideways smile. "Let's just say you have allies who want you back in the family, but there's nothing they can do about it now."

"Why tell me this? You're a Vessel. Are you admitting there's disagreement among the Muses about me?"

Galeo's cloak-projected gray eyes stared at Kaeso as if willing him to take one more mental leap to the truth.

Before Kaeso could ask another question, a distant rumble came from the connector tube, growing stronger and louder by the moment. Kaeso looked at the console screen. The outer camera trembled that showed the way station corridor. People ran in every direction, knocking over vendor stands and trampling each other. In the distance, down the vast corridor, an orange light grew larger.

Fire. The way station atmosphere was burning.

Kaeso leaped toward the console and slammed the button that closed *Caduceus's* connector hatch. The door began to slide closed, but too slowly.

"Gods..." Galeo breathed, staring at the outer camera display.

Kaeso ignored him. The rumbling grew to a roar, and the air in *Caduceus* rushed out through the closing hatch, feeding the fire racing toward them at the speed of sound. Just as the hatch closed and sealed itself, the fire exploded into the connector tube and slammed into *Caduceus's* hatch. The whole ship buckled, knocking Kaeso into the metal walls. Kaeso rolled into the middle of the corridor, trying to stay away from the bulkhead. Galeo did the same.

Kaeso tapped his collar com. "Lucia, what's happening?" He remembered her com didn't work, so he called, "Nestor!"

No response. "Any crew respond!"

Silence.

Galeo's eyes stared at the floor, then he looked at Kaeso. Kaeso had not known many Vessels during his time with Umbra, but the ones he knew were always calm, always in control, for the Muses knew what was happening in any location another Vessel was present.

So the abject horror on Galeo's face made Kaeso more frightened than he'd ever been in his life.

"What's happening?" Kaeso asked Galeo. The ship jumped again, tossing Kaeso and Galeo almost a foot off the floor.

When they steadied themselves, Galeo said, "I don't know."

"If this is more of your Vessel secrets—"

"You don't understand," Galeo cried. "*I don't know* what is happening. *They're not talking to me.*"

Kaeso grabbed Galeo's arm. He pulled the stunned Vessel toward the command deck ladder. Galeo climbed without protest.

When they reached the quarters deck, they almost ran into Lucia who dove for the ladder rungs as another shockwave slammed into the ship. She wore a sleep tunic and no pants.

"Are we under attack?" she asked.

Before Kaeso could respond, Blaesus, Flamma, Daryush, and Nestor filled the corridor with the same questions.

"Get to your delta couches," Kaeso yelled above the din as he climbed the ladder to the command deck.

They all got in line at the ladder to rush to their couches, Nestor and Lucia followed Kaeso and Galeo to the command deck, while Blaesus, Flamma, and Daryush descended to the engine room and cargo bays.

On the command deck, Kaeso strapped himself into his couch. Lucia jumped into the pilot's couch, while Nestor secured himself at the delta sleep controls. Galeo slumped into a passenger couch behind Nestor.

"Talk to me, Lucia," Kaeso said.

"There are multiple fires on the way station...blessed Juno...a quarter of the outer ring is gone."

"Is the gap near us?"

"No. Maybe a mile to our port."

"Disengage the connector."

Lucia moved a few sliders on her console and then cursed. "It's locked from the way station side."

"*Cac*," Kaeso swore. He thumbed the internal ship's intercom. "Blaesus, Flamma." Kaeso's voice echoed through the ship over the internal speakers behind him. "Our coms aren't working, so listen up. The connector to the way station won't disengage. One of you has to blow the emergency locks at the hatch console. There's an intercom at the console, so yell back to acknowledge."

Kaeso waited a few agonizing seconds as explosive waves shook *Caduceus* so hard that he wondered if the ship would break free from the way station before they could undock.

"Blaesus here, Centuriae," the old senator's voice resounded through the ship. "We're at the hatch console and about to blow the connectors."

Orange light outside the command window caught Kaeso's eye. He looked up to see a large tear in the way station's wheel fuselage rending its way toward *Caduceus*. Fire, debris, and bodies erupted from the tear.

"Now, Blaesus!"

"It's done, we're free," Blaesus shouted.

There was momentary weightlessness as *Caduceus* disengaged from the gravity generators of the way station, and then weight returned when the ship's grav came on. As soon as the ship was free, the violent shockwaves stopped, and the ship floated away from the doomed way station.

"Get us out of here, Lucia."

"Working on it."

The ship's thrusters turned *Caduceus's* nose up ninety degrees. The ion drives kicked in and the ship shot upward just as the tear consumed the connector tube where the *Caduceus* had been docked. The view out the command deck was space and stars, but a haze of metal shards slammed against the hull, sending loud pings shooting up and down the ship.

"We're clear of the way station, sir." She studied her console. "Some wreckage punctured the hull."

"Did repair foam plug the holes?" Kaeso asked.

"Yes, but I can't tell if any systems were dam—"

Proximity alarms blasted from the consoles. A large freighter appeared in front of them from the starboard side, its cargo containers reflecting a hellish orange light from the flaming way station behind them.

"*Cac!*" Lucia yelled. She slammed the controls on her console in a violent pitch to the port side, a move the ship's aging inertia cancelers failed to negate completely. The momentum flung Kaeso's body against his couch's restraints so hard that he feared he'd broken some ribs.

The freighter disappeared from view to be replaced by another fleeing ship, this one a passenger liner. Lucia slammed the controls again, weaving below the liner, and then around several cargo ships the size of *Caduceus*.

"Too many," Lucia grunted after another violent maneuver. Every other ship connected to the way station was trying to escape without way station control to guide them. There could be hundreds of ships out there, all fleeing at the same time in multiple directions.

A brilliant flash filled the command deck windows as a private yacht slammed into the middle of the passenger liner. The huge liner seemed to absorb the impact, but then tears spiderwebbed along its hull, and the liner broke in two. Flotsam and bodies spilled from the two sections.

"Stay away from the way line," Kaeso said. "Everyone else is going there."

"Not everyone," Lucia yelled. "Too many ships have the same idea we do."

Another white light erupted on their port side. After the command deck's windows dimmed to compensate, Kaeso searched for the light source. The region near the way line was clogged with ships trying to enter from all directions rather than the single, orderly line procedure mandated. But the ships that were once right in front of the way line were gone.

Another light erupted from the way line, and Kaeso had to look away. After blinking away the spots before his eyes, he saw that another layer of fleeing ships had turned to vapor. The ships making for the way line veered away, many of them colliding with each other.

"Lucia, get a reading on those blasts."

Lucia moved some sliders on her console. "Antimatter plasma."

Bile rose in Kaeso's throat. Someone was clearing the way line entrance with antimatter drones. Libertus was about to be invaded.

"Two Roman Eagles just jumped out of the way line!" Lucia yelled. "Make that four...eight...gods, it's a whole battle group."

Kaeso's console showed twenty Eagles and two Imperium carriers materialize from the way line. From the Roman Imperium ships, dozens of Pinnace fighters shot out to take on the limping survivors fleeing the two antimatter explosions. The beacons from the running civilian ships began winking out.

"They're slaughtering civilians," Nestor exclaimed.

"They're eliminating anyone who can give away their numbers," Kaeso replied grimly. "Which will be us if we don't get out of this system now."

"The way line's blocked," Lucia said, "and we can't outrun a shuttle, much less an Eagle. They'll get us sooner or later." She slammed her hand on the console. "Where are the godsdamned

Liberti? You'd think they'd have defense patrols around their own way line. It's their damned home world!"

Even more disturbing, where's Umbra? He turned his couch around to Galeo. The once proud and confident Vessel was slumped in his couch, despair and shock on his face.

"We need your engines, Navigator," Kaeso said. "Navigator!"

The man closed his eyes, shook his head. "They're gone," he said with a half-sob. "I can't feel them anymore."

"What's he talking about?" Lucia asked.

Kaeso unbuckled himself, jumped up, and unbuckled Galeo. He half-dragged the Umbra Vessel out of the command deck and made him climb the ladder down to the crew quarters. Once on the crew deck, he turned the man around and slammed him against the bulkhead. Galeo continued to stare past Kaeso, his eyes wide and darting.

"We need those engines or we all die," Kaeso said. "How do we run them?"

Galeo closed his eyes and began to cry. Kaeso slapped him once across the face. Galeo opened his eyes, and Kaeso was relieved to see anger there.

"How do we run the engines?" Kaeso asked again.

Galeo blinked away his tears and set his jaw. "You can't run them from the command deck. I haven't set up the automated systems yet. We have to engage them from the engine room."

"Then do it," Kaeso ordered. "Daryush is in a delta couch down there. He'll help you if you need it. Can you do this?"

Galeo gave a shaky sigh and then nodded his head. He turned around and descended the ladder to the engine room.

When Kaeso returned to the command deck, Lucia said, "We've got two Eagles headed our way. They'll be in missile range in fifteen minutes."

Kaeso buckled himself back into the couch and then thumbed the intercom. "Engine room, you have less than fifteen minutes to get those way line engines up."

To Kaeso's surprise, his collar com chimed. His elation over the com system working again melted when he heard the shock in Blaesus's voice. "Centuriae, we have a casualty."

"Flamma?"

"That dear, stupid boy..." Blaesus's voice choked. Nestor jumped from his couch and hurried to the ladder, practically sliding down. "He hurt himself trying to save me during your maneuvers. I don't know if he's alive."

Lucia's brow furrowed and her teeth clenched.

"Nestor's on his way," Kaeso said. "Keep me informed." He turned to Lucia. "You worry about those Eagles. Understand?"

She nodded slowly. "Yes, sir."

Kaeso's console showed the Eagles closing fast. There were six other ships following *Caduceus*, four freighters, a passenger liner, and the massive cargo hauler *Caduceus* passed during their initial escape. Kaeso watched as an Eagle shot six missiles at the cargo hauler. A minute later, the hauler's beacon winked out.

"Navigator," Kaeso called through his com, "what's your status?"

After an agonizing pause, Galeo said, "Five minutes." He sounded calmer, without the arrogance to which Kaeso had grown accustomed.

"We don't have five minutes."

"It would've been ten without the help of your Persian. Five minutes."

A flash of light came from the window above Kaeso, and he looked down at his console. Three of the freighters had turned into a plasma cloud. The explosions were close this time, and the external temperature around *Caduceus* rocketed to barely tolerable levels.

"Nestor, how's Flamma?" Kaeso called on his com.

"Alive, but his back is broken."

Kaeso felt the air leave his lungs. When he could breathe again, he said, "Can you get him to a couch? We need delta sleep in five minutes."

"Doing that now."

"The liner and freighter are gone," Lucia announced.

His console had blips for just *Caduceus* and two Eagles in the immediate sector. One of the Eagles veered off and headed back to Libertus, but the other one continued after *Caduceus*.

"They have laser lock," Lucia said.

"Navigator!"

"Engines online, Centuriae. Waiting for delta sleep control."

"Missiles launched!" Lucia yelled. "Twenty seconds till impact!"

Nestor climb up the ladder behind Kaeso and hurried to the delta couch. "Delta generators online, acknowledge way line engine control. Delta sleep control routed to command."

Without acknowledging command control, Kaeso moved the slider on his console to engage delta sleep for the crew. Lucia slumped in her couch, her eyes closed. He cast a brief glance at the incoming missile blips on his console. If the new engines didn't work, at least he would wake up in Elysium.

He engaged the delta sleep.

Chapter Twenty-Three

Ocella and Cordus arrived at the Mars Trading Fields on foot. Ocella did not want to chance a taxi ride after the murder she committed at the Temple of Empanda. Taxis had lockdown mechanisms if a suspected criminal entered them. Ironically, a drunken ex-soldier's murder would draw greater public attention than the Consular Heir's kidnapping. The Praetorians had kept quiet their search for the Consular Heir. But a murder would put her on every street lictor's watch list.

Not that walking all the way to the Mars Trading Fields made Ocella feel safer. Ocella made sure she and Cordus kept their hoods up at all times, and that they took back alleys whenever possible. She got so good at avoiding human contact that she sometimes felt as if she and Cordus were the only two people in the city.

They arrived at the Fields before dusk, so Ocella decided to stay in an alley across the street from the gates until nightfall. When she told Cordus this, he sat down, his eyes lowered. Cordus had not spoken since they fled the Temple of Empanda, and he avoided eye contact with her as they waited for sunset behind a large trash bin in the dank alley. It had been eight hours since they'd left the Temple, and they had not risked stopping at another temple for food. She had only eaten half her meal before the soldier appeared, so she was hungry. Her mouth watered as she eyed the moldy tavern leftovers in the trash bin next to them.

Ocella tried to make conversation with the boy, but he ignored her, and then finally closed his eyes. She did not disturb him. She knew he must be exhausted since he had not slept more than an hour here and there since they left Scaurus's house. She struggled to keep her eyes open, for she had not slept at all in the last two days. When they moved, she was weary but alert. Now that they stopped, the damp stone alley was like a feather mattress. When she nodded off, she jerked herself awake, then stood and paced the alley until nightfall. Cordus opened his eyes when she stood, but shut them again.

Ocella kept her mind occupied by studying and memorizing every person that went through the Fields' column gates, every ground car that parked outside the gates, every taxi. She didn't notice any person or car that lingered, but that meant nothing. The Praetorians would switch out teams to not only avoid suspicion, but to keep their teams well rested. That was not a luxury Ocella had, and she worried her fatigue would doom her and Cordus.

If everything had gone according to plan, the Consular Heir's extraction should have taken two days to complete, from the moment they escaped the Consular Palace to the moment he left Terran soil.

It had now been three weeks. Everything had gone wrong. The transport they booked had broken down. Their contacts backed out at the last second. Scaurus's death.

Umbra was better than the Praetorians, but the Praetorians were good. She used every skill she'd been taught in her evasion training. She thought she had done rather well up until the Temple of Empanda. The murder had complicated things, forcing her to avoid all taxis and most public places where she knew security cameras monitored the crowds.

The murder. She couldn't erase the man's surprised look from her mind, his wide eyes, the betrayal. The blood still staining her shirt.

She shook her head, blinking away the tears. She turned and watched the boy sleep. His mouth hung open, his breathing steady, eyes moving beneath their lids. She wondered if the Muses, or gods, or whatever the Roman elite called the virus, kept him from having bad dreams. No child should have to endure the things he had endured the last three weeks. Even if they did escape, what kind of life would he have? He was humanity's best hope for freedom, and he was only twelve years old. Most adults would crumble beneath that responsibility. He was a good kid, with a good heart. He did not deserve this.

It took another hour before darkness covered the sky and the street lamps flickered on. Though the street in front of the Mars Fields was as well lit, the shadows were stronger and would better conceal their faces within their hoods.

The round clock on the bas-reliefs above the column gates across the street said it was near the twenty-second hour. She put a hand on Cordus's shoulder. His eyes flickered open, and he shut his open mouth.

"It's time," she said.

He blinked away the sleep, then nodded. He stood, stretched, and then pulled his hood over his head without Ocella reminding him. Ocella scanned the street one last time for anything suspicious, then they both left the alley and crossed to the Trading Fields.

Once inside, Cordus's mouth fell open at the exotic sights, smells, and sounds. Ocella had to drag him along when he slowed to stare at some alien animal in a cage, or pornographic holos that would make a Legionnaire blush. They finally reached the foreign quarter and descended the rock stairs down the hill toward the vendors at the river's edge. The same old man from Atlantium Auster was at the *xocolatl* stall, packing his wares for the night when she approached. He looked up at her without even glancing at the boy.

"How can I serve you, my lady? Looking for something your taste buds have never experienced? I have just the thing right here."

The old man rubbed his right finger under his nose, then reached for a tea canister labeled as being grown on Atlantium's southern continent. He handed her the canister and then pulled off the lid.

"Take in the scent of this fine tea, my lady. Just the thing to wake you up after a night of revelry. That *kaffa* the Ethiopians drink is no match for this brew's stimulative properties."

Ocella leaned forward and sniffed at the tea leaves in the canister. "Not bad. Do you have anything else? Perhaps *xocolatl*?"

The merchant frowned, then ran his left index finger under his nose. "Unfortunately not, my lady. I sold the last canister this morning. A popular item, and growing more popular by the day. I do have tea that combines the essence of *xocolatl* with a hint of cinnamon. No merchant in the city does it better. Would you be interested?"

Ocella shook her head, her chest tightening and her stomach turning to ice. "No thank you."

She gave the merchant one last glance and then guided Cordus toward the stairs up to the main Trading Fields. The boy frowned, but did not say anything until they were at the top of the stairs.

"What happened?" he asked. "I thought we were going with him?"

"He's compromised. He can't help us."

The boy's mouth fell open. "Compromised? You mean the Prae—"

"Shh!" Ocella said. A lictor strolled down the walkway toward them fifty feet ahead. When he stopped to chat with a vendor, she pulled the boy toward a different aisle.

"Yes, the Praetorians," Ocella said. "He can't help us anymore."

"How do you know?"

"Hand signals," she said. She had assumed the contact was another Saturnist, but the contact had used clear Umbra hand signals. The right finger under the nose meant they were being watched. The left finger under the nose meant she was being tracked. So her greatest fear was true. The Praetorians allowed her to wander free so they could see where she went for help.

Cordus walked along with her for a while and then asked, "What do we do now?"

"I have an idea."

She said no more.

Somehow the Praetorians had attached a tracking device to either her or Cordus. Since they had not arrested her, she assumed they had time. The Praetorians *wanted* her free so they could wrap up the remnants of the Umbra and Saturnist networks in Roma. To complete the work she started with her initial betrayal. Her only choice now was to go to the one person left in Roma who might help her remove that tracker and get them off Terra.

Unfortunately her life was in just as much danger with that one person as with the Praetorians.

Lepidus and Appius stepped down from the Atlantium merchant's small cargo ship once the woman and the boy had disappeared up the rock stairs. The merchant stood near his table of teas, his back to Lepidus, watching the hill where the two fugitives had disappeared.

"I did my part," the merchant said without turning. "Now I want assurances that my family will live."

"I swore an oath they would live, and so they shall," Lepidus said. "The Picus Reach has numerous worlds filled with valuable metals and way line fuel. They always have a need for slaves to work the asteroid belts. I hear conditions have improved over the last twenty years. Your wife and two sons should live at least another ten years. Fifteen if they have the strong will and stamina for which your Atlantium tribes are famous."

The merchant's head dropped slowly as Lepidus spoke.

When Lepidus finished, the merchant said quietly, "My only regret is that I will leave them alone in this world."

The merchant turned around, his chin up, eyes steady. His arms dangled at his side, inviting the killing strike. Lepidus walked to within a few paces. In one fluid motion, he thrust his long knife up beneath the man's sternum. He pulled the knife free, and a gout of blood flowed from the wound. The merchant grunted, then crumpled to the ground. Blood continued to pump from his wound as his open eyes glazed.

Appius stooped and checked the merchant's pulse. He looked up at Lepidus, confused. "Could we not have obtained more information from him?"

Lepidus wiped his knife on a silk fabric ream. "He wouldn't tell us anything. He knew his family's fate regardless of what he did for us. Along with his own fate."

"Then why did he help us at all?"

Lepidus regarded the dead merchant. "*He* was willing to die, but he would not sacrifice his *family*. A life of slavery for some is better than no life at all."

Appius nodded, then stepped back from the pooling blood. "Why not just shoot him with a pulse pistol? It's cleaner."

Lepidus stared at his apprentice. "If you have to kill an honorable man, show him respect by using your own hands."

Lepidus sheathed his knife and strode from the merchant's stall. "Call the lictors and tell them there's a body here. We need to see which traitor Marcia Licinius Ocella reveals to us next."

Chapter Twenty-Four

Flamma Africanus was the first person to die under Kaeso's command.

Kaeso stared at the young Egyptian. He appeared to sleep peacefully in his bunk, with his eyes closed, his face relaxed. There was no sign his neck and back were broken in six places. Kaeso was no stranger to death. He was an Umbra assassin, after all. But this was the first time someone he was responsible for keeping alive had died.

Blaesus stood beside Flamma, staring at him with puffy red eyes.

"Brave, stupid boy," Blaesus said over and over.

Blaesus told Kaeso a way line plasma storage shelf had broken loose in Cargo Two when Lucia evaded the panicked ships around the Liberti way station. The shelf had broken through the Cargo Two window where Blaesus would have been standing if Flamma had not pushed Blaesus to safety. The shelf's seven hundred pounds slammed into Flamma's back, throwing him into the bulkhead the same moment Lucia did another maneuver that launched him to the other side of the corridor.

Kaeso put a hand on Blaesus's shoulder, squeezed, then left Flamma's quarters. He entered the corridor, then leaned his back against the wall and rubbed his eyes. *First Dariya and now Flamma. Seems I'm better at killing than commanding.*

"Centuriae," Galeo said from down the hall.

Kaeso straightened as Galeo came down the deck ladder. He still looked pale and his eyes darted as if he were a mouse wary of a hawk.

Galeo paused. "I'm sorry about your crewman."

Kaeso nodded.

"Are you all right?"

"I could ask the same of you," Kaeso said. When Galeo didn't respond, Kaeso asked, "Do you know where we are?"

Galeo looked away. "No. We're in a corner of space no human has ever been, so there are no navigation charts on record. It's slow work."

"Then the work needs to speed up," Kaeso said. "I won't lose Dariya as well."

"I'm aware of the emergency."

"What can I do?"

"Do you have a Valkyrie 11 navigational tabulari in your cargo bays?"

"Sadly, no."

"Then there's nothing you can do."

"So much for the ultimate Umbra engines," Kaeso said.

"The engines would have worked fine if a four inch chunk of the Liberti way station hadn't lodged itself in your navigation dish. We'll need to do an EVA to remove it and repair the dish. First, we need to do some things inside. If you come down to the engine room, I'll show you."

Kaeso watched Galeo as they descended the ladder to the engine room. Galeo was not his confident self, but neither was he in shock like during their escape from Libertus. Kaeso had not asked Galeo about that for fear his implant might punish such questions. But if he was to trust Galeo with the repairs to his ship, he had to know if Galeo was mentally present.

Daryush was staring at a console when they entered the engine room, and looked up when they arrived.

"Daryush," Kaeso said. "Blaesus could use some company."

The big Persian nodded, then walked past them into the corridor. Once Daryush ascended the ladder, Kaeso turned to Galeo.

"What happened to you during the attack?" He let an involuntary sigh when no pain came from his implant.

Galeo stared absently at his console. "I'm surprised it took you this long to ask me."

"I've been busy. I'm asking now."

Galeo was quiet, but Kaeso waited, the question hanging between them.

"Same thing that happened to your collar coms," Galeo said finally. "I lost communication with other Vessels."

"I didn't think that was possible. Vessels don't communicate through implants. Their Muses talk to each other."

Kaeso never understood the physics behind Muse communication because it was never taught to him. It was an Umbra secret that only Vessels knew. What Kaeso did know was that a Vessel anywhere in the universe could communicate instantly with any other Vessel in the universe. It was a com method bordering on the mystical, the thought of which made Kaeso uncomfortable. The Muses were a sentient, alien virus. They were not gods, though he could understand how some could think so. They had a collective wisdom and intelligence going back millions of years, and they could overturn all known laws of physics with each new technology they revealed to the Vessels.

"So now the Romans can block Muse communication?" Kaeso said. "If they can do that..."

"Libertus won't survive." Galeo gave him a weak smile. "Now you know why I was so shocked at the time."

"Can you communicate now?"

"Only with Vessels outside the Libertus system. But Libertus is a black hole to me."

With *Caduceus* in a corner of the universe humans had never seen, their only connection to Libertus was now cut off. Had Libertus fended off the Roman attack? Had general war broken out with the other Lost Worlds? There was no way to know if Umbra ships had taken on the invading Romans, or if they had suffered the same com failure as Galeo. If Umbra ships were neutralized, then Libertus was defenseless. Libertus and the Lost Worlds had a defense pact, but the pact envisioned Libertus defending other Lost Worlds. If Libertus was under siege, Kaeso doubted the rest of the Lost Worlds could muster a force strong enough to take on the Romans.

"Your scowl tells me you think the situation is as dire as I think it is," Galeo said.

"I just realized something," Kaeso said. "You never released the concealment protocols on my implant. Why can I talk about this? Why can I say...Umbra?"

There was no stabbing pain behind his right ear. Kaeso smiled.

"Don't celebrate your freedom just yet," Galeo warned. "You're discussing secrets that could tear your mind apart once communication with Libertus is restored. Your implant still records every conversation you have, even if it's no longer able to censor you. Once the Muses on Libertus learn what you revealed, and to whom..."

"I won't tell my crew about my past, if that's what you mean." *I won't kill the rest of them.*

Kaeso wouldn't know the first thing to tell them, anyway. How could he tell people who trusted and respected him that he used to be an assassin? That he had killed hundreds to save millions of Liberti?

"See that you don't," Galeo ordered. "For their sake and ours. Communication with Libertus has never been disrupted like this. Once it's restored, which could be at any moment, your actions will be revealed and your punishment the same as it would have been before the cut."

Kaeso nodded, not wanting to know how a week's worth of "punishment" felt all at once.

"Why *did* the Romans attack Libertus? It makes no sense."

Galeo worked at his console without responding.

"Who was Ocella extracting?"

"The Consular Heir to the Roman Republic, Marcus Antonius Cordus."

The Consular Heir... Kaeso closed his eyes.

"You were going to find out once the mission was underway. I suppose that's now."

"You fools. The Romans won't let Libertus take one of their gods without a fight!"

Galeo frowned. "The Romans are worried about their image after the bloody nose they took in their "victory" over Kaldeth. They are a declining power, yet still prideful, so we believed they wouldn't make public the fact they lost their Consular Heir. We didn't anticipate their reaction to be so extreme. That means the boy is every bit as important as we think he is. The Romans would not risk an attack on Libertus for a regular boy, even if he is the Consular Heir. That means he is a threat to them. A big threat."

No kidding, Kaeso thought. The other Lost Worlds would immediately slap a trade embargo on Roma that would hurt them worse than any military strike. The Zhonguo would embargo Roma as well, and would probably jump into the fight—not out of solidarity with Libertus, but to keep the Romans from taking the rich Libertus system in one piece. The scientific, economic, and cultural output of Libertus was far greater than all the Lost Worlds combined, and rivaled the major empires. A Roma that possessed Libertus intact would become a hyperpower no other human nation could match, and that was just too much for the

Zhonguo to risk. No, Roma would never have attacked unless it was desperate.

Then a thought twisted Kaeso's stomach.

"Ocella's betrayal helped them neutralize Umbra," Kaeso said. "Roma has wanted Libertus for a hundred years but never knew how to take her. Now they can. Because of Ocella."

"Many factors culminated in this attack," Galeo said, returning to his calculations. "Our main concern right now is getting to a friendly way station."

"We're not going to Terra?"

Galeo shook his head. "I'm a Vessel. If they can detect Umbra implants, they'll detect me as soon as I enter the system. We'll go to a Liberti-allied way station first. You can make your repairs and continue to Terra while I stay behind."

"You'll take my crew with you."

Galeo looked at him. "Unbelievable. You still think you can do this on your own? You're not an Ancile anymore. You need to learn how to work with other human beings, Centuriae Aemilius."

"The deal was I do this alone," Kaeso said. "Arrange their transfer. Give them their citizenship. They've earned it."

Galeo sighed, then returned to the console. "Perhaps you should discuss this with your crew. Your man Blaesus just snuck up the ladder to your command deck. I imagine he's about to tell your first officer what we said."

Kaeso whipped around, ran to the door, and looked up the ladder just in time to see Blaesus's feet disappear into the corridor above.

Kaeso turned and lunged at Galeo. The Vessel was ready for him. He dodged Kaeso's reach, swung Kaeso around, and slammed his head against the console, holding it there. The numbers on the console were bright in Kaeso's eyes, almost as bright as the starbursts from Galeo's unexpected move. He was just as angry with himself for letting his rage dictate his tactics as he was at Galeo for dooming his crew.

"You bastard!" Kaeso yelled, his cheek against the console. "You've killed them!"

"Maybe," Galeo said. "Maybe not. If you complete this mission, maybe Umbra will show mercy and let them live with what they know."

"Umbra doesn't do that! You know what the policy is!" Kaeso had enforced that policy on Roma many times.

"Will you stop fighting and listen to me?" Galeo said into his ear. "I'm tired of holding you. You're strong for a starship centuriae."

Kaeso stopped struggling.

Galeo released Kaeso's head slowly and then stepped away. Kaeso glared at Galeo as he stood. "You've killed them."

"You need your crew. The only way I can get you to take them is if you feel you have to protect them from, well, me. You will take them with you, use their skills. Even the Persian, though dull in speech, is a genius when it comes to starship engines. You will need them all for this mission. Now their only chance to survive this is for you to complete your mission. After that, I forget they know about Umbra."

"I don't believe you," Kaeso said. "The Muses have never made exceptions before. They'll never agree to this."

"They just have. The Vessels outside Libertus now know of our deal. The Libertus Vessels will agree as well once communication is restored."

Kaeso narrowed his eyes. "You may see my crew as game pieces on a board, but they've been my family for the last five years. The Romans will kill them if they're caught."

Galeo cocked his head. "See that they don't get caught. I'm sorry, old friend, but this mission is now the only thing that can save Libertus from a Roman ground invasion. If we can secure the Consular Heir, find out what he knows, then we can perhaps blackmail the Romans into lifting the siege."

"So this cure for the Cariosus? Was that all a lie to get me to go?"

"The Consular Heir has knowledge that could lead to a cure. That is the truth."

"He's just a boy, what could he know?"

Galeo looked away for just an instant, but it was enough to tell Kaeso he was hiding something. "Can I get back to work?"

Kaeso moved away from the console, staring at Galeo. "Re-activate my implant."

Galeo laughed. "If I do, the pain will knock you out for hours. Implant reactivation is not a pretty procedure. Besides, you cannot land on Terra with an active implant. We've already been over this."

"The only way I can know if you're telling me the truth is through my implant," Kaeso said. "After I've verified the deal, you can de-activate it again." Kaeso grabbed Galeo's arm, and the Vessel flinched. "Activate the implant, or we float in this gods forsaken corner of the universe for eternity."

"Don't be so dramatic. I thought your crew was precious to you. You'd let them die in the middle of nowhere?"

"If you're lying to me, they die anyway. At least I get to take you with us."

Galeo stared at Kaeso several moments, then sighed. "You'd better have your medicus tie you down. You don't want to injure yourself once we start."

Lucia stared at Blaesus after he finished telling her what he'd heard in the engine room. She didn't know whether to laugh, throw Blaesus off the command deck...or believe him.

"You're sure?" Lucia asked. "You know how your hearing is these days."

Blaesus scowled. "My hearing is perfectly fine, young lady. Bouts of ringing notwithstanding. Kaeso is a Liberti spy, or used to be, and he's going to Roma to kidnap the Consular Heir."

Lucia looked out the command deck window, unable to believe what she heard. She knew Kaeso had a past he refused to reveal—they all did—but she never suspected he was a Liberti spy. An actual on the ground, secret agent, assassin, spy. Kaeso Aemilius, the same man who had taken in a motley crew of runaways and criminals because his honor would not let him turn them away.

"I can't believe this," she said. "Kaeso's an honorable man."

"Don't let our Roman revilement of spies blind you," Blaesus said. "Romans may look on spies as dishonorable, but we've used them quite happily throughout our history. Spying is just another form of warfare. One in which Libertus is unparalleled, apparently."

"This explains much," she said. "Maybe he thought we wouldn't follow his orders if we knew he was a spy. Maybe that's why he didn't want us going to Terra."

Blaesus snorted. "Or because he's kidnapping the Consular Heir! I've never been the religious sort, but you know how the Consular Family is worshiped. Perhaps he thought we'd never kidnap one of our gods?"

"Why the Consular Heir? Does he really have this cure for Dariya?"

Blaesus shrugged. "I don't know. Which is why we need to have a talk with our Centuriae."

Lucia nodded. "He can't worm his way out—"

The inhuman screams from the crew quarters made Lucia jump. Blaesus started as well. She jumped from the pilot's chair and slid down the ladder to the crew quarters. The screams came from Kaeso's quarters. She charged up the corridor. Inside, Kaeso was strapped to his bunk, thrashing and screaming. The Navigator stood over him, his hand on Kaeso's head.

Lucia rushed toward the Navigator. But Nestor, standing near the door where Lucia could not see him, grabbed her arm. Lucia was about to elbow him in the face when Nestor yelled, "Wait! The Centuriae wanted him to do this!"

Lucia yanked her arm out of Nestor's grip, then drew her pistol and aimed at the Navigator. "Why? He's killing him!"

The Navigator stood over Kaeso with a serene expression, unmoving, his eyes glazed.

"No," Nestor said. "Centuriae said this would happen and not to interfere. He said he would be all right."

The waver in Nestor's voice told Lucia he was not so sure, considering Kaeso's awful, ragged screams.

Lucia stepped forward, put the gun against the Navigator's head. "Stop what you're doing right now."

The Navigator blinked, then looked at her. "If I stop now, he will die."

"What are you doing to him?"

"What he asked me to. Now I suggest you let me continue."

Lucia looked from the Navigator's serene eyes to Kaeso, straining against the straps over his chest, arms, and legs.

"The more you distract me," the Navigator said beneath Kaeso's shrieks, "the longer this takes."

"Lucia," Nestor said, "let him finish."

Lucia ground her teeth, and then lowered the gun. "If he dies..."

"I know," the Navigator said, then turned his glassy stare back to Kaeso.

Blaesus and Daryush now crowded the hatch to Kaeso's quarters asking Nestor what was happening. Lucia ignored them, only watching Kaeso's agony. Every scream clawed at her heart, every thrash made her want to hold him tight, to keep him from hurting himself. If she could, she would have taken his pain and made it her own.

She was confused and helpless. She clenched and unclenched her fists around the pistol, not knowing whether to trust the Navigator or shoot him. Why was this man causing her centuriae so much pain? And why did Kaeso agree to this? Questions burned on her tongue, but she didn't want to scream them at the Navigator for fear he told the truth, that any distraction would cause Kaeso's death.

Kaeso stopped screaming. His red face, streaked with tears, began to relax. His eyes were still shut, but he stopped straining against the straps, his whole body settling into the bunk. For a terrible moment Lucia thought he was dead, but his chest rose and fell quickly as if he'd just run a sprint.

"I want answers," she said to the Navigator. "Now, or you're going out the airlock."

The Navigator lifted his hand off Kaeso's forehead. "Your centuriae just did a stupid thing." The Navigator's gaze swept the whole crew. "For all of you."

He tried to slip past Lucia, but she grabbed his arm. "What did you do to him?"

The Navigator smiled. "I suggest you ask him when he wakes up. He'll tell you more than you ever wanted to hear."

"When will he wake up?"

The Navigator pulled his arm from Lucia's grip and then shrugged. "Tomorrow. His body needs time to adjust to what he asked me to do."

Lucia raised the pistol again and pointed it at the Navigator's head. The Navigator didn't flinch, only stared at Lucia with those preternatural eyes. It galled Lucia that she couldn't intimidate him, not even with a pistol aimed at his head.

"Why won't you tell me anything? You and your people just board our ship, destroy our engines, force us to take a mission that I don't know why it's so damned important for *us* to take. Now we're lost and my centuriae is strapped to his bunk after screaming his lungs out. I want answers. Who are you people?"

The Navigator sighed. "You're not a murderer. Besides, you need me to get those engines running again."

"One, if you read anything about my past, you know that's not true. Two, Daryush has watched you since you boarded. He'll do just fine with the engines."

Lucia tried to ignore Daryush in the hallway behind the Navigator, emphatically shaking his head.

"Once again," the Navigator said, "ask your centuriae when he wakes up. I am not authorized to give you the answers you want. He is."

Lucia stared at the Navigator. Her impulse was to shoot him in the head, be done with him, and then they could figure out the engines themselves. Maybe she'd wake Dariya to help Daryush. They could make it work.

Her grip tightened on the pistol. The Navigator must have seen her resolve, for his eyes widened slightly. *Good*, she thought. *Now he's afraid.*

A groan came from behind. "Lucia, put the damn gun down."

She half turned and saw Kaeso staring at her.

"Are you okay, sir?"

"No," he said with a raspy voice. "But I will be. Put it down."

The Navigator looked over Lucia's shoulder at Kaeso. "The re-activation worked, Centuriae. You can verify the terms of our deal now, if you remember how to do it."

"I remember," he said. His eyes glazed a moment and then refocused. He looked at the Navigator. "Good."

"Tomorrow we deactivate it," the Navigator said. "Agreed?"

"Agreed," Kaeso said.

Lucia put the gun in her holster and then turned to Kaeso. Nestor was already unbuckling the straps. Her once strong, invincible centuriae looked so pale, haggard, and weak. Her worry battled her rage at not knowing what in Dis' hell was going on.

"What," she asked in a trembling voice, "did he do to you, sir?"

Kaeso smiled weakly. "It's a long story. I promise I'll tell you. Later." He closed his eyes, and seemed to fall instantly into a deep sleep. His face relaxed and a bit of color returned to it.

Nestor put a hand on her shoulder. "I'll watch him."

Lucia clenched her teeth, then said, "Let me know when he wakes up." Then she nodded toward the Navigator. "And let me know if *he* comes back."

The Navigator smiled. "I have an engine to repair, remember?" He turned and brushed past Blaesus and Daryush.

She left Kaeso's bunk as well, watching the Navigator descend the ladder to the engine deck. She turned to Daryush. "Pay attention to everything he does. I want you to know those engines as well as him."

Daryush cocked his head, as if to say he'd been doing that all along, but he nodded and hurried down the corridor to the ladder.

"Now what?" Blaesus asked. "I for one do not trust that Liberti thug."

"Agreed," Lucia said. "For now we play his game. But if he hurts anyone else on this ship, or sneezes the wrong way, I will kill him. No matter what the Centuriae says. Will you back me?"

"Of course. He's the reason we're here. He's the reason Flamma..." Blaesus paused, blinking away tears. "Kaeso has not been himself since Menota. These Liberti have done something to his mind. They're known for that."

Blaesus stared at the ladder where the Navigator had descended. "I'm willing to go to Roma if it means finding a cure for Dariya. But I think whatever bargain Kaeso struck with these Liberti may have cost him too much. I would feel better doing this on our own. Without their help."

Blaesus gave Lucia a meaningful stare, and then he walked away and entered his hatch.

Lucia went to the ladder and was about to ascend to the command deck when she stopped. She thought about what just happened and what Blaesus said. She cursed, then descended the ladder to the engine room.

She found the Navigator working at the console next to Daryush. She activated her pistol and pointed it at the Navigator.

"Daryush, please leave the engine room," she said. Daryush sighed at the interruption, but gasped when he saw her aiming at the Navigator. He hurried out and ascended the ladder.

"I want to know what you did to the Centuriae," Lucia said. "No more games, Liberti."

The Navigator stared at her with blank eyes. "Ask him when he wakes up."

"Not good enough," Lucia said. "I know your kind. There were people like you in the Legions. People so arrogant in their power they thought nothing could harm them. It's people like you who killed my friends during the Kaldeth Rebellion. People like you who forced me to—"

The Navigator turned back to the console. "I don't have time for this. I need to get these engines repaired and calibrated or we're never going home. I'm sure there's something you could be doing on the command deck. Attend to your duties, trierarch, and stop bothering me."

Attend to your duties.

Those words slammed into her mind again after more than ten years. It was her greatest humiliation, one she never told the *Caduceus* crew. One she tried hard to convince herself never happened. She could not blank out the image of her former centurion's red face above her, an open grenade in his hand, his promise to release it and kill them both unless she lay there and let him finish. *Attend to your duties,* he had whispered in her ear over and over again until he was through with her.

The next day, while patrolling the Kaldethian forests, she slit his throat while he urinated behind a tree, and left his body in the woods for the planet's native carnivores to devour. Her century always suspected her, but never had any proof. Many of the women and men in her squad had approved. They had suffered the same way, and gave her knowing smiles.

Attend to your duties.

Lucia raised her pistol and shot the Navigator.

Chapter Twenty-Five

Ocella stood across the street from the house of the Julii matron. Once again she hid in an alley, for the grimy clothes on both her and Cordus would stand out among the finer dressed residents of the Caelius Hill. She watched slaves, better dressed and fatter than most Roman citizens, walk in and out of the house's back entrance. Some carried grocery bags while others carried rakes and auto-shears for the vast garden within the home's walls. It was quite a luxury to have such a large property on the wealthy Caelius, but then the Julii had been wealthy since Roma's founding. They had fallen far in social status among the other patricians after Marcus Antonius deposed Octavian Caesar, but they had at least retained their wealth.

Ocella told Cordus to hide behind a large trash bin, and then she trotted across the alley to the Julii back entrance. A large private lictor guarded the entrance, his massive forearms folded over his equally massive belly. He wore a red tunic over white pants, with a pistol holstered in a shoulder strap under one of his arms. He stared at Ocella from beneath a wide-brimmed white hat as she ran toward him, and did not move when she stopped in front of him.

"I'd like to inquire about work," Ocella said. "I'm good with gardening."

"The *domina* does not hire citizens for the garden," the bored lictor said. "She has slaves for that."

"I'm also a good cook," Ocella continued. "In fact, my recipes for jellied sardines are the talk of the Capitoline. Please tell the *domina* that a gardener cook with recipes for jellied sardines is at the door."

The lictor frowned. "I told you, the *domina* does not hire citizens. Now leave, beggar, before I get annoyed."

Ocella was getting annoyed herself. Her former Umbra contacts had assured her that the coded phrases would get her through the doors of the Julii household. Obviously this idiot had never learned the codes, or he had forgotten.

"Please tell the *domina*, or at least her head slave, that a woman talented in both gardening and cooking is at the door seeking work. My jellied sardines—"

The lictor sighed, unfolded his arms and tried to give Ocella a backhand slap with one beefy hand. Ocella ducked beneath the slap and put all her weight behind a punch to the lictor's chest. His eyes bulged and he gasped for air. He doubled over and reached for his pistol. Before he could grab it, Ocella pulled it from his holster (where the fool had not fastened it) and aimed it at his head.

"Call your *domina*," Ocella said, "and tell her what I told you."

The lictor nodded, holding his hand up, gasping. She gave him a moment to collect his breath and then cocked the pistol when she thought he took too long. He thumbed his collar com and said, "Memnio, it's Desitus."

"What?" a man with a Germanic accent said over the com.

"There's a woman here wanting work as a cook or gardener," Desitus said in a strained voice.

Ocella cursed under her breath at the lictor for mixing up the code's order, and she wanted to hit him in the face with his pistol.

"The *domina* does not hire citizens, Desitus, you know this."

"She's insistent."

"I prefer gardener," Ocella said loudly so Memnio could hear, "but I am also a cook. My jellied sardines are a delicacy on the Capitoline."

Seconds passed, and she began to think this Memnio didn't know the codes either. She was about to call out again when Memnio's voice returned.

"I said the *domina* does not hire citizens." Memnio paused. "But you might find work at the Aeneas Cafe. They have their own garden and always need good cooks."

"Where is the Aeneas Cafe?" Ocella asked.

"Via Rumina, two blocks east."

"Thank you, sir." Ocella backed away from the lictor, still aiming his gun at him. The lictor glared at her with murderous eyes.

"Can I have my gun back?"

"Pick it up at the Aeneas Cafe," she said.

She turned and trotted across the alley back to Cordus. He saw the gun and gave her a questioning look. Ocella threw it in the trash bin behind him. She scanned the alley behind her to ensure they weren't followed and then motioned him toward the Via Rumina at the other end of the alley.

It was midday but the dark clouds forming above threatened rain and storms. Most of the well-dressed patricians strolled down the sidewalks with umbrellas. Ocella still felt conspicuous in her dirty clothes, but there was no avoiding it. It was only a two-block walk, but two blocks was enough for a stray patrician to recognize Cordus. She couldn't eliminate a nosey patrician as easily as a drunken Legionnaire.

She clutched Cordus's hand as they walked onto the street. In Ocella's previous cover as a Praetorian, she had patrolled streets like these during her investigations of potential traitors among the patrician ranks. But she never noticed until now—with a grumbling stomach—how many gourmet food shops were interspersed among the high fashion clothing boutiques, jewelers, and fine porcelain stores. The scents of roasted pistachios, honeyed cakes, and even imported teas made her mouth water. Cordus wasn't faring well either, for he craned his neck at each little food store and cafe they passed.

Most patricians on the street tried their best to ignore the beggar mother with her son. Some wrinkled their noses and gave them a wide berth. So far, no one seemed to recognize Cordus.

Ocella found the Aeneas Cafe two blocks from the alley just as Memnio said. The cafe had polished oak doors, colorful potted flowers arranged in front of the windows, and an austere glowing sign above the door without dancing images like the other businesses along the street. It was small, classy, and crowded with people sipping their drinks from porcelain cups as they read scroll pads.

She passed the front entrance and went around the block to the alley behind the cafe. Its supply entrance was blocked by a truck from which men were unloading crates of bottled drinks. They gave her passing glances as she and Cordus approached the door, but continued pulling crates off the truck without saying a word to her.

She drew Cordus aside and bent down to whisper in his ear. "This should only take a few minutes. Hide behind the trash bins."

"I know the procedure," Cordus said in the same whisper. "Keep out of sight, run to our rendezvous if someone attacks me."

Ocella smiled, then nodded. "I suppose you're the evasion expert by now."

"I am having the time of my life."

She couldn't tell if he was joking or serious. His eyes gleamed, and a slight grin tugged at the corners of his mouth. She was glad to see his old excitement for this "adventure" return after the business at the Temple of Empanda. *Excitement, but now tempered by brutal reality,* she thought. *He might just survive this.*

Ocella walked through the supply door and into the kitchen. A woman stood at a counter chopping carrots, her back to Ocella. The woman wore a gray smock and apron, and Ocella almost dismissed her as a slave, but noticed she wore expensive leather shoes and figured her for the cafe's owner.

"Excuse me," Ocella said, "I was told I might find work here. I'm an exceptional gardener, and I also cook. My jellied sardines are considered a delicacy on the Capitoline."

Without turning, the woman asked, "Do you have references?"

Ocella hesitated. "I don't have a list with me, but I can get you one later."

The woman turned around and looked at her shrewdly. She was in her early fifties, with elegant cheek bones, dark hair, and a Roman patrician's olive skin. She wasn't wearing makeup that Ocella could see, but the woman's skin and lips had the glow that only came from an expensive salon.

"What makes you think I'm the owner of this cafe?"

"I'm sorry, *domina*, I assumed—"

"I'm joking," the smiling woman said. "I'm Gaia Julius Rutila, the owner. You are?"

Ocella bowed, surprised to meet the Julii matron in a kitchen chopping carrots. "I am Vibia Minius."

The matron put down her knife and wiped her hands in a towel. "So, Vibia Minius, can you tell me why I shouldn't have you killed?"

There was movement behind Ocella. She turned to see one of the men who had been unloading the truck pointing a pistol at her. The other man held Cordus just outside the door, his hand over the boy's mouth. Cordus's eyes bulged and he grunted as he fought against the man's arms. Another man came from the cellar door behind Ocella, patted her down, and took the pistol from her coat pocket.

Ocella turned back to Gaia Julius, and licked her lips. She had known this would be a dangerous tactic. Gaia Julius had been an Umbra contact for almost twenty years, since she became head of the Julii after her father's death. She obviously knew that every Umbra Ancile on Terra had been killed, and she must've had a good idea it was Ocella's fault. Would Gaia seek revenge?

But Gaia's Umbra connections were not the reason Ocella sought her help. Ocella heard rumors about the Julii when she was under cover in the Praetorians. Rumors that they were Saturnists, the same as Scaurus. Nothing was ever confirmed, and Scaurus himself never revealed to Ocella whether the rumors were true. He was protective of Saturnist members, even with Ocella.

Gaia Julius was the only choice Ocella had left. Without her, Ocella and Cordus were dead anyway.

"You know who I am," Ocella said slowly. "I assume that makes me valuable."

The lady snorted. She made even that outburst seem dignified. "Yes, you are quite the wanted woman. You and...the boy. The question is: to whom do I give you?"

She raised her right palm. "On one hand, the Romans would be quite appreciative if I handed over the Consular Heir and his kidnapper. Imagine that. It would return my family to its rightful place among the Roman elite. A thousand years is a long time to be treated like *cac* on the bottom of a slave's shoe."

Ocella stared at the Julii matron, her body and mind a tightened coil.

Gaia Julius raised her left palm. "Or I could give you to our Liberti friends. They would be most grateful, considering you had every one of their associates slaughtered. They took that rather poorly, I might add. I'm sure they would give me a suitable reward"—her eyes gleamed—"and you a suitable punishment. Especially with the current hostilities."

"What hostilities?"

Gaia arched an eyebrow. "You don't know?"

"We've been on the run for three weeks. We've stayed away from any—"

"War, my dear. Roma attacked Libertus yesterday."

Ocella blinked. "Attacked? That's impossible."

But with a sickening realization, Ocella knew it *was* possible. *She* had made it possible. Umbra's only defense against a Roman assault was to kill it within the Roman government before the idea could be implemented. The attack was her fault.

Ocella swallowed the bile rising in her throat. "Is Libertus fighting back? The Romans haven't..."

"No, the Romans have not bombed the planet," Gaia said, "but they've set up a blockade, and according to the newscriers, it's going rather splendidly for the Naves Astrum."

Ocella shook her head. That didn't matter right now. She forced herself not to worry about something she couldn't control.

Even though it's your fault.

Through clenched teeth, Ocella said, "The boy is important."

"Of course he is. He's the Consular Heir."

"You have a third option." *If she is a Saturnist, she'll know what I mean.*

Gaia stared at Ocella, her face revealing nothing. Her eyes flitted from Cordus to Ocella.

"You know what he can do," Ocella continued. "Neither the Romans nor the Liberti should have him. Get him off-world." She swallowed. "Give me to whomever you want."

Gaia Julius stared at her a moment longer, then sighed and returned to her carrots. "Put them in the cellar."

The man behind Ocella jabbed her with the pistol and pointed her to the cellar door behind her. She glanced at the man, then at Cordus. The boy no longer struggled, but the man behind him still held Cordus's arms in an iron grip. He stared daggers at Gaia Julius's back.

"Julii coward," Cordus growled.

Gaia Julius stopped cutting and turned to Cordus, the knife still in her hand. "Sire," she said sweetly, "it's been a long time since we last saw each other. You were five or six, but it was at the wedding of my niece Sephilia to one of your cousins. Titus, I believe. Or should I say, "almost" wedding. Young Titus backed out just before the ceremony after last-minute pressure from your father. After all, it wouldn't do to have an Antonii marry a Julii. The shame and embarrassment my beloved niece felt as she stood at the podium waiting for her groom was…well, it was like she'd been flayed alive. Socially speaking, of course."

Gaia Julius held up the knife and inspected its edge. "Because, obviously, an actual flaying would hurt much, much worse."

Cordus's jaw clenched, but he maintained his defiant stare. Ocella tensed, ready to leap if Gaia Julius made any move toward Cordus. The man behind Ocella seemed to feel her tension, and he pushed the pistol further into her back.

Gaia Julius looked from the knife to Cordus. She bent down so her eyes were even with the boy's. "Sephilia drowned herself in the Tiber two days later. I've been quite upset with the Antonii ever since. So do not provoke me, *sire*."

Gaia Julius turned around and resumed her chopping. The man holding Cordus pulled him toward Ocella, while the man with the pistol pushed Ocella again toward the cellar stairs.

The stairs were ancient and worn, as if they were hewn from the rock when Romulus was king. She descended into the dark, dank cellar with the gunman and Cordus behind her. The gunman touched a pad on the wall, and ceiling globes illuminated the rough stone corridor. The gunman told her to go left and then had her stop at a wooden door with iron bands. He opened the door and motioned her in. Ocella entered a room filled with plastic wine barrels. The man holding Cordus shoved the boy into the room, then slammed and locked the door. The only light in the room came from the crack beneath the door, which disappeared once the gunmen went back upstairs. Ocella and Cordus stood in the center of the room holding hands in pitch-blackness.

"What is she going to do to us?" Cordus asked in a quiet voice.

"She won't turn us over to the Praetorians," Ocella said, putting more confidence in her voice than she felt. "She hates your family. She won't let Roma keep you."

"I think she hates *me*. Did you see what she was doing with the knife?"

"She was just trying to scare you. She won't hurt you."

At least a sane *person who knew Cordus's secret wouldn't hurt him*, Ocella thought. But the anger in Gaia Julius's eyes when she told the story of her niece made Ocella wonder.

"So she'll give us to Umbra?" Cordus asked. "I cannot go with them either."

"If my guess is right, she won't do that either."

Cordus was silent and then asked, "Are you sure she is a Saturnist?"

Ocella sat down on the cold stone in the middle of the cellar, and Cordus sat next to her. He was shivering, so she put her arms around him.

"I don't know yet."

"What will she do to you?"

Give me to Umbra so they can flay me alive for what I did to their Ancilia here, not to mention starting a war with Roma that Libertus could not hope to win.

"I don't know," she said.

They were both silent for a while, and then Cordus asked, "Do you want to play a game?"

"What game?"

"I tell you the name of a city, country, or planet, and you have to name another city, country, or planet whose first letter begins with the last letter of the one I gave you."

She smiled in the darkness. "Sounds fun."

"I'll go first."

Ocella held him closer as he began.

Chapter Twenty-Six

Kaeso didn't know how long he'd been out, but he knew it was a long time. Every muscle in his body was sore, his empty stomach rumbled, and he had a terrible urgency to urinate. He eased himself on his elbows and then brought his feet off the bunk and to the floor. He didn't pass out, so he stood. Lightheadedness assaulted him, and his vision tunneled, but he held on to the bunk until the feeling passed. He got up, shuffled into the corridor, and entered the latrine a dozen paces away. After urinating for almost a minute, he left the latrine and ran into Nestor standing outside the door.

"Feeling better, Centuriae?"

"Sure."

His vertigo and pounding head was light years "better" than his implant's agonizing reactivation. Kaeso had wanted to die, anything to end that searing pain. After his discharge from Umbra, he'd been unconscious when they deactivated his implant. Now he knew why.

But it had been worth it. His brain was still adapting to the reactivation, so there were many things he couldn't yet do with the implant. One thing he could do was see the contract Galeo had made with him regarding his crew's safety. Most importantly, he could see the endorsement given to it by the Vessels who were not trapped on Libertus. The Muses would keep secrets, to be sure, but contracts were religiously upheld. The pain was a fair trade for knowing his crew wouldn't be killed to protect Umbra's secrets.

Kaeso was tempted to push his implant to see what else he could do. It had been a long time since it was active, and he missed its clarity, wisdom, and power. *No. I can't get addicted to this thing again. Not when it's going to be taken away from me so soon.*

"You should lay down for a few more hours at least," Nestor said.

Kaeso ignored him. "How long was I out?"

"Nine hours."

"Lucia hasn't killed the Navigator yet, has she?"

Kaeso's last lucid memory was waking up after Galeo had reactivated the implant to see Lucia pointing a pistol at Galeo's head. Kaeso said something to her—he couldn't remember what—and then his memories faded. Interesting that Kaeso could now remember in crystal clarity every mission he ever took for Umbra, yet he couldn't remember what happened nine hours ago.

Nestor frowned. "Well..."

Kaeso looked at Nestor. "What did she do, Medicus?"

"She, um, shot him and then locked him up in Cargo Two."

Kaeso cursed. He turned around and was about to storm up the ladder when a wave of vertigo hit him. He staggered forward, fell to his knees, and then all fours.

"He is all right," Nestor said, helping Kaeso up. "She shot him in the liver, but the bullet went through his body. I cleaned the wound and was about to surgically repair the liver but...well, the liver was almost healed. I thought he might be a golem, but he is human. That's not all. His skin is covered with a fabric that *projects* a different skin." Nestor stared at Kaeso with haunted eyes. "He is a different man beneath that fabric."

The ship continued to spin, so Kaeso squeezed his eyes shut. Nestor helped him up and back to his bunk. Kaeso lay down without resisting. He knew the implant reactivation would take at least another six hours to complete. But Kaeso couldn't wait six hours. Not with a mission to prepare for, a crazy first officer, and a wounded Vessel in his cargo bay, who happened to be his crew's only hope to survive after this mission.

"Stay here and sleep," Nestor said. "That's an order from your medicus. There are no emergencies at the moment. I'll check on you in an hour."

"Nestor," Kaeso croaked, "don't mention the Navigator's skin to the crew."

Nestor clicked his tongue.

"You already told the crew, didn't you?"

Nestor nodded, then left Kaeso's quarters.

Kaeso screamed in his mind. Why had Lucia shot Galeo? The bastard could be arrogant and bossy, but those were not reasons to kill him. Was it self-defense? Had *he* attacked *her*? Kaeso doubted he'd sleep until he found out. All he could do was wait out the vertigo so he could storm up to the command deck without vomiting all over it.

And now Nestor had seen Galeo's Umbra cloak and told the crew. If the deal Kaeso made with Galeo was off, then his crew was dead.

To occupy his mind while the vertigo receded, Kaeso concentrated on his newly reactivated implant. The neural connections with his brain continued to build, and the implant's information was already seeping into his mind. The implant had all the memories from his years with Umbra: every mission, procedure, wondrous Umbra tech, contact he developed in Roma. The confidence, the wisdom, the bravery. It was all there. Despite his body's weakness from the reactivation, Kaeso wanted to go to Roma now and use those dormant skills. Skills he missed more than he ever realized.

The Magisterium, however, was still a "black hole" in his mind. It was the Magisterium that fed all Umbra Ancilia their mission intelligence. Through Muse tech, the communication traveled light years in an instant, whereas the fastest communication the rest of humanity used were starship couriers via the way lines. The implant com was more like a broadcast, however. Kaeso could not send a message back to Libertus, even though his body's vital signs were. Umbra explained this was for security—if the enemy ever caught an Ancile and figured out the implant, he could send an electronic virus back to Libertus to wipe out the implant network.

Kaeso now understood the caution. The "black hole" proved the Romans could at least jam Umbra coms. From there, it wasn't too much of a leap to access them. Kaeso hoped Libertus was simply being jammed. He didn't want to think the Romans had slagged the entire planet.

Memories of Claudia suddenly flashed through his mind. Her laughing, six-year-old face while she and Petra played fake instruments to the tune of some popular new song. Then tears streaming down her eight-year-old cheeks, the orange and yellow flames of her mother's funeral pyre reflected in her eyes. The snarl on her ten-year-old mouth when she told Kaeso she hated him and wished it had been him who died in that explosion. It was his last memory of her.

Kaeso closed his eyes, opened them, and found the room no longer spinning. He knew it wasn't an hour since he lay down, but he couldn't sit still. Sleep was elusive, especially when he didn't know what was happening to his crew and his ship. He could have used his collar com to call Lucia, but he didn't want to give her time to collect herself and come up with an excuse for what she did. A surprise visit would throw her off balance, which would most likely get Kaeso the truth.

Once again he stood up from his bunk, the vertigo all but gone, and left his quarters. At the ladder to the command deck, he said a silent prayer to Fortuna that the vertigo would not return while he climbed and then began to ascend.

Lucia sat in the pilot's couch, her chin in one hand and her other hand scrolling through data on her console.

"Why did you shoot Galeo?"

Lucia flinched, then turned to him. "You should be in your bunk."

"Why did you shoot Galeo?"

"I didn't kill him."

Kaeso slammed his hand on the wall, making a loud reverberation through the deck. Her eyes were wide like a child who'd been caught stealing candy. "Godsdamn you, Lucia, give me a straight answer."

"Me?" she asked. "What about you, Kaeso? You're the one who sought out these Liberti agents. You're the one who won't bring your own crew on some job you won't tell us the half of. You're the one who let this Navigator aboard the ship and let him turn you into some bootlicking slave who jumps when he lifts a finger. Never mind he has some holographic fabric covering his entire body. I think *you* are the one who owes me—and your crew—straight answers."

Kaeso knew he should have been angry. *I'm her centuriae and she is bound by honor and law to obey my orders.* But that was not his first thought during her rant.

Freedom was his first thought. With Umbra no longer broadcasting from Libertus, there were no concealment protocols on his implant. Days ago he would have been doubled over clutching his head for merely considering to tell her what he knew. Now he felt nothing. And it was the greatest feeling of freedom he could remember.

"You're right," Kaeso said. "You deserve answers. You all do."

Her eyes narrowed.

Kaeso tapped his collar com. "All crew meet in the galley."

He glanced at Lucia, who didn't move. "Do you want answers or what?"

She stood up, walked past him, and descended the ladder. He followed her down.

Nestor and Blaesus were in the galley when Kaeso and Lucia arrived. Daryush was the last to enter, and the big Persian stood in the corner, his arms folded. It was the same location and stance Dariya adopted for the all-crew meetings.

With all of them sitting there, Kaeso was suddenly uncomfortable. He was used to giving orders, not bearing his soul and his past to them. He wondered what they'd think of him when they found out what he once did, especially Blaesus and Lucia.

Just to break the silence, he turned to Nestor. "How's the Navigator?"

"He's lost a lot of blood and he's still unconscious. He should have died."

Kaeso glared at Lucia, but she did not meet his gaze.

"But the way he's healing," Nestor continued, "I'd say he's only going to have a small scar in a few days. I can't explain it. Not even golems heal that fast. I would love to know who...or what...he is."

Nestor left that non-question hanging as he studied Kaeso. "Dariya?" Kaeso asked, avoiding Galeo for now.

"She sleeps," Nestor said. "All vital signs are normal except her body temperature. It increases a tenth of degree every twelve hours. I believe this is due to the virus."

Kaeso nodded. The sleeper crib would give Dariya another week if she stayed in it the whole time. The crib wouldn't stop the virus from spreading, only delay it. Her best chance was Ocella's alleged cure. Kaeso didn't want to think about what he'd have to do to Dariya if that cure didn't exist.

Kaeso looked at the crew. "You want answers. I don't blame you. I've wanted to give you answers for a long time. So now is your chance. Ask me what you want."

The crew glanced at each other, as if they all had a jumble of questions, but didn't know where to start. As always, Blaesus spoke first.

"Just who is this Navigator, Centuriae?"

Even without the implant's concealment protocols in place, Kaeso hesitated. He realized if he told them what he knew of Umbra, he was potentially killing them. Kaeso verified the deal Galeo had made, but he didn't know if that deal was off because of Lucia's attack. If it was, and he told them what they wanted to know, then maybe not today or tomorrow, but some day an Ancile would kill each one of them. It was a brutal policy, but one that kept Libertus safe for over two hundred years. Once the jamming was lifted from Libertus, his implant's restrictions would return and it would send back everything Kaeso had done while out of contact. And he and his crew would be marked.

But if the deal still stood, then Kaeso could tell them whatever he wanted, and they would not be harmed. During Kaeso's years with Umbra, he knew the Muses to be brutal when the situation called for it, but they *always* honored their deals.

He had to trust that now.

"An organization called Umbra Corps is what has kept Libertus free for over two centuries," Kaeso began. "The simple fact that I told you its name may have put your lives in danger."

The crew stared at him.

"I was once an Umbra Ancile," Kaeso said. "I was stationed in Roma. I spied on Roman Senators, bureaucrats, generals, patricians, and centurions. I also assassinated Senators, bureaucrats, generals, patricians, and centurions. Among others. I did many things to prevent Roma from gobbling up Libertus. Things with tools so amazing you'd think they came from the gods. Like the Navigator's Umbra cloak."

"Umbra cloak?" Nestor asked.

"Ancilia wear it to conceal their identity," Kaeso said. "It works well unless it's torn or examined by a medicus."

Kaeso looked from one set of eyes to another. "Six years ago I was discharged from Umbra. Well, you never really leave Umbra. I have an implant in my brain that let me communicate with Umbra when I was an Ancile. Once I left, my implant was mostly deactivated. Except for one function, which prevented me from talking about Umbra or my service with them."

"Why?" Blaesus asked. "Every planet has its spy agencies, and every planet makes their names known. It builds the mystique. Any one of you would quiver in fear if you knew the Praetorian Guard were after you. So why is this Umbra so different that it kills anyone who learns its name?"

"Umbra *has* built a mystique. You've heard of the Liberti *numina*, right?"

Blaesus chuckled. "You're saying Umbra Ancilia are *numina*?"

"No, but Umbra can do things that would make some think they're *numina*."

"Kaldeth," Lucia said. "The 'spirit' I saw on Kaldeth. Was that...?"

Kaeso nodded. "Roma was in an expansionist mood. They'd craved Libertus for almost as long as it's been settled, so Umbra knew it was high on Roma's wish list. Umbra did what it's always done: divert Roma's attention elsewhere."

Nestor furrowed his brow. "But Kaldeth started that war. The religious castes had been calling for 'death to Roma' for decades. Kaldethian terrorists even set off bombs in Terran cities..."

Nestor's voice trailed off as he realized what he'd just said. "That was Umbra?"

"I don't know the operational details," Kaeso said, "but I know Umbra had a hand in starting the conflict. Umbra instigated the Kaldethians without them knowing it."

Blaesus shook his head. "I always thought the Kaldethians were mad for provoking Roma. Apparently they weren't mad. They were puppets."

"I know this sounds dishonorable," Kaeso said, "but Libertus doesn't have a large space fleet. It cannot withstand a direct assault, as we all witnessed two days ago. That's why it must protect itself in other ways."

Kaeso didn't know how to make his crew understand what it was like to live on Libertus. Yes, it was a wealthy world. Its economy was bigger than all the Lost Worlds combined, its cultural output one of its largest exports, its cities and islands a source of tourism revenue that kept it from taxing its own citizens like every other world or nation.

But it lay between two hostile empires—Roma and the Zhonguo—who would like nothing better than to take the Liberti jewel for their own treasure vaults. As a school child, Kaeso endured constant drills of running to bombardment shelters. He remembered speeches from Liberti Senators thanking the gods and the *numina* for protecting Libertus from foreign invasion. Without a large space fleet, the only weapons Libertus had were economic, cultural, and diplomatic. Those seemed like a flimsy shield to most Liberti. Since they could not fathom why Libertus was still free, they just assumed the planet had the gods' favor. In some ways the Liberti were more religious than the Romans. Their "religion" was to work hard and make a lot of money. If they did that, they would continue to enjoy the gods' protection.

"That's why Umbra encourages those *numen* legends," Kaeso continued. "To make other nations think twice about attacking. Umbra is in almost every nation in human space. It listens to politicians, military leaders, and the ruling classes. When someone advocates an aggressive policy toward Libertus...Umbra takes care of the problem. No need for large space fleets or wars when you can take away your enemy's desire to attack you."

Blaesus frowned. "I suppose it is more humane than targeting entire cities and worlds. Dishonorable, but humane."

Nestor asked, "How did Umbra get all this 'magical' technology to fight its secret wars? I've been to Libertus. It is more prosperous than most worlds, yet its technology is not that different. Are you saying the gods have favored Umbra with tech that not even the Romans have?"

Kaeso hesitated. Speaking of Umbra, a crime worth assassination under normal circumstances, was one thing. But to discuss the Muses, secret alien allies of Libertus since its founding, would be stretching Fortuna's grace. Kaeso decided to be cautious and keep the Muses to himself.

"Libertus is a prosperous world," Kaeso said. "Prosperity brings many things most worlds don't have, like a good education system. What can I say, the Liberti are clever."

Blaesus snorted. "My Roman heart takes offense, since it's widely known Romans are the most clever race in the universe. But my Roman brain concedes that if half of what you say is true, then the Liberti must be *very* clever."

Kaeso grinned. "Only you could admit a shortcoming while also complimenting yourself."

"One of my many talents."

"So why does Umbra *really* want us to go to Terra?" Lucia asked. "It's sure not out of concern for Dariya."

"You're right," Kaeso said. "You heard some of it yesterday."

Kaeso glared at Blaesus. The old Senator shrugged. "It's not my fault you don't know how to keep your voice down."

"So it's true," Lucia said. "They want us to kidnap the Consular Heir. They must be mad. It's impossible. There's no way we can get close to him."

"The Consular Heir wants to defect to Libertus," Kaeso said.

The crew stared at him in stunned silence. Blaesus and Lucia shifted in their seats. While they did not practice most Roman religious rituals, they were still Roman, taught from birth that the Consular Family, especially the Antonii, were gods. That was a hard faith to abandon. Even when the belief was no longer there.

"The Consular Family," Blaesus said, "rarely leaves their walled palace on the Palatine. An army of Praetorian Guardsmen protects them. They cannot just come and go as they please. Many attempts have been made to infiltrate the Consular Palace over the centuries. None have succeeded."

"None that you know of," Kaeso replied.

"Well perhaps your Umbra comrades have found a way, if they're as all-knowing as you say they are. But getting in is one thing. Getting the Consular Heir out is another."

"He's already out," Kaeso said. "Three weeks ago, an Ancile got him out of the palace. They've been on the run ever since. At least, that was their status before the Romans attacked Libertus."

"That is why the Romans attacked Libertus?" Blaesus asked. "Because they think Umbra has the Consular Heir?"

"It's not just that," Kaeso said. "Being the Consular Heir, he knows things about the Roman government even Umbra doesn't know. Supposedly he wants to tell Libertus everything. Including this cure for Cariosus."

Lucia shook her head. "It just doesn't make sense. A member of the Consular Family doesn't defect. Especially the godsdamned Heir. Why does he want to leave Roma? It's never happened."

"We don't know," Kaeso said, "but whatever information he has, the Romans are willing to go to war with Libertus to get him back."

Nestor asked, "Our deal for Liberti citizenship? Does that still stand after..." He glanced at Lucia, who frowned.

"There are few things Umbra believes in," Kaeso said. "One of them is sticking to their contracts. They will honor the deal I made with Galeo."

The rest of the crew seemed unconvinced. Blaesus drummed his fingers on the table, Lucia stared at her hands, and Daryush kept glancing out the door. Kaeso himself was unconvinced. *I have to trust in the deal I made with the Muses. It's the only way I can save my crew...and get back into Umbra.*

Nestor nodded thoughtfully, then said, "What if I told you there was another way?"

"What do you mean?"

"There may be a third party that would like to meet the Consular Heir."

"The Zhonguo?" Kaeso asked. "Of course they'd love to get their hands on the Heir."

"Not the Zhonguo."

Kaeso stared at Nestor, who held his gaze without speaking. A strange look came over the medicus, one Kaeso never saw before. The medicus usually avoided eye contact with those whom he conversed. This time the medicus stared directly at Kaeso, and it was Kaeso who wanted to turn away from those hard eyes. But he held Nestor's gaze and asked again, "What do you mean?"

"I will tell you," Nestor said. "But first you must tell us the whole story of Umbra. And do not forget the Muses."

Chapter Twenty-Seven

Kaeso stared at Nestor as if seeing him for the first time. He sat straighter in his chair, and seemed more confident. This was not the skittish medicus Kaeso had known for two years.

"Who are you?" Kaeso asked.

Nestor licked his lips. "I am the same man you've always known, Centuriae. I'm Nestor Samaras, a medicus from New Athens and a Pantheon priest. I also belong to a society that wants to free humanity from slavery."

Blaesus grunted. "You're an abolitionist?"

"Yes, but that's not the slavery I'm referring to," Nestor said, staring at Kaeso.

Kaeso narrowed his eyes. "You're a Saturnist."

Nestor nodded once, then smiled.

Over 150 years ago, the Saturnists popped up on Libertus with stories that the government had aliens inside their brains. They were a joke to most Liberti, but Umbra took them seriously. Over the next few decades, Umbra systematically wiped them out so that now hardly anybody on Libertus knew what a "Saturnist" was.

Blaesus threw up his hands. "Am I the only one on this ship who's *not* in some secret organization?" He looked at Lucia. "Are you in a secret organization?"

Lucia turned to Nestor. "What is a Saturnist?"

"Centuriae," Nestor said to Kaeso, "it would make more sense to them if you told your story first."

Umbra conditioning taught Kaeso to distrust or ignore Saturnist propaganda. When Kaeso was in Umbra, they knew Saturnists still existed, but the group was so marginalized and scattered that Umbra didn't think them worth the resources to hunt down.

Now Kaeso had a self-professed Saturnist on his ship.

"No," he said.

Nestor shrugged. "I am going to tell them my side of the story, and it will leave them with questions you'll have to answer sooner or later."

"Jupiter's cock," Blaesus exclaimed. "*Somebody* start talking!"

Kaeso glared at Nestor. The Greek medicus returned Kaeso's glare with a nonplussed gaze.

How fast could I kill him before he—?

Kaeso shook away that thought, horrified it even came to him. *Why?* the old Ancile in him asked. *It's what you were good at.*

Kaeso ground his teeth, keenly aware Nestor and the crew were watching him. "If I tell you what Nestor wants me to tell you," Kaeso said, looking from Daryush to Blaesus to Lucia, "then it's possible you will have a permanent death mark on your heads. Umbra may track you down and kill you for hearing this."

All three looked at each other. Blaesus asked, "What are the chances they won't kill us for knowing their name?"

"The deal I made with the Navigator might prevent that. The key word is *might*, especially after..." Kaeso glanced at Lucia again.

She slammed one hand on the table. "If I could take it back I would, but I can't. He's going to live, so could we just move past it and figure out what to do now?"

Kaeso knew she was right about focusing on their future plans and not the past. But he would not let her off as easy as she wanted.

"If I tell you the rest," Kaeso continued, "I don't know if my deal with the Navigator will protect you when they find out what you know."

"How will they know?" Lucia said. "Who will tell them?" Lucia glanced around the room, her gaze resting on Nestor.

Nestor shook his head. "You have nothing to fear from me. Umbra would kill me too if I went to them with this. Never mind the fact they would kill me for being a Saturnist."

"It's me," Kaeso said. They all turned to him, and Kaeso explained how his reactivated implant worked.

Blaesus sighed. "So according to you, our only hope to survive this is to extract the Consular Heir from Roma and hand him over to your Umbra people."

"Yes," Kaeso said.

"But even then," Blaesus continued, "they may still kill us for knowing about these 'Muses.'"

"Yes."

Blaesus turned to Nestor. "And you, whoever *you* are, say we can avoid an assassin's bullet and give the Heir to your 'Saturnist' friends."

"I cannot guarantee against a bullet from Umbra," Nestor said, "but, yes, you will be more protected by my people than if you work with Umbra."

Blaesus sat back and folded his arms. "Well I don't trust either of you."

They all stared at each other for several long moments, and Kaeso didn't have long before Nestor began spewing whatever Saturnist propaganda his people assumed about the Muses. Then Kaeso would have to refute those claims, but from a defensive position.

They're going to know anyway, he thought. *They should at least know the truth.*

He looked at his crew and said, "The Liberti are no more clever than any other human nation. But we were lucky, because we colonized a planet with intelligent alien life."

Blaesus and Lucia leaned forward in their chairs, while Nestor settled back with a satisfied smile.

"We call them the Muses," Kaeso said. "They've never told us their real name. They seem to like being compared to the gods of inspiration."

"How has Libertus kept this secret so long?" Blaesus asked. "*Bona Dea*, people have been searching for alien intelligence since before humans left Terra. What do they look like?"

"A bit like influenza."

"Wait," Lucia said. "They look like a giant virus?"

"No, they *are* a virus."

Blaesus's eyes widened. "The Muses are an intelligent alien *virus*?"

"That's right," Kaeso said. *I pray to the gods I've not just killed you all.*

"Fascinating," Blaesus said. "So they infect people? How do they communicate? When did the Liberti discover—?"

Kaeso held up his hands. "It would take days for me to tell you everything. Here's what you need to know right now. Umbra's tech comes from the Muses' ancient wisdom. The Muses infect human volunteers—we call them Vessels—and pass that wisdom on. The Vessels communicate tech designs to Umbra engineers who make it a reality."

Lucia stared at him. "Are you a, um..."

"No I'm not," Kaeso said, "but the Navigator is."

"The Navigator has this alien virus in him right now?" Lucia asked. "Is that why he's healing so fast?"

Kaeso nodded. "Among other things, the Muses transform their host's metabolism and cellular structure. Makes them virtually immune to other diseases, and helps them heal faster than normal humans."

Kaeso turned to Nestor. "There. Now your turn."

Nestor cleared his throat. "A succinct description of an intelligence that has enslaved humanity."

"'Slavery,'" Kaeso grunted. "I call it protection. You cannot deny that Libertus has enjoyed unprecedented freedom and prosperity with the Muses' help."

"Of course you're prosperous," Nestor said. "For now. But you are not free. Have you ever asked what the price will be? Did you ever ask what the so-called Muses want from you? I can assure you they're not helping Libertus out of the goodness of their nucleic hearts."

"They thrive on experience, on wisdom," Kaeso said. "Every Vessel they infect gives them a lifetime of memories the Muses record in their collective consciousness. Experience to them is like gold to us. That is how we pay them."

"Ah, Centuriae," Nestor said, "you've bought the lie as well."

"Fine," Kaeso said. "What do *you* think they want?"

Nestor smiled. "That is the question we Saturnists have been trying to answer for the last thousand years."

"I told you, the original Liberti colonists discovered the Muses when they settled the planet two centuries ago."

"True," Nestor said, leaning forward. "But the Muses have been with *humanity* a lot longer. My friend, the Muses infected Roma first."

Chapter Twenty-Eight

"You don't believe me, do you?" Nestor said.

"It's impossible," Kaeso said. "The Muses would know if there was another strain on Terra. Umbra would know."

Nestor shook his head. "Centuriae, of course the Muses know. Of course Umbra knows. How could they not? Why do you think a Vessel is forbidden to land on Terra? Because the Roman Muse strain would immediately detect them."

Kaeso swallowed. It was true, Vessels were forbidden to land on Terra. Umbra said Vessels were too valuable, that it would be a disaster if they fell into Roman hands. Kaeso had accepted the Umbra explanation without question.

Or maybe his implant *prevented* him questioning it...

"Why then?" Kaeso said. "If what you say is true, why would the Liberti Muses want to fight the Terran Muses? If they're the same virus—"

"They're the same virus, but different strains," Nestor said. "The Liberti strain is different from the Terran strain. They fight each other for the same reason humans fight each other. Aggressiveness is inherent to all intelligent species."

When Kaeso stayed silent, Nestor continued. "Over the centuries, we've learned the two strains have different 'personalities,' if you will. The Liberti strain prefers working behind the scenes, secretly moving events to their liking. It makes them feel safer. Whereas the Roman strain prefers hosts that are worshiped like gods. That's why only the Consular Family and the Collegia Pontificis are infected."

Blaesus leaned forward. "So it's these Muses that give the Consul and the Collegia the technology they pass on, as if it came from the gods?"

Nestor nodded. "It has been that way since Marcus Antonius deposed Octavian Caesar."

"Antonius was infected?" Blaesus asked. He ran a hand through his thinning white hair. "How did this all happen?"

"We don't know for sure," Nestor said, "but Saturnist legend says Antonius was infected while in Egypt during the Second Triumvirate years."

"But *how* was he infected?" Blaesus asked.

"That is lost to history," Nestor said. "As every human knows, Antonius returned to Roma after a decade in Egypt, his legions armed with the first crude muskets and cannons. He claimed he was the Voice of the Gods, who gave him this wondrous technology to bring Roma into a permanent Golden Age."

Kaeso glanced at Lucia, who looked like someone whose entire faith was crumbling before her eyes. Blaesus was interested, but he also seemed uncomfortable, even for a self-proclaimed agnostic. Kaeso could not blame them. Everything they'd been taught their whole lives—things *all* Romans were taught—was turning out to be a lie.

Kaeso's stomach leaped. "That is the secret," he said, without realizing he spoke aloud. Everyone turned to him. "When the Navigator first explained this mission, he said the Consular Heir had a secret that could bring down the Republic. If that's the secret, that the 'Voices of the Gods' are an alien virus, then it would cause complete chaos in the Republic."

Blaesus nodded grimly. "Say what you want about the Republic, but it's a stable institution that has lasted over fifteen hundred years. If Roma crumbles...well, a third of humanity would dissolve into bloody anarchy. And not just in Roma. Most worlds worship some gods of the Roman Pantheon, even the Zhonguo. This revelation would touch every human being, and not in a good way."

"But humanity would be free to worship the *real* gods," Nestor said. "Yes, the Muses have given us prosperity, but what if they go silent and stop giving us their technology? What if they do what every other deadly virus does and begin killing people? Do you think we could stop a *sentient* virus from doing what it wants to us?"

"You would reveal this horrible secret despite the cost in lives?"

"Of course," Nestor said. "Because the only way humanity will be free is if we stand on our own, without these aliens. Maybe then we will rediscover the *true* gods of the Pantheon, not these viral pretenders."

"Who's to say these 'viral pretenders,' as you call them, were not the inspiration behind the gods we worshiped?" Blaesus asked. "Who's to say the 'gods' were not always the Muses?"

Nestor shook his head vehemently. "No, the gods exist. This virus took them away from us by pretending to be gods."

Lucia muttered into her hands, "This is insane."

Kaeso glanced at Daryush, who stared out at the corridor, as if checking on Dariya just down the hall.

"Nestor," Kaeso said, interrupting the argument with Blaesus. "You haven't told us what *you* want, and what you're doing on this ship."

Nestor said, "The Muses took the true gods from humanity. They made us turn to false gods like the Consul and his dogs in the Collegia Pontificis. Worlds who worship the Pantheon still see the Consul and Collegia as authoritative voices in religious doctrine, even if they have no wish to be part of the Republic. Saturnists want to free humanity from Muse domination, to return us to the natural order of things. Where humanity makes its own choices, without interference from these aliens who call themselves 'gods.'"

Nestor turned his brown eyes on Kaeso. "My people have been hunted since the days of Antonius. We've been called many names over the centuries, but Saturnist is our most recent. We are wanderers. We travel the way lines searching for a cure to this virus that enslaves humanity. That is our mandate from the true gods of the Pantheon." Then he grinned. "For me personally, I signed on to your ship because I assumed your, ah, business would take me to some interesting corners of the universe. Corners that might have a cure. Turns out I was right."

"So you want us to hand the boy over to you?" Kaeso said. "What good would that do us?"

"For one," Nestor said, "an alien virus does not control me. Second, a Vessel of one strain does not up and move to a world infected with another strain. It has never happened. The strains hate each other. That is why this boy must be special. It suggests one of two things: the boy is not a Muse infectee, which seems impossible since he's the Consular Heir, or the boy can somehow *overrule* the virus within him. Which suggests—"

"The boy himself may be the cure," Kaeso finished for Nestor.

The recent actions of both Roma and Umbra now made perfect sense. Now Kaeso could see why Roma desperately wanted the boy back. And Umbra would do anything to get their hands on a way to control the Consul and the Collegia, not to mention hide any "cure" for the Liberti Muses. Kaeso's implant ached with the knowledge and thoughts he was having. *Sedition, Ancile. That's what you're thinking, and that's what your implant hates. You know how Umbra repays sedition.*

"It's a theory," Nestor said, leaning back in his chair, "but it makes the most sense given the information we have."

Blaesus said, "If you can use the boy to kill these alien viruses, how would it affect their hosts?"

Daryush raised his eyebrows and turned to Nestor expectantly.

Nestor shook his head. "I don't know. The Vessels could gain control over the Muses within them, or the Vessels might die as the Muses die. The Muses are so integrated with their hosts that any attempt to remove them might prove fatal to the host."

Daryush groaned.

"Fine, you want him because everybody else does," Kaeso said. "Again, how does that help us? And by 'us,' I mean my crew who has not lied to me about their identities."

Nestor laughed. "You're one to talk, Centuriae. But to answer your question, the Saturnists can protect you. How long do you think you'd last on your own with both Praetorians and Umbra chasing you?"

We'd live longer lives staying right here, Kaeso thought. But neither was he eager to jump into the arms of a third group that he thought just a few minutes ago was made up of crackpots at best, seditionists at worst.

"We've become good at protecting ourselves," Nestor went on. "We have colonies in the Lost Worlds and in Roman space. We've even hid from Umbra, which is no small feat."

"So you can protect us," Kaeso said. "What else?"

"My, you are greedy, Centuriae."

"Nestor, you've been a part of this crew for two years. Aren't you the least bit concerned for Dariya?"

Nestor's eyes softened, and for the first time since he revealed what he was, he turned away from Kaeso. "Of course I'm concerned," he said. "This crew is family to me just as they are to you." He looked back. "That is why you must give the boy to the Saturnists. If you give him to Umbra, they will hide him in a hole so deep he'll never be found. Then they will kill you. You know this."

"Enough," Lucia said, staring at Nestor. "The things you're saying... What proof do you have? How can we believe anything you say?" She looked at Kaeso. "Either of you?"

Kaeso realized how hard this must be for his crew to accept. He was used to outlandish stories, since he'd seen and done outlandish things with Umbra. It was easier for him to accept the plausibility of Nestor's stories. Daryush wasn't Roman, so these revelations did not seem to bother him, except where it concerned Dariya. For Lucia and Blaesus, however, Nestor's allegations struck at their identity.

Nestor regarded her sympathetically. "I know this is all hard to take, and there's nothing I can say that will make you believe me. If anything, you should trust the fact that Kaeso can corroborate much of my story."

Kaeso shook his head. "Much of what you just said is news to me, as well. How do I know you're not a Roman agent? An Umbra Ancile? A freelancer for the Zhonguo? You could be anybody, Nestor Samaras. If that's your real name."

Nestor smiled sadly. "It is not the name I was born with, but it is my name for now."

"I agree with Lucia," Blaesus said. "How can we trust you both now? Seems I don't know either of you."

Kaeso wanted to protest that the implant, and the threat of immediate death to anyone who learned about Umbra, always prevented him from revealing his past. But he knew mere words could not gain back trust. He spent the last six years building that trust with his crew. He had just destroyed it in the last six days.

Nestor stared at his hands. His eyes suggested he struggled with the same dilemma as Kaeso. Kaeso didn't know if he believed Nestor's story, but he would have believed anything said by the Nestor he knew fifteen minutes ago.

"Remember last year," Kaeso said, breaking the silence, "that courier job for Salisius?"

Nestor, Lucia, and Blaesus looked at each other and then at Kaeso.

It was supposed to be simple job: pick up a small package of *kriat* tusk powder from Salisius's covert lab in the mountains of a moon orbiting the Lost World of Titanus, then transport it to a Roman patrician vacationing on a beach on Titanus. *Kriat* tusk powder was illegal on Titanus due to its narcotic effects, so Salisius couldn't very well mail it to the patrician.

There were no landing sites near the lab, so Kaeso landed *Caduceus* at the foot of the mountain nearby. Lucia volunteered for the hike up the mountain path to Salisius's lab, and Nestor offered to go with her. On the way Lucia broke her leg in a fall off a ledge, where she caught a branch and hung on for her life. Below her was a hundred foot drop where she would have died if she let go.

"Do you remember what Nestor did?" Kaeso asked Lucia.

She nodded.

"He climbed down that rocky hill without a rope and pulled you off that ledge," Kaeso said. "Blaesus, remember two years ago when you caught the furies pox on Concentus?"

Blaesus paled. "How could I forget?"

"Nestor stayed in the quarantine zone with you on the planet until you recovered."

"Where," Blaesus said, grinning at Nestor, "he caught the pox himself. I returned the favor by entertaining him while he recovered."

"I would've recovered much faster if not for your polemics on the virtues of Republican rule," Nestor said, smiling back at Blaesus.

"My point," Kaeso said, "is that we *do* know each other. Nestor has had ample opportunity to cause us harm, through not only his actions but inactions too. But as long as I've known him, he's only risked his life for us all. He didn't have to risk death to climb down that hill and pull you up, Lucia."

"I ordered him not to," Lucia said quietly. "Just shows he doesn't know how to take orders." A small grin tugged at the corner of her mouth.

"And he didn't have to listen to your complaining, Blaesus," Kaeso said.

"I was a model patient," Blaesus said, his chin up. Then he shrugged and said, "I *may* have uttered a mild criticism here and there, but I was very brave overall." When Nestor snorted, Blaesus frowned. "I had black pustules covering my entire body for a week. Let that happen to you, Centuriae, and see how well you stay calm."

Nestor said, "I appreciate what you're doing, Centuriae. What you said of me can also be said of you. You've risked life and pain for us as well." Nestor looked from Daryush to Blaesus to Lucia. "We all have secrets, but that does not change who we are. My secrets have *never* prevented me from doing my duties as a member of this crew. It won't now. All I'm giving you now are options."

Blaesus sighed, and looked from Daryush to Lucia. Daryush simply shrugged, while Lucia rolled her eyes.

"So what do we do?" she asked.

Tension seemed to leave the room, and the crew turned to Kaeso as if he was about to brief them on another job. It was the happiest feeling he'd had in a long time.

Don't begin to consider staying, you fool. You're not a centuriae.

A shadow fell over Kaeso's heart just as he was getting used to connecting with his crew again. Umbra was where he belonged. Umbra was what he was good at. *You'll get these people killed if you keep leading them.*

Lucia, Blaesus, Daryush, and even Nestor turned to him expectantly, waiting for his orders. Their expressions said they still trusted him to get them through anything.

What will happen when I abandon them?

He shook those thoughts from his mind. He had too much to do to submit to his doubts right now. Ancilia never doubted their abilities or the mission. It was time he remembered what he was.

"First," Kaeso said, "we get the engines running. Daryush, you've worked with the Navigator. Can you do it without him?"

Daryush's eyes grew wide. He licked his lips, then gave a slow shrug.

"Can any of us help you?" Kaeso asked. "We can't get to Terra much less anywhere else until those engines work."

Daryush nodded again, then patted his chest to indicate he could do it.

"And our Umbra friend?" Blaesus asked. "He won't be happy when he wakes up. Does he have any secret god-like powers we should know about?"

"He's not a god," Kaeso said. "He's just a man."

"Considering the stories you and Nestor just told us," Blaesus said, "I'm not taking anything for granted."

"Technology and the Muses give him certain advantages," Kaeso said, "but he can be hurt and killed. And to answer your first question, we'll have to wait until he wakes up."

Lucia said, "We should figure it out now."

Her grim face told Kaeso what she had in mind. Kaeso's reactivated implant gave him many of those advantages he just mentioned to Blaesus, but it also came with rules. Number one, he could not harm a Vessel, nor allow a Vessel to be harmed if he could prevent it. His implant's punishment for violating that rule would make the concealment protocols seem like a minor headache.

"We will keep him locked up if we have to."

"But how can we trust him," Lucia asked, "especially after what I did? I'd hold a grudge."

"He's a Vessel," Kaeso said.

When she shook her head in confusion, he forgot that simple declaration had no meaning to Lucia.

"Vessels will do anything the Muses want them to. The Muses don't think as individuals. Their intelligence comes from the combined thoughts of every virus cell in their strain throughout the universe, no matter how far apart they are. They could care less about an individual Vessel. If they decide that it's more important for the Navigator to help us—despite the fact you shot him—then the Navigator will cheerfully help us."

"If they don't want him to help us?" Lucia asked. "We keep him locked up, he could still pass information to them. They'd still know where he is. I'm sorry, sir, but I don't think we can trust him even if he says he'll help."

Kaeso knew Lucia was right, but he also knew he could never allow them to throw Galeo out the airlock. It was partly because of the implant, but Galeo was also an old friend and former mentor. He wouldn't kill Galeo just because he didn't trust him, not while he had a shred of honor left in him.

"We keep him locked up, and that's final. Once the engines are fixed, and we find a nice remote planet in the outback, we'll dump him off there. Satisfied?"

Lucia hesitated, but then nodded.

"All right," Kaeso said. "Daryush, you will get those engines running. Lucia, help him if he needs it. Nestor and Blaesus, you two and I will figure out how in Hades we're going to get the Consul's son off Terra."

"And then?" Nestor asked.

Kaeso paused. "Can we agree the best thing right now is to get the boy?"

The Greek nodded slowly, keeping his gaze locked with Kaeso's.

"Then we concentrate on that for now."

Nestor frowned, but didn't say anything.

As his crew hurried off to their tasks, Kaeso felt like he had a purpose and a mission. A mission that did not make him feel used, and potentially discarded afterwards. He was working for himself and his crew, just as he had before.

And the comfort of that role disturbed him.

Chapter Twenty-Nine

Ocella was staring into the darkness, her back against a plastic wine barrel and the boy leaning against her, when she heard a scrape at the door. She sat up, and Cordus awoke with a start. When the door opened, she squinted against the light from the hallway. A large man stood in the door, his silhouette blocking most of it. Two other men stood behind him, their hands resting on the pistols in the holsters around their chests.

"The *domina* wants to see you," said the man in the door.

She had no idea how long she and Cordus had been in the room, but she knew it was hours. She was hungry and had a terrible urge to urinate. She assumed Cordus felt the same.

She stood on cramped legs and then helped Cordus up.

"Just you," the man said.

Cordus looked up at her, his eyes wide.

"It'll be fine," she assured him.

Cordus's face said he didn't believe her. She turned to the man in the door. "Can you at least take him to the bathroom? Otherwise he's going to piss all over your *domina's* wine."

The man frowned at her. Then he turned to the man behind him and nodded to Cordus. The man brushed past the larger man and grabbed Cordus's arm. Cordus yanked it free and said, "I need no assistance walking."

Ocella hid a smile.

"So sorry, *highness*," the man said, then grabbed his arm again and pulled him from the room. Ocella jumped forward, but the man in the door put a hand on her chest.

"Don't be stupid," he said. "He's going to the bathroom, like you asked."

"Make sure your dog doesn't hurt him, all right?"

The man grunted, then said, "Let's go."

The man led her up the stairs, through the kitchen, and out the back door. It was night, and the city lights made the sky glow orange beneath a canopy of clouds. Her captor took her to a van with its engine running, its side door open. Gaia Julius sat in the passenger's seat with her window down.

"We're going for a ride, Ancile," Gaia said.

Ocella stopped. "Not without Cordus."

"He'll be fine. Get in."

When Ocella didn't move, Gaia said, "I'd rather not force you."

Ocella jerked her arm free and smashed her elbow into the face of the man holding her. He stumbled back, blood spurting from his broken nose. She kicked the other man in the crotch, and he fell to the ground gasping. The third man drew a jolt gun and jabbed the prongs into Ocella's chest. White-hot pain screamed from every nerve in her body. Her muscles seized, and the world turned black before she fell to the ground.

Ocella came to slowly. She felt the fire in her muscles before she even opened her eyes. She blinked away the cloudiness over her vision.

She was in the van strapped to a heavy wooden chair that was bolted to the metal floor. She was completely naked. Her arms were fastened to the armrests, and her ankles to the base of the chair. A surge of fear banished Ocella's grogginess. She jerked at the straps, but they did not give.

"Good, you're awake."

The Julii matron sat on the floor next to Ocella, tapping on a tabulari in her lap. The flat device showed a column of streaming numbers on the display's left side, and a human outline on the right.

Without looking up, Gaia said, "It's a wonder you've survived this long, dear. You're being tracked."

It confirmed Ocella's own suspicions, but she did not want to take the Julii matron's word without proof.

"How?" Ocella asked with a hoarse voice.

"Your implant was my guess."

Ocella frowned. Scaurus's device, coupled with Cordus's talents, should have deactivated her implant. She had not been able to access it since that day. How could it still produce a signal?

"But when I tried to deactivate it myself," Gaia continued, "I found it was already dead. Nevertheless, you're emitting a signal similar to an implant's."

Ocella tried to keep calm and not let the van's leering driver bother her. His eyes wandered over her body from his rearview mirror.

"We were careful leaving the Consular Palace," she said. "And even if we had trackers in our clothes, we destroyed them the moment we left the palace."

"Your clothes were clean," Gaia said. Then she wrinkled her nose. "Of trackers, at least. No, the signal I'm picking up is either on your skin or inside you. The chair you're sitting in will tell me where it is."

"You could have told me this earlier," Ocella growled.

"I was about to before you assaulted my men," Gaia said. She put a small web of wires over Ocella's head that reminded her of the webbing Scaurus had used to deactivate her implant. "Of course, I wasn't sure how you'd react to getting strapped naked to a chair. Not to mention the discomfort of this procedure."

"I'd have reacted better if I didn't think your goons were about to rape me." Ocella eyed the driver again, who continued to stare at her with hooded eyes.

"Ah, forgive me," Gaia said. "We had just finished buckling you in when you woke up. Tiberius, hand me the blanket."

The man in the front passenger seat handed Gaia a rough blanket, which Gaia draped over Ocella. The driver's eyes in the rearview mirror looked disappointed as he turned back to the road.

"Satisfied?"

Ocella ignored the question. "What are you going to do?"

"We had to remove your clothes to ensure they were not tracked. We did the same to the boy."

Ocella gave an involuntary jerk in her straps. "If you hurt him—"

"He's in a bath right now. We took his clothes while he soaked, and he'll get a fresh set once he's done. He's rather enjoying it, so relax. I assume it's been a long time since his highness's last bath."

Gaia turned back to her tabulari and moved some sliders. "Now we need to find that tracker. Unless you'd prefer to tell me where it is."

"If I have one, I have no idea where it is."

"Hmm," Gaia said, returning to her tabulari. "In that case, please relax your muscles. This won't hurt as bad as the jolt gun but it's not going to be pleasant either. Shall we begin?"

"Do I have a choice?"

"Not if you want live," Gaia said. She moved some sliders on the tabulari keyboard, and the human outline on the screen began to pulse green.

Ocella ground her teeth as a burning sensation began at her scalp. It felt like a thin, hot line moving down her head, neck, and torso. Above and below the line there was no pain, but everything that line touched was on fire. It crawled down her abdomen and legs. Gaia was right that the pain was nothing like the jolt gun, but Ocella wished it would end soon. When it reached the tips of her toes, she exhaled with relief.

Then the line moved back up her feet. She tensed her already aching muscles as the line of pain made the return trip up her legs, torso, and then head. She relaxed a bit when it stopped at her scalp.

Ocella glanced at the tabulari display on Gaia's lap.

"There," Gaia said. "The tracker is on the back of your neck. On the skin."

A purple dot pulsed on the neck of the human outline.

"How?" Ocella said.

She had ensured she was clean of trackers when she left the Consular Palace, and once again when she and Cordus discarded their clothes after they escaped. Scaurus had ran his own scans to ensure they were not tracked. Someone in the crowds Ocella and Cordus passed through over the past three weeks must have attached the trackers.

"Lean your neck forward," Gaia said. When Ocella did so, Gaia's cold fingers ran up and down the back of her neck. Ocella felt something no larger than a fingertip blocking Gaia's touch. Gaia scratched at the spot, and a layer of adhesive peeled off the back of Ocella's neck.

Gaia held the tracker in front of Ocella. It was a piece of clear plastic, with no visible circuitry. It was the most sophisticated Roman tracker she'd ever seen.

"This little thing was sending Muse-based signals," Gaia said. "Did you give this to them?"

"Absolutely not," Ocella said, her mind racing.

How could the Romans have created something like this so soon? Cordus assured her the Romans did not possess any

Muse-based com besides that which exists between one Vessel and another. Did they get it from the Ancilia they captured? Ocella felt sick, her nakedness forgotten. It tore Ocella apart to know she had doomed her former colleagues on Terra. They did what they thought was right, just as she did for years before she met Cordus. But keeping Cordus away from any organization controlled by a Muse strain was far more important than the lives of several dozen Ancilia. At least that's what she kept telling herself.

"Then how did they get it?" Gaia asked, still holding the tracker before Ocella.

"I don't know," Ocella answered truthfully. "Look, I don't care what you do to me. Just don't give the boy to the Romans. Or to Umbra. I have money."

Gaia laughed. "Do you think I need money? My family may be social outcasts, but we are still quite wealthy." Her smile melted. "If you don't want me handing the boy over to the Romans or to Umbra, then who *should* I give him to? I certainly can't adopt him."

Ocella studied her. It was time to see just whose side Gaia Julius was on. "Scaurus said you could be trusted."

Her left eye twitched, something Ocella would have missed if she had blinked. "Scaurus. Should I know that name?"

"He was Prefect of the Praetorian Guard twenty years ago."

"Ah, yes," Gaia said. "I haven't talked to him in years. How is he?"

"Dead."

Gaia's left eye twitched again. "Unfortunate. He was a Roman patriot. What happened?"

"It's a long story, but he said you were...of like minds when it came to the Romans and the Liberti."

Gaia folded her arms. "If Scaurus said we were "of like minds", then he must have explained what our similar opinions were, did he not? Because I'm confused as to why the former Prefect of the Praetorian Guard would mention my name to you."

"I'd be more comfortable talking if I was out of this chair," Ocella said. "You found the tracker."

Gaia smiled and leaned forward. "Tell me more about Scaurus and I'll consider it."

"He was a Saturnist," Ocella said.

Gaia raised an eyebrow. "Well, that is surprising, considering the level he reached within the Guard. So he accused me of being a Saturnist, is that it?"

Ocella stared at Gaia. "Aren't you?"

"Saturnists are killed on the spot in both Roman and Liberti space. It's the one thing on which both nations seem to agree. Why would I admit to you the one crime that would negate my rights as a citizen?"

"Do you think I'm a Roman spy after I just kidnapped the Consular Heir? Do you think I'm still Umbra after I single-handedly destroyed their Terran corps? The Saturnists are my only hope to get Cordus to safety."

"You've fallen far from your Umbra loyalties, my dear," Gaia said. "What made you defy years of Umbra training? What turned you?"

"Unshackle me and I'll consider telling you."

Gaia watched the streets of Roma roll by the van's darkened windows. Ocella noticed they were in the Suburba—small discount shops lined the streets along with cheap, fastfood taverns. The people were not as finely dressed as the residents of the Palatine.

"So Scaurus told you I could be trusted," Gaia said without looking at Ocella. "Trusted to do what?"

"This sparring wastes time we don't have," Ocella said. "Are you, or are you not a Saturnist?"

Gaia sighed. "As I understand it, a Saturnist would be careful to whom she admits that sort of affiliation."

Gaia stared at Ocella, and she got the impression Gaia waited for—and wanted—Ocella to say more. Ocella had gambled when she mentioned Scaurus. *The Julii have been a strong friend of my family since the days of Caesar,* Scaurus had told her the day she and Cordus arrived at his door. She assumed that friendship, and the fact Scaurus kept a bust of Caesar in his entry, meant the Julii were also Saturnists.

Gaia's behavior implied she knew Scaurus as more than the former Prefect of the Praetorian Guard. But was *Gaia* a Saturnist? Was she waiting for a secret code word? Some gesture that Saturnists gave to each other to identify themselves? Ocella racked her mind thinking of every conversation with Scaurus, searched for a clue that would—

She looked up at Gaia. "Scaurus kept a bust of Gaius Julius Caesar and Marcus Tullius Cicero in his entry way."

Gaia smiled, relief softening her hard eyes. "Really? And what did he say about them?"

"That Caesar reminded him of Roma's excess, and that Cicero reminded him to laugh."

Gaia exhaled. She leaned down and unbuckled the shackles around Ocella's ankles and then her wrists. Ocella wrapped the blanket around her body and then rubbed her wrists where the straps had chafed.

"So you are a Saturnist," Ocella said.

Gaia's smile turned to a sad frown. "My family has been Saturnist for as long as Scaurus's. It grieves me to know he is dead. How did it happen?"

Ocella explained how she and Cordus had fled to Scaurus's home, where he hid them in his secret basement for two weeks. She described the night the Praetorians arrived.

Gaia stared at the Umbra device she'd used on Ocella, her eyes not really seeing it. "He killed himself. He knew how the Praetorians worked. He knew he'd break eventually."

"So you can get Cordus off Terra?" Ocella asked.

"I will try. First we need to get you and the boy to a safe place. You were tracked to my cafe. The Praetorians will be watching it soon, if not already." Gaia inspected Ocella's hair. "Your hair is already too short for cutting, but we could dye it."

"I already have," Ocella said, touching her short brown hair. It was one of the first things she did when she and Cordus arrived at Scaurus's safe house. "It used to be black."

Gaia sighed. "Not much else we can do with your Indian skin tone, then, and not attract attention. You will wear your hooded cloak, and I'll get you some clothes once we arrive at the safe house."

"Will you bring Cordus there?" Ocella grew more anxious every moment the boy was out of her sight.

Gaia nodded. "After we've made sure he has no trackers as well."

Ocella frowned at the thought of Cordus enduring the scan, but she knew it had to be done. She just wished she could be with him when they did it.

"Another thing," Gaia said. "Except for Tiberius and Brocchus up front, my employees don't know I'm a Saturnist. They think I'm an Umbra sleeper agent. Which in most respects I am. I would appreciate if you'd keep the Saturnism to yourself. It could make things difficult if they knew. Their morale is not the greatest right now."

"What's wrong with the morale of your men?"

"My men blame you for the war with Libertus. It was all I could do to keep them from killing you. And now a new development. The government has officially admitted the Consular Heir was kidnapped. The Consul and the Collegia Pontificis have been on the bands for the last few hours demanding that Liberti agents return the Heir. If he's not in Roman hands within two days, they will slag Libertus."

CHAPTER THIRTY

Kaeso's collar com chimed.
"He's awake," Nestor said.
"I'll be right down."
Kaeso stood up from his command couch. Lucia sat in her pilot's couch reviewing Daryush's navigation charts. She didn't look up.
"Time to see if he'll help us," Kaeso said. When she ignored him, Kaeso turned and descended the ladder to the crew deck.

Lucia had done her job as she and the crew had agreed to yesterday, but she still didn't trust him, Nestor, and especially Galeo. He remembered how long it took her to integrate with the crew when she first came aboard. She was always professional in her duties, but she had kept her distance emotionally, staying in her quarters when the rest of the crew visited taverns on whatever planet they did business. It was only in the last six months that she dropped her shields and began trusting the crew. Kaeso and Nestor had just destroyed that, and he could not blame her for her wariness.

But Kaeso had no time for her to return to her shell. He needed his trierarch at his side, running the ship smoothly, anticipating his needs and orders. He needed that more than ever, and he hoped Lucia understood that.

Kaeso landed on the crew deck and glanced down the ladder to the engine room. Daryush's shadow moved about as the big Persian tried to figure out the new way line drive. He had made great strides in the last twenty-four hours in deciphering the systems, but it was not fast enough. At this rate it would be another few days before Daryush figured out how to find a quantum way line, much less get *Caduceus* to ride one to Terra. They didn't have a few more days. Libertus was under siege and Ocella was stuck in Roma with the Consular Heir. Every moment they wasted was another moment the Romans could win.

Kaeso entered the ship's small infirmary. Galeo lay strapped to a bunk, a sensor cuff wrapped around his arm. Nestor was checking the monitor next to Galeo. The Vessel was shirtless, with fresh white bandages wrapped around his abdomen and chest. There were no bloodstains from the wound just below his left lung. The Umbra cloak still functioned, displaying the pale, Germanic complexion. But patches of olive skin peeked from where the cloak was torn near the bandages.

Galeo's eyes opened, and they followed Kaeso when he entered the room. Galeo had no expression and regarded Kaeso as if studying a blemish on the wall.

"He's still groggy," Nestor said, "but the wound is almost healed. I changed his bandages just before he awoke, and the hole is only a scab now."

Kaeso nodded. "Give us a moment, Medicus."

Nestor hesitated. "Centuriae, he's a Vessel who happened to reactivate your implant just before he was shot."

Galeo eye's darted from Kaeso to Nestor, and then slowly returned to Kaeso. Galeo sighed, his gaze turning sad.

"He can't control my mind, if that's what you're thinking. Please close the hatch when you leave, Medicus."

Nestor frowned, then turned and left the room, shutting the hatch behind him.

"You told them everything," Galeo said in a weak voice. "I didn't think you would."

Kaeso nodded. "How could I not with your Umbra cloak hanging open. I had no idea your true skin was so tan."

"Kaeso."

"My crew is safe. That's the deal we made, right? I help you get the boy, and you keep Umbra away from my crew. That's the deal *you* forced me to make."

"The deal stands," Galeo said. "The Muses never break a contract." Galeo stared at him through half-closed eyelids. "Does your crew know about Petra and Claudia? You seem to have told them everything else."

Kaeso tensed at the sudden question. "No. They don't need to know."

"Why not? They're the reasons you joined Umbra in the first place."

"I said they don't need to know." Kaeso saw no reason to reveal his greatest pain and his greatest shame.

"We need your help with the engines," Kaeso said, bringing the conversation back to what he intended. "It'll take Daryush a week to figure the damned things out. We don't have a week."

"No we don't." Galeo moved against the straps holding him in the bunk. "Revenge for me strapping *you* in?"

"Precaution," Kaeso said. He moved to Galeo's side and unbuckled the straps. "Lucia doesn't seem to trust you."

"Ah," Galeo said, sitting up slowly. "How is Lucia? I hope she at least cleaned my blood from the engine room floor."

"Nestor did that." Kaeso tossed one of Nestor's green tunics to Galeo, who eased it over his bandaged chest. He winced as he pushed his left arm through, so Kaeso helped him. "Did you know he's a Saturinst?"

"Yes."

Kaeso looked at Galeo. He hoped the revelation would throw Galeo off balance.

"Come now," Galeo said, "we knew every little secret about your crew days before we met at Menota. You know how it's done."

"Why didn't you take Nestor out then? I thought Saturnists were killed on sight."

Galeo winced as he slipped on the green pants. "Saturnists are no longer a threat. We've done a good job marginalizing them. We needed him as part of your crew more than we needed him dead."

"Another expendable crewman."

Galeo was silent as he looked for his shoes.

"So only the Romans fear Saturnists now," Kaeso said, picking up Galeo's bloody shoes from near the hatch and handing them to him.

"Why would the Romans fear them?" Galeo asked. Galeo didn't seem surprised at Kaeso's question.

"Maybe because the Romans are also infected with the Muses."

Galeo chuckled. "You've been listening to Nestor too much."

"Maybe," Kaeso said. "But it got me thinking. Why is it so important that the Consular Heir come to Libertus?"

"You really have to ask? He's the Consular Heir. He knows things."

"He's a twelve-year-old boy. What's he know that's so damned important to Libertus? And why would Libertus risk open war with Roma to get him?"

Galeo rolled his eyes. "Do you want me to fix these engines, or do you want to talk mythology all day?"

"Seems to me that it's not what the boy *knows* that's so important. It's what he *is*."

"'What he is?'" Galeo said, then laughed. "Don't tell me you think he's a god?"

"No. But maybe he's a cure."

"Our sources say he knows something about a cure for the Cariosus," Galeo said, "not that he *is* the cure. How could a *boy* be a cure for anything?"

Galeo is either very good at this or he actually believes what he's saying, Kaeso thought. He doubted he'd get Galeo to admit anything. But if Nestor's allegations were true, and the Romans were infected with a different Muse strain, was it possible Umbra knew nothing about it? Kaeso didn't think so. Umbra had Ancilia in every corner of Roman power centers. If a Roman Muse strain existed, Umbra knew about it.

If Nestor's claims were true, that is.

Kaeso stared into Galeo's Umbra cloaked eyes. "Never mind. I'm sure it's all a story."

Galeo grunted. "Look, the boy is important, but he's just a boy. He's not a god. He simply has information that's important, not to mention the priceless value of him publicly defecting to Libertus."

"That's it?"

"Can we get started on these engines?"

You never denied it, old friend.

Kaeso nodded, then motioned Galeo toward the infirmary hatch.

"Oh, before we go," Galeo said. "Your implant."

Kaeso frowned and then nodded. He knew this was coming once Galeo woke up. He had asked for his implant's reactivation to verify the Muses had approved Galeo's contract, but he had also wanted a brief taste of his old life. He needed the power, wisdom, and confidence it gave him more than ever now. It grieved him to lose it again, and he worried he couldn't complete the mission without it.

However, with all he learned in the last few days, he wasn't sure he wanted the strings that came with it.

"Get Nestor this time," Kaeso said as he lay down on the bunk. "I *want* to be knocked out."

Galeo smiled. "Wise choice."

Chapter Thirty-One

Kaeso strapped himself into the command couch and then tapped his collar com.

"All crew to your delta couches for way line jump."

The crew finished numerous repairs the previous day, so they were all anxious to leave whatever corner of the universe they were in. Even if it meant going to Terra.

Galeo had the engines running two hours after waking up. Kaeso praised Daryush, who did most of the work calibrating the systems while Galeo was unconscious. Galeo doubted Kaeso's praise, but was surprised when he saw the progress and complimented the Persian, even half-jokingly offering Daryush a job with Umbra. Daryush looked horrified at the prospect, which drew a proud smile from Kaeso.

Kaeso glanced outside the command deck window at the green gas giant they'd found in this unknown system. Though *Caduceus* was more than 500,000 leagues from the planet, the giant was a swirling green wall to the left of the command window. Galeo said its quantum way lines were strong and that it would give them a clear passage to Pandisa, a Lost World two alpha way line jumps from Libertus. Galeo wanted *Caduceus* to leave him there, where he would rendezvous with other Umbra Vessels on the planet.

Kaeso watched his tabulari lights turn green as his crew secured themselves in their delta couches. Kaeso noticed Flamma's light was still off and for an instant wanted to call him. Then he remembered the young Egyptian's body was in the Cargo Two freezer. A cold lump grew in Kaeso's throat. Before he allowed the guilt to consume him, he focused on the last remaining red light. Kaeso was about to call Nestor when the medicus hurried up the command deck ladder. He climbed with one hand, while the other juggled the way line sacrifice bowl and a knife.

"Nestor, we ate the last chicken yesterday," Kaeso said.

"I know," he said, arranging his ritual supplies on his cutting board. "I'm not using a chicken."

He took the knife in his right hand and ran the edge down his left palm. A bright line of blood gushed from the wound.

"Nestor!" Lucia cried.

"We didn't make a sacrifice on our last jump, and look what happened," Nestor said, squeezing his left hand over the bowl. Scarlet blood dripped from his fist into the pewter bowl. "The gods require a blood sacrifice for way line jumps. I hope *my* blood satisfies them."

Lucia grunted, and shook her head.

Kaeso frowned at him. "If this boy is what you say he is, then I think the gods will give you safe way line passage your whole life."

Nestor grinned. "Let us pray that is so."

Nestor closed his eyes and chanted way line passage prayers. When he finished, he took a skin glue tube from his pocket and squeezed the clear gel into the wound. He wrapped his hand in gauze, taped it tight with practiced precision, and then strapped himself into his couch.

Kaeso tapped his collar com. "Galeo, are the coordinates set?"

"They should be on your tabulari now," Galeo said from his engine room couch.

Though unrecognizable to Kaeso, the quantum way line coordinates streamed down his tabulari display, and he transferred them to Lucia's station.

"Medicus, engage delta sleep," Kaeso said.

"Acknowledged," Nestor said.

Kaeso watched Galeo's delta indicator until it turned green. Kaeso waited another moment and then tapped his collar com. "Daryush, is Galeo asleep?"

The Persian grunted an affirmative from the engine room.

Kaeso opened another file on his tabulari, this one with the coordinates he, Daryush, and Blaesus worked out while Galeo was still unconscious. Though they weren't 100% confident in their accuracy, they were reasonably sure the coordinates would take them where they wanted. And it was not Pandisa.

Kaeso transferred the coordinates to Lucia's pilot tabulari, who entered them into the quantum way line jump program. She smiled as she did so. "This'll be fun when he wakes up."

Kaeso said, "Medicus, engage delta sleep for the crew. For real, this time."

"Engaging delta sleep now," Nestor said. "For real this time."

Kaeso saw Lucia's eyes close and her body slump into her couch. He checked his tabulari. Daryush and Blaesus also slept.

"Transferring delta control to you, Centuriae," Nestor said formally.

"Acknowledged. See you on the other side, Medicus."

Kaeso moved Nestor's slider on his tabulari, and Nestor's delta indicator turn green. Kaeso started the quantum way line jump countdown, watching the numbers tick down to five seconds. He blinked...

...and faced another swirling gas giant through the command deck window. This one had red, brown, and pink bands, along with a large red storm in the lower hemisphere. It had been years since he'd last seen the planet Jupiter.

Lucia was awake and already running diagnostics. "Ship integrity normal, position two light-seconds from Jupiter." She looked at Kaeso. "Right where you wanted us."

Kaeso exhaled. "I love these engines."

Panicked shouts issued from his collar com. "Kaeso, what have you done! Why did you take us to Jupiter? We were supposed to go to Pandisa!"

Lucia smirked. "Uh-oh."

Kaeso tapped his collar com. "Calm down, Galeo, I'll be down in a second."

"You damn well better explain," Galeo yelled, "because you may have just killed us all!"

Kaeso unstrapped himself from his couch and went to the ladder behind the command deck. Nestor said, "Do you want me to go with you?"

Kaeso scowled. "I'm Centuriae. It's my duty to take care of unruly passengers."

Nestor smiled, then turned to his tabulari displays.

When Kaeso entered the engine room, Galeo was out of his delta couch and frantically working the interface on the main tabulari. From what Kaeso could see, Galeo was scanning for ships in the Jupiter system. Roman Eagles didn't worry Kaeso since there was no alpha way line near Jupiter. Foreign threats only came from the alpha way line orbiting Terra, so there was no reason for Roman patrols out here other than policing the system's gas and mining guilds. And those guilds had their own security, so *Caduceus* would likely be ignored unless they got in a mining ship's way.

Daryush stood behind Galeo. The Persian eyed Kaeso, and shrugged.

"Go check on Dariya," Kaeso said. Daryush frowned, then left the engine room.

Galeo spun around. Not even the Umbra cloak could hide his anger and fear. His normally pale cheeks and forehead were tinged red. If the Umbra cloak showed Galeo's anger, then Kaeso knew his plan had struck home.

"Why did you bring us here?" Galeo yelled. "Just what are you trying to prove?"

"I want answers," Kaeso said. "I don't like being lied to and I don't like going into a mission without all the facts. You're holding out on me, Galeo, and I want to know why."

"You're talking nonsense, Kaeso!"

"Then why are you so scared? Aren't Vessels always in control?"

Galeo snapped his mouth closed and put greater effort into calming his Umbra cloak features. The redness on his face subsided, the snarl around his mouth relaxed, and he took on the look of someone mildly put out by a flight delay.

But the calm demeanor did not hide the rage in Galeo's voice. "You can't land on Terra with me, you fool! Why do you think we wanted *you* to go? No Vessel can go to Terra because of what your old lover did."

"No Vessel has *ever* gone to Terra," Kaeso said. "I want to know why. There is a Vessel on almost every human world *except* Terra. Only Ancilia are placed there. Terra is the capital of the Roman Republic, humanity's birthplace. Seems the Muses would be interested in seeing it."

Galeo closed his eyes and shook his head, his control slipping again. "You don't know what you're doing..."

"Then tell me. Once you do, I'll take you to Pandisa. But your explanation better make sense."

Galeo considered Kaeso, fear and doubt warring on his face. "I...I can't..."

Kaeso grabbed Galeo's shoulders and looked into his red-rimmed eyes. "Does a Roman Muse strain exist?"

Galeo stared at Kaeso, trembling in Kaeso's grip. "Kaeso...I...they..."

Galeo jerked violently, and then his eyes rolled up into his head. Kaeso tapped his collar com. "Nestor, engine room, now!"

Kaeso laid Galeo on his back, and tried to keep him still, but the seizure made Galeo bang his head repeatedly against the floor.

Kaeso put all his weight into holding Galeo's shoulders. Nestor came from behind and said, "Hold his head!"

Kaeso jumped toward Galeo's head and held it tight while the rest of Galeo's body spasmed and flailed. Galeo suddenly arched his back high, then a gurgle escaped his throat and bloody spittle seeped from the corner of his mouth.

"He can't die!" Kaeso said.

"We have to let the seizure pass. There's nothing we can do."

Kaeso clenched his teeth in impotent fury. Eventually the spasms slowed and Galeo grew still. His pupils rolled back down, but with a dead man's glassy stare. Nestor put his fingers on Galeo's neck, then put his ear to Galeo's mouth. He knelt beside Galeo and started chest compressions.

Kaeso stood and slammed his hands against the bulkhead. This wasn't supposed to happen. He only wanted to scare Galeo into admitting what he knew about the Muses and Roma. He thought potential capture would frighten Galeo so much that he'd tell Kaeso everything. And Kaeso believed Galeo was going to talk, but he had no idea the Muses would try to kill Galeo before he could. He'd never heard of a case where the Muses killed their Vessel, for that would mean the Muses in the Vessel would also die.

Perhaps that was the point. Rather than suffer capture by another strain, or admit another strain existed, the Muses in Galeo chose death.

After several minutes of chest compressions, Nestor sat back and sighed. Galeo's eyes stared at the ceiling, and his chest was still.

"I'm sorry, Centuriae," Nestor said, standing up. "There was nothing—"

Nestor's eyes widened as he looked down at Galeo. Where once there was a man with blond hair and pale skin, now lay a human form whose skin and head was covered in a fine silvery mesh. The mesh disintegrated into an ashy substance that sloughed off Galeo's naked body. It floated away in the engine room's mild air currents. Within minutes, not even the ash would exist.

Kaeso saw his former mentor's face for the first time. He appeared a few years older than Kaeso, with black hair and olive skin. Two scars ran down his left cheek, as if from a wild animal. Galeo never mentioned such an attack. Kaeso tried to ignore the accusing brown eyes that stared at him.

"What happened to his cloak?" Nestor asked, bending down next to Kaeso.

"The implant powers it," Kaeso said thickly. "If the wearer dies, then the cloak and implants deactivate. Turn to ash." The implant in Galeo's brain, along with the Muses, had likely dissolved already into his cooling blood.

Nestor put a hand on Kaeso's shoulder. "He was your friend. I am sorry."

"They killed him," Kaeso said. "He was about to tell me everything, but they killed him. They killed themselves."

"Makes you wonder what they didn't want us to know."

Kaeso didn't respond. *Where did you get those scars?* It was a strange thing to wonder right now, but the scars reminded Kaeso that he really knew nothing about a man he called friend for almost ten years.

Reminded him that Umbra had no room for friendships.

Nestor asked, "What of the mission, Centuriae?"

Kaeso stood. "The mission is still on. The boy scares them. Both strains. That's why we need to get him before they do."

Kaeso and Nestor carried Galeo's body into Cargo Two and placed him in the same freezer where they had wrapped up Flamma's body. Kaeso gave both friends a long look before shutting the freezer door.

He also checked on Dariya, where she slept blissfully unaware of what happened the past few days. Her skin was pale, almost translucent, and it was not a function of the sleeper crib.

The Cariosus Muses were devouring Dariya cell by cell. The Roman Muses killed Flamma during their attack on Libertus. Now the Liberti Muses murdered Galeo. They were taking his friends, one by one.

It was time Kaeso Aemilius took things from them.

Chapter Thirty-Two

From his disguised taxi, Lepidus watched the woman and boy leave the Aeneas Cafe. They were both cloaked with their hoods up. The tracker Appius placed on the woman still functioned, but had had winked out for a moment and then came back. It concerned Lepidus, for he did not like surprises or events he could not explain. Everything had a reason. Even winks.

"I cannot believe Gaia Julius would help them," Appius said from the seat next to Lepidus.

"You didn't believe Scaurus would help them either, yet here we are."

"Scaurus was a washed up old man without friends," Appius said. "Gaia Julius is one of the wealthiest patricians in the city. Her family's only now gaining the respect it lost because of Octavian. Why would she throw it away?"

"Perhaps *because* it's taken her family a thousand years to regain that respect," Lepidus said. "Never underestimate human pride."

"Or perhaps the woman and boy simply wanted something to eat?"

"Dressed like they were? Doubtful. They'd attract too much attention among the bathed patrons. Ocella would find another Temple of Empanda first. No, Gaia Julius is a traitor. It feels right." He looked at Appius. "I've succeeded more when I act on my feelings rather than facts. Trust that. It's the gods communicating with you."

Appius frowned. "I thought the gods only talked to the Consul and the Collegia."

"Talk, yes," Lepidus said, "but there are more ways to communicate than words. Be mindful of the augurs around you, Appius. Be mindful of your feelings. Unlike the Consul and the Collegia, you and I are mortals. We cannot hear the gods directly. But they still show us the proper path if we see and listen."

Appius nodded. Lepidus told the boy things he should have already known, if not through the Pantheon *flamens* then through his own intuition. Appius just began his training, though. In time his intuition would attune to the will of the gods. It took Lepidus many years to open his mind to the gods, to accept the order of things. He was bound by honor and faith to obey the Consul and the Collegia, for they were infallible. Once he truly accepted that, he found the gods favored him with clear signs to guide his path. He served the gods and their Voices faithfully since the day he was punished for the Battle of Caan. Since that day, the gods showed him mercy by giving his family prosperity and granting him talents to protect and expand the glory and light that was the Republic.

Yes, if Appius followed Lepidus's instructions, he would know that joy and prosperity as well.

"If you're correct, sir," Appius said, "then Gaia Julius is the high-level traitor we've sought. Should we not arrest Ocella and the boy now? Not to mention Gaia Julius?"

Lepidus considered the same idea ever since they tracked the woman to the Aeneas Cafe. The wealth of the Julii could get Ocella and boy off-world. And while it was possible there were higher placed traitors, Lepidus didn't think he had time to root them all out before Ocella escaped. Besides, Gaia Julius's interrogation would reveal any other traitors she knew or suspected. Not to mention interrogations of the woman and the boy.

"Very well," Lepidus said. "Have the Praetorians secure the Aeneas Cafe and the house of Gaia Julius. If they find her there, they will keep her under guard until we arrive. You and I shall take the woman and boy."

Appius nodded and then gave orders into his com. The Praetorian centurions on the other side acknowledged the orders. Lepidus started the taxi and merged into the street traffic.

According to the tracker, the woman headed east on the Via Rumina. Lepidus drove the taxi to a parking lot a block ahead of where Ocella fled. Lepidus told Appius the plan, and the young man nodded his understanding.

Appius stepped out of the taxi and stood next to the door of a small bookshop. He pretended to browse the books and scrolls displayed in the window, but his eyes searched the reflection to his right, watching for the cloaked woman and boy.

Lepidus walked several dozen paces up the sidewalk in the direction where Ocella would approach. When he saw their hooded heads bobbing toward him on the crowded street, he stopped before a butcher's shop and examined the live eels swimming in a cloudy glass tank. The female attendant asked if she could help him. Lepidus asked her about the freshness of the eels, where they were caught, and whether they were free of the diseases that plagued the farmed eels last year. As the attendant answered his questions, Lepidus watched the reflection in the fish tank of two hooded figures passing behind him and toward Appius. Lepidus thanked the attendant for her time and fell in behind his prey, maintaining a comfortable distance of ten paces.

Ahead of the two, Appius's large frame turned away from the bookshop window and stood in the center of the tight alley. People flowed around him with annoyed glances, but he kept his eyes on the woman and boy approaching him.

When Ocella and the boy came within six paces of Appius, Lepidus called out, "Marcia Licinius Ocella."

The woman and boy continued on as if they didn't hear him. When Appius stood in front of them with a jolt gun in hand, they finally stopped. "Answer the man," he growled.

Her head swiveled from Appius to the boy and then to the street around them. Lepidus chose this spot because of its close confines. They could not retreat, they could not go forward, and the alley walls kept them from going left or right. They were trapped.

"Marcia Licinius Ocella," Lepidus said again, this time two paces from them. "We have questions for—"

The woman turned, lowered her hood, and said, "I'm sorry, *dominar*, are you talking to me?"

She was not Marcia Licinius. She was much older, her graying brown hair wrapped in a single braid. She was pale, with the complexion of a Norseman. The boy was probably her grandson. The same pale skin and light brown hair shown from beneath his hood.

"Who are you?" Lepidus asked, regaining his voice.

"I am Hestia Gruen and this is my grandson, Kel," the woman said, her eyes lowered but fearful. "We are slaves of Gaia Julius. We're delivering her post."

"Give it to me," Lepidus said.

The woman handed Lepidus a wrapped package, and Lepidus grabbed it. He waved his hand-held tracker over it, but the package was clean. He ran the tracker over Hestia Gruen's cloak as the woman tried to shrink away. Appius growled, "Don't move."

Lepidus found the tracking strip near the cloak's left sleeve. "Give me the cloak."

"*Dominar*, it's cold."

"Now, slave!"

The woman took off the cloak and handed it to Lepidus. He reached into the sleeve and found the sticky tracking strip. He held it up to his tracker, and the device gave off the telltale blips. He clenched his teeth and then tossed the cloak at the woman, which she quickly put back on. He studied the slaves. The woman kept her eyes lowered, while the boy alternated his wide gaze between the woman and his feet.

"Did you see a woman with short brown hair and a twelve-year-old boy with the same colored hair in your *domina's* cafe? She would be of Indian descent."

The woman nodded. "Yes, they gave us these cloaks. They were much nicer than the old cloaks we had. Not that the *domina* isn't generous to us. Gods be praised, she treats my family better than my old master, but sometimes she overlooks simple things, like cloaks that are fraying at the edges—"

"The woman and the boy," Lepidus interrupted, fighting the urge to shoot the slave. "Do you know where they went?"

The woman cast her gaze to the ground again. "I'm sorry, *dominar*, I did not see where they went after they gave us the cloaks. They were still drinking tea when the *domina* gave me the post and told me to deliver it."

"Did they talk with your *domina*?"

The woman shrugged slightly. "I didn't see them speak to each other, but I wasn't in the cafe the whole time." She gave Lepidus a furtive glance. "Can me and my grandson go now?"

Lepidus waved his hand absently, and the two Norse slaves hurried down the alley and around the corner. Lepidus stared at the tracking strip on his finger.

"So maybe it was a coincidence," Appius said. "Perhaps Marcia Licinius found the tracker, went into the cafe, and gave the slaves her cloak."

Lepidus shook his head. "It is not a coincidence. Any cafe on Via Rumina would've thrown them out looking and smelling the way they did. And it's unlikely that slaves of Gaia Julius would accept dirty cloaks from street beggars. The slave lied."

"How could you tell?"

Lepidus looked at Appius. "Feelings. Now that we've shown ourselves, we'd better question the Julii before they have time to coordinate a story."

Hestia Gruen pulled out her com pad and called Gaia Julius. When the *domina* answered, Hestia said, "They stopped us, *domina*."

"What did you tell them?"

"What you told me to tell them."

"Did they believe it?"

"I don't think so," Hestia said. "They'll come for you soon, if they haven't already."

"I know. Thank you, Hestia."

"Yes, *domina*." Hestia put the com pad in her cloak pocket, then smiled down at her grandson. The boy stared at her expectantly.

"Fine," she said, "we'll go to the bakery. You earned it."

Kel smiled. "Can I have *two* cinnamon rolls?"

"The deal was *one* roll," she said. "And let's take off these rags."

She bunched the cloaks into a ball, including the com pad, and tossed them into the lap of a sleeping beggar.

Chapter Thirty-Three

Roma.
Kaeso watched the city grow larger through the window of the commercial dropship he and Nestor rode. It was almost ten years since Kaeso last saw the Eternal City. No building could exceed the height of the Temple of Jupiter Optimus Maximus on the Capitoline, so instead of building up, Roma built out. Its sprawling *suburbas* covered most of central Italia, making the peninsula's center one large city when viewed from the dropship. Gleaming white temples dotted the entire city and the *suburbas*. The familiar ovals of coliseums almost matched the quantity of temples. Cars zipped along roadways streaming into and out of the city. While the roads outside the city lay in straight lines, the roads in Roma itself twisted and curved to follow the ancient streets and alleys that grew up before Roma dominated the world.

Despite fighting the Republic during his days in Umbra, Kaeso had always loved the city. How could any human not feel some grudging nostalgia for Roma? For good or bad, it was the center of human culture, the cradle of modern civilization. Roma had created a worldwide commercial commonwealth before way line travel gave humanity the stars. Though never conquered outright, even the Zhonguo of eastern Asia took on aspects of Roman culture. Today humanity was fractured into dozens of nations and independent worlds, but human culture still rotated around Roma like stars around the black hole of a galactic core.

Nestor leaned near Kaeso and looked out the window. "I've never been to Roma," Nestor said.

"I thought a man with your interests would've visited by now."

"Things got in the way."

When he didn't say more, Kaeso said, "There's no other city like it in the universe. You're going to enjoy it."

Nestor gave him a wry smile. "After our recent travels, I'd enjoy any planet with a breathable atmosphere."

Caduceus had left the Jupiter system after Galeo's death and arrived at the Terra way station two days later. When the way station authorities challenged them, Kaeso used the credentials Umbra prepared for them: cargo hauler from the Lost World of Llahsa running the Terra-Jupiter trade routes. After several tense minutes, the Romans allowed *Caduceus* to dock at the massive Terra way station.

During the two-day journey from Jupiter to Terra, Kaeso and his crew hid the bodies of Flamma and Galeo refrigeration crates they used for transporting produce, and then hid them in the ship's smuggling holes. It was an awfully big risk keeping them. If Roman agents boarded and inspected *Caduceus*, Kaeso could say Dariya was a patrician using the sleeper crib to slow her aging (a common practice among the wealthy). Finding two dead bodies, however, would be trouble.

But Kaeso couldn't stomach jettisoning old friends as if they were trash. If they succeeded in this mission, he would return Galeo's body to Libertus, and Flamma's to his father in Egypt. If they didn't succeed, it wouldn't matter what happened to the bodies.

Kaeso ordered Blaesus, Lucia, and Daryush to stay on board *Caduceus*. It was an order he probably didn't need to give: Blaesus was an exile, Lucia a known deserter, and Daryush an escaped slave. Though Umbra gave them fake credentials and gene coatings, the off chance that someone would recognize them was too great a risk. As long as they did not leave the docked ship, they would not encounter Roman authorities.

Unless, of course, the Romans decided on an abrupt ship inspection. Umbra was very thorough, so Kaeso had faith that *Caduceus's* credentials were in order. An inspection was unlikely. He relied on the fact that Roman bureaucracies were like every other throughout human history: They did not take on more work than they had to.

The winged dropship glided onto the airport's runway and then rolled to the orbital terminal where the other dropships docked. Along the way, they passed terminals designated for planetary air traffic. Dozens of airplanes sat on the runways or waited in line at the terminals to dock. Kaeso reminded himself that while this airport was incredibly large and busy, it was only one of eight in central Italia. The crush of 120 million people in the greater Roma region still amazed Kaeso, himself a native of Avita, the largest city on Libertus with three million residents.

Once the dropship finished docking, Nestor and Kaeso made their way through the crowded cabin toward the exit. Inside the terminal, the crowds were just as thick as Kaeso remembered. Romans in business attire mixed with people of all ethnicities and colorful clothing: Africans with light flowing robes; Indian women with the red *bindi* on their foreheads; Gallic men with their traditional long hair and beards; and bronze-skinned men from the Atlantium continent with rings in their ears and noses, yet dressed in the business togas favored by Roman merchants. There weren't many places in the world, much less human space, with such a diversity of people crowded into one place. Roma was the center of human civilization, and five minutes in the interplanetary terminal proved it.

Kaeso and Nestor carried their small shoulder bags through the teeming crowds. Kaeso noticed a large visum wall with a male newscrier in front of a picture of Libertus from space. Kaeso made out the planet's familiar brown and green continents floating on blue oceans beneath a sprinkling of clouds. He stopped among a crowd of people watching the visum wall.

"...the duplicitous Liberti have once again reiterated their claim that they did not kidnap the Consular Heir, or know his whereabouts, despite the proof the Consul and the Collegia Pontificis recently presented. Their denials have forced Lord Admiral Gneaus Cocceius Nerva to destroy another Liberti city."

Sickness rose in Kaeso's stomach when the image zoomed to Taura, a continent in the southern hemisphere of Libertus. Taura looked like a sideways horseshoe. Clouds floated above the green and brown continent, the sun glistening off the blue waters of the Mare Pavo within the horseshoe's curve.

A white light erupted from the horseshoe's southern tip. Clouds expanded away from the explosion like ripples in a pond. When the light dissipated, a dark smudge glowed with orange fires where the Liberti city of Dives once sat.

The crowd surrounding the visum wall cheered.

"As you can see," the crier said, "the Liberti city of Dives is no more. Maybe now the Liberti will give the Roman people back their Consular Heir. But that is doubtful judging by the Liberti government's stubbornness so far. They've already let two cities die, Agricola and now Dives."

Not Avita, Kaeso thought. *Thank the gods, Claudia is still safe. For now.*

"If the Liberti government has such a low regard for its own people," the crier continued, "the Roman Republic urges the Liberti people to rise up and overthrow their government and install one that is more reasonable. One that does *not* kidnap children, or let its citizens perish in fire."

The crowd cheered again.

"Serves the bastards right for kidnapping Cordus," said a young Roman man in a white toga in front of Kaeso. "I say slag the whole planet."

"Cocceius Nerva won't do it," said another young man with a half-beard. "He's too soft. Besides, what if Cordus is on the planet?"

"True. Even if we don't get Cordus back, though, at least the Liberti are getting what's coming to them. They've been acting like a power for a hundred years. Time we showed them what a true power is."

Kaeso tightened his grip on his shoulder bag to keep from breaking their necks.

The man with the half-beard frowned, then said in a low voice, "You shouldn't say such things. The *numina*..."

The man in the toga laughed. "You're such an old woman. The Liberti *numina* are fairy tales. The Liberti are no more protected by *numina* than the Kaldethians. Look what happened to them."

Half-Beard still seemed uncomfortable and didn't say anything.

Nestor put a hand on Kaeso's shoulder, guided him away from the crowd and the visum wall. He must have sensed Kaeso's anger, for he gave Kaeso a meaningful look once they'd walked several paces from the wall.

"Are you all right?" Nestor asked.

"Fine. Let's leave before I strangle someone."

Two armed lictors with pulse rifles stood at the terminal exit. They only eyed the crowds and did not check credentials. Nestor and Kaeso walked past the lictors and through the terminal exit archway without sparing them a glance.

Kaeso and Nestor stepped outside into a chilly gray dawn and made their way, with hundreds of other people, to the central Roma train. They found two seats next to each other in the last car and sat down amid the cacophony of different languages and crying children.

As the train glided out of the station, Nestor watched the Roman metropolis speed by. The train ran along side the ancient Appian Aqueduct, its stone arches and brightly painted frescoes still sharp after twelve hundred years.

"Do they still use that?" Nestor asked, marveling at the ancient structure.

"No," Kaeso said absently. "Their water comes from underground pipes, just like any other city. They keep the Aqueduct for historical and religious purposes now. It still empties into a fountain in the old Forum Boarium."

Nestor nodded, his eyes taking in the sights. Kaeso smiled to himself, remembering the first time he came to Roma. He had wanted to see everything. The city was so vast and historic, vibrant and seemingly eternal. But Kaeso arrived that first time as a spy for Umbra. His cover was a local Roman merchant, so he had to contain his overwhelming desire to gawk at everything.

Now that he thought about it, Kaeso realized he'd *never* toured Roma's more famous sights, even though he lived in the city for five years. Ancilia always worked, always noted subtle hints of surveillance, and always sought out Romans willing to help Umbra. It never left time to see the places that gave birth to humanity's ascension to the stars. He remembered how Petra had wanted to bring Claudia to Roma to see the museums, plays, horse races—

Kaeso blinked away the tears clouding his vision. It was easy to think of his family now, after all those years of forced and intentional forgetfulness. It was also painful, and would be the rest of his life. He missed the mundane things most: eating dinner with them, watching a holo together, going to the market, the hugs and kisses when he went to work.

Petra was long dead and he might as well be to Claudia, but at least he could ensure she lived. His daughter would *not* become a Roman slave or turn to ash under Roman guns. He vowed to fix this. He vowed to find Cordus and give the Roman Muses something to fear.

The train arrived at the Forum Boarium station. Colorful frescoes covered the station's cavernous ceiling. Stained glass windows twenty feet tall lined the walls, casting rainbow hues down on the teeming crowds. Nestor's wide eyes echoed Kaeso's thoughts. From temples to coliseums to train stations, it seemed the Romans didn't know how to build things small.

They left the station and walked west along the Via Nova. They were in the heart of the Roman commercial district, and the three-story visum walls flashing images and blaring music from every large building confirmed it. Kaeso focused on the mission, but Nestor had a hard time. He stared open-mouthed at the visums, the gleaming white columns of courts and temples, and the statue-adorned arenas.

"You'd think you'd never seen a city before," Kaeso said.

"I've seen many cities," Nestor said, "but there is only one Roma, as they say."

"Well try not to trip over your feet," Kaeso said, just as Nestor bumped into a toga-clad older man talking on his com pad. The man glared at Nestor, but Nestor ignored him, continuing to take in Roma.

They walked another three blocks before turning onto the Via Ludus, which was far less noisy and loaded with visum walls. The crowds still existed, but the buildings and business were smaller and more ubiquitous. Niche clothing shops sat next to gourmet food stores, which sat next to jewelry stores neighbored by cafes and taverns. Kaeso found the Scipio Tavern next to a shop selling tobacco from Atlantium. Kaeso opened one of the old-style wooden doors for Nestor.

The tavern's interior was dark, smoky, and smelled of decades of wine. Music from forty years ago drifted from the speakers, while a golem gladiator match played on the visum wall in the tavern's rear. Three older men threw dice on a concave table in the near corner, giving occasional half-hearted cheers. To Kaeso's right, four white haired men concentrated on their *latrunculi* boards as they sucked on pipes filled with tobacco.

"So this is where the old men of Roma come to die," Nestor whispered to Kaeso.

"Old men of all nations come to places like this to die."

He motioned Nestor toward the barkeep in the center. He was a large, middle-aged man with a pregnant stomach and a shaved head. He eyed Kaeso and Nestor when they approached the counter.

"What's your drink, my lords?"

Kaeso put both hands on the counter. "I heard this place brews an amazing *posca*. I could go for a pint."

The barkeep frowned. "Sorry, we haven't had *posca* in months. Got too expensive with the pepper shortage last year. Maybe in another few months when the prices come down a bit."

"*Posca* isn't hard to make," Kaeso said. "Only takes sour wine, some water, and a few herbs."

"Ah, but the secret to a good *posca* is the herbal mixture. Pepper is a key ingredient. Won't sell sub-standard *posca* at my tavern. Would ruin my reputation."

Kaeso nodded. "Can't fault you there, friend, but I'm sorry to hear that. Business has kept me off-world for months. Know where I can find the second-best *posca* in the city these days?"

The barkeep grinned. "Well you can find the *second best posca* at The Triclinium, west end of the Mars Trading Fields. Not as fancy as it sounds, but it'll satisfy your cravings until I can get it back on the board."

"Thanks, friend," Kaeso said and then turned and walked out the door with Nestor behind.

Outside, Nestor asked, "Was that, Umbra code?"

"The place is being watched," Kaeso said, easily falling into his old habit of scanning the street for surveillance without acting paranoid or like a tourist. He decided to run his evasion exercises to ensure he wasn't followed.

"Now what?"

Kaeso thought back to the conversation. He'd known the barkeep Tiro for years, and had worked with him many times to move the secrets Kaeso stole off-world. The man was more professional and steady then some Ancilia Kaeso had known.

Kaeso had put his hands on the bar counter and asked for *posca*, a clear code that he was in trouble and needed access to an emergency equipment and money cache Umbra stored throughout the city.

But Tiro greeted him as a stranger, telling Kaeso the tavern was watched. If Tiro had greeted Kaeso as an old friend, he would have defaulted to his usual cover as a Roman merchant coming in for a cup of red wine.

Tiro also told Kaeso he should go to The Triclinium for the second best *posca* in the city. That bothered Kaeso, though he expected it. It meant Tiro didn't know which caches were safe anymore. Since all Ancilia in Roma were dead or missing, it stood to reason the Romans found the caches as well.

"So what now?" Nestor asked.

"I don't know," Kaeso said, pretending to watch a visum wall while scanning the street. Tiro was the only Umbra contact he had in Roma who was not also an Ancile with an implant. If Galeo was correct, all the Ancilia Kaeso had known were gone. Which meant the odds of finding Ocella dropped to virtually nil.

"I know where we can get help," Nestor said.

Kaeso looked at him, and Nestor smiled. "You're not the only one who has contacts in Roma."

"I thought you'd never been to Roma."

"I haven't. But I never said I didn't know anybody here."

"Who's the contact?"

"A sister."

"You have a sister in Roma?"

Nestor gave Kaeso a steady look, and Kaeso assumed he meant a Saturnist "sister."

"Can you trust her?" Kaeso asked.

"Of course. She's my sister. How do we get to Via Decianae on the Aventine?"

"It's two miles south along the river," Kaeso said. "Rough neighborhood."

Nestor grinned. "My sister is a rough woman."

Chapter Thirty-Four

"That's the third time that lictor's passed the hatch," Lucia said, watching her tabulari screen from the pilot's couch on *Caduceus*. The camera feed showed the way station terminal outside the connector tube. The brass-capped lictor, with a pulse rifle slung over his shoulder, strolled up the way station corridor without glancing at *Caduceus's* hatch. The fact he'd looked at every other nearby hatch made Lucia suspicious.

"He's just walking his beat," Blaesus said, sitting in Kaeso's command couch. He had one leg draped over the edge of the couch as he used the command tabulari to watch Roman entertainment channels.

"He's trying too hard to ignore us," Lucia said. "I know he's watching us."

Blaesus sighed. "My dear, you need to relax. Stop watching that feed and take in a good Roman comedy or maybe a drama. They've gotten much better since the last time we were home."

Lucia frowned at the old man. "How can you watch comedies and dramas?"

"Because I'm bored?"

"You know what I mean," Lucia said. "The Praetorians could storm this ship at any moment and arrest us both. Aren't you the least bit worried?"

"Of course I am. I don't want to be arrested any more than you, but what can we do? We won't leave Kaeso and Nestor on Terra, so we'll sit here and wait for them. In the meantime, I will distract myself from imminent crucifixion by watching a comedy. Laughter can heal the most sour mood. You should try it."

Lucia turned back to the corridor feed. She hated sitting still. She joined *Caduceus* because they never stayed in one star system longer than a month. It satisfied Lucia's restlessness and her desire to stay ahead of any Roman bounty hunters wanting to haul in a Legion deserter. Doing nothing while her friends were in danger made her want to pull out her one inch of Legion-style hair. Though Blaesus's nonchalance annoyed her, she knew he was right. She should relax, escape her anxiety through comedies and dramas.

But she continued studying the corridor feed. An armed lictor talked to a maintenance worker across the corridor from *Caduceus's* hatch. She wasn't sure if it was the same lictor who already passed the ship. They all looked the same with their brass helmets and dark blue uniforms.

She sighed. Maybe she was paranoid. Maybe Blaesus was right: The lictor was following his assigned patrols. With the siege of Libertus, *Caduceus's* Roman docking attendant told them security was the tightest it had been since the Kaldethian war.

Now if she could only make herself believe it.

She rose from the pilot's couch. "I'm going to check on Dariya."

"Why? She's not going anywhere."

"Then I'm sick of listening to your shows. Satisfied?"

Blaesus shrugged, then turned back to his comedy.

Lucia slid down the ladder to the crew deck and then slid down to the cargo and engine deck. She glanced into the engine room and saw Daryush napping in his delta couch. She shook her head. One man watched comedies while the other napped. Was she the only one who knew what Roman arrest entailed? Obviously so, or Blaesus and Daryush would pace the ship, too. She had seen Roman "justice" firsthand on Kaldeth.

She arrived at the cargo bays and placed her palm on the pad for Cargo One. The hatch slid open with a grinding of metal. The hatch had been grinding for months, and no amount of oil or grease seemed to quiet the noise for long. It was on Kaeso's repair list, but "minor" things like food and fuel took precedence.

She went to the sleeper crib and looked through the window on top. Dariya seemed dead. Her skin was pale, almost translucent, which enhanced the death pallor considering her normal skin tone was a west Persian bronze. Her chest did not rise, at least not that Lucia could discern. The cribs did not freeze sleepers, *per se*, but slowed their metabolisms to just a few percentage points above clinical death. Dariya could stay like this for a hundred years before the sleep took its toll on her body.

"I'm sorry for this, Dariya," Lucia said to the pale woman inside. "I'm sorry I wasn't quick enough on Menota. You're a pain in the ass, have been since I met you. But you didn't deserve this."

Lucia placed her hand on the window above Dariya's face. The window was cool, more from the chill of the cargo hold than the well-insulated sleeper crib.

"Kaeso and Nestor are on Terra looking for the Consular Heir who supposedly has a cure for you. Can you believe that? It's insane. I guess I'm not optimistic, to be honest with you. I know you appreciate honesty. I know you'd be the same way with me."

Lucia smiled. Dariya was nothing but honest with Lucia since the day Kaeso hired her and Daryush. In most cases, it was her honesty that made them fight more often than they got along. Lucia understood why; Dariya was just like her.

"But if anyone can do it, the Centuriae can," Lucia continued. "You wouldn't believe the things he's told us over the last few days, or the things that've happened."

Lucia shook her head. "All we wanted to do was stay out of everyone's way. Now we're in this international crisis and going up against both sides. I don't know what we're thinking. Of course, I don't know what else we could do."

Lucia surveyed the empty cargo bay. It had been far too empty the last few months. That was why Kaeso took the Menota job. She could not fault him. All he wanted to do did was keep his crew fed, his ship flying. He was being a centuriae. Lucia longed for those days again, where their biggest worry was finding a job. Looking back, she realized that despite the fights with Dariya, or the breakdowns, or even hunger, those were the happiest days of her life.

She looked back at Dariya. "Whatever happens, I just wanted you to know that I always respected you. Even when we fought. I...well, I just wanted you to know that." She grinned. "Because I'd never tell you this while you're awake."

Lucia was about to leave when she noticed something on Dariya's left ear. A fine webbing of hair-thin red veins covered the entire lobe. Lucia moved to the other side of the sleeper crib and saw the same thing on Dariya's right ear.

She tapped her collar com. "Blaesus."

"My dear."

"Did Nestor mention the first signs of Cariosus infection?"

"I believe he said blood-shot eyes and pale, almost translucent skin."

There was no way Lucia could check Dariya's eyes. Her skin was more pale than usual, but it still might be a symptom of the sleeper crib.

"What about the ears?"

"Let me check Nestor's files," Blaesus said. "Here we are. One file says if red veins appear on the ears, the Cariosa has 48 hours before full symptoms manifest." Blaesus paused. "Please don't tell me you see that on Dariya."

"Both ears."

"Not good," Blaesus said. "It's progressing while she's in the crib. No known disease does that. We should tell Kaeso."

"No," Lucia said. "They know time is short. They're going as fast as they can."

"But maybe Nestor knows—"

"Nestor can't cure the Cariosus," Lucia said. "The sleeper crib was our only chance to delay it. All we can do is wait for them to get back with this cure. I'll tell Daryush, though."

Lucia gave Dariya one last look and then left Cargo One.

She disturbed herself when she realized she was wondering how to dispose of Dariya once the Cariosus took her.

Chapter Thirty-Five

Kaeso and Nestor walked the two miles to the Via Decianae at the base of the Aventine along the stinking banks of the Tiber River. Sewage odors wafted from the river just beyond the dilapidated townhouses on his left. Few people walked the cramped streets, as almost all the buildings were either boarded up or abandoned, a rare sight in a city as overcrowded as Roma. Kaeso had never been to this neighborhood, but he knew it to be one of the city's poorer.

The closer they got to the river, the more it smelled. Many of the steel mills that once lined the Tiber and supplied Roma with its meteoric growth had closed and moved to other locations in Italia and Europa. But waste from the last one made this neighborhood a cesspool. He even heard the humming mill machinery a mile upriver.

"So which house is it?" Kaeso asked.

The rundown townhouses stood on the right side of the street, while a sidewalk and the river were on the left. On the Trastevere across the river, lights twinkled from elegant apartment buildings. But on Kaeso's side of the river, the homes were dark and vacant. There were just as many overgrown lots as there were buildings. Crude graffiti covered whatever structures still stood.

At least the area has one thing going for it, Kaeso thought. *It'll be easy to spot surveillance.*

Nestor strode down the street, peering at the numbers on each townhouse. Sometimes he had to walk up to the doors and clear away some ash or dirt to read the numbers.

Midway down the street, Nestor stopped on the sidewalk in front of a dark townhouse. "This is it."

"You're joking."

"I wish I was."

Kaeso grunted.

The townhouse was mostly intact, but a fire had blown out all the windows and doors years ago. Weeds and saplings grew all over the yard. A dim glow seeped into the front room from a hole in the roof—

The glow vanished.

"There's someone in there," Kaeso said.

A man's voice yelled from the house. "Get on the ground now, or you die."

Kaeso and Nestor froze, glancing at each other.

A pulse bullet tore the ground to Kaeso's right.

"Now!" yelled the voice from the house.

Kaeso and Nestor slowly lay on the broken concrete sidewalk.

"Put your hands your heads."

Kaeso and Nestor complied. The fact they were alive, and the absence of Praetorians swooping down from flyers, suggested the people in the house were either criminals or Nestor's Saturnists. The man spoke with a Roman patrician accent, so Kaeso bet on the latter.

Once Kaeso and Nestor were on the ground, two men emerged from the house with pistols aimed at them. They wore workmen's clothes, and while they seemed to know how to hold their guns, they did not move with the predatory grace of a Praetorian.

"Easy, friends," Nestor said. "I think we have a misunderstanding. Tell me, how many children did Cronus have?"

The men paused. While Kaeso couldn't see their faces in the shadows, their silence said they thought about Nestor's question.

One of the men took out a com pad, tapped a few keys, and then held it to his ear.

"They asked how many children Cronus had." The leader listened and then said, "Understood."

"Get up," the leader said, putting his com pad away. "Keep your hands on your heads."

Kaeso and Nestor obeyed his commands. While the leader kept his gun aimed at Kaeso and Nestor, he motioned for them to follow the second man into the house.

The house looked just as bad on the inside as the outside. Blackened debris crunched beneath their footsteps. In the gathering room, a cracked video screen covered the south wall. Burned couches lay on their sides, and soot covered the once colorful frescoes on the walls. A thick smoky odor blanketed the room's dampness and rot.

The man in front of Kaeso led them further into the house to what was once the kitchen. A door sat open door in the back, with stairs dropping into blackness. The man pulled out a small light and shined it down the steps, then descended. Kaeso followed.

The basement was in much better shape than the house above. Although garbage from its years as a haven for the drug addicted littered the corners, at least the walls and floor were not cinders.

The man's light illuminated a woman standing in the far corner with folded arms. Kaeso started. She was well-dressed and every bit the Roman matron, adding to Kaeso's surprise. The man turned off his light just as the woman turned on an electric lantern. It emitted a harsh white light that cast sharp shadows on the walls. She walked to Kaeso, held the lantern up to his face. Kaeso returned her stare, trying not to squint in the light. She then studied Nestor the same way.

"Who asked about the children of Cronus?"

"I did," Nestor said. "So, my lady. How many children *did* Cronus have?"

She paused. "Who is Cronus?"

"Forgive me," Nestor said quietly, "I meant Saturn."

The woman nodded. "Put your hands down."

Kaeso dropped his hands and asked Nestor, "Saturnist code?"

Nestor grinned. "Umbra isn't the only outfit with secret codes."

The woman raised an eyebrow. "Where do you think Umbra got the ideas for its codes?" She turned back to Nestor. "So, brother, what brings you to this lovely sanctuary?"

"We're searching for a woman and a boy," Nestor said, then gave her a hard look. "The boy resembles the Consular Heir."

The woman gave him a tired smile. She turned and went to a power conduit on the wall behind her. She pulled the unit back on hidden hinges to reveal a door pad. She put her left hand on the pad. It glowed, and then a click sounded from the wall to Kaeso's left. The woman ran her hands over a stone block and then pushed open a door built into the wall.

In the room beyond, light globes on the ceiling bathed the room in a soft orange glow. The room was twenty feet wide and long. A tabulari sat on a desk to Kaeso's left, several chairs and a couch on the right. In the back of the room was a larger couch where two forms lay wrapped in a blanket. A brown-haired woman slept on her side facing the door, her arm draped over a sleeping boy in front of her.

Kaeso would not have recognized Spurria if not for her eyes. They were set wide apart, with thin brows. The same as Petra's.

Chapter Thirty-Six

Lepidus raised the dead man's head by the hair and looked into his dilated eyes. He checked the man's pulse. Nothing.

"Servius!" he shouted into the man's ear.

Disgusted, Lepidus let Servius's head loll. He'd only taken two fingers, and the man drops dead of a heart attack. Lepidus wanted the foreman's screams to last much longer than two minutes. He was not surprised, though. Nothing was going right today.

"Get another one," he told Appius. "Someone younger."

Appius untied the old foreman's arms from the chair's armrests, hoisted him over his shoulder, and carried him out the office door. He dumped him in the middle of the room where the other Julii employees sat on the floor, their hands on their heads and Praetorian Guardsmen with pulse rifles pointed at them. Through the office door, Lepidus saw the terror in their eyes when they noticed the bloody stumps where their dead comrade's fingers used to be.

Appius studied the employees and then pointed to a blond-haired man in his twenties.

"You."

The blond man gasped as two Praetorians lifted him off the ground and dragged him into the office where Lepidus waited. They sat him down in the chair where the older man died and tied him to the bloody armrests. After securing him, the Praetorians left the room. Appius shut the door and then leaned against it with folded arms.

The blond man's breathing came in gasps and tears brimmed in his wide eyes. Lepidus thought Servius's two minutes of screams might be enough for this one.

Lepidus finished wiping his bloody hands in a dishtowel, then tossed it on the desk behind him. He clasped his bloodstained hands in front of the blond man. The man couldn't take his eyes off Lepidus's hands.

In a kind, patient voice, Lepidus asked, "What is your name?"

"De-Demeter, my lord."

"Demeter, do you know why I'm here?"

"N-No, my lord."

"I'm here because your *domina* has betrayed the Republic, the Consul, and the gods. I need to find her. Where is she?"

Demeter's brimming tears spilled down his cheeks, and he sobbed. "I don't know, my lord, I wish to the gods I did, but I don't. The *domina* bought me three days ago, she's rarely spoken to me, I only get my orders from my foreman." Demeter glanced at the pool of blood on the floor next to the chair. "Oh, blessed gods, don't kill me."

Lepidus leaned forward and gently stroked the young man's hair. "Shh, Demeter, I don't want to kill you. To tell you the truth, I hate killing. But it is not up to me to decide these things. I am a tool of the gods, and if it is their will that I kill a man to obtain the information I need, then I will do it."

Demeter continued to cry.

"If you tell me anything about Gaia Julius that helps me find her, the gods will reward you a thousandfold in Elysium." Lepidus raised Demeter's chin. "And I will let you live."

"I don't know," Demeter said through sobs.

"Think," Lepidus said soothingly. "Do you remember a woman and a boy? Both have dark hair. They were dressed like beggars, but the boy would've acted like a patrician."

Demeter continued to sob, but then his eyes darted back and forth, as if thinking hard. His sobs calmed, and he looked at Lepidus. "I remember them. Yes. They came into the cafe through the back entrance, the slave entrance, I mean. I thought it odd because the boy did not carry himself like a slave. More like a patrician, as you said."

"Good," Lepidus said. "Do you remember when they left?"

Demeter nodded. "The woman left in the night, and the boy left a half hour before you arrived."

"Which way did they go?"

"They got in a van," Demeter said, thinking back. "A white van w-with a Borum Meats logo on the sides."

Lepidus looked at Appius. His apprentice tapped a few keys on his com pad and spoke to the Praetorian on the other end, quietly issuing a bulletin for a white Borum Meats van.

As Appius spoke, Lepidus continued questioning Demeter. "Do you remember which direction they went?"

Demeter paused. "I didn't see the woman leave, but I did see the boy. I was pruning the flowers and wondered why they drove away so fast."

"Direction?" Lepidus repeated.

"They turned left up the Via Nostrumae. After that, I don't know."

Lepidus smiled. "You've helped me tremendously, Demeter."

Appius finished his call and motioned Lepidus into the kitchen. Lepidus said to Demeter, "Excuse me. This will be over soon. You've done well."

Demeter nodded, relaxing a bit with Lepidus's assurances.

In the kitchen, Appius said in a quiet voice, "Traffic cameras show a Borum Meats wagon going in the direction the slave said. But the van entered the Murcia Tunnel an hour ago and didn't come out."

"Any cameras in there?"

Appius shook his head. "They've been down two days for maintenance. Fortuna was with them when they took that tunnel."

"Or they knew its maintenance schedule. Send a detail to search the tunnel."

"On their way now."

"They'll find the van, but it'll be empty. Tell your men to track all vehicles that left the Tunnel after the van entered."

"Time range?"

"Half hour."

"Could be hundreds of vehicles."

"I know," Lepidus said, "but it's all we have."

Appius nodded, then pulled out his com pad and made his calls. Lepidus went back to the office where Demeter looked up at him hopefully.

"Can I go now, my lord?"

"In a moment. First we need to settle a formality."

Lepidus pulled out the hand-held bolt cutters he'd used to dismember Servius.

Demeter gasped and squirmed in the chair. "B-But my lord I told you what I knew!"

"I know, Demeter, but the law states that a slave's confession is valid in court only if obtained through torture. It's an archaic law, going back a thousand years, but it is still the law. I don't want Gaia

Julius gaining an acquittal off a technicality. Now. Do you want to lose a finger or a toe?"

Chapter Thirty-Seven

Ocella thought she was dreaming when she saw the man standing next to Gaia Julius.

"This man says he knows you," Gaia said.

The man stared at Ocella, a nervous smile playing on his lips. "The name's Kaeso Aemilus. For now."

When Ocella found her voice, she said, "But not ten years ago."

He nodded slowly. "Our former employer doesn't let us keep old names."

No they don't. How long did it take me to get used to the name Marcia Licinius Ocella?

Ocella did many things in Umbra, things she never imagined when she was a civilian. But seeing Petra's "dead" husband—and Ocella's first love—standing before her was the first time she felt shock since she joined Umbra. She attended his funeral only a year after Petra's. She watched his body go up in the flames of his funeral pyre. This was a dream.

But she knew she was awake and staring at the man she once loved. He was older and skinnier, but he had the same deep-set eyes, the same strong cheekbones, the same erect posture. Umbra had changed his mouth and nose, made them both sharper. Small scars crisscrossed his forehead, scars she didn't remember him having. She wondered if he was an Ancile wearing an Umbra cloak, that Gaia had turned her over to Umbra after all. But when "Kaeso" opened his mouth, she heard his voice and knew it was him. Umbra cloaks could do many things, but they could not mimic another person's voice.

But this man *was* an Umbra Ancile. He just said so. Ocella was suddenly alarmed, and the urge to embrace this man melted away. If he was Umbra, that meant he was here to take her back to Libertus. She could not allow that.

"We need to talk," he said, then went into the basement beyond the safe room. Cordus awoke and gave her a questioning look. She told him it would be all right, and then she followed Kaeso into the basement. He walked up the stairs without turning to see if she was behind him. She was still too shocked to do anything but follow.

When she came to the top of the stairs, he walked into the gathering room and then stood to the side of one of the blown out windows. He stared at the river and the lights on the Trastevere beyond.

"You're supposed to be dead," Ocella said.

"You, too," he replied. He turned. Shadows from the city lights behind him masked his features. "Why did you join Umbra?"

"Why are you here?" she countered.

He sighed and then folded his arms. "I was once Umbra, too."

"Not anymore?"

Kaeso shook his head.

"You selfish bastard..."

"Don't start with me, Sp— Ocella."

"Too, bad," Ocella said. "Do you know what your 'death' did to your daughter? She lost both parents within a year. She was devastated."

"You don't have to tell me what I already know."

"I don't think you *do* know. Did you know she tried to commit suicide six months after you "died"?"

His form stiffened.

"Yes," she continued, "your ten-year-old girl tried to jump off the Hestium Bridge. She thought it was her fault you died. She said you two had an argument the night before your "accident"."

"We did..." Kaeso whispered.

"She said you'd still be alive had she not said she hated you."

"I thought she did."

"You are such a fool, *Kaeso*. She was ten-years-old! She'd just lost her mother a year before. It was an argument. She didn't mean it!"

Kaeso turned around and stared at the river. "I know that. Now. I've made many mistakes, ones I'm not proud of. But there's nothing I can do about them now. All I can do is avoid the same mistakes."

Ocella shook her head in amazement. "You haven't changed at all. That's the same thing you always say after you hurt someone who loves you."

Kaeso turned around. "I didn't come here to get lectured on my faults. I'm here to get you and that boy off this planet."

Ocella clenched her fists. "I'm not taking him to Libertus."

"Not Libertus."

She paused. "Where then?"

"I don't know, but it has to be far from the reach of Roma and Umbra. From what I hear, the boy has talents both sides want."

Ocella walked over to the window so she could get a better view of Kaeso's face. She wanted to see his eyes. *Is he the same man I knew?* she wondered. *Or is he now Kaeso Aemilius, Umbra Ancile?*

"What do you know of his talents?"

"My handler told me Cordus knew how to cure the Cariosus, though I think he can do much more. I think he might know how to cure the *Muses*."

Ocella waited for more. Either he was a good liar or he actually didn't know the boy's full potential.

"Are you still with Umbra?" she asked.

"Like I said, not anymore."

"Then why did they send you?"

Anger flashed in his eyes. "Because every other Ancile is dead."

Ocella looked away.

"Why did you do it? Why did you give away your world's only defense against Roma? Do you know what they're doing to Libertus right now? Claudia could be dead right now because of you."

"It was the only way to get the boy away from..." She stopped. "Are you here to take him away from me or not?"

She studied him. She was able to detect his moods, once, no matter how much he masked them, and she always called him out whatever his emotion. It was that ability that ended their relationship. He hated how she could tell what he thought simply by studying his face. Not that he habitually lied to her, but he was a private man who kept his thoughts and emotions to himself. He couldn't be with a woman who would not give him that privacy. So he chose Petra, who in many ways did the same thing as Ocella. She at least had the wisdom to let Kaeso think otherwise.

Kaeso shook his head, his gaze holding hers. "No. But I don't know where we can be safe with the most deadly security forces in the universe after us."

"I do," Ocella said.

"Where?"

She shook her head.

"I know you don't trust me," Kaeso said, "but I'm your only option."

"Gaia Julius has promised to help us. We don't need you."

"Gaia Julius is being hunted. She'll be recognized wherever she goes. Same with you and the boy. The Romans announced to the universe the Consular Heir was kidnapped. They may not show his picture publicly, but you can bet every security force in Roman space has it."

"Yes, but they've said the Liberti have him. People won't expect to see him right here in Roma."

"But the Praetorians will," Kaeso said, exasperated. "They'd be foolish not to search for him here unless they had solid proof he was off-world. And he's obviously not. I can get you off Terra, because nobody is looking for me."

Ocella knew Kaeso was right. It was bad enough she and Cordus were the most hunted people in Roman history. It would be foolish to also associate with Gaia Julius, another face now on the Praetorian most wanted list.

"To do this, though, I need to trust you," Kaeso continued. "I need to know you won't throw me to the wolves like you did every Ancile on Terra. And the only way I can trust you is if you tell me everything that's happened to you since you took this mission. I want to know why you sold out Umbra, and I want to know how you got the boy out of the Consular Palace."

Ocella looked at him. "Umbra should have told you that when they brought you back into the fold."

Kaeso gave a cynical laugh. "We both know Umbra doesn't tell Ancilia what they need to know, much less want to know."

"They thought you could bring me back because of our history, right?"

Kaeso was quiet a moment. "Yes. They said I was the only one who knew you *and* had the skills to get you out."

"You were retired. Why did you agree to this mission?"

Kaeso looked away. "I own a small cargo ship. I caused one of my crew to get infected with the Cariosus. Umbra said the boy may have a cure, so here I am."

"That's it?"

Kaeso turned back to her. "And you're the only family I have left that I'm...allowed to talk to."

Emotions warred in his eyes, something only she could see. She saw his grief over not being able to hold his daughter again, not being able to tell his parents he was alive. She saw his anger at himself for joining Umbra and leaving behind all he loved. She saw the confusion he felt every day he woke up, looked in the mirror, and forced himself to memorize a new name and to forget another. Knowing that Umbra was the only family he could have, and the only family he deserved.

She saw these things because they were the same feelings she once had, before she decided to escape Umbra. Ocella joined Umbra because she lost the two most important people in her life: Petra and "Kaeso." Umbra Corps was her escape from the pain, to a new life without attachments. She could not imagine the pain Kaeso had tried to escape. Or the pain from which he still ran.

Ocella wrapped her arms around Kaeso's neck and pulled him close. He kept his arms at his sides and did not return her embrace.

"I miss them so much," he whispered in her ear, his voice catching.

She tried to pull him closer, but he shrugged away and retreated to the other side of the room. He cleared his throat, and said, "It's my turn for questions. Why did you betray the Ancilia in Roma?"

Ocella sighed. "You already know one reason. I needed the Praetorians' trust. I spent four years in their academy excelling at all the tests. To get close to the Consular Family, however, I had to stand out in a way they couldn't help but notice. A way that made my loyalty unquestionable."

Kaeso paced the floor, his anger building. "So you threw away your world's only defense just to stand out?"

"I didn't betray my world just to stand out. I came to understand that Umbra was just as dangerous to Cordus, and humanity, as Roma."

"How was Umbra dangerous?" Kaeso said. "They would've given you every resource to extract the boy."

Ocella shook her head sadly. "Umbra didn't send me to extract Cordus. They sent me to kill him."

Chapter Thirty-Eight

Ocella paced on the other side of the room from Kaeso in the townhouse's burned out gathering room. He tried to remind himself she indirectly killed Ancilia who were once good friends.

But all he could see was his beloved wife's sister. A woman he once loved himself. She was a link to his past before Umbra, a happier time that didn't seem so then. Though Umbra had altered her facial features in subtle ways, there was no mistaking the woman he once knew so well. She still curled her fingers at her sides when she was anxious; she still chewed the inside of her lower lip before she said something she knew Kaeso wouldn't like.

He would not kill her.

"I would've done it, too," Ocella said, referring to her Umbra mission to assassinate the Consular Heir. "It wouldn't have been my first kill...but it would have been my first child. That didn't matter to me, though. I was a well-trained Ancile. I didn't question orders. I had faith the Muses knew what was best for Libertus."

Ocella smiled grimly. "But then Numerius Aurelius Scaurus helped change my mind. He headed the Praetorian Guard for twenty years. He retired ten years ago, but was still respected in Guard circles. Even the Consul invites him to dinner parties now and then. Or, he used to."

"Scaurus is dead?"

Ocella nodded. "Cordus and I were in the safe room beneath his house. The Praetorians did it. I don't think they got anything out of him, because they never found us. At least I didn't think so at the time."

Scaurus was the Praetorian Guard Prefect when Kaeso was in Roma. Kaeso never met the man, but he knew Scaurus was one of Umbra's highest placed contacts. The information he funneled to Umbra prevented many Roman attacks on Libertus before they even hit the planning stages. Why would such a highly placed contact betray Umbra? Did his loyalties switch back to Roma? It happened from time to time, but Umbra always found out and eliminated the contact before he could give the Romans anything useful.

But Kaeso didn't say any of this to Ocella, mostly out of old habits. Ancilia never talked about their work or contacts, even with other Ancilia.

"How did he persuade you to turn on Umbra?" Kaeso asked.

Ocella smiled and then surprised him by giving up her contacts easier than he. "Did you know Scaurus was an Umbra contact? Forty years in the Guard, twenty as the Prefect, and the Romans never suspected. He knew my mission because Umbra asked him to help me. He got me into the Praetorian Academy, and then a post in the Consular Palace."

Ocella walked to a half-burned couch and sat down without wiping away the debris.

"Scaurus was a complex man," she said. "He was also a Saturnist."

Kaeso shook his head. "Praetorian. Umbra. Saturnist. Complex or confused?"

"Scaurus was anything but confused. His life's purpose was to stay close to the Consular Family and watch them. Saturnists have this theory—or prophecy, considering their religious devotion to it—that one day humanity will evolve to a point where the Muses could no longer control us. That human beings would one day control *them*. He watched the Consular Family for such a person, just as other Saturnists watch the infectees in the Collegia Pontificis. While still others watch Umbra Vessels. The Saturnists have watched infectees for a thousand years."

Ocella looked up at him. "Scaurus believed Marcus Antonius Cordus was the first human with such an ability."

"How did he know this?"

Ocella shrugged. "Scaurus knew the Consulars well. He knew how they acted, or rather, how the Muses inside them forced them to act. But Cordus was different."

"How?"

"He had no interest in politics, for one. The Consulars—at least the Muse-infected—eat, drink, and sleep politics. It's in their Muse strain's nature. Cordus also hated being treated like a god. That really got Scaurus's attention, because the one thing the Consular's love above politics is their godhood. Scaurus confirmed his suspicions through careful observation and secret talks with Cordus."

Kaeso scratched his three-day growth of beard. "So Scaurus managed to persuade you to betray Umbra with that?"

"Of course not. He didn't come out and say "I'm a Saturnist and, oh, by the way, the Consular Heir is a one in a billion child." He was more subtle than that."

Ocella arose from the couch and paced the floor. "One day he brought me into the Consular Palace to meet the Family. They were like Umbra taught us: cold, distant, calculating. They were polite and they smiled when I bowed before them, but they treated me like a commodity they could buy or sell or kill should the fancy strike them.

"All of them except Cordus. He acted the same way as his family while he was with them. On his own, however, his eyes wandered and he looked bored. The Consulars never look bored. They either stand there like deactivated golems or they give orders. They don't fidget. They don't even laugh. But Cordus did all that. In other words, he acted like a human being.

"Scaurus introduced us during a private dinner one night. And by private, I mean over a hundred Senators and powerful patricians. Cordus sat at a table by himself reading a book when we approached. I tried to keep my emotional distance: I didn't want to know the boy I was supposed to kill. But he disarmed me with a simple question."

When her pause continued, Kaeso asked, "What was the question?"

Ocella sighed, then turned her eyes to him. "'Will you protect me?'"

Kaeso held her gaze. She said, "I told him I was a Praetorian. It was my duty and honor to protect him. I gave him all the assurances a Praetorian would give her client. I played the part well." Ocella smiled. "Then he laughed and said, "I meant, will you protect me from this dinner party?" He explained he wanted to talk about anything other than politics, and I had to talk to him so the sycophants at the party wouldn't approach him. Those were his words."

"Why didn't you kill him that night?" Kaeso asked. "You had an Umbra cloak. You could have finished your mission and slipped out." Kaeso watched Ocella as she stared at the floor with a soft gaze. "He got to you, didn't he? After just one meeting."

She turned away as if he'd accused her of something shameful. "He's a good boy. Brave, smart, kind. He has a great sense of humor. Yes, I'm fond of him. And that bastard Scaurus knew it would happen."

"But your mission..."

"I told myself the timing wasn't right. That my escape plan wasn't perfect. That I couldn't just slit the boy's throat in front of a hundred nobles and an army of Praetorians."

"Yes, you could have," Kaeso said. "Unless Umbra training has taken a complete turn since I left."

"I know I could have completed the mission had I wanted to. But after meeting him...I didn't want to. I came up with all kinds of excuses, but my mission failed when Cordus asked me that first question."

"One question made you give up Umbra?" Kaeso asked.

Ocella's face tightened. She continued pacing the room, debris crunching under her shoes.

"At another dinner party a few days later, the boy and I were talking about some gladiator match when Scaurus came over and said Cordus had a unique talent he wanted to show me. I turned to Cordus. The boy smiled, took my hands, and..."

Ocella shuddered. "Thoughts *exploded* from my implant. Memories that weren't mine. Memories of ancient Roma, when Marcus Antonius sacked Roma and deposed Octavian. *Only I saw things through the eyes of Marcus Antonius Primus.*"

Kaeso stared at Ocella. What she described was impossible. There was no known way to transfer another person's memories from one implant to another. Not even Vessels could send their memories to an implant.

At least, that's what Kaeso was always told.

"I know this sounds ludicrous," Ocella said, "but it happened. In a flash, I saw the entire history of Roma from the time the Muses came to Marcus Antonius in Egypt to the second Cordus released my hands."

"Are you sure it came from your implant? Perhaps the boy's Muses—"

"It came from my implant," Ocella said firmly. "You know that buzzing you get behind your ear when your implant receives orders from Libertus? That's what I felt with these memories. Only more powerful than anything I ever experienced."

Kaeso still wondered if Cordus somehow used Ocella's implant to manipulate her, but he decided to avoid that argument for now. "What did you do?"

"After I recovered my wits, I left the Consular Palace as fast as I could without looking suspicious. Scaurus tried to stop me, but I ignored him. I ran back to my Praetorian apartment at the base of the Capitoline. I took a long hot shower. I told myself my implant must have malfunctioned, because what I saw in those memories was too unbelievable. Because if those memories were true, all human history was a lie.

"An hour later, Scaurus, came to my apartment and offered to answer my questions. I still reeled from my experience. Everything was so vivid, like watching a video wall in my mind. I could use my implant to recall every memory Cordus gave me. Not even Umbra orders were so clear. It all opened my mind to the possibility these things were true. Without those memories, I would've killed Scaurus for being a double agent when he came to my apartment. Cordus's 'transfer,' if you want to call it that, was just part of Scaurus's plan to recruit me. He showed me copies of ancient documents on his com pad. He told me the originals were in a secret basement beneath his house, which I confirmed when Cordus and I fled there. He told me the Saturnist mission, how they sought a way to free humanity from the Muses."

Ocella stared at her empty, soot-covered hands. "That's when we came up with a plan to rescue Cordus. That's when I decided to betray Umbra, so I could stay close to Cordus."

Kaeso shook his head. "What is so awful about the Muses that made you turn away from everything you believed in? They've made Libertus prosperous and safe. They lifted Roma and humanity from a muscle-powered civilization to one that lives among the stars."

"But it's not real. We have all this technology and prosperity because of *them*. We did not discover it ourselves."

Kaeso shrugged. "Well again, so what? I can live with the fact we got a little help from the Muses. You haven't given me any reason to fear them."

"I thought the same way," Ocella said. "I thought we should be thanking the Muses for what they did for us. Then Scaurus showed me ancient testimonies from infectees. When an infectee dies, whether it be from trauma or a disease or anything, the Muses die first, giving the infectee his mind back for only minutes before his death. Over the centuries, the Saturnists gathered these testimonies bit by bit and discovered what the Muses have planned for us. And it is something you should fear."

Lepidus accepted the binoculars from Appius and trained them on the dark townhouse across the Tiber River at the base of the Aventine. From the Trastevere, he saw two figures standing in the townhouse's gathering room, their heat signatures glowing in bright reds, oranges, and yellows.

"Are you sure they're not opium addicts?" Lepidus asked.

"No, Evocatus," Appius said.

Lepidus frowned. The Borum Meats wagon was abandoned in the Murcia Tunnel under the Circus Maximus. Public lictors obtained street camera footage of all the vehicles that left the Tunnel minutes after the Borum wagon entered. The lictors were identifying every vehicle that left within thirty minutes of the wagon entering, but progress was slow.

But by the grace of the gods, a lone street lictor on the Aventine noticed a red van stop two blocks from the townhouse Lepidus watched. A woman matching Gaia Julius's description had exited the van, along with two men and a boy, and then made their way down to the riverfront. The lictor notified his commander, who notified Lepidus.

And here we are, Lepidus thought.

"It couldn't hurt to question them, whoever they are," Appius said.

"I don't want to send in a Praetorian squad just to round up drug addicts," Lepidus said. "We might tip off Julius if she's hiding nearby. Disguise your men as beggars and have them scout the area."

"Yes, sir," Appius said. He took out his com pad, but it chimed before he could place his orders. Appius listened for several moments, then ended the call.

"There's something else, sir."

Lepidus continued watching the two figures. "What?"

"Terra Way Station Control reports a ship of Liberti manufacture docked early this morning, but their credentials say they're a Llahsa ship."

"Liberti exports cargo ships to all Lost Worlds. So?"

"The ship is eighty years old, yet its manifest records only go back twenty. Under normal protocols, the Way Station checks back ten years. With wartime protocols, however, they check thirty. They thought we should know this ship is missing its first ten years."

Lost World centuriae were notoriously poor record keepers, unlike professional and meticulous Roman centuriae. They traded, sold, and gambled away their ships all the time, usually without giving the new owner past manifests. This ship was likely one of those.

Or it could be Ocella's escape.

"Tell Way Station Control to send crew profiles and to maintain a discrete surveillance on the ship. Have any crew members left?"

"Two."

"Get their pictures and give them to your recon team. Wouldn't it be interesting if they were in that house?"

Appius smiled. "Yes, sir."

"Oh, any word from Lord Admiral Cocceius?"

Appius shook his head. "The courier ship should have arrived at the siege fleet four hours ago. Won't be long now."

"Good. Get up there now. Fortuna be with you."

"And you, Evocatus." Appius took out his com pad again and relayed Lepidus's instructions to his recon team as he strode toward the waiting flyer.

Lepidus brought the binoculars up to his eyes again and watched the two figures in the house. His job was about paying attention to the feelings the gods gave him. He had no evidence Gaia Julius was in that house across the river. Nothing proved the Llahsa ship docked at the Way Station was there to pick up Ocella.

But he had faith the gods were with him tonight. He could feel it.

Chapter Thirty-Nine

"There," Lucia said, pointing to the security guard on her tabulari display. He wore civilian clothes and sat at a table outside the tavern across from *Caduceus's* dock hatch.

Blaesus squinted at the display.

"And here's the guard from an hour ago," Lucia said. She brought up a split screen. One side showed the guard now, while the other showed the same guard two hours ago in his Way Station Security uniform, patrolling the corridor in front of the hatch. The guard's face wasn't clear, but she recognized his posture.

"I don't know, my dear," Blaesus said, studying one side of the display and then the other. "I suppose it could be the same man..."

"It *is* the same man," Lucia said. "Your eyes are old."

Blaesus looked wounded. "Maybe it's the end of his shift and he likes that tavern. Maybe he's trying seduce the barmaid."

Lucia shook her head. "They're watching us."

Blaesus sighed. "Maybe, but we can't leave Kaeso and Nestor behind. If they have us under surveillance, then Kaeso and Nestor are in danger."

"I know."

He looked at her. "Should we contact them?"

"You know we can't."

Kaeso gave strict orders to maintain com silence, since the Romans could track their com signal to him on Terra. But she had to tell Kaeso somehow that the ship was being watched. If he came back with the boy, they'd stop him for sure.

The man in the tavern stood up from his table and strode toward the hatch. As he neared the hatch, a squad of way station security rushed into the camera angle wearing flak vests, black helmets, and pulse rifles held ready.

Blaesus groaned. "Oh..."

"*Cac!*" Lucia yelled, then lunged for the connector controls and closed the ship's hatch. Blaesus jumped into the command couch to Lucia's left.

"Are we leaving?" Blaesus said as he strapped himself in.

"If we can."

She entered the commands to retract the connector, but they didn't respond. She cursed again. Only the way station could retract the connector once the ship docked. When she hit the controls again, the com panel lit up.

"*Caduceus*, this is Terra Way Station Control," the Roman controller said. "You are ordered to power down your engines and prepare for boarding."

Lucia growled, "You can stick your orders—"

"They're through the outer hatch!" Blaesus shouted.

Lucia glanced at the camera feed on her panel. The security team had opened the locked hatch on the way station and was inside the connector working on *Caduceus's* hatch.

"Daryush," Lucia yelled into her collar com, "get the way line engines spooled up, now!"

He replied with a grunt, which she hoped meant he was on it.

Lucia fired the ion thrusters. If they couldn't disconnect from the tube she would tear the ship away and send the whole godsdamned security team into space.

"Lucia," Blaesus breathed, staring at the outside sensors.

Lucia looked at her panel. Two Roman Eagles floated less than a half mile from *Caduceus*.

"*Caduceus*, stand down," the Way Station Control said again. "If you try to run, you will be destroyed."

Even if she managed to tear the ship away from the connector, she'd never make it past two Eagles. They'd turn the ship to plasma before she made it a mile from the way station.

"*Caduceus*, acknowledge or we will fire."

"It's over, my dear," Blaesus said quietly.

She glared at him. "It's not over."

The old Senator's eyes widened as she reached for her controls, but she entered the commands to turn off the thrusters. She tapped her collar com and said, "Daryush, power down the way line engines."

"What now?" Blaesus asked.

A siren warbled throughout the ship. Lucia looked at her display. The security squad had bypassed the ship's locks and opened the outer hatch. They rushed into the ship with their pulse rifles against their cheeks.

Lucia turned to Blaesus. "They'll do everything they can to make us talk."

Blaesus swallowed. His pale skin turned even sicklier.

"Everybody breaks," she said, "but hold out as long as you can. Kaeso and Nestor might still be alive. They might still get away."

Blaesus gave her a wan smile. "I was a Senator, my dear. I can talk for hours without saying anything."

Lucia nodded. "There's still a chance we can... If you can get away without me or Daryush, do it. I'll do the same."

Blaesus licked his lips. "May the gods—"

"Command deck," barked a voice from the ladder tube behind them. "Come down slowly. You have ten seconds before we toss in flak grenades."

Lucia closed her eyes. She reached down beneath her couch and put her hand on the pulse pistol strapped there. She swore to herself the Romans would never take her. She knew what they did to deserters—she was assigned crucifixion and flogging duty many times—and told herself a quick death would take her first.

But now, faced with that choice, she found she was a coward.

She let go of the pulse pistol.

"Five seconds," the voice yelled.

Blaesus stood. "Let's go, Lucia."

She unbuckled herself from the pilot's couch and went to the ladder tube.

"We're coming down," she said, then climbed down the ladder with Blaesus behind.

Three men in black helmets stood at the base of the ladder, two with their pulse rifles pointed at Lucia, the third with his rifle trained on Daryush. The terrified Persian knelt on the floor with his hands on his head. She stepped down, and put her hands on her head. Behind the security guards was the blond-haired man she'd seen in the tavern across from the ship. He held up a com pad, looking from the pad to Lucia. When Blaesus came down, he did the same thing.

The man returned the com pad back to his vest. "Are you Lucia Marius Calida and Gaius Octavius Blaesus?" he asked with a patrician Latin accent.

Lucia and Blaesus remained silent.

The man frowned. "No matter. I think you're the people I want."

He took a pulse pistol from his vest and shot the first two guards in the back of the head. Their heads exploded in a spray of blood, tissue, and plastic. The third guard turned, but the blond man shot him in the face, the remains of his head splattering on the walls.

Lucia stared in shock.

The man put his pistol back in his vest. "I assume you want to leave?"

She didn't move. She felt her jaw gaping, but was too stunned to close it.

"Close your mouth and get to the command deck. Engineer," the blond man said to Daryush, "back to your post and ready your engines."

Daryush nodded, his face screwed as if waiting to be shot. He stepped around the bodies on the floor without glancing at them and went down the ladder to the engine deck.

"Who are you?" Lucia finally managed to ask.

"Get up there and I'll explain. You, too, Senator."

Blaesus lunged for the ladder and climbed as fast as his old legs could carry him. Lucia went next, followed by the blond man.

Once on the command deck, the blond man pushed past Lucia and tapped the com panel on her pilot's tabulari.

"Way Station Control this is the Centurion of Praetorian Guard Unit 202," he said. "The ship is secure. Stand down your patrol Eagles and recall the men in the connector."

"Acknowledged, Centurion," Control said.

"By authority of the Praetorian Guard," the man said, "I'm taking command of this ship and transferring it to a guarded facility on Terra. You will erase all records of this incident, as it is red level security status. Authorization code 988-89-WSW. Acknowledge, Control."

Control paused for a long time. Lucia watched the blond man. He stood before the com panel with a serene expression, despite flecks of blood on his face and light brown vest.

"Authorization accepted, Centurion," Control said. "You have the ship. We're clearing a flight path for you. Do you need an escort?"

"Negative, Control," the man said. "Your Eagles are not authorized to know the coordinates of the Praetorian facility."

Control paused again. "Will Unit 202 accompany you?"

"Yes," the man said without hesitating. "They will guard the prisoners until I reach the surface. They'll come back on the next shuttle."

"Very good, Centurion. Your flight path is cleared. You can undock at anytime."

The man turned to Lucia. "The ship is yours to fly, Legionnaire."

Lucia stepped into the pilot's couch and strapped herself in. The blond man went to the command couch, and told Blaesus, who continued to stand in the back slack-jawed, to take the delta controller's couch. Blaesus complied.

"Undocking from way station," Lucia announced. Once the ship cleared the connector, she checked the flight path the way station gave them. It took them right into Roma.

"Where do we go once we get to Roma?" Lucia asked, setting the flight coordinates into *Caduceus's* nav port.

"I'll let you know," the man said.

Lucia eyed him. The man tapped the command tabulari, reviewing the ships in the area. She had the sudden urge to throw him out of Kaeso's post.

"Who are you?" she asked again.

He continued to tap at the tabulari. "Someone who just threw his life away for you. So I'd appreciate some gratitude in your tone." He raised his eyes to her and said, "My name is Gnaeus Hortensius Appius. I'm a Praetorian Guardsman, and a Liberti agent."

Lucia blinked. When she didn't say anything, Appius asked, "Where's your tongue, soldier?"

She studied him, then asked, "Are you with Umbra?"

Appius raised an eyebrow. "What's 'Umbra'?"

Of course he wouldn't say if he was. *Damned Liberti and their secrets.* "How did you get past the tests, the security checks, the—"

"I did, and we'll leave it at that," Appius said, watching Kaeso's tabulari. "All you need to know now is this ruse won't last long. Way Station Control will eventually double-check my codes with the Praetorian Guard, and the Guard will say they issued no such order."

"How long do we have?"

"Less than an hour. What kind of beacon does this ship have?"

"Same one it had out of the docks."

Appius smiled. "Good. This bucket's age might just save your lives."

Blaesus said, "Ship beacons can't be altered."

"The newer ones can't," Appius said, moving some sliders on his tabulari, "but the old ones can, if you know how."

"I suppose you do, Praetorian?" Blaesus said.

Appius nodded, still searching the tabulari. "Among the first things they teach us in our sabotage courses."

Lucia asked, "So you can change *Caduceus's* beacon. Then what? We still can't get off the planet without landing records. Roman flight controls are strict."

"Only applies to private or commercial traffic. Praetorian beacons are a different matter."

Lucia checked her tabulari. Appius scanned the way line plasma conduit specs, and paused on Umbra's modifications. His eyes widened slightly, but he kept scrolling.

"How will you give us a Praetorian beacon?" she asked.

Appius focused on a schematic showing where the plasma way line conduit intersected the communications conduit.

"Watch," Appius said.

Appius sent a surge of way line plasma into the plasma conduit. Lucia watched the surge drive up the power overload indicators to dangerous levels. A siren warbled from her tabulari.

"You're going to slag our com! Shut it down!"

"Wait," Appius said as the indicators continued rising.

"If you slag our com, we can't replace it," Lucia said. When he didn't respond, she said, "I'm shutting it down."

Appius pulled his gun and aimed it at her. "I said, wait."

Lucia froze. He was fast. She'd never get to the pistol under her couch before he killed her. She ground her teeth, clenched her fists, and watched the overload indicators rise to maximum levels.

But before they hit catastrophic levels, the communications conduit overloaded and then shut down. When that happened, Appius reversed the plasma flow, and it fell back down to normal levels. Lucia checked the communications conduit and saw ship's com still functioned. She sighed. Then she noticed the beacon signal was silent. A window popped up on her display saying the beacon was disabled due to a power surge, and it needed resetting.

She understood.

"A power surge in the com conduit resets the beacon?" she said.

Appius nodded, putting the pistol back in his vest. "Simple in concept, but tricky to implement. Timing has to be perfect, or, as you said, you slag the com system. And now a new Praetorian beacon code"—he tapped the keys on his tabulari—"makes us a covert Praetorian freighter with a commercial cover beacon. Your ship's new name is *Vacuna*. The way station won't bother us when we take off again."

"You're sure this will work?" Lucia asked. "Won't Way Station Control think it odd that our beacon changed mid-flight?"

"No, because they took us off their sensors once I gave them Praetorian authorization codes. Officially we no longer exist. They cleared a flight path for us so no ships would wander into our trajectory."

Blaesus said, "Won't other ships in the area see the change on their sensors?"

"Maybe, if they were looking at us the moment we changed. They don't know this trick is possible, though, so they'll think it's a glitch in their sensors. I've done this many times on other worlds."

"Where are we going?" Lucia asked. They entered the Terran atmosphere above Asia, and their collision with the air formed plasma sparks at the front of the ship. "We enter Roman airspace in fifteen minutes."

Appius tapped his tabulari. "Land the ship at these coordinates."

The coordinates came across Lucia's display. She read them and then checked them again. "My friends are in Roma."

"For now," Appius said. "But they're about to be caught, and they will be taken to those coordinates."

Blaesus must have read the coordinates on his tabulari. "The South Pole?"

"The Praetorians have a secret facility there for high profile prisoners," Appius said. "Prisoners they don't want people to know they have."

"Like the Consular Heir," Lucia said.

"Like the Consular Heir."

"So he really wants to defect to Libertus. Why?"

Appius smiled. "If I told you, you wouldn't believe me."

"My boy," Blaesus said, "you'd be surprised at what we believe now."

Chapter Forty

Kaeso glanced at the chronometer on his wrist. It was midnight. He'd been talking with Ocella for a half hour, but it felt like five minutes.

"Humanity has been in space for more than five hundred years," Ocella said. "Why do you think we've never encountered any alien beings?"

"Space is big. Humanity has traveled to an infinitely small corner of it."

"Traveled, yes. But we have telescopes and scanners on almost every inhabited world searching the stars for intelligent alien life. In five hundred years we've never found any sign."

"Maybe we're just alone."

"We may be alone now, but we were not the first intelligent life in the universe."

"The Muses."

"Yes, the Muses came before us. Yes, they're intelligent, but they're a virus. How did they know how to build starships?"

"What are you saying? Because I can't pretend to answer these questions."

Ocella licked her lips. "I'm saying humanity is not the first intelligent race the Muses found. There were nine others before us. All were infected with the Muses; all were given knowledge the Muses learned from previous races. And all died when the Muse strains began fighting each other."

"Fighting each other?" Kaeso said.

"Yes. It all starts out benign. The Muses infect a race, give them technology enabling them to cure diseases, increase fertility. Populations explode. Eventually each race is given the technology for space travel, and each race colonizes other planets using the way lines.

"Then they find another race infected with a *different* Muse strain. Or sometimes different strains infect the same race, like they did us. Either way, the Muses seem to go insane and force their hosts to slaughter each other. It's a brutal fight to the death, and every race used this way is extinct."

Kaeso rubbed a hand over his shaved head. "So somehow the Muses came to Terra? They've been with humans since the beginning?"

"Not since the beginning of humanity," Ocella said. "Since Marcus Antonius Primus found them in Egypt."

It made a crazy kind of sense. Antonius took Roma because he developed gunpowder weapons while in Egypt. Antonius's gunpowder weapons were a world-changing innovation...the kind that came from the Muses on Libertus. Antonius obliterated Octavian's naval fleet at Actium with cannons, sailed his armies to southern Italia, and marched up the peninsula with few casualties on his side. After Antonius took Roma, the Republic entered a Golden Age that some say still existed.

"Why did the Muses infect Marcus Antonius?" Kaeso asked. "If they were in Egypt, why didn't they infect Cleopatra, or the Ptolemy kings or the pharaohs before them?"

"I asked Cordus the same thing. He said it was a chance encounter Antonius had while exploring an Egyptian ruin outside Alexandria. He opened a sealed tomb where several vials of the Muses were stored. Egyptian priests said the tomb was that of an ancient god, and the vials contained the god's powers. Octavian had just declared war on Antonius, so he was desperate...and very drunk. On Antonius's orders, the priests mixed the vials' powdered contents with water, placed the solution on the tip of a dagger, and then Antonius cut himself with the dagger."

"So Antonius was the first human infectee."

"At least the first modern human. The alien race the Egyptians knew as gods came to Terra over fifteen thousand years ago to escape their war with the Liberti Muses. That race infected some humans, but those early humans died out due to natural disasters and primitive conditions."

"You're saying the Terran Muses uplifted humanity just so they could find the other strains and wipe them out?"

"*I'm* not saying this," Ocella said. "I'm just telling you what's in the memories Cordus gave me."

"Cordus," Kaeso said skeptically. "Who is the Roman Consular Heir."

"How could those memories lie? What would Roma have to gain by giving me a story like this?"

Kaeso laughed mirthlessly. "I don't know, maybe get you to destroy Umbra?"

Ocella sighed and stared at him. "This is all true. The memories, Scaurus's texts, Cordus. I've never been more sure of anything in my life. Even Roman and Umbra actions so far confirm what I'm saying."

"Fine," Kaeso said, "let's assume what you're saying is true."

"It is."

"Then what is *your* plan? You get Cordus off Terra, then what?"

"We get him to a Saturnist stronghold."

"And then?"

"They use his blood to develop a cure against the Muses."

"And after that?"

"Gods, I don't know! I don't have a detailed mission brief for this. I'm making it up as I go. I know I have to get Cordus away from Roma and Umbra. He's the only chance humanity has to avoid extinction."

A noise outside the window made Kaeso look. He and Ocella stepped to either side of the window facing the street and peeked around the corner. An old woman in filthy rags pushed a cart filled with old blankets, cans, and other dingy items. The sound of her cart's squeaky wheels floated over the sounds of waves and boat traffic on the river.

"This street is filled with beggars," Ocella whispered. "I don't think the Praetorians recruit old women." The doubt in her eyes and rigidity of her posture belied her confident words.

"Maybe not," Kaeso said. The old woman shuffled down the street, pushing her cart, without glancing at the townhouse. At the next street corner, she turned right and out of Kaeso's sight.

"Then again..." Kaeso said. He pointed to a large, overflowing trash bin across the street from the corner on which the old woman had turned. "Seems like a tempting target for a real beggar."

"Maybe she'd already found what she wanted," Ocella said, taking a pulse pistol from her cloak and scanning the street. "Maybe she was tired and wanted to go...to where ever she slept."

"Or maybe she has a disguised camera in her cart and was scouting the block," Kaeso said. "I think we should leave."

Ocella hesitated, then said, "Agreed."

"Go warn the others. I'll keep watch."

Ocella nodded, then left the gathering room. Kaeso turned to the window and watched for other "beggars."

Lepidus studied the man's face on his pad. The picture from the recon unit was washed out due to the darkness, but the black and white image matched the one the way station took of the Llahsa freighter's centuriae. Same shaved head and scarred forehead, same sharp nose and dimpled chin.

Lepidus smiled. *The gods are with me tonight.*

He turned to the Praetorian centurion next to him. "Take them."

Kaeso heard noise behind him. He turned to see Ocella enter the room, but she was alone.

"Where are they?" he asked.

"Downstairs. Gaia Julius has another idea."

"We have to leave now, the Praetorians are here."

"There's a way out through the basement. Best we use it instead of the front door, don't you think?"

Kaeso nodded and was about to follow Ocella when blinking lights from across the river caught his eye. He turned and realized they were not blinking lights. Two flyers, black and silent, glided over the river toward the townhouse, momentarily blocking the lights on the Trastevere.

He cursed, then pushed Ocella to the kitchen. They ran down the stairs and into the basement just as a house-shaking crash came from upstairs.

Everyone in the basement—Nestor, Cordus, Gaia Julius, and her two men—turned to Kaeso and Ocella as they charged down the stairs.

"We need to leave!" Kaeso yelled to Gaia.

Boots stomped on the floor above them.

"In there," Gaia said, motioning to the secret room. After they all rushed in, Gaia put her hand on the palm pad next to the door. The stone entry slid shut. Cordus ran to Ocella, who put a protective arm around his shoulders.

"Please tell me we're not trapped in here," Kaeso said to Gaia.

"Give me some credit, Ancile," Gaia said. She hurried to the other side of the room, pushed aside a bookcase to reveal a hidden door. She opened the door, and a dark tunnel appeared. She turned back to Kaeso with a smile.

"Secret doors upon secret doors," Kaeso said.

"Saturnists are *much* more paranoid than Umbra," she said, then hurried into the tunnel. Gaia's men followed.

Ocella glanced at Kaeso, and then she pulled Cordus into the dark tunnel.

On the other side of the wall, boots charged down the stairs into the basement. Kaeso went to the wall and put his ear to it.

"Centuriae!" Nestor said in a whisper. Kaeso waved him into the tunnel. Nestor frowned, looking from the tunnel to Kaeso. When Kaeso waved more insistently, Nestor shook his head and approached the wall. Kaeso wanted to throw Nestor into the tunnel, but that would make noise. Besides, the voices behind the stone wall were muffled. Nestor might pick up bits Kaeso missed.

"All clear...empty...yes, sir...search the house...secure the block..." Boots stomped up the stairs back to the first floor, and then all was silent in the basement.

Kaeso caught Nestor's eye, then jerked his thumb back at the tunnel. They both stepped quietly to the tunnel and pulled the door closed behind them. The tunnel was pitch dark for a moment until Kaeso's eyes adjusted and he could make out a white glow up ahead. It was enough to outline the contours of the tunnel and enable him to move forward. He heard the shuffling footsteps from the others and followed the sounds.

"What did you hear?" Kaeso asked Nestor.

"The house was clear and they're searching the entire block."

"That's what I got, too. How secure are Saturnist secret doors?"

"Should be shielded to prevent any power or heat signatures."

Kaeso kept his hands on the rough-hewn walls to guide him along. The white glow ahead grew brighter as they closed on the others. The odor of dirty water grew stronger, overpowering the tunnel's mustiness.

"We have to assume they'll find it," Kaeso said. "And we have to find a way to warn Lucia. *Caduceus* is in danger."

Before Nestor could answer, they turned a corner to their right and found the rest of the escapees. They stood near an opening from which Kaeso smelled the stagnant water. He made his way to the front, where Gaia Julius pointed her electric torch over the edge. The beam illuminated brown water three feet below the opening. Black and green mold covered the ancient stone walls and arched ceilings.

"It's an offshoot of the Cloaca Maxima," Gaia said. "It's no longer used, so don't worry about walking through raw sewage."

"Where will it take us?" Kaeso asked.

"If we go that way"—pointing to the right—"the Tiber. If we go that way"—pointing left—"the main line and the Forum Romanum. I suggest the river."

"Agreed. Won't the Praetorians know this line?"

"I'm sure they'll figure it out," Gaia said, "so our best chance is to be out of here before they do. Ready to get wet, Ancile?"

Gaia jumped into the brackish water with a splash. The water came up to her waist, and she waded down the passage to the right. Gaia's two men jumped in after her, as did Nestor.

Cordus stared at the water. "I-I don't know how to swim."

"It's not deep," Ocella assured him. "It only comes up to your chest. See where it is on Gaia?"

"What about the river?"

Impatient, Kaeso said, "It's either the sewer or you take your chances with the Praetorians. Which is it?"

Cordus glanced at the dark tunnel behind Kaeso, and then the water below his feet. He still hesitated.

"I can't believe you're scared of a little water," Kaeso said. "I thought Romans were a brave race. Isn't that what you always tell us barbarians?"

The boy shot Kaeso an angry look. The fear in his eyes turned to determination, and he jumped into the water. He gasped, but quickly righted himself and followed Gaia.

Kaeso grinned. *Romans are so easy to manipulate.*

Ocella's eyes flashed at Kaeso, then she jumped into the water after Cordus.

Kaeso was the last to jump. The water was brutally cold and Kaeso gasped despite himself. He followed Gaia's small torch beams ahead. They passed side tunnels, and even turned down a few, making Kaeso pray that Gaia knew where to go. Just to be sure, he waded up to her and asked where they were.

She smiled. Her once perfectly styled patrician hair hung in wet strands down her back. "The walls are marked," she said, but did not elaborate.

Kaeso didn't recall any markings on the walls where they turned, and he had checked. *But then the Saturnists have become good at hiding things in plain sight.*

"What happens when we get to the river?"
"We swim."
"I was hoping for a better plan."
"Our plan was to wait in the safe house until my contacts could secure passage off-world. Your arrival made us flee before they could secure that passage."

Kaeso bristled at her implication that he brought the Praetorians down on them, though he knew he likely had.

Ocella waded up to them. "You have a starship, Kaeso?"
"Yes."
"But how do we get to it?" Gaia asked. "The Praetorians won't let us ride a shuttle to the way station. Our pictures are on every security watch list on Terra."

"We never planned to take a commercial shuttle," Kaeso said. "I have a contact who can get us on a cargo shuttle to the way station. You just need to get us out of this sewer."

"Working on it, Ancile." She then gave him a sideways glance. "How did you make it through the way station? I thought the Praetorians killed every Ancile they found."

Kaeso was silent, then said, "They can't find Ancilia with deactivated implants."

Gaia eyed him curiously, and Kaeso said, "Let's just say Umbra brought me out of retirement."

"Well," Gaia said. "Ocella's betrayal has made Umbra desperate."

Kaeso refused to take Gaia's baiting. Instead, he said to Ocella, "By the way, how did you deactivate your implant?"

Ocella watched Cordus. The boy and Nestor were engrossed in a conversation on Roman history and the days after Antonius became Consul. "Cordus did it."

"How?"

"Scaurus had a device that enabled communication between me and Cordus. Apparently Roman Muses need it to deactivate an implant developed by the Liberti Muses."

"What about these memories Cordus gave you? Can they help us find a way out of Roma?"

Ocella shook her head. "The memories went away when Scaurus deactivated my implant."

Gaia chuckled. "Implants or not, Roma will find you or Umbra will kill you. Saturnist resources are considerable, but you'll need to stay on the run. Your best hope is for that siege to last as long as possible, keep them both distracted, and give you a head start."

Claudia's tear-streaked, ten-year-old face flashed in Kaeso's mind. "That siege is killing my home. It has to end."

"My aren't we ambitious?" Gaia said. "Kidnapping the Consular Heir and lifting a Roman world-siege. You enjoy impossible tasks, don't you?"

"Enjoy isn't the word I'd choose," Kaeso said. "But Libertus must win. I can deal with the consequences here."

"*You* might be able to," Ocella said in a low voice, "but what about Cordus? We need to protect him. Gaia is right. Keeping Roma and Libertus distracted helps to get us off Terra. I can live with the siege lasting a few more days."

"Libertus doesn't have a few more days. The Roman fleet has already slagged three major cities. That's over six million people dead."

"I know," Ocella said, "and it breaks my heart. But Cordus is important..."

"So is my daughter," Kaeso growled. "Your niece. You might be here to save humanity, but all I want is to save my world and my daughter from incineration. If the siege ends, then I can handle a little pressure from Umbra and the Praetorians."

"You are so short-sighted," Ocella said, her voice rising. "Umbra may have changed your face, but you're the same man you were before Petra died. You never look beyond your current mission. You never think what happens next. Or who it hurts."

"When you sentenced every Ancile to death, did you wonder who *that* would hurt?"

"They would've killed me and that would've killed Cordus," Ocella snarled. "I hate what I did. I hate myself more than you know. But I made the right decision, because that boy is the only thing that will keep *every human alive* from ending up like the six million dead Liberti."

Gaia cleared her throat. "Perhaps you two should continue your conversation when you have more privacy?"

Kaeso glanced at the others. Gaia's men were a little too focused on the tunnel ahead. Nestor and Cordus had stopped talking—Nestor frowned at Kaeso, while Cordus looked from Kaeso to Ocella with sad eyes.

Ocella glared at Kaeso, then waded back to Cordus and spoke quietly to him.

Kaeso exhaled. "How much further?" he asked Gaia.

Gaia pointed her torch at the walls to the right. Another small tunnel trailed off into darkness, but she trained her light on scratches carved into the wall on the side. Kaeso did not recognize them.

"Another hundred feet ahead, we should find a large pipe that empties into the Tiber, but..."

When she didn't finish, Kaeso asked, "What?"

"We should feel a current from the outflow. I don't feel anything."

Gaia was right. Kaeso felt no more current than he did in a bath pool.

"The pipe is blocked."

Gaia nodded. "Which means we need another way out."

"Do you know one?" Kaeso scanned the small tunnel on the right as they passed it. The Cloaca Maxima tunnels ran under the entire city. They could be lost for days without finding a way out.

Gaia didn't say anything, but moments later her torch illuminated the pipe that was supposed to lead to the Tiber. The pipe's entrance was sealed with blocks and mortar, and the work looked relatively recent. The blocks were more square, and the mortar more evenly placed, than the ancient blocks around them. Kaeso guessed this was done within the last two hundred years, after the newer systems were constructed.

Gaia scowled at the new wall. She panned her torch back the way they came and waded in the opposite direction.

Kaeso turned and followed.

A boom reverberated down the tunnel. The water sloshed and mortar dust rained down on them. Gaia stopped, then said, "Damn."

"We take another tunnel," Kaeso said.

"I don't know where they go."

"I don't think we have a choice. What's your best guess?"

Cordus waded up and pointed to the tunnel back near the walled up pipe. "I think we should take that one."

"Why?" Kaeso asked.

"Because I have memories of when this pipe was sealed. The offshoot near it empties into the modern systems."

"Very good, sire," Gaia said. "A modern system has manholes from which we can escape."

Kaeso stared at Cordus doubtfully.

Another boom sounded from the safe house.

"I know the way," Cordus said. He held Kaeso's gaze with determination. Either the Muses made this boy a good actor, or he really wanted to prove his bravery.

A third boom made up Kaeso's mind.

"Fine," he said, waving his hand to the walled pipe. "Lead the way, *sire*."

Gaia walked beside Cordus, focusing her light ahead. Ocella said to Kaeso in a low voice, "Thank you for trusting him."

"Nothing to do with trust," Kaeso said. "It's either go with him or wait for the Praetorians."

Ocella frowned and then followed Cordus.

Chapter Forty-One

The helmed Praetorian emerged from the smoking hole in the wall. "The room is empty, Evocatus."

Lepidus frowned.

"But we found a tunnel behind a book shelf," the Praetorian said. "The tunnel leads to an ancient storm drain system. No sign of them, though."

Lepidus thought for a moment. "The old Cloaca Maxima runs under this area." He turned to another Praetorian holding a com pad. "Bring up the Cloaca Maxima system. Highlight its outlets."

The Praetorian tapped some keys on his tabulari then showed it to Lepidus. As he suspected, the system was no longer used, but it did drain into more modern systems. He could see only three outlets through which any human could escape. The other outlets were either pipes only a baby could crawl through, or they were sealed.

He studied the three outlets. The first went under the Forum Romanum, the second ran under the Jupiter Fountain, and the third connected with a more modern system. From there the Liberti could go anywhere.

Lepidus pointed to the pad. "Centurion, your teams will guard the three outlets here. Arrest anyone who emerges. I will lead a team into the Cloaca Maxima."

After he explained his plan to the centurion, the man nodded. "Yes, Evocatus."

The centurion spoke into his helmet com and ordered teams to secure the outlets Lepidus noted. Lepidus gathered his men and led them into the secret room.

He peered inside the smoking hole that was the secret room's block-covered door. He wished he had more time to study the door's mechanisms, or the room's contents. Both would teach him so much about the Liberti presence in Roma. Lepidus did not frighten easily—his faith in the gods assured him his life or death would serve a purpose—but it scared him to know how badly Liberti agents had infiltrated the Roman government. Marcia Licinius Ocella exposed dozens of agents in high places, but he assumed there were more. This room and its records could lead him to those other agents.

Later. Right now he needed to find the boy and discover why he had betrayed his people and his gods by going with Marcia Licinius. Then Lepidus would do what was necessary to protect Roma.

He entered the dark tunnel.

※※※

Ocella hadn't heard any booms from the tunnel behind them in over fifteen minutes, or even sounds of pursuit. At least not from her position at the column's front beside Cordus. Kaeso was back there now listening for the Praetorians. She trusted his ears, though right now they were the only things about him she trusted. He'd help get them off Terra, but after that...would he give them to Umbra or let them go with Gaia and the Saturnists?

"I bet you are wondering," Cordus said abruptly, "why I can hold my breath so long, and yet I do not know how to swim."

"What?"

"Well, I can hold my breath for three minutes, yet I cannot swim. Strange, yes?" His voice had a slight tremble from the cold water.

Ocella shrugged. "I suppose holding one's breath has nothing to do with the water."

"But don't you want to know why?"

Ocella grinned. "So tell me why you can hold your breath for three minutes, yet can't swim."

"Because of my father's gas."

Ocella burst out laughing before she could stop herself. Gaia turned and gave her the severe look of a school matron disciplining a child. Ocella snapped her mouth shut. It was not Gaia who ended her laughter, but the realization that any loud noise could bring the Praetorians down on them.

Ocella whispered to Cordus, "Your sense of humor is going to kill us all."

Cordus shook his head seriously. "It is not a joke. The gas my father emits from his skin is something all Roman Vessels can do. My family calls it an "aura." It is odorless to mundanes, but it soothes them, makes them more compliant and worshipful. Only Vessels can smell it, and it is rather vile. So I learned to hold my breath when I am around my father as he manipulates mundanes."

Ocella didn't know whether to laugh or be disgusted. No wonder people worshiped the Muses' human hosts as gods. But Ocella wondered why she never felt the same way around Roman Vessels during her Praetorian days—

The implants.

Umbra would not send their valuable Ancilia to Roma without a defense against the so-called "aura" of Roman Vessels. The implants were ostensibly for communication. Now Ocella realized their secondary purpose, if not their primary.

"Is it just Roman Vessels that can do it?" Ocella asked.

"I believe so. Though I do not know if the Liberti Vessels have evolved the ability since the Roman Muses last encountered them. It has been 15,000 years."

"Do they do this at all times?"

"It is voluntary," Cordus said. And then with a shy smile, "Otherwise Vessels would never have descendants."

"Are you...did you ever...?"

"I only did it around my father, since he expected it of me. I have never used it on you or anyone else since we left the Palace. It disturbs me."

Ocella noticed Gaia had stopped a dozen paces ahead. Her torch illuminated a recently sealed wall. Like the blocked pipe to the Tiber, the mortar and blocks were more modern than those around it.

Cordus shook his head. "I do not remember this."

"Did we take a wrong turn?" Ocella asked.

"No, this is the way I remember—er, my Muses remember. It should not be blocked."

"Well it is now," Kaeso said, wading up to the front next to Ocella. "Do you remember another way?"

Cordus bit his lower lip, then slowly shook his head.

Kaeso let out a breath. Ocella thought he would yell at Cordus, but he pressed his lips together when he saw her glare. "We go back, then," he said. "Gaia, we'll need your light."

Gaia waded toward Kaeso, frowning at Cordus as she passed him. Cordus lowered his eyes slightly, which for him was the ultimate sign of defeat.

Ocella put a hand on his shoulder. "It's not your fault."

"It is," Cordus mumbled. "I told them to go this way. Now we might be trapped in this section if the Praetorians are following us."

"You're right. It's all your fault."

Cordus furrowed his brow at her.

"I mean, how could you not realize a wall you didn't know about was built here?" she said. "You're so incompetent."

His mouth fell open to protest, and then he closed it. "Maybe I am being foolish about the wall. I suppose I am feeling guilty about this whole situation. Nobody would be here if it were not for me. And that *is* my fault."

How do I explain that it's just beginning?

Ocella caused more deaths than she wanted to think about. If she survived this, the guilt over those deaths would make a sound night's sleep impossible for the rest of her life.

Every time she closed her eyes, she saw the faces of the Ancilia she gave up to maintain her cover in the Praetorian Guard and ensure Cordus's safety.

She remembered Scaurus's face when he walked up those stairs from the secret room in his house. He knew he was going to his death, yet he went to protect them.

She saw the Legionnaire in the Temple of Empanda. All he wanted to do was pay his respects to his god. Ocella rewarded his devotion with a dagger in his heart.

It was likely more people she cared about would soon die because of her. She glanced at Kaeso as he spoke with Gaia.

Cordus sought reassurance that he would not cause more suffering. How could she tell Cordus everything would be all right when more people would likely die before this was all over? Perhaps people in this tunnel?

"I've never lied to you about our chances," Ocella told Cordus. "We talked about this before we left the Palace."

Cordus nodded. "Talking about it and living it are quite different. I know it is childish, especially since I have the memories of a thousand years of Consuls. You would think I knew what I was getting into. The Consuls of old did many dangerous things before they consolidated their power over humanity. They led men into battle all the time. I can barely keep my wits about me in a cold tunnel."

"Out of all those memories," Ocella said, "how many were from Consuls who actually cared about their people?"

Cordus snorted. "The Consuls never cared about "the people." The people were only a means to get to space and find the other Muses. They gave "the people" prosperity because they knew a happy population was a productive and virile one. But that will all change someday. Someday soon."

"Then you are the first Vessel to worry about other human beings. So *of course* you never knew what you were getting into. You never had the memories of Consuls who cared."

Cordus thought about this, and then he nodded. "You may be right. The Muses do not let Vessels become emotionally attached to mundanes."

Ocella looked down at him with a grin. "So you've become emotionally attached to me?"

Cordus blushed, and Ocella gave him a playful punch to the shoulder. He glanced at Kaeso and Gaia, who were studying the next tunnel junction with the torch. Cordus whispered to Ocella, "Do you trust him?"

"I used to," she said. "I want to again. He was the most resourceful man I ever knew, and that was *before* Umbra trained him."

The group approached Kaeso and Gaia, who were arguing over the correct tunnel.

"If we go back the way we came," Kaeso said, "we'll run into the Praetorians."

"And if we go forward," Gaia said, "we'll wander these tunnels for days before finding an exit. It's only another hundred yards to the next junction. Then we can take the west tunnel which will take us to the river."

"Aren't you listening? The Praetorians are coming that way!"

Gaia's two men, Tiberius and Brocchus, watched Kaeso with narrow eyes. Ocella assumed Kaeso wouldn't attack Gaia, but she hoped Gaia's men wouldn't shoot Kaeso if he twitched the wrong way.

Kaeso and Gaia argued a few moments when Cordus suddenly said, "Quiet!"

Both Kaeso and Gaia looked at Cordus, surprised. Kaeso said, "You had your chance to—"

"Listen," Cordus said.

The whole group stopped talking and then stopped moving. Ocella heard the gentle lapping of the water against the walls from their movement, drips echoing down the tunnel from behind them...and a low hissing.

"Do you hear it?" Cordus whispered.

Ocella whipped her gaze to Kaeso. His eyes widened as he also recognized the hissing.

"*Cac!*" Kaeso swore. "Turn off the light! Go back!"

Gaia clicked off her torch, and the tunnel turned pitch black. Ocella heard Kaeso lunge through the water, then felt him push both her and Cordus back the way they came. They all rushed through the water back toward the far end of the tunnel, though she knew it would not be far enough.

"What is it?" Cordus asked, then coughed.

Damn, Ocella thought, smelling the gas, *it's already on us.* And then she coughed herself. Soon everybody was coughing.

It's over, Ocella thought. *I failed. All those deaths for nothing...*

She felt Cordus begin to drag behind her, and then his body went limp in her arms. She struggled to push him onto the small ledge on the wall that served as more of a shelf than a walking platform. Stars burst at the corner of her eyes despite the darkness as she continued coughing up whatever gas the Praetorians pumped into the tunnels. There was an extra set of hands next to her, and she heard Kaeso grunting as he helped her get Cordus onto the ledge. Between his own coughs, he said, "Get up there."

He pushed her up as she dragged herself onto the ledge next to Cordus. She stopped coughing, but her limbs were as heavy as marble blocks and she couldn't keep her eyes open. She curled up on the ledge next to Cordus and whispered to him, "I'm sorry."

Her last thought was that at least they would not drown in the sewer water.

Lepidus waded through the murky water, refusing to allow the cold to affect him. At least his breath mask blocked out the water's stench. He eyed the ledges on either side of the tunnel, dismissing them as an optional way to get through because they would force him to walk stooped. He would endure the frigid water. The walk would be worth it if he found the quarry he pursued the last several days.

Lepidus kept his eyes on his Praetorian team's lights a dozen yards ahead. He increased his speed as he neared the team's centurion, his heart thumping with victory rather than the exertion of moving through waist-deep water. His smile broadened beneath the breath mask.

The centurion stood near the entrance to another tunnel on the right, his pulse rifle held high above the water. He tilted his helmeted head toward the tunnel.

"They're in there, Evocatus," he said through his own breath mask.

"How many?"

"We count seven. Four men, two women, and one boy."

"Alive?"

"Yes, my lord. All unconscious."

Lepidus entered. Six Praetorian commandos illuminated the tunnel with their lights. Seven people lay on the ledge above the water in a jumble, some on top of each other, but all asleep. Then Lepidus noticed the woman and the boy.

Praise the gods. I've saved the Republic again.

He studied the boy's features in the harsh commando lights. Cordus had his father's dark eyebrows and wavy black hair. Lepidus gently stroked the boy's hair.

I hope you've been kidnapped, sire. I really do.

Chapter Forty-Two

When Kaeso awoke, he thought he was still recovering from his implant reactivation. He was groggy and his head pounded with the force of a plasma cannon, just as it had during the reactivation. But he opened his eyes, and the memories came back to him in a rush.

He lay on a cot in a small room with bare, stone-block walls painted with a tan gloss. The room was eight feet by eight feet, with a tan door and a small steel-mesh window in the center. There was no handle on the door, only a palm pad on the wall next to it. A window on the wall behind him was neck-high. Bright sunshine flooded the room, feeding his headache all the more.

Kaeso sat up slowly. A wave of vertigo hit him, so he lowered his head between his legs. He took several deep breaths and fought down the nausea. Once the sickness passed, he sat up straight. That's when he noticed he wore prison garb, a loose-fitting yellow tunic and matching pants. He was barefoot, and the smooth stone floor chilled his feet. A faint, orange stain spread beneath the cot toward a small drain in the center of the floor. He stood anyway.

The vertigo returned, but he closed his eyes and he leaned on the smooth wall until it passed. When the vertigo faded, he opened his eyes and turned to the window.

A man's frozen body was nailed to a wooden cross just outside. It was Tiberius, one of Gaia's men. The cross stood a dozen feet from the window, so Kaeso only saw Tiberius's upper torso. Kaeso moved closer, squinting against the sunshine and blue sky beyond the wooden cross. Tiberius was naked, his wrists nailed to each end of the cross, his feet nailed to a pedestal at the bottom, and coarse ropes wrapped around his arms. Tiberius's entire body was purple, and his face was a frozen mask of agony. Black blood and mucus streamed in a solid river from his nose and mouth. Kaeso wondered where they got the wood for the cross. They must've kept a supply of wood for this purpose. The expense alone of transporting wood to the South Pole just for—

Kaeso bit his lip to refocus, lest his panicked thoughts paralyze him.

When he tore his gaze from Tiberius's tortured face, he noticed the desolate white landscape beyond the horror in the foreground. Jagged gray rocks punched through the rolling hills of white snow that stretched to the horizon under a blue, cloudless sky.

Kaeso leaned forward and looked to the right and left. Twenty feet from Tiberius's cross on the right stood another cross. Brocchus, his body in the same condition as Tiberius's.

Kaeso sat on the cot and stared at the wall in front of him, relying on his Umbra training to assess the situation.

He assumed the Praetorians brought him to their prison at the South Pole. He knew tales about it that made him struggle to stamp down his growing despair. It was not a large complex, but its seclusion gave the Praetorians privacy to interrogate prisoners they didn't want the Senate or public to know they had. In an age where travel across the universe was an every day occurrence, the South Pole Praetorian facility was harder for native Terrans to visit than a trip to Libertus. The facility did not officially exist, so only the Consul or the Collegia Pontificis could approve a visit.

He studied his room some more and dismissed any thoughts of escape. The door was metal with barely a hair's width between it and the wall. The palm pad was built into the wall, with no seams from which he might pry it loose with a knife, much less his fingers. He assumed a camera in the pad watched him right now.

A small ventilation grate above the window interrupted the smooth tan ceiling. He didn't know the strength of the window glass, but even if he could break the glass, escape would be pointless. The South Pole would kill him in minutes.

He suspected the Praetorians placed the crosses of Tiberius and Brocchus for better viewing from the cell windows to Kaeso's right. He assumed Ocella, Nestor, and Gaia occupied those cells. They had not been crucified—at least, he didn't see their bodies outside—because they had information the Praetorians wanted. The Praetorians likely hoped the crucified corpses would "open" them to revealing that information.

That left Cordus. Was he also in a cell? Would Cordus give the Praetorians all they wanted? No doubt a normal twelve-year-old boy would under these circumstances, but Cordus was obviously not normal. If he resisted questioning, would the Praetorians dare torture the Consular Heir?

Or, was Cordus back in his Palace, having successfully completed a mission to root out traitors to Roma?

He stared at the sky through the window, doing his best to ignore Tiberius. Had *Caduceus* been captured too? He and Lucia prepared a plan for an emergency run from Roman space, and he gave her strict orders to do so if she sensed imminent capture. He hoped her sense of duty to Blaesus, Daryush, and Dariya would convince her to do the right thing and flee. But if it were Lucia herself, she'd never leave Kaeso and Nestor behind.

He checked his implant and found its concealment protocols were deactivated. The siege was still on. He wondered if the Romans had destroyed any more cities. He wondered if Claudia still lived.

He found it hard to concentrate on anything. He had his share of "hopeless" situations during his time with Umbra, but he always had the confidence, the mental focus, and the knowledge his implant provided to get him through.

But his implant was useless, and it was all he could do to keep from screaming obscenities and pounding on the door. Kaeso closed his eyes and tried to calm his racing heart.

No need to advertise to the wall pad camera they were close to breaking him.

Chapter Forty-Three

Ocella sat on the cot with her back against the wall near the door, staring at Brocchus's crucified corpse through the window. He was the one who leered at her while she was strapped naked to Gaia's scanning chair. She found it hard to have any sympathy for him. If the Praetorians hoped the sight of his frozen body would soften her up for interrogation, they had failed laughably.

But laughable failure described her present situation.

Her own fate mattered little to her. She was going to die—had known it was likely when she agreed to help Cordus escape. It was only a question of how long she'd last under interrogation. She knew Praetorian methods well. They were patient. Everyone broke. And once they were done with her, once she told them everything, then they would kill her.

No, what mattered to her was Cordus. She tried to rescue the boy and give him a life where he could explore his abilities, and perhaps give humanity a fighting chance against the Muses. But she'd only succeeded in revealing his true nature to the Romans. He was probably locked away in the bowels of this prison, strapped to a cot and prodded with the needles of a Praetorian and Collegia medicus team. His own father would likely have given the order.

All those deaths you caused, she told herself, *all for nothing.*

The door next to her cot clicked and opened outward. A Praetorian security guard with a shaved head and black commando uniform entered the room holding a stun baton. A second guard stood outside the door with another baton.

"On your feet," the man in the room said.

Ocella stood up, eying the batons. She shivered when her bare feet met the cold stone floor.

"Hold out your hands," he said. When she did so, he tied plastic wristbands around her hands and cinched them tight.

He then took a black hood from his belt and draped it over her head. Faint light filtered through the hood's threads, but she saw nothing else.

"Let's go," he said and then guided her outside the cell.

She knew any resistance would be met with a debilitating jolt of electricity from the batons. She considered resisting anyway. If she was struck, the jolt would paralyze her for several minutes. *Then the bastards can* carry *me*, she thought. Though she relished resisting any way she could, she still had no desire to feel electricity ignite every nerve in her body.

Better to save her strength for what awaited.

Once outside her cell, the men led her to the left. With her sight gone, she concentrated on her other senses to remember where she went. She heard nothing besides the soft whisper of the commandos' uniforms and her bare feet slapping the smooth stone floor. She began counting her steps.

At step twenty-two, they stopped. There was a click and the sound of a door receding into the wall. The guard behind her grabbed her left arm tightly, and the other guard prodded her back. They guided her forward into the room beyond the door.

"Steps," the guard warned her, his voice echoing in a stairwell.

Ocella felt around with her feet until she found the steps, then proceeded down with the help of the guards. The stone here was rougher, but just as frigid as the floor in the cell corridor.

She counted eighteen steps to the bottom. They stopped at another locked door, and after opening it, the guards led her down another hall to her right. They stopped after she counted seventeen steps, and then they opened a door to her left.

The room into which they pushed her was much warmer than the corridor. The guards walked her six steps forward and sat her down in a hard wooden chair. They cut the plastic cinch around her wrists, then forced her arms onto the armrests and her legs against the chair's supports. Her arms and legs were fastened down with coarse rope that dug into her skin. She wondered at the wooden chair, since it felt similar to the one Gaia Julius used to locate the tracker on her neck.

None of it mattered, though.

Make them work for your screams, she told herself.

The guards yanked the hood off.

The first thing she noticed were the candles. Dozens of them sat on tiered tables along all four walls in the small square room. All were lit, bathing the room in an orange glow and giving off more heat than Ocella had felt in hours. The candles illuminated what looked like Egyptian hieroglyphs decorating the walls. Not for the first time, she wished she still had the memories Cordus gave her. Maybe she could have translated the glyphs.

The two Praetorian commandos moved to stand behind her chair. When they stepped away, she saw two female *flamens* in the back of the room. Each wore a dark red woolen cloak with gold fringe, and an apex leather skullcap strapped beneath her chin. One *flamen* held her hands upturned at her sides and chanted in Egyptian. The other *flamen* held a bronze bowl, her head bowed and her eyes closed. She also chanted, though her voice barely rose above a whisper.

This would not be a standard Praetorian interrogation.

The door behind her opened, and a tall man in a black commando uniform strode in. He glanced at the *flamens*, gave them a respectful nod, and then turned to Ocella. He was in his lower fifties, his graying blond hair cut to within an inch of his scalp.

Then she recognized him. He was the man she saw in the camera feed outside Scaurus's door. He killed Scaurus.

"I am Lepidus," he said. "I've chased you and the boy for the last two weeks. Now I have you."

"Congratulations," Ocella said.

She expected a smirk or even a laugh at her attempted sarcasm, but instead he frowned. *Can he be this easy to anger?* she wondered.

Lepidus opened his mouth again, then paused. His eyes moved around the room. "This is not the sort of room the Guard uses to interrogate criminals like you. We prefer a more...austere setting. Too many petitions to the gods." He leaned forward. "The gods should not witness the things we do."

"Depends on which gods you mean," she said. "Some might enjoy Praetorian interrogations."

Lepidus leaned closer so he was inches from Ocella. She smelled soap on his skin; saw zealous danger in his eyes. "Don't presume to know the will of the gods, Liberti," he whispered. He glared at her a few moments, then straightened.

"I'm ordered to prepare you for a ritual that will make you more compliant to the will of the gods and the Consul." Lepidus glanced around the room. "The decor is too barbaric for my taste, but my orders were explicit."

"When did Romans start worshiping Egyptian gods?" Ocella asked.

Lepidus shrugged. "The room is decorated with Egyptian writing. Doesn't mean the Egyptian gods are here. After all, you're in the company of two Roman *flamens*."

The two robed women swayed in time to their chants.

"They don't look Roman to me. Where are their blue robes?"

Lepidus continued staring at her with a blank expression.

"What's going to happen?"

Lepidus raised an eyebrow. "I don't know."

Either Lepidus really didn't know, or he played the mind games all interrogators played with their subjects. Ocella had steeled herself for torture. She knew the Praetorian procedures for interrogation—had participated in them—and was ready to resist at least their beginning tortures. Her knowledge gave her strength.

But now fear of the unknown crept into her mind and body. Were the room and the *flamens* and Lepidus's apparent confusion supposed to throw off her concentration? If it was, it worked. Just what were they going to do to her? Her mind began to imagine other horrors the Romans could inflict on her, and she struggled to keep her focus. If she lost focus, she would panic and then give them everything they wanted without making them work for it.

"I did not come here to gloat," Lepidus said, his hands clasped behind his back. "I wanted to ask you a question."

Finally, Ocella thought. *Something I can resist.*

"Did you kidnap the boy, or does he really wish to defect to Libertus?"

The soft desperation in his voice made Ocella pause. It was as if he asked her this question for personal reasons, not as part of the interrogation. She almost wanted to tell him the truth just to shatter his faith in the gods and the Consul, to strike back at her captor in any way she could.

An act. He knows he's more likely to get quick answers from me with gentle questions than torture. Give him nothing.

But what did it matter at this point? They knew she could never take the Consular Heir—and keep him hidden—against his will. So why not give them something they already knew?

Because they want you to.

Ocella closed her mouth and turned away.

The com on Lepidus's sleeve chimed. Lepidus sighed and then tapped the bud in his ear.

"Yes," he said. He listened and then said, "Very good, we're ready here."

Lepidus looked at Ocella, his confusion returning. "I suppose you're about to learn the purpose of all this, Liberti."

He studied her a moment longer and then walked out the door. The two Praetorian commandos exited the room and shut the door.

She turned to the *flamens*. "What's going to happen to me?"

They didn't acknowledge her or skip a beat in their chanting.

"Which god do you serve?"

No response, just more chanting.

Ocella pulled against the ropes fastening her to the chair. They were tied in such a way to cause the rough fibers to dig into her flesh whenever she moved. If she struggled too hard, the ropes would leave the skin around her wrists and ankles in bleeding rags.

So she sat and waited. Making a subject wait was also Praetorian strategy, though Ocella supposed it was universal to all interrogators. It gave subjects time to think about the nightmares that would befall them if they didn't give the interrogators what they wanted.

Ocella knew the game, so she cleared her mind by focusing on an old prayer to Juno her grandmother taught her when she was young. She said the prayer over and over again, tapping her fingers to keep count. She had made it through forty-two recitations when the door behind her swung open.

Ocella recognized the man who glided into the room, for she always thought him to be rather short considering his lineage and his position as leader of the Roman Republic. He wore a plain, cream-colored coat without any adornment. His trousers of the same color were crisply pressed and his shiny dark brown shoes reflected the twinkling candlelight.

He stopped in front of her, hands clasped behind his back, and stared at her with ethereal blue eyes. His hair was as black as Cordus's, with the same firm set to his jaw, but Marcus Antonius Publius had a serene air that Ocella assumed was aided by the Muses. His angular face was freshly shaved, without a hint of shadow. The faint scent of an expensive cologne entered the room with him.

"What did you do to my son?" the Consul of the Roman Republic asked with a gentle, yet commanding voice.

Ocella's first impulse was to bow her head before this great man. He was a god on earth, someone who could answer her every prayer. He deserved adoration, sacrifice, and worship on par with Jupiter himself. He was Jupiter incarnate.

Because of my father's gas, Cordus's voice repeated in her mind.

Then she laughed. She laughed for a long time; tears of mirth and terror streaming down her cheeks. Ocella's desire to bow before the Consul proved Cordus's story was true: she never would have been tempted to grovel had the Consul not been emitting his Vessel aura. Ocella's Umbra implant had protected her when she'd met the Consul before, but she had not encountered another Vessel since Scaurus deactivated her implant. The desire to grovel was subtle, but there. Now that Ocella knew what it was, she found it easy to resist.

Most importantly, she realized that Cordus told her the truth earlier: he never used the aura on her, for she never felt this way around him. The boy's honesty suddenly gave her strength.

The Consul cocked his head, his expression curious. Ocella had spoken to the man three times before, and his face was always placid. She'd been in the same room with him many more times, and he'd worn the same non-expression. That's why the curiosity on his face was tantamount to a screaming fit.

"What did you do to my son?" he asked again.

"Nothing," she said, forcing herself not to add "sire" to the end of her statement.

"Why did he run away from his family?"

"You should ask him, sire—" Ocella frowned and clenched her teeth. The effort it took to resist him proved harder than she thought.

"I did," the Consul said. "His answers did not make sense. He is Antonii; he should want to stay with his family. He should want to serve the Roman people as their heavenly representative, as I have done my whole life, and his ancestors before him."

Ocella wanted to please the Consul, to tell him whatever he wanted. She had to force her tongue to do the opposite.

"Perhaps that's not what *he* wants."

The Consul cocked his head. "Why would he want something different?"

Ocella paused. The Consul seemed genuinely confused, as if Cordus wanting to leave Roma opposed the laws of nature. As with Lepidus, Ocella wondered if a well-rehearsed drama was happening here. Each time Ocella met the Consul, he seemed aloof, and she assumed that was how he acted around those he considered beneath him. Now she wondered if it was simply who he was: The Muses had addled his brain to the point where he had no personality left. He was a mouthpiece of the Muses.

"What he wants is irrelevant," the Consul said. "He was born for a purpose. To serve Roma. Any other desire conflicts with that purpose."

"He is serving Roma. In his own way."

"There is one way to serve Roma, and it is the way of the gods and the way his ancestors served. What did you do to make him forsake his purpose?"

"I did nothing to him."

"Why did you take him?"

"I did not take him," Ocella said. "*He* came to *me*. He wanted to get away from Roma because he knew it was not the gods who controlled Roma. We both know that, Consul."

The Consul blinked. "Of course the gods guide Roma. I hear their voices myself, as have all my ancestors, as do the Collegia Pontificum. You are a mundane, so it is not your fault. You cannot know the bliss that comes from feeling the love of the gods, from hearing their wisdom. The gods love humanity. I know this because they tell me."

Ocella gaped at him. Did he believe it was the gods who talked to him and not the Muses? The man had a steadiness in his eyes that said he was serious. How could he not know? Umbra Vessels knew what the Muses were because the Muses told them. Perhaps the Roman Muses told their Vessels they were gods, and the Vessels believed it.

"I don't know what you want me to tell you, Consul. Your son is special. He can hear...the gods, but he has a choice as to whether or not he obeys their orders."

The Consul's head gave a slight jerk, and Ocella thought it was how this emotionless man scoffed.

"The gods give us direction. It is not up to us to *choose* a different direction. The proof is in Roma's greatness. If my ancestors had disobeyed the gods, they would not have given Roma and all of humanity such prosperity."

"You really don't know, do you?"

The Consul stared at her. She tried to maintain eye contact, but it was like looking into a puppet's eyes.

Before she turned away, the corners of the Consul's mouth upturned in a smile. Life came to his eyes, and his grin widened.

"We know more than you think."

And just like that, a different man stood before her.

"So my influence does not work on you. He told you about it, yes?"

Ocella stared at him.

"There are other ways to influence you." He held his hand out to the *flamens* behind him.

A *flamen* stopped chanting, reached into her vestments, and produced an ornate curved dagger that gleamed in the candlelight. The *flamen* who held the bronze bowl hurried beside the Consul.

Now it begins, Ocella thought, taking a deep breath and clenching her teeth. Her heart thundered in her chest and ears.

The Consul rolled up the sleeve of his cream coat, exposing his pale wrist. He moved his wrist over the bronze bowl the *flamen* held and sliced it from the base of his hand almost four inches down his forearm. Blood flowed in rivulets down the Consul's wrist into the bowl, sounding like a faucet left slightly open.

The Consul watched her as his life seemed to drain from him.

After filling the bowl halfway with his blood, the Consul grabbed a nearby candle and held it directly onto his open forearm. His skin sizzled, and the smell of cooking meat filled the room.

He continued staring at her with the same relaxed grin.

The candle cauterized the wound, but the Consul's wrist was a gruesome mix of black and red flesh.

"Our pain threshold is quite high," the Consul said, rolling his coat sleeve over his wrist. "So are our healing abilities. Not even a blemish will remain tomorrow."

The Consul dipped the knife's blade in the bowl, turning it over until he covered every part of it in his blood.

"The Muses, as you Liberti call them, are really quite stupid. Yes, they are a marvelous source of knowledge and physical power, but they do not control us. We are free to make our own choices. Except in one small instance."

Ocella's throat was dry, but she managed to ask, "What is that?"

The Consul smiled, straight white teeth showing. "You'll see."

With a fluid movement, he pulled the dagger from the bowl and plunged it into Ocella's heart. As her vision faded, she lamented she never made him work for her death.

Lepidus frowned when the two *flamens* wheeled Ocella's body from the room. She lay on a long wooden board adorned with carved Egyptian glyphs. A white gauzy shroud covered her entire body, and a dark red stain filled the area around her heart. The Consul strode from the room, and Lepidus fell into step slightly behind him.

"Sire, I don't mean to question your—"

"Then don't. Have you followed my instructions, Quintus Atius?"

Lepidus cleared his throat. "Yes, sire. Though I am confused as to what—"

The Consul stopped and regarded him with dangerous eyes. "Quintus, you are questioning me again. When you question me you question the will of the gods."

"My apologies, sire," Lepidus said, his gaze cast down. "I would never question you or the gods. I was just hoping for...clarification."

"All you need to know is what you do today will please me and the gods. They know of your service, Evocatus. Your reward will be great."

Lepidus lifted his head higher. All his life he wanted the approval of the gods, to know he did the right thing. If his place was not to know the entire plan, then so be it. He would gladly perform his part and trust his role would contribute to the greater good. Just as he had on Caan.

Lepidus bowed his head. The Consul regarded him a moment more and then strode away following Ocella's body.

Lepidus strode in the other direction. He had to contact Appius. He'd not heard from his apprentice in hours.

Chapter Forty-Four

Lucia and Appius dragged the three bodies of Praetorian Unit 202 into Cargo Two and stripped off their uniforms. Lucia tried not to look at their headless necks or the bloody trail they left behind. One uniform was somewhat less bloody than the others, so Lucia removed it from the body, took it to the washbasin, and scrubbed it with a heavy brush. Fortunately the material was a black, waterproof mesh that resisted stains. All it needed was a few splashes of water and a quick scrub.

Their plan was to go at "night," which on the South Pole meant they'd approach the Praetorian compound in broad daylight. It was mid-summer, and the sun shown the entire day. Appius told Lucia the compound still had a day and night watch.

"If we enter during the shift change," he explained, "we'll have a better chance getting in and out."

The plan made sense to Lucia, but she still didn't trust Appius. Yes, he had killed his own men. Yes, he got them through Terra's electronic shields. He had done a lot to help them. And if he wanted to capture her and the ship, he could have done it on the way station.

But it took a long time for Lucia to trust anyone, especially strangers who just hopped onto her ship.

After they stripped the bodies, she and Appius stacked them in a corner and threw a red plastic tarp over them.

"These rifles are older models than what the compound Praetorians use," Appius said, handing Lucia a pulse rifle, "but they will do at a glance. Just try not to let anyone get a good look at them."

Lucia checked the magazine, pulled back the firing mechanism, and then chambered a pellet. She sighted the rifle on a point at the far end of the bay.

"Better than what they gave you in the Legions, eh?"

"What makes you think I was—?"

"I read your file before I was sent to kill you."

Lucia stared at him, wondering whether she should turn the rifle on him now and silence her doubts. He never gave her concrete proof that Kaeso and Nestor *were* at the South Pole compound. But how could she doubt him after what he'd done?

If there was even the slightest chance she could rescue Kaeso and Nestor, she would do it. She couldn't get into the Praetorian compound without Appius, so for now she had no choice but to trust him. Actually "trust" was the wrong word. She would follow him in. If things went bad, he would be the first to die.

Blaesus came down to Cargo Two carrying an armload of his white Senatorial togas.

"I can't decide which toga I'd rather be captured in," he said. "This one I wore when I first took the Senatorial oath, or this one when the Senate censured and exiled me. Which do you think would give a more dignified appearance?"

Lucia sighed, then decided to play along with the old man's theatrics. It could be the last time she got to banter with him. "I like the gold frills on the second one. Makes you more regal. It shows you've returned to Terra as you were on the day they censured you—undefeated."

Blaesus nodded with a determined set to his jaw. "Absolutely. Well, back to the storage closet with you," he said to the older toga. He scooped them up and left the cargo bay.

"He's not really going to wear a toga, is he?" Appius asked from behind.

"No," Lucia said, then returned to her uniform.

Lucia and Appius went back to the command deck after they both secured their thermal uniforms. The ship was on autopilot, just crossing the shore of Terra's southern continent at 40,000 feet. The Praetorian compound's guidance systems took control of the ship's flight once they'd reached the southern Mare Atlantic, so all Lucia could do was watch the ship obey the compound's commands. It was always hard for her to give control to any planetary guidance system. But her nerves were all the more jittery knowing the Praetorians had control.

Appius strapped himself into the command couch. "Any questions before we land?"

"No."

"Tell me the plan again."

She glared at him. "I'm not some green draftee. I've completed missions before."

"I know. But tell me the plan again."

Lucia exhaled, then related the plan as they had worked it out. Appius nodded.

She put her pulse rifle on her lap, the barrel pointed at Appius. "Now tell me why you're doing this?"

Appius raised an eyebrow. "We're going to land in six minutes. Do you really want to discuss this now?"

"Be quick."

"I told you, I'm a Liberti agent."

"How did you know where *Caduceus* was docked? How did you know we were here to extract the Consular Heir?"

Appius rolled his eyes. "I'm also Praetorian, soldier. I've been hunting Marcia Licinius Ocella and the Consular Heir with another Praetorian named Lepidus. Your centuriae met with another Liberti agent in Roma named Gaia Julius. She contacted me and asked for my help to keep you out of Roman hands. Now are we through with the interrogation? If I wanted to capture you, I could have done it much easier on the way station. Without killing my own men."

He was very convincing. But her service in the Legions taught her Praetorians had their own agenda. Everyone else, including their own people, were pieces in a *latrunculi* game. Every piece was expendable.

She continued pointing the barrel at him, but she turned away and monitored the flight into the Praetorian compound. She caught Appius's frown from the corner of her eye, and she took some satisfaction in that.

The landscape below the ship was a flat white plain that gave off a painful glare from the bright sun. Lucia enhanced the ship's window filters to shield her eyes. She watched the feed from the ship's external cameras as they approached the compound. The main structure looked like a brown letter "E" that sat on stilts, which Lucia guessed prevented snow build-up. Steam billowed from a separate block-shaped power plant near the compound. There were no fences because they weren't needed—nobody could escape into the frozen desert and hope to survive more than a few hours, even with cold weather gear. Lucia glimpsed several crosses with bodies just outside the compound's bottom prong, but the ship's descent soon blocked the view.

A long runway for airplanes sat on the compound's east side, and two large jets were docked at the top "E" prong. On the compound's west side sat six grav-powered starships on a flattened landing area. Four were standard cargo freighters. While not of the same manufacture as *Caduceus*, they had a similar spheroid structure. The two other ships were passenger shuttlecraft from the way station, the red paint on their streamlined wings contrasting sharply with the white pad on which they sat.

The compound's guidance system flew *Caduceus* to the starship landing area. The ship touched down near the other spheroid cargo freighters with a slight bump. Lucia's stomach lurched when the ship's grav deactivated and the planet's gravity took over.

Lucia powered down the engines and then spoke into her collar com. "Blaesus, Daryush, meet in Cargo One."

Appius unbuckled himself from the command couch and stopped Lucia before she could leave the command deck.

"I don't expect you to trust me," he said. "I wouldn't either in your position. Just remember your friends are dead if I *don't* help you. You have nothing to lose here."

Lucia slung the pulse rifle over her shoulder, walked past him, and descended the ladder to Cargo One.

Blaesus and Daryush were already in the bay. Blaesus wore gray thermal coats and a thermal head mask. Daryush was similarly dressed, but standing in front of Dariya's sleeper crib staring at his sister through the crib's portal. Lucia put on her black coat and mask. Though the sun shined bright outside, the cold air would freeze exposed skin within minutes. Once she secured her coat and mask, she took out plastic wristbands and placed them on the outstretched gloved hands of Blaesus and Daryush.

"I don't mean to question your professionalism, my dear," Blaesus said, his voice muffled through the mask, "but I take it you've ensured these bands are loose."

"Even you should be able to break them, old man."

The old Senator's eyes crinkled from a grin.

Daryush allowed Lucia to place the bands on his wrist, but he stared at them with furrowed brows.

"You know what you need to do, right?" Lucia asked.

Daryush nodded. He made a motion to break the bands. Lucia patted his arms.

She turned to Appius, who had donned his thermal coat and mask. "Ready?" he asked.

"Lead the way," she said.

Appius turned, moved a few sliders on the tabulari near the cargo doors. Red lights flashed in Cargo One and a small alarm buzzed. The door ramp at the end of the hold clanged and hissed, and then lowered. A cold blast shot through the opening, and it felt good to Lucia. It had been weeks since she'd smelled fresh air and not the ship's stale, coolant-tinged, body-odoriferous air. Appius marched down the ramp, leading Blaesus and Daryush in their bindings, while Lucia came last, serving as the rear guard with her pulse rifle cradled in her arms.

The air was even colder outside, and she had to lean into a sharp bitter wind. A wave of fine snow blew off the ground and into her face. She blinked constantly to keep the moisture on her eyes from freezing. In front of her, Blaesus grunted from the effort of steadying himself in the frigid gusts. Daryush bore the cold in silence, but he bent his head low into the wind and flying snow.

Ocella thanked the gods the march to the compound wasn't long. They entered a tall, white cylindrical structure that looked like a grain silo. Appius went to the controls on the left side of a metal door at the base of the silo and said through his mask, "Outer door: open. Authorization: Gnaeus Hortensius Appius."

The controls chimed, then in a male voice, said, "Voiceprint acknowledged."

The lock clicked, gears whirred, and the door slid open. A second set of doors was just inside the structure. Once they were all inside, Appius said, "Outer door: Close."

The outer door whirred shut, and Lucia was instantly warmer, though the temperature inside the vestibule was well below freezing. The inner doors clicked and slid open. Appius led them through the doors to a guard station on the other side. One guard sat at a desk with camera displays showing various parts of the compound. Another guard stood to one side, his pulse rifle cradled in his arms, eyes trained on the new arrivals. Both young men seemed fresh out of the Praetorian Academy, which made sense to Lucia. South Pole duty did not seem like a coveted post for veterans.

Appius pulled back his hood, removed his thermal mask, and withdrew a com pad from his coat pocket.

"Prisoner transfer. Authorization code 988-89-WSW. You should have received documentation from the way station and a copy of my voice print."

The Guardsman at the desk scrolled through his terminal, then nodded. "Yes, sir. I have Way Station Control approval and your voiceprint checks out. However, your prisoners have not yet been processed. I will need their names, and I'll need a skin sample and pictures."

Appius narrowed his eyes. "Do you understand what a 988 code is, Guardsman?"

The Guardsman blinked and then glanced at his partner. The Guard shifted his stance. Lucia forced herself not to move her free hand to her rifle's trigger.

"Yes, sir, but my orders are to—"

"Obviously you *don't* understand a 988 code because you're still speaking. 988 prisoners are high-risk, high profile prisoners that are *not* documented. They do not exist. In fact, if they took their masks off right now, I'd have to kill you and your partner to keep their identities secret."

The Guardsman swallowed. The other Guardsman's eyes widened, and the right side of his face twitched.

"Of course, sir. I will not log their arrival. B-But, sir, should know the whole 988 wing is closed by order of Praetor Quintus Atius Lepidus. We'll need to house your prisoners in another wing, sir. That's why I assumed I'd need to run them through the standard prisoner transfer procedures."

"Why is the 988 floor closed?"

"Other 988 prisoners were brought in this morning, sir."

Appius nodded. "Arrange two cells in another wing. I want them on a deserted floor. These men are dangerous manipulators and cannot be underestimated. I don't want them talking other prisoners into a riot."

The desk Guardsman nodded quickly. "Yes, sir. There aren't many prisoners here, so I can put yours on an empty floor. With your approval?"

"Fine," Appius said. "Transfer the protocols to my com."

"Yes, sir." The Guardsman typed on his terminal, while Appius watched his com for the protocols. Satisfied, Appius put his com into his coat pocket.

"Er, one more thing, sir," the Guardsman said. "Compound regulations require you surrender your weapons while in the prison wings." A fine sheen of sweat materialized on the Guardsman's forehead.

But Appius unslung his rifle and placed it on the desk, and then pulled the pulse pistol from the holster at his side and lay it next to the rifle. Appius motioned Lucia forward. It went against every instinct in her blood, but she laid her weapons on the table next to those of Appius. He said they would ask for the weapons. She hoped they wouldn't insist on a body search and find the small pistol inside her coat.

The relived Guardsman stood, collected the weapons, and stacked them in a storage cage behind him with racks of rifles and pistols. The Guardsman sat back down at his terminal and said, "I've arranged two cells in wing two on the third floor. You go through the doors behind me to—"

"I know where it is, Guardsman. I've been here before. Just open the doors so I'm not delayed any longer than I already am."

The Guardsman nodded, then tapped a few keys on his terminal. The thick glass doors behind him clicked, then slid open to the right. Appius strode through the doors, while Lucia made a show of prodding Blaesus and Daryush to follow. They entered a small, doorless corridor that led to an elevator at the end.

Lucia leaned close to Blaesus and asked, "How are you doing?"

"Sweating like a gladiator," he replied in a harsh whisper. "These thermal masks are lovely outside, but hotter than—"

Appius turned with glare. "Quiet."

They entered the elevator without another word. Appius pressed the button for the first level rather than the third.

"Your friends should be in the 988 section on level one," Appius explained.

"Will the guards be any trouble?" she asked.

"No," he said. He pulled his own hidden pistol from his black vest, checked the rounds, and then returned it to his vest. "Getting in will be easy. Getting out will be the challenge, as we discussed."

When Appius had told Lucia the plan, she thought its chances for success were slim. Now that she was here, she wondered if the plan wasn't suicidal. Yes, the compound was lightly guarded due to its remote location. But these were still Praetorian Guardsman, the elite Roman security force. They would be hard to kill; even the green men downstairs were trained to deal with attempted breakouts.

Blaesus tested his wristbands. "Are you sure these will come off when I pull? Because they seem tight to me."

"I cut them myself," Lucia snapped. "A good tug will do, but wait until we get past the guards."

Daryush regarded his wristbands and gave them a gentle pull. They snapped and fell to the floor.

Lucia cursed and picked them up just as the elevator door slid open.

One guard sat at a terminal in front of glass doors that led to the prison cells. The Guardsman looked up as they exited the elevator. He also seemed like a fresh recruit, and he had the bored gaze of a man lulled to complacency by a dull post.

"Prisoner transfer," Appius said, stepping forward to hand the young Guard his com pad.

The Guard eyed his terminal. "Yes, sir. I'll just need to see—"

Appius brought his pistol up with his other hand and shot the young Guard in the head. The Guard fell backward in his chair and hit the floor, his skull and brains dripping down the glass doors behind him.

Appius rushed around to the Guard's body, pulled a large knife from his coat, and hacked off the Guard's right hand. He stood up, placed the bloody hand on the desk, and then punched a few keys on the Guard's terminal. The glass doors behind him clicked open. "Let's go," he said, grabbing the bloody hand and bolting into the cell corridor.

Lucia swallowed. Blaesus pulled apart his wrist bands and retrieved a pistol from his coat. Daryush stared wide-eyed at the dead Guard, now handless and, for the most part, headless.

"Come on, big man," Lucia said from behind him. He tore his gaze from the Guard and moved to follow Blaesus and Appius into the corridor.

All four checked the narrow rectangular windows on each door. Lucia counted twenty cells, ten on each side of the corridor. She peeked through the windows on the left side while Appius and Blaesus took the right.

The first three cells were empty. In the fourth one she saw Kaeso.

"In here," Lucia cried out. When she said that, Kaeso leaped up from his cot and stared astonished at Lucia through the window. He shook his head and grinned.

Appius rushed over, placed the Guard's bloody hand on the door pad, and the door clicked open. Kaeso, dressed in yellow prison garb with no shoes, pushed the door open and charged out.

Before she could open her mouth, he said, "Nestor, Ocella, and Gaia Julius should be next to my cell."

"Nestor and who?"

"Later," Kaeso said, then rushed passed her and hurried to the cell next door.

"Glad to see you, too," Lucia muttered.

She stood beside Kaeso and looked into the fifth cell's window. A middle-aged woman stared back at her, trying to get a glimpse of the commotion outside. Appius opened the door with the Guard's hand, leaving a bloody smear on the pad. Though she was also dressed in yellow prison coveralls, the woman stepped out as if she had entered the Senate. She held her chin high, regarding Lucia, Appius, Blaesus, and Daryush with cool eyes and a frown. Her lip curled when she saw how Appius was opening the doors. They were obviously not the rescue she expected.

You must be Gaia Julius, Lucia thought.

"Don't forget the boy," Gaia said.

"Where is he?" Appius asked, looking through the next cell's window.

"Is he not here?" Gaia asked.

"Haven't seen him yet."

Appius placed the hand on the door pad, leaving another bloody smear. Nestor stepped out and took Lucia in a large hug.

"I knew you were crazy," he laughed, "but I had no idea you'd attack a Praetorian compound. I cannot wait to hear your story."

Blaesus and Daryush came over to Nestor, both smiling. Blaesus slapped Nestor on the shoulder. "It is a long story fraught with peril and perdition, my good medicus."

"Later," Kaeso growled. He nodded toward Appius who was still checking cell windows. "Who's he?"

"Another long story," Lucia said.

"I found Marcia Licinius," Appius announced. He opened the door with his gruesome key. "Time to leave," he said to the occupant. He did a double take, and frowned. "Do you want to leave or not?"

"Of course," a woman's voice said from inside the cell. "Lead the way, Praetorian."

An Indian woman with short brown hair, who appeared to be Lucia's age, stepped out of the cell. She carried herself with the same haughtiness as Gaia Julius, which made Lucia wonder if she was also a patrician.

"Ocella?" Kaeso said with concern.

"Where's Cordus?" Ocella asked calmly. "We cannot leave without him or this was all for nothing."

"He's not here," Appius said, reaching the end of the corridor.

"Where else would they keep him?" Kaeso asked.

An alarm blared in the hallway. They all winced at the piercing wail. Appius ran past Lucia. "Let's go!"

Lucia glanced at Kaeso, then followed the Praetorian, with the rest in pursuit.

In the Guard station, Appius hurried over to the storage locker and yanked it open. Over a dozen stun batons hung from hooks inside.

"How are we getting off the compound?" Kaeso asked. "And could I have a weapon?"

"First question, the roof," Appius said. "Second question, knife or baton?"

"Knife," Kaeso said. Appius handed Kaeso the bloody knife he'd used to cut off the Guard's hand. Kaeso wiped it on the Guard's pants, and tucked it through his coat belt.

Ocella grabbed Appius's arm. "We cannot leave without Cordus," she said firmly.

"If we don't leave now, none of us will."

"The Liberti is right," Gaia said. "We can't leave the boy. Better to die rescuing him than leave him with the Praetorians. They will use him to find us anyway."

Lucia couldn't believe what she heard. "Are you two insane? Praetorian commandos are going to charge through that door any second and you want to take them on?"

"Wait," Blaesus said from the Guard station. He stared at the terminal, reading the text that scrolled down the screen. "It's not us. It says 'all available units assemble in exit 3 to repel imminent assault.'"

"They're under attack?" Kaeso asked, rushing to where Blaesus stood.

Appius leaned forward. "Impossible. Nobody can get within a hundred miles without being detected."

Lucia was about to ask if it was Umbra Ancilia when her collar com vibrated against her neck. She'd switched the com to vibrate out of habit when off the ship, even though nobody was on *Caduceus* to call her.

She tapped the collar com. "Who is this?" she asked.

"Uh, is this the trierarch of the Liberti ship?" a young voice asked.

The eyes of everyone in the room swung to Lucia.

"Who is this?" Lucia repeated.

"Cordus," Ocella said, and moved to Lucia. "Where are you, Cordus? Are you all right?"

"Ocella! I am fine, for now, but I am on the Liberti ship. I assume this is the one rescuing us?"

Ocella laughed. "A lucky assumption, but yes. Stay there, we're on our way."

"I will not leave without you."

Lucia stared at Ocella. "How did he...?"

"We'll ask him later," Kaeso said. "Let's get to the ship."

Once they all crowded into the elevator, Appius slammed the button for the first level. When the elevator reached the ground floor, the escapees pushed themselves against the sides of the elevator, and Appius held up his pistol. The doors slid open. Appius scanned the area, then lowered his weapon.

"Clear," he said, hurrying out. He rushed to a locker behind the deserted guard station, whipped the door open, and threw jackets, thermal hoods, and boots onto the floor at the feet of the former prisoners. "They keep these for transfers outside the compound. Lucky for us they don't use off-compound clothing."

They dressed within seconds. Appius pushed through the glass doors and into the vestibule in front of the metal door. He pulled his thermal mask over his head and neck, then slammed his hand on the door pad. The door slid open with a metallic grind. Lucia had just pulled her thermal mask over her head when a blast of frigid air hit her. Appius raced out the door and toward *Caduceus*.

A shot cracked from behind them. Blood sprayed from Appius's neck and he went down. He did not move. Lucia blinked and then knelt down next to Appius while the others raced toward the ship. Kaeso stopped with Lucia.

"He's gone," Kaeso yelled as more shots kicked up snow around them.

"I know." She pried Appius's gun from his hand. "We might need this."

Kaeso pulled Lucia up and they both raced toward the ship, pulse bullets cutting the air around them.

Lucia was startled to see Appius go down, but she never trusted him anyway. That was cold considering how he helped them, but it kept any regrets at bay while she tried saving her centuriae and crew.

The escapees had all entered the cargo bay, and Blaesus shut the Cargo One ramp door as Lucia and Kaeso leaped into the bay. Lucia kept running past the others and up the ladder to the command deck. Kaeso followed, as Daryush hurried to the engine room.

On the command deck, a boy jumped up from her pilot's couch. A part of her wanted to bow to the boy. He was the Consular Heir to the Roman Republic!

And the host of a psychotic alien virus. That thought made it easier to push past him and jump into her pilot's couch.

"Are they shooting at us?" he asked.

"Yes," she said.

Kaeso strapped himself into his command couch and tapped the ship's intercom on his display. "All crew find a delta couch and strap yourselves in. We're going to delta sleep as soon as we clear the atmosphere."

Lucia ran the engine startup, her eyes flitting to the window, watching for commandos. The ship's ion engines roared to life, and she saw that Daryush had started spooling the way line engines.

"Um, where should I sit?"

Without glancing back, Lucia said, "Go to a cabin on the second level. Use a delta couch there."

"Can I use this—?"

"That's Nestor's. Get off the command deck."

The boy sighed, but then hurried away just as Nestor entered the command deck and strapped himself into his delta couch.

"This is all moot," Nestor said, working his delta controls. "We won't get a two miles before the orbiting Eagles shoot us down."

"How *did* you get down here?" Kaeso asked Lucia.

"Appius did something to the beacon." She quickly explained what the former Praetorian did. "Welcome to the *Vacuna*, Centuriae."

Kaeso raised an eyebrow. "Can you do it again?"

She shook her head. "Almost destroyed the com system. Ship can't take that kind of overload again. Ion engines are online."

"Wayline engines?" Kaeso asked.

"Daryush is spooling them. They'll be up before we leave atmosphere."

"How long?"

A series of pings came from the outer hull, and she looked out her window. Six black-clad commandos rushed toward them, all firing at the ship with pulse rifles.

Lucia didn't wait for Kaeso's command to lift off. She tapped the sliders on her pilot's control board, the ship lurched, then the inertia cancellers kicked in and the ride turned smoother. Pings still resounded off the hull until they were two hundred feet in the air.

"Course?" she asked Kaeso.

He pulled a collar com from a basket next to his couch, clipped it to his yellow prison tunic, then said, "Gaia, Ocella, Cordus, if you're in a delta couch, pick up the receivers."

A few moments later, Gaia's voice came over the com. "I'm here, Centuriae."

"Ocella here."

Then, "Cordus here, too."

"Where are we going?" he asked. "And we need to know now."

Gaia said, "There's a Saturnist planet."

"No," Ocella said, "we can't waste any more time. Cordus? We need to go to the planet we talked about. We need the proof before the Romans find us again."

"What planet?" Gaia asked.

"Cordus?" Ocella asked again.

There was a pause, then Cordus said, "Centuriae?"

"Yes."

"When I was on the command deck, I noticed your engines are a bit...untraditional. Can you get us to a specific planet without using the main way lines? If you can, I can give you the exact numbers."

Lucia gaped at Kaeso. *How did that kid know our engines can do that?*

Kaeso said, "Yes. Give me the way line numbers."

Cordus relayed a set of numbers and Lucia entered them into the reconfigured way line navigation system. She frowned at the numbers as she entered them. When Cordus read the last number, Lucia shot a look at Kaeso.

"Centuriae, that's—"

Proximity alarms blared. Lucia's radar showed two Roman air fighters, a hundred miles away, screamed toward them at three times the speed of sound.

"Two Falcons approaching from the north— Missile launch!" Four, then six, then twelve missiles popped up on Lucia's display.

Kaeso tapped his com. "All crew prepare for delta sleep."

"Centuriae," Nestor said, "engaging way line engines in the atmosphere will tear us apart."

"Those were the old engines," Kaeso said.

Nestor just exhaled.

The alpha way lines every school child knew always began at a point two thousand miles from a planet's atmosphere. No one ever determined why two thousand miles, so the priests attributed it to divine calculation, and said any way line jump attempts outside that jump point would meet disaster. Subsequent experimentation confirmed it.

But *quantum* way lines intersected with a planet's core. Could the new engines find them while still in atmosphere?

They were about to find out. "Course set, Centuriae. Piloting controls transferred to your terminal."

She leaned her head back, waiting for delta sleep. She turned to Kaeso and watched his grim determination until her eyes closed.

Lepidus exited the compound's main entrance near the landing yards when a deep boom rumbled across the landscape. The shockwave hit him a moment later, a blast of hot wind out of place in this frigid land.

Did the Falcons kill them? If they did, the Consul would have the pilots crucified before the day was out.

He walked to where Appius lay in the hard packed snow, blood turning the white ground a dark crimson around his head.

"They're gone," he said.

Appius blinked behind his thermal mask. Lepidus held out a hand, and Appius took it to rise to his feet. "The bitch took my gun."

"We'll get you a new one," Lepidus said. "Let's get inside before that pig's blood freezes solid on your neck."

"Yes, sir."

As they strode back to the compound, Lepidus noticed Appius's frown.

"What is it?"

"We lost good men today."

"You doubt the wisdom of the Consul?"

"No, Evocatus. I understand why the escape had to appear real. I just...hope they will receive proper funerals."

Once they entered the metal doors to the compound, Lepidus turned to Appius. "They are Roman heroes. The gods will welcome them all to Elysium with triumphs. Besides, they were young and inexperienced, so their loss will not terribly damage the state. They were sacrificed for that reason."

Appius nodded. "I don't understand how letting the Liberti go will aid us. Once they take a way line, we'll lose them."

Lepidus sighed. "It sounds to me you are doubting the Consul again."

When Appius was about to protest, Lepidus raised a hand. "I know how confusing this must seem. There are parts of the plan to which you are not privy. All you need is faith in the Consul and the gods that the part you play will keep Roma safe from her enemies."

Appius nodded, but his eyes told Lepidus the boy did not have the faith Lepidus required in his apprentices. He was certainly good at what he did, but without faith, he would never serve the gods and the Roman state with the unquestioning devotion they deserved. Lepidus feared that when this mission was over, he would need to search for another apprentice, and Appius would be relegated back to the Praetorian commandos from which Lepidus plucked him. It saddened Lepidus and frustrated him, but he would not give the gods and the state a successor that did not share his loyalty.

Now he had to hurry to the shuttle that would take him to the orbiting Eagle fleet assigned to follow the Liberti ship. He didn't know where the ship was going, or even how the Eagles would follow it.

Those were parts of the Consul's plans to which even he was not privy.

Chapter Forty-Five

Ocella screamed, but the Muses would not let the sound come from her own mouth.

She awoke from the delta sleep and immediately tried to seize control of her body. But her attack had as much impact as a snowflake against a mountain. The Muses awoke before she did and stopped it.

Her body was no longer hers from the moment she awoke after the Consul's murderous attack. At first she thought her spirit had gone to the Underworld, that this was punishment for all the deaths she'd caused, all the misery she left behind.

Millions of tiny whispers soon convinced her she still lived. They told her to be calm, to give up control, to let the gods do with her body what they will. It was easier if she just submitted. If she did, they whispered, they would give back her body, and she could be as powerful as the Consul.

She fought them with every shred of mental and spiritual energy she could muster, yet she still could not break their control. They were too powerful, too entrenched in her brain. She was a prisoner.

During their escape, she had rejoiced when Appius opened the door to her cell. This strange man would help free her from the Praetorians and from her own body. But then dawning horror when the Muse whispers rejoiced, saying "the plan" worked. Her mouth formed words. Sounds came from her throat that were not of her choosing. She fought to scream at Kaeso and the others, to tell them this was all a trap.

The Muses wouldn't even let her blink.

Her heart leaped when she heard Cordus's voice. *He's alive!* Her joy turned to anger when the Muses used her voice to urge Cordus to take them to the planet that held his precious evidence.

Evidence that would prove to humanity what the Muses had done to other civilizations. The Muses whispered to each other. The planet must be found, and the evidence destroyed. Then they would turn their full fury on the Liberti Muses.

The Muses made Ocella's body sit up from the delta couch, exit the cabin, and walk down the cramped corridor.

Ocella could see the memories the Muses held, going back millions of years. She saw the intelligent species they'd used to fight each other. She still did not understand why the strains fought. All she could feel was their anger toward the Liberti Muses: irrational, violent, savage. It was a mindless drive for domination that had gone on since the dawn of their existence. It would continue until the other strains were wiped out.

What then? she asked them.

The whispers combined into one voice. *We will be the only gods.*

Ocella would have shivered if the Muses had allowed it.

The Muses moved her body to a ladder, which she ascended to the command deck. On the deck, Nestor unbuckled himself from his delta couch, gave her a grim look, then brushed past her and descended the ladder. Kaeso and his pilot Lucia scrolled through readouts on their terminals. The view outside the command windows showed a planet covered in gray clouds, with patches of brown and black poking through. A thin brown ring surrounded the planet, and she could make out glints from the floating raw ore mixed with gray and brown rock.

"I assume we arrived in one piece," the Muses forced her to say.

It's not me talking! Ocella screamed. *This is all a trap!*

"Not exactly," Kaeso said. "Our jump through Terra's atmosphere fried the way line engines. They need repairs if we want to jump anywhere again."

"What about your alpha way line systems?" the Muses asked.

Kaeso shook his head grimly. "Umbra took the old ones out. The Romans attacked before we got our backups." He turned back to the tabulari. "Daryush is checking the new ones, but it'll take time. Time I assume we don't have."

The Muse whispers were jubilant, and she felt them pass this information along their mysterious connections to Muses on the other side of the universe. She wanted to shake Kaeso. *They're tracking you through me! They're coming!*

Lucia unstrapped herself from her delta couch. "I'm going to help Daryush with those engines. Maybe we can…I don't know…"

When she passed Ocella, the Muses made her turn to Lucia. "Thank you for rescuing us. That was very brave."

Lucia looked at her, then glanced at Kaeso. "I don't leave my crew behind."

In other words, she didn't do it for me or Cordus. Ocella wondered if Lucia and Kaeso were together. A twinge of jealousy sparked in her, which increased the whispers of the Muses as they discussed her emotion with clinical detachment. Their cold interest in her emotions made her more angry, and she mentally flailed against the prison they had constructed around her mind.

Her screams almost made her ignore Cordus.

"Ocella!" he yelled, just coming up the ladder. He launched himself toward her with a tight hug. The Muses forced her body to return the hug with equal force, though she would have done it by choice.

But she noticed a curious thing. For the first time since she'd awakened from the Consul's attack, the whispers in her mind had stopped. The Muses still controlled her body, but they were silent.

"I thought they killed you," he said into her shoulder.

"Obviously they didn't," the Muses made her reply. "How did you get away from them?"

"Yes," Kaeso asked, his eyes narrowed at Cordus. "That's something we're all wondering."

He's not the one you should be worried about, Ocella wanted to say. *It's me!*

Cordus broke away from his hug, looking sick. "I-I *made* my guards let me go."

Kaeso stared at him, confused. Ocella didn't need the Muses to figure out what he did. A source of amusement to her in the Cloaca Maxima had saved Cordus's life. He had released his Muse pheromones to manipulate his guards into releasing him. Though the Muses no longer whispered, she could feel their ironic pleasure.

Because it had also been part of their "plan."

"You did what you had to do," the Muses said. "You should have no regrets."

Kaeso leaned forward. "What did you do?"

Cordus flushed and shook his head. "Never mind. I escaped."

Kaeso nodded slowly. "So how do we find this proof you mentioned? We don't have much time."

As if to underscore the point, the ship's proximity alert chimed ominously. Kaeso turned back to his tabulari and cursed. "A squadron of Umbra ships just jumped into orbit. They used the quantum way lines."

Anger exploded from the Muses, and they began whispering violent curses.

Cordus gasped and backed away from her, his eyes wide. Ocella wanted to scream, *Yes, they have me! You know! Tell the others!*

"How?" he stammered.

The Muses turned her lips into a sneer. "I suppose it was a matter of time before you found out, your grace. Now it is too late."

Kaeso stared at her. "Ocella?"

"She's one of them," Cordus said. "She's a Vessel. She's infected."

Kaeso jumped up from his couch, but the Muses spread Ocella's hands. "Worship me."

The Muses pushed the aura from her skin and breath. The chemicals shot toward Kaeso and enveloped him in a vapor cloud he could not see.

Kaeso paused, his eyes fluttering as he fought to control the overwhelming desire to do whatever the Muses told him. He exhaled sharply, then gritted his teeth, staring at her venomously.

Fight it, Kaeso!

The vapor dissipated around Kaeso, and before the Muses could send forth another one, Kaeso's right fist came around in a lightning undercut to her chin. Ocella screamed in triumph as she blacked out with the Muses.

Chapter Forty-Six

Kaeso shook his right hand as he stared down at Ocella. Whatever she'd used to try and stop him was wearing off, but he still felt overwhelming guilt over what he did. *You cannot hit a god!* Such an unnatural thought only confirmed it was not his.

He eyed Cordus. "Is that how you escaped?"

Cordus still leaned against the bulkhead, staring down at Ocella. Then he looked up at Kaeso and nodded.

"Was she always a Vessel?" Kaeso asked.

Cordus shook his head. "They could not have hidden that long. I would have known. It must have happened at the compound."

Kaeso tapped his collar com. "Nestor, Daryush, command deck."

Lucia climbed up the command ladder. "Centuriae, twelve more Umbra ships just—" She stared at Ocella on the floor. "What happened?"

"She's a Vessel," Kaeso said, climbing into his command couch. "Get us moving."

"*Cac*," she breathed, stepping over Ocella as if avoiding a snake.

"Centuriae," Cordus said. "She may have told the Praetorians where we are."

"Likely."

"Then we do not have much time. We need to retrieve the records or they will destroy the planet."

Kaeso nodded. "Let's hope they'll try sooner rather than later."

Cordus frowned, opened his mouth to speak, but Lucia cut him off.

"Roman Eagles just jumped from the alpha way line!"

Kaeso grinned and thanked Fortuna for her luck. He compared the Umbra ship headings with those of the Eagles. Both squadrons converged on his location, their flight paths forming a "V" with *Caduceus* at the tip.

"Cordus," Kaeso said, "if Vessels are aboard the Umbra ships and the Eagles, will they fight each other?"

"Under normal circumstances, yes. But it depends on how bad they want me."

"Then let's give them something to fight over."

Lucia glanced at Kaeso. "What do you mean?"

Kaeso heard Daryush and Nestor arrive. Without turning, he said, "Take Ocella down to a cabin and strap her into a delta couch. Make sure she's tied down tight. She's a Roman Vessel."

"What?" Nestor said.

"Just strap her in, and then you two do the same once you're done. We're entering the atmosphere. Cordus, those coordinates?"

The boy recited a longitude and latitude on the planet. Lucia gave Kaeso a sharp look, and Kaeso shook his head.

"Unbelievable," Kaeso muttered.

"Why?" Cordus asked.

Kaeso exhaled. "Nothing. Lucia, set a course."

He hoped the weather on Menota, and the city of Pomona, had improved since their last visit.

Chapter Forty-Seven

Lepidus stood on the navigation deck of the command ship *Fury*, grinding his teeth. He watched the holographic display of the space surrounding Menota, the Liberti squadron approaching *Caduceus*, and the Roman Eagle squadron racing to the same coordinates.

"Once again, Lord Navarch," Lepidus said to the squadron commander, Vibius Laelius, "the Liberti war ships are irrelevant. We should focus on the—"

"I'd hardly call them irrelevant," Laelius snapped from his command couch in the center of the deck.

Vibius Laelius was a large man with a quiet, yet deep voice. He was a member of the Collegia Pontificis, which made the unusual decision to make him the mission's Navarch. Lepidus understood why, considering the mission's sensitivity. Not only were they chasing the Consular Heir, but Menota was a world the gods and the state had declared off limits to all humanity after the Roman Fleet irradiated it. Even the godless Liberti refused to allow landings there. Why would the Consular Heir want to come to this godsforsaken, plague-infested planet?

"The Liberti have come for a fight, and we will give them one," Laelius declared. Lepidus frowned at the irrational anger dripping from Laelius's words. Did he not realize the Consul himself had ordered them to *follow* his traitorous son? The Lord Navarch's desire to engage the Liberti not only wasted time, but also went against the Consul's orders.

Do not question the Collegia, he reminded himself. *They are Vessels of the gods. They are infallible.* If Laelius decided it was wiser to attack the Liberti ships, then Lepidus had to trust in the Lord Navarch's decision.

"Missile range in four minutes, my lord," said the weapons officer to the right of the Lord Navarch's couch.

"Sir," Lepidus said, "please allow me to take a ship and follow *Caduceus*."

"Are you mad? I'm about to blow a squadron of Liberti to Hades. I need *all* my ships."

"Then at least let me take a shuttle, my lord. The Consul's orders were clear: I am to follow his son, no matter what."

Laelius frowned as he stared at the holographic display, then he waved his hand. "Very well. You may have an unarmed shuttle."

Lepidus bowed his head and then retreated, Appius following him. He gave the holographic tactical display one last glance before leaving the command deck.

"Let's get off this ship before they destroy each other," Lepidus said to Appius under his breath.

"Yes, sir," Appius said.

Lepidus never commanded an Eagle, but even he could see the trajectories of the opposing squadrons would result in a vicious point-blank shootout. Conventional space battles were fought from long distances, each ship firing missiles and then using their short-range plasma cannons to destroy approaching enemy missiles at close range. Missiles fired at close range caused just as much damage to the firing ship as the target ship.

This is madness, Lepidus thought, surprising himself with his doubts. He quickly stamped them down. Lord Navarch Laelius was a prominent member of the Collegia Pontificis, and therefore in constant communication with the gods. The gods would grace him with the wisdom needed to win this battle, for they would not abandon one of their prophets to inglorious death. If the Lord Navarch's destiny was to die in this battle, then it would be for a divine reason.

Just because Lepidus couldn't see the reason did not mean there wasn't one.

As soon as Lepidus and Appius entered the shuttle wing, missile alarms blared through the ship. Lepidus found the closest shuttle hatch, opened it, and descended a ladder into the shuttle's cockpit. The shuttle had no gravity, so Lepidus and Appius floated hand over hand to the pilot couches. Once they strapped themselves in, Lepidus told Appius to fire the engines and disengage from the Eagle. It took Appius a few minutes to prep the shuttle and get the engines started.

"Disengaging," he announced.

The shuttle was a miniature version of the Eagle, with a long fuselage and glide wings on either side for atmospheric flight. It was attached to the Eagle's wing, so when the shuttle disengaged, there was a jerk, then the shuttle dropped away from the ship, revealing space, the stars, and the gray outline of Menota to the starboard side.

Lepidus searched the port window for the Liberti ships and their missiles. He couldn't see them, but they lurked out there several hundred thousand miles from the Eagle. The missiles traveled a quarter of the speed of light, so he'd never see them when they struck. He pulled up the sensor display of the space around the planet. They had less than a minute to clear the Eagle before the missiles hit.

Appius noticed the same thing and engaged the shuttle's ion engines. The acceleration felt like Lepidus was kicked in the chest by a horse. Eagle shuttles did not have anti-gravity or inertia cancellers, since they were too small for such large systems. Lepidus clenched his teeth at the four gravities pressing him into the command couch. He rarely experienced more than two gravities during a passenger shuttle launch and had not endured this many since his Academy days. But it was either this or vaporization when the antimatter missiles hit.

"It'll be close," Appius said with a strained voice. The shuttle accelerated another gravity. Darkness crept into the corners of Lepidus's eyes. He tensed his muscles to increase blood flow, but he'd soon black out if the acceleration did not cease. He couldn't lift a hand or move his head to see if Appius was still conscious.

A white light filled the cockpit window from behind them. Lepidus made a supreme effort to move his eyes to his terminal and check the hull temperature. The temperature rocketed higher than during atmospheric re-entry. The air grew hotter in the cockpit. Beads of sweat popped on his forehead, then rolled off his head and into his hair.

"Appius..." he groaned.

"Almost clear," Appius grunted back.

The white light faded, and the hull temperature began to fall. Appius eased the acceleration to match the dissipation. Once the light faded, Appius brought the shuttle down to a meager half-gravity acceleration.

Lepidus raised his arms and shifted his legs in his couch to stretch out the kinks in his muscles. He'd be sore for a week, as if he'd spent a day lifting five times his weight in bricks.

He checked his display. Eight of Lord Navarch Laelius's twelve Eagles were gone, including the command ship *Fury*. Of the surviving four, only two maneuvered for another assault on the Liberti ships. The disabled two continued on their old trajectory toward interstellar space without correction. The Liberti squadron lost six ships, two were disabled and four moved to engage the surviving Eagles. Thankfully the Liberti did not seem interested in a lone shuttle flying toward the planet.

Lepidus ground his teeth. If they destroyed each other, he would not have a way home. The shuttle did not have way line engines or a delta sleep system. Not even an old-fashioned sleeper crib. Shuttles transported personnel and cargo from ship to ship, and ship to ground. He would need a starship to get back to Terra, and if those fools—

He took a deep breath. *The Lord Navarch had a plan.* He could not see it now, but the gods did this for a reason. Lepidus had a role to play, and he would follow orders. The gods would either allow him to succeed, or they would not. Either way, he accepted his fate.

"I have *Caduceus* on sensors," Appius said.

On Lepidus's display, a ship called *Vacuna* descended into Menota's atmosphere. The burning air surrounding them would make their instruments useless during re-entry. With Fortuna's help, the antimatter explosions may have hidden them from before "*Vacuna*" began re-entry.

"We can still surprise them," Lepidus said. "What is their heading?"

Appius checked his terminal. "If they continue on their current heading, they should land near the city of Pomona."

Lepidus frowned. Why did they flee to a dead world like Menota? A thriving black market existed for Pomona artifacts. But the pursuit of treasures seemed a frivolous act for *Caduceus*, considering the Praetorian Guard was chasing them. Lepidus assumed they would flee to some well-defended Liberti stronghold. Why had they come to a planet where they could not hope to defend themselves?

Unless they knew the Liberti would be here.

"Three Eagles just came off the way line," Appius announced. "One has the Consular beacon."

Thank the gods, Lepidus thought. *A sane man will now command the battle.*

"They're engaging the Liberti ships," Appius said.

Lepidus looked at his display. All three Eagles fired their missiles at the remaining Liberti. At their distance from the Liberti, the missiles would not hit their targets for another ten minutes.

Lepidus breathed easier. The more Eagles there were, the greater chance they'd destroy the Liberti warships. And the greater chance he'd have a way home once he found the boy. The Consul's presence did not surprise him, considering this was the Consul's plan.

Though the Consul said Ocella was no longer a threat, Lepidus would treat her as an enemy until she proved otherwise. She'd been his prey for a week, not to mention she betrayed the Liberti, then Roma, and now the Liberti again. He told himself he did not doubt the Consul, only Ocella. Her accidental death would be most unfortunate.

"*Caduceus's* heading to Pomona is confirmed, Evocatus. They're landing near the city center."

Lepidus brought up a display of Pomona and zoomed in on the buildings surrounding *Caduceus*. "Set us down on the Hospital of Angita's landing pad a half-mile southeast of their location."

"Course set," Appius said. "Entering the atmo— Sir, two more Liberti ships just appeared!"

"Off the way line?"

"No, sir. They appeared next to the fleeing Eagles, but they did not come from the way line. They must have the same engines as *Caduceus*. They're firing missiles."

The two new Liberti signatures were almost on top of the Eagles fleeing the opening salvo with the Liberti. Several dots flew from the Liberti ships and then, seconds later, expanded into a cloud of plasma vapor enveloping all five ships.

He was surprised the godless Liberti sacrificed themselves. He was even more surprised they would sacrifice themselves in a situation that did not call for it. The fleeing Eagles were damaged, no longer a threat to them. He imagined numerous tactics the Liberti could have used against the Eagles without killing themselves in the process.

Before he could wonder more, his display blanked out. A white plasma cloud blossomed outside the window. They were entering the atmosphere, and their instruments were useless while the ship's collision with Menota's air engulfed it in several thousand degrees of white plasma. The deceleration pushed Lepidus into his couch straps, but it was no where near as bad as the acceleration.

He would have to wait to find out the battle's outcome. He spent the next ten minutes praying to Jupiter for the strength and wisdom to accomplish his mission.

Oh, Jupiter Optimus Maximus, grant me and my apprentice your strength to do the will of your servant, the Eternal Consul Marcus Antonius. I pledge to follow the path you would have me follow, to destroy all those who would harm your people, and to give you glory and honor through my deeds today.

Lepidus opened his eyes and looked upon the bright clouds surrounding the shuttle. Dark blue sky reigned above, and the billowing cloud formations rose in miles-high columns all around them. Menota's sun shown through one such formation, shining rays on the blanket of clouds below.

A sign from Jupiter. *I have lit the way for you, child.* Lepidus's heart sighed, and peace flowed through him. The peace of a man whose path was set.

"We have instruments again," Appius said.

Lepidus brought up a sensor view of the space above Menota. Two more Eagles came off the way line and engaged with another pair of Liberti warships.

The Consul had committed almost two squadrons to this battle. So had the Liberti. Where did these ships come from? Lepidus thought most available Eagle squadrons surrounded Libertus. The Consul viewed his son's retrieval a top priority, but Lepidus assumed it was a secret priority. The Roman people could not know the Consular Heir was a traitor. It would shake the faith of those whose faith was not as strong as Lepidus's.

But it wasn't heresy to note the Roman Fleet was weaker than it once was only a decade ago. It took most of its strength to lay siege to a single star system, while its reserves protected strategic planets and waystations throughout the Republic. Could the Consul afford to commit this many squadrons to retrieve his traitorous son?

Could he afford *not* to, considering the upheaval it would cause if the truth were known?

Lepidus considered these things as the shuttle descended into Menota's perpetual cloud cover. The strong winds buffeted the shuttle, but it plowed through the clouds and emerged three thousand feet above the planet's gray, brown surface.

"Nearing the landing pad," Appius said.

They flew over the ruins of Pomona and then hovered over an ash-covered landing pad on Pomona's former hospital. When

they landed with a heavy jolt, Lepidus unbuckled the belts on his couch.
The gods' will be done.

Chapter Forty-Eight

Kaeso put the EVA helmet over Cordus's head and then sealed the bindings. He tapped a key on Cordus's wrist pad, which began the airflow from the small tank on his back.

"Feel the air?"

The boy sniffed, then nodded.

"Good. You ever use an EVA suit?"

"Not one this old," Cordus said.

"Right. It operates the same way as the fancy ones you patricians use. It responds to your eye movement the same way, but you adjust air flow on your wrist pad."

"It is heavier than I am used to."

"I don't have a child-sized suit, so you'll have to make do with this one. Can you manage?"

Cordus nodded. Kaeso grinned and then donned his helmet.

Lucia entered Cargo One just as Kaeso sealed his helmet and enabled the airflow. "The Roman shuttle landed on an old hospital pad about a half-mile southeast."

Kaeso frowned, then nodded. They knew about the Roman shuttle since it left its Eagle mother ship and had hoped it was destroyed in the battle between Umbra and the Eagles. But when *Caduceus's* re-entry plasma dissipated, they saw the shuttle had survived and continued to follow. Kaeso chose to land in Pomona and proceed with the plan anyway. If they didn't retrieve Cordus's evidence now, they never would.

Kaeso sighed, thinking of the plan they dashed together as they fell through Menota's atmosphere. *I have a better chance getting back into Umbra than making this work.*

Lucia zipped up her EVA suit and fastened her helmet. Kaeso watched her and then said, "Daryush could get the engines fixed faster with your help."

"Probably," Lucia said. "They'd get done even faster if *you* helped him, but we both know that won't happen, right, Centuriae?"

Kaeso grunted. He was once an Ancile. Besides a Vessel, he knew the Muses as well as any human could, and he was trained for unpredictable situations. He had to go. But Lucia was right. He could not explore the vaults while keeping an eye out for Cariosa *and* Praetorians *and* Cordus *and* the proof. Kaeso needed help. Daryush had to fix the engines. Gaia Julius had surprising technical knowledge for a patrician, so she was helping Daryush. Nestor and Blaesus were brave, but they wouldn't stand a chance in a fight with Praetorians. The only other person on the ship that came close to his training was Lucia.

Besides Ocella, that is.

Kaeso checked the ammunition in his pulse pistol, holstered it, and then slapped his hand on the cargo controls. The cargo ramp descended. Eddies of ash and dust swirled into the bay.

Kaeso activated his ship's intercom with his eyes. "We're leaving Cargo One now. Make sure she's sealed up tight. If the Romans attack—"

"Trust me, Centuriae," Blaesus said, "we will not let them in for eels and garum."

"I was going to say, if the Romans attack, I want you to leave. They will destroy the ship if you resist them."

Blaesus snorted. "And you think our chances are better against the Eagles above us?"

"Yes. The Eagles are preoccupied right now. You can get away."

Blaesus snorted again, but didn't say anything.

Gaia Julius weighed in. "Get that evidence, Centuriae. We need to give the Muses something to fear."

Nestor said, "That evidence is worth my life. We're not leaving without it."

"Speak for yourself, Greek," Blaesus said. "I don't know if I'd die for some theoretical evidence." Then he paused. "But I would die for my crew."

Daryush grunted an affirmative over the com.

Kaeso shook his head in his helmet. "You're all going to disobey a direct order from your centuriae?"

"Yes," Nestor and Blaesus said almost simultaneously.

Gaia said, "You don't command me, Centuriae. So I shall ignore you as I wish."

"Fools," Kaeso said. Lucia chuckled over her com. He turned to her and said, "*You* don't have that option. If you're coming with us, you *will* follow my orders. Clear?"

"Yes, sir," Lucia said, a glint in her eyes.

Kaeso regarded Cordus. "I don't care if you're the Consular Heir, you'll do what I say, too."

Cordus nodded. "I will defer to your judgment."

Kaeso turned and led them down the ramp into the swirling clouds of particulates. The weather and the landscape had not changed since their last visit. Empty buildings stood like crosses along the street. Ground cars sat in an eternal traffic jam on the city's main thoroughfare. Just as before, Kaeso saw no bodies in either the cars or the roads and sidewalks.

But as he learned last week, the underground was different.

Kaeso brought up the map of the city center on his helmet display. The coliseum was straight ahead, and the theater across the street. Lucia landed the ship in virtually the same place as last week, so he knew the obstacles between him and the vaults.

He gave the southeast a quick glance to see if anyone followed them. The Roman shuttle had landed on a hospital a half-mile from their location. It would take the Praetorians several minutes to navigate through the ruined hospital, then several more minutes to reach *Caduceus*. They had time, but not much.

Kaeso maintained a quick pace and soon heard Cordus breathing heavy over his open com. He wasn't surprised, considering the suit was built for an adult and Menota's gravity was ten percent greater than Terra's.

He half-turned to Cordus. "Need to slow down?"

"I can keep up," he said between breaths.

"Tell me something," Kaeso said. "How did the Cariosus survive in the vaults? Infectees attacked us just last week. The irradiation should have left nothing alive on the planet."

"Shielding," Cordus breathed. "The Cariosa Muses set up shelters against irradiation in case the Terran Muses found them."

Lucia asked, "They knew the Romans would irradiate the planet?"

"They knew it was possible. The Cariosa Muses did it to the Roman Muses two million years ago."

"Long memories," Lucia said.

"You have no idea."

Kaeso grunted. "I assume these vaults will give us an idea?"

"Some. At least enough to show humanity what the Muses are and what they did to other species."

"I thought your Muses were of the Terran strain. How do you know this evidence is here?"

Cordus was silent a moment. "I...I am guessing."

Kaeso stopped, turned around and glared at the boy. Cordus took a step back when he saw Kaeso's face.

"We fled to this planet on your assurance it had evidence of Muse influence on Terra. We could have gone anywhere else, but we came here. Because of you. Are you saying this evidence may not even be here?"

The boy's mouth opened and closed. "I admit I do not know for sure the evidence is here. But I know the alien species that hosted the Cariosa strain before humans arrived were meticulous record keepers. This planet was one of their bases, so they would have kept records here on the Terra strain and its locations. And the Saturnists believe those records are in these vaults."

"Meticulous record keepers," Kaeso said. "You're risking the lives of my crew because you *think* there might be evidence here. Gods..."

"Ocella agreed with this plan."

"Ocella's not here. She never will be again."

Kaeso turned and stalked ahead.

"Where are you going?" Cordus asked.

"To the vaults. What choice do I have? We're committed now." Kaeso whirled around and pointed a finger at Cordus. "But you'd better be right. If not, we're all going to die because of your *guess*."

Cordus glowered at him. "I *am* right."

Kaeso turned and proceeded down the thoroughfare. He realized blaming the boy was shameful. It wasn't going to bring back Flamma or Dariya. Flamma's death and Dariya's infection were on him. It was his decision to take the Umbra mission to Terra. If he hadn't, Flamma would still be alive. It was his decision to come to Menota in the first place. If he hadn't, Dariya wouldn't be dying. Kaeso lashed out at the boy because he couldn't lash out at himself. Completing the mission was the only thing he could do to give some meaning to the death and suffering of his crew.

Kaeso did not need the map on his helmet display, for he remembered the way up the dead streets. He led Lucia and Cordus around ruined cars and debris from the crumbling buildings. The wind still howled through the cavernous streets, sending dust and ash at them in gentle clouds one moment, then blasts that staggered them the next. All the while, Kaeso noticed the sun to his right—a hazy glow in the western sky—descending behind Pomona's buildings, creating shadows every bit as dark as night. In another hour, the whole thoroughfare would be covered in darkness, and they'd have a hard enough time making it back to the ship through the constant gales.

Kaeso found the theater and entered through the front door. He strode through the garishly decorated lobby, into the theater, and through the torn curtains to the elevator backstage. Mummified bodies lay in heaps on either side of the elevator, exactly where his crew left them last week.

Flamma's rigging of the elevator control panel was still there, so all Kaeso had to do was attach Flamma's battery to the nodes protruding from the panel. He took the battery from a pocket on his suit, connected it to the nodes, and pressed the door controls. The doors slid open, and Kaeso went inside followed by Cordus and Lucia. Kaeso hit the controls inside and the door slid shut. Small emergency lights bathed them in a dark red haze. All three turned on their helmet lights, illuminating themselves and the dust floating around inside. The elevator gave a jerk and then descended.

Lucia unslung her pulse rifle, ensured it was charged, and then held it in a firing position aimed at the cracks in the door. Kaeso unholstered his own pulse pistol and chambered a round.

Cordus regarded them nervously. "How bad were they?"

Without glancing at him, Lucia said, "Let's hope Dariya fried them all. Otherwise we have problems."

The elevator's level indicator descended past the ground floor and continued to drop.

"What are we looking for?" Kaeso asked Cordus. He'd asked the boy before, but Kaeso would rather ask repetitive questions than wait in silence for the elevator to reach the vaults.

"A tabulari," Cordus said. "It would not be of normal Roman design, but it will have a similar interface."

"Will we be able to read it?"

"Most likely. All the Muse strains speak to their hosts in their native language. The hosts would have created the tabulari with the language and tools the hosts knew."

"And if we can't read it?" Lucia asked.

"I can read it."

Kaeso shook his head. "That's not good enough. If you want people to believe you're more than a traitor with a fantastic story, you'll need proof that doesn't rely on your own interpretation. You're trying to overturn a thousand years of doctrine and culture."

Cordus bit his lip, but didn't say anything. Kaeso was not encouraged.

The elevator jerked to a stop. Kaeso and Lucia both held up their weapons as Cordus moved behind them.

The door opened to blackness. Dust floated out of the elevator with their movements and settled on the hallway floor. Kaeso and Lucia shined their helmet lights on the blackened floor ten feet from the elevator.

But the charred bodies of the Cariosa were gone.

Lucia cursed and scanned ahead with her pulse rifle in a firing position beneath her helmeted chin. "Maybe the Romans took them?"

"Does it matter who did?" Kaeso asked.

"Yes. That would mean other Cariosa didn't."

Kaeso kept his pistol pointed down the corridor. "Where do we go?" he asked Cordus.

Cordus said in a tight voice, "I suppose we should start with these first doors."

"Just garbage in there," Kaeso said. The first door on the right held the marques he risked his crew's lives to obtain, unless *Corus's* Lady Centuriae took them. If so, the marques were now atoms floating above Menota. Kaeso didn't care to check the room to make sure. They were nothing but bloody bits of paper to him now.

"We never got to the control rooms at the end of the hall," Kaeso said.

"Infectees might be there," Lucia said nervously.

"And our proof," Kaeso said.

He stepped into the blackened hallway. Footprints disturbed the area where the charred bodies once lay. Some prints came from boot treads and some from bare feet. The door to the marque holding room was still open, and Kaeso swung his pistol around the corner, ready to fire at anything that jumped at him.

No one was in the room. The marques were gone as well. The empty way line canisters Kaeso and Dariya had set up to fool the Romans lay near the wall. A bitter taste arose in Kaeso's mouth; he fought the urge to spit.

They continued to the next room. The door to the kitchen hung on its hinges, and the interior was just as ransacked and devoid of life as when he last saw it.

They moved on. Beyond the kitchen door was unknown territory. There was a wide open door on the right. Both Kaeso and Lucia aimed their weapons and helmet lights inside. It was a meeting room. Couches, tables, and chairs lay on either side of the door, as if they'd been piled against it, but something had pushed them inward. The room was empty of Cariosa or bodies.

"What will this tabulari look like?" Kaeso asked. "Could it be hidden in one of these rooms?"

"No," Cordus said. "Like all the Muses, the Cariosa strain treats their histories with religious devotion. The tabulari would be in a place similar to an altar."

"No altars back there," Lucia said.

"So we move on," Kaeso said.

They came to a locked door on the left. A nondescript control pad hung on the wall next to the door handle. No sign indicated what was inside. Kaeso inspected the door and the handle, then turned to Lucia.

"Shoot the handle."

Lucia studied the door. "We might attract attention."

"We can't leave any doors unchecked. Shoot it."

Lucia frowned, aimed her pulse rifle at the door handle, and fired a single shot into it. The shot exploded the door handle and its lock. The door swung inward. Lucia brought her rifle back up and aimed it inside. Their lights showed a room filled with tabulari terminals, all of them dark and dusty.

"Is this it?" Kaeso asked.

Cordus studied the terminals doubtfully. "This is too utilitarian for the Muses. I think this is a mundane data monitoring room. We should keep going."

Kaeso, Lucia, and Cordus found more rooms, all empty of Cariosa and all used for mundane purposes: a bunk room, bath room, and more pantries with nothing left but empty boxes, cans, and packaging strewn about the floor.

At the end of the corridor, another hall ran left to right, a perpendicular cap to the first corridor. Kaeso shined his helmet lights in both directions. More doors lined the hall within the reach of his lights, and then darkness beyond.

"So which way?" Kaeso asked.

Cordus turned left and right, shining his helmet lights down each corridor. "Right."

"Another guess?"

Cordus didn't say anything. Kaeso grunted and led them to the right.

All they found were more doors; some open, some locked. No Cariosa attacked them. They found no tabulari altars, only mundane rooms common to any fallout shelter. The monotony of their inspections weighed on Kaeso's focus, and his mind wandered to the fate of his crew rather than the task before him. He struggled to return his attention to the inspections. A lack of focus in this place would kill them all. *This was all so much easier with that damned implant.*

A blank wall greeted them at the end of the corridor.

"Left corridor it is," Kaeso said. Cordus was quiet again, and Kaeso saw a scowl through his helmet. The boy looked as frustrated as Kaeso felt. They were wasting time with all these room checks, time that allowed the Praetorians to either attack *Caduceus* or follow them down here.

When they got back to the main corridor, Kaeso said, "We're going all the way to the end before we check any doors."

Cordus nodded. "That might be best."

Lucia said, "What if we pass a room with Cariosa and they cut us off from the elevator?"

"We have to take that risk," Kaeso said. "We're running out of time."

Lucia frowned, then nodded. She proceeded down the left corridor.

This one was as long as the right one, with the same ratio of open and closed doors. They took it slow despite Kaeso's urge to hurry to the end. They shined their helmet lights into the open doorways just to ensure the rooms were empty. He wanted to get to the end of the corridor quicker, but he still shared Lucia's fear that the Cariosa could cut them off. A token inspection was better than no inspection.

At the end of the hall, an open metal door hung on one hinge. Their helmet lights illuminated a stairwell.

Kaeso paused. "Everyone still," he ordered.

Lucia and Cordus stopped moving.

He used his eyes on his helmet display to enhance the external sound in the corridor. He heard the breathing systems on the suits of Lucia and Cordus, but beneath them, a low hum rose from the stairs.

"Enhance your external audio," Kaeso said. "What do you hear?"

Their eyes flit about their helmets as they adjusted their audio, then they listened.

"A generator?" Lucia said.

"No," Cordus said, staring wide-eyed at the stairs. "Voices."

"Are you sure?" Kaeso asked. When he concentrated further, he thought the sound could be voices, but it seemed more mechanical to him.

"Yes. I am a Vessel, remember?"

"You know what they're saying?"

Cordus took a few steps toward the door. "It is chanting, but I cannot make out the language or if they are saying words at all."

Cordus took a few more steps forward.

"Careful," Kaeso warned.

"Light is coming from down the stairs," Cordus said. "I think this is the place."

Lucia exhaled. "Are we really going into a den of Cariosa?"

Cordus looked at Kaeso. "This is where we need to go. I am sure of it."

Kaeso's mouth turned dry. He shuddered as he remembered the hideous faces leaping out of the dark, sunken eyes, swollen necks, pale, hairless skin, their teeth yellow with purple gums. In all the missions he'd performed with Umbra, he'd never been as terrified during any of them.

Kaeso swallowed once and then said, "Turn off your helmet lights."

He switched off his light, as did Lucia and Cordus. A dim green glow came from down the stairs. As he watched, the light seemed to flicker and change to red, then blue, and then various other colors.

"Let's go," he said. He held up his pistol and entered the stairwell.

"Wait!" Cordus said, startling Kaeso. "I hear something from the main corridor."

Kaeso enhanced his external audio again and pointed his helmet back toward the T-intersection. It was completely black that way, so he closed his eyes to focus his hearing. He barely picked out the sound, but he knew it immediately.

He turned and hurried down the stairs. "Time to move. Someone just activated the elevator."

Chapter Forty-Nine

Kaeso hurried down the stairs as fast as the darkness and his own caution allowed. The farther down they went, the brighter the lights grew and the more varied they became. The humming also grew louder. Kaeso could tell the voices made most of the sound, but not all—antimatter generators, which would've powered the whole complex, reverberated beneath the voices. Between the voices and the generators, he no longer heard the elevator motors bringing down their unwanted guests. Kaeso hoped they wasted time searching every damned door in the corridors just like he had.

Kaeso stepped onto a landing and descended one more flight of stairs. At the bottom was a half-opened door. Beyond it were the bright flickering lights, the voices, and the generators. Lucia pulled Cordus behind her and against the wall, then aimed her pulse rifle at the door. Kaeso lifted his pistol and peeked through.

A metal landing overlooked a vast cavern. A staircase descended to the left, but the door blocked his view of the cavern floor. The lights and the humming came from below. To see them he'd have to open the door further. He pushed against it, and it inched forward, scraping the metal grate below it. The sound did not overpower the humming or the voices in the cavern, so Kaeso pushed a little more until he could fit his whole body through the opening. Once through, Kaeso eased his head over the edge of the grate.

"Gods," he breathed.

In the cavern's center, a holographic projector displayed a large translucent globe fifty feet in diameter. Videos flickered inside the globe, showing images Kaeso didn't understand at first. Creatures like land-based octopeds slaughtered other octopeds with small axes in each tentacled hand. The video shifted, and the octopeds now destroyed each other with cannons. The video changed again, and the octopeds fought in starships.

Starships that looked exactly like the first bulky freighters Roma built for way line travel.

Those starships rained bombs on a planet until the whole world seemed covered in white antimatter plumes. After the bombing, the octopeds were slaughtered by a bipedal species with feathers and long beaks in vicious hand to hand combat. With the octopeds out of the way, the bird-like species started fighting each other, obliterating a planet with antimatter bombs, and then in turn being slaughtered by another alien species.

The videos went on, through dozens of species, each more exotic and strange than the last. Each following the same pattern of events.

Surrounding the holographic projector and filling up the vast cavern were hundreds of sleeper cribs filled with human beings. Some cribs were broken and destroyed, and Kaeso quickly saw the reason. In between the sleeper cribs, dozens of Cariosa stood or swayed before the projector. Some watched the videos with enraptured gazes on their pale, sunken faces, while some gnawed on the bones, dry entrails, and other human remains they took from the broken sleeper cribs.

Answers the survival question, Kaeso thought, trying to keep the bile from rising in his throat. Had he not worn an airtight, stench-free EVA suit, he doubted he could've kept from retching.

Kaeso looked to his left. The metal staircase wound its way down along the cavern wall to the bottom. To his right, the walkway snaked along the cavern wall and ended at a platform that appeared to have a control station.

Lucia and Cordus stared at the spectacle below. Lucia seemed grimly disgusted, while Cordus looked more sad than horrified. Kaeso nudged them and motioned to the control station to the right. They nodded and followed Kaeso past the open door.

The control station was a hundred paces away. Kaeso glanced down at the Cariosa, bracing himself for the inevitable screams once they noticed the mundanes creeping along the walkway above them. He also watched the holographic projection they worshiped. It flickered and changed, displaying new alien events, mathematical formulae, and diagrams he did not understand.

A way line node map suddenly displayed. The map showed alpha way lines connecting one node with another in a pattern Kaeso did not recognize. But after studying the map a moment, he recognized the patterns in one quadrant—it was the same pattern that made up human space. He recognized the nodes of the Roman Republic, the Zhonguo Sphere, and the Lost Worlds. Kaeso determined that all human populated space was connected to the unknown way line nodes of previous civilizations through one node.

Menota.

There must be other alpha way lines in this star system, Kaeso thought. Maybe next to one of the six gas giants that made up the outer—

He placed his right foot into empty space where the metal walkway should have been. He waved his arms, dropped his pulse pistol, and lunged for the railing to his left to avoid plummeting to the cavern floor dozens of feet below. His pistol hit a sleeper crib, producing a clang that echoed throughout the cavern. Kaeso whipped around toward the Cariosa.

They all looked up at him as one. They stared at him for a breathless moment and then screamed with one voice. The Cariosa who were chanting around the projector rushed through the rows of sleeper cribs, while the ones feasting on the sleepers dropped their grisly meals and joined the chanters.

They raced to the stairs leading to Kaeso, Lucia, and Cordus.

Chapter Fifty

Kaeso looked from the open door to the infectees charging up the stairs. He, Lucia, and Cordus *might* make it through the door before the infectees got there. Might...

He turned back to the chasm in the walkway and the control station beyond. The railing and support beams on either side of the walkway were still intact, but twenty paces worth of metal floor grating was gone. To get to the control station, they'd have to creep along the six-inch wide beams while holding the railing.

Lucia cursed, then brought her pulse rifle up and aimed at the landing near the stairway door where the infectees would emerge. "Orders?" she yelled.

"Control station," Kaeso said. "We won't make the door in time. Go!"

He shuffled along the support beam, keeping a tight grip on the railing. He stepped around areas where the railing connected to a vertical pole welded into the support beam, but those areas only delayed him a few seconds. Cordus followed him closely, while Lucia slung her rifle over her shoulder and followed Cordus. Both moved in jerking motions with a vice grip on the railing.

With ten paces to go, the infectee screams grew louder, and Kaeso felt the support beam shake. He looked back to see the infectees on the platform racing past the open door toward them. Cordus tried to look, but Kaeso yelled, "Ignore them! Move!"

Cordus whipped his eyes back to the railing and his feet. He shuffled faster to keep up with Kaeso.

Kaeso reached the end and leaped onto the grating where the walkway continued to the control panel ten paces away. He turned, grabbed Cordus's hand, and yanked the boy behind him. He then took Lucia's hand and pulled her to safety.

Lucia turned, unslung her rifle and aimed at the oncoming horde. They charged forward, high-pitched shrieks echoing throughout the cavern, their footfalls shaking the walkway so badly that Kaeso wondered if it would collapse.

No second-guesses now.

When the first infectees came within range, Lucia fired. Two shots blew apart the heads of two infectees. They fell to the grate, the infectees behind them tripping over their twitching bodies. A pileup ensued which delayed the horde's progress a moment.

Kaeso pulled Cordus toward the control station, jumped up two steps and looked down at the terminal. Fortunately the interface was in Latin, but he had no idea how to get the information he needed.

"What do we do?" he asked Cordus.

The boy stepped up to the terminal and studied the interface. A terrible shriek came from the infectees, making him wince. Kaeso glanced behind him and saw the infectees arrive at the chasm. The crush of infectees from behind caused several in front to plummet off the platform and splatter on the broken grating and sleeper cribs below. Some attempted to jump the chasm, but the distance was too great even for their Plague-enhanced muscles. They howled and screamed as they made it less than halfway across before falling. Lucia held her fire as they jumped.

He turned to Cordus. The boy brought up file structures on the terminal screen and methodically opened each one.

"What can I do?" Kaeso asked.

"Stop distracting me."

Kaeso looked back up at Lucia. The infectees shuffled along the support beams now, just as Kaeso had done. Lucia easily picked them off when they got to the middle, but Kaeso worried about the charges left in her pulse rifle. Dozens more infectees waited for them on the other side of the chasm. What happened when Kaeso, Lucia, and Cordus were ready to leave? Would they have enough ammunition to get through those swarming infectees and back to the ship?

"I think I have it," Cordus said. He had brought up a list of files that looked to be in the hundreds.

Kaeso watched the file sizes with growing dismay. "It'll take hours to upload those to *Caduceus*."

"We do not need them all," Cordus said. "Just those linking Roma with the Muses."

"Do you know which ones we need?"

Cordus studied the file list. "I think so. Cariosus naming conventions appear similar to the Terran strain."

"How long?"

Cordus glanced at the howling infectees. "Fifteen minutes."

"Get as much as you can in five."

Cordus turned back to the terminal, his eyes losing focus. This was the part—among many—where failure was most possible. If the Cariosus hosts built their interface to only be accessed by Cariosus Muses, then the whole mission was for nothing. Cordus would not be able to direct his Muses to upload the terminal's contents to *Caduceus's* tabulari.

Cordus's lip curled, and his eyes twitched with effort. He stood like that for almost a minute. Lucia's pulse rifle continued firing behind him, and the infectees howled and screamed. Kaeso wanted to put a hand on Cordus's shoulder, to see if he was still awake, but it was pointless to disturb a Vessel while communicating with the Muses. They ignored everything while the Muses had them.

Cordus blinked, sucked in a breath, and then grinned at Kaeso. "I am in."

The infectees stopped shrieking at once. Kaeso turned to see them standing still on the walkway staring at Cordus, their hollow faces blank. Lucia fired at three more infectees stopped midway across the support beam. Their bodies dropped to the cavern floor, but the other infectees did not flinch.

"Lucia, hold your fire," Kaeso ordered.

Lucia stopped shooting, but continued aiming at the infectees on the support beam. "What's happening?" she asked without turning around.

"Cordus?" Kaeso asked, but he looked as confused as Kaeso felt.

"Centuriae!"

Kaeso's eyes darted to the infectees across the chasm. A woman with the same swollen neck and hairless body as the others stepped forward while the infectees around her stepped back.

Cordus said from behind him, "I hear you."

Kaeso turned to him. The boy stared at the woman, his brow furrowed.

"You should speak so my friends can hear you," Cordus said.

"Terran," the infected woman said in a clear voice. Her voice sounded sane and human, though with the robotic cadence Kaeso heard in other Vessels while the Muses spoke through them. But what made him shiver was how all the other infectees around the woman whispered "Terran" at the same time.

"You are of the Terran strain," the woman, along with the other infectees, continued, "but they do not speak through you. How is this?"

"I do not know," Cordus said. "I was born this way."

"Are the Terran strain coming to destroy us?" The woman's voice and the whispers of the infectees sounded fearful.

"They do not know you are here," Cordus said. "They think they destroyed you already."

"Yet you are here," the woman said. "They will find us soon. We are all that is left. We have been reduced to this. To feed on our own kind. It has driven us mad."

"You were already mad," Cordus said. There was no sarcasm in his voice, only sadness at stating a simple, heartbreaking fact. "You were incompatible with humanity. You drove them to...this."

The woman stared at Cordus. "Perhaps we erred. That is irrelevant. We do not want to die." The woman cocked her head. Then her voice, and the whispers of the infectees, said, "We cannot let you tell the Terrans we are here. We cannot let you leave this cavern."

Chapter Fifty-One

Lepidus and Appius methodically checked each door and room in the vaults with the heat sensors built into their helmets. They found nothing. Their infrared filters let them go through the corridor without lights to announce their presence. When they met no resistance, Lepidus began to wonder if the Liberti had somehow left the vaults through a different exit.

Then the howling began.

Lepidus and Appius trotted down the corridor toward the howling as fast as their EVA suits allowed. Lepidus had read intelligence reports on Cariosa and knew they were strong for people with a virus that destroyed their humanity. The chilling shrieks could not have come from the throats of sane humans. Lepidus could not fathom why the gods would curse people with such an affliction. But then, he reminded himself, the gods did many things he could not fathom. It was hubris and blasphemy to assume he knew how to run the universe better than the gods.

Lepidus and Appius reached a door with a stairwell beyond. Lepidus aimed his pulse rifle down the stairs, but did not see any targets. The shrieks were definitely louder and coming from the bottom of the stairwell. Lights flickered from the bottom; he turned off his helmet's infrared filter to see their varied colors.

After switching his infrared filter back on, he descended the stairs while holding his rifle in a firing position. Appius didn't say a word and followed Lepidus with the same posture. If he feared what made the inhuman screams, he did not show it. Lepidus nodded in satisfaction. The screams would test any man's faith in the gods and obedience to his commander. Appius was performing admirably.

They had descended two flights when the screaming stopped. Lepidus paused and then raised his hand to stop Appius. The screaming was a horrid, animalistic cacophony moments ago, but had ceased as if switched off. Lepidus frowned. Like any soldier, he hated unknowns, and this whole situation stank of unknown.

Lepidus listened for a moment, turning his external audio up. He still heard the soft hiss of his air filtration system. With a flick of his eyes, he filtered out the hissing and enhanced the sounds coming from down the stairs.

Voices, accompanied by what sounded like whispering.

Lepidus motioned Appius forward.

※※※

Kaeso stared at the emaciated woman, his fists clenching, waiting for the screams and attacks to begin again. He glanced at Lucia, who continued aiming at the woman.

"We are not here to kill you," Cordus told the woman. "We only want to copy your sacred archives."

The woman cocked her head, as if listening to someone behind her, but no sound came from the animated corpses. "Why?" she asked, along with the Cariosa whispers.

"We want to hurt the Terran strain," Cordus said. "This information will prove the Consul and Collegia Pontificis are like golems controlled by the Terran strain. You know how Roman culture worships the Consul and Collegia. You know that if the Roman people knew this, things would go badly for the Terran strain."

The woman cocked her head again. "The Roman people will not believe. They are too conditioned to believe what the Consul and Collegia tell them. Our hosts built this archive to convince the leaders of this world, and they could not even do that. Our strain is Keeper of the Archive. We failed in our mission. The Roman people will not believe."

"Enough will believe. Things may not change tomorrow, but they will change. It may take months or years, but the truth will spread, and not even the Consul or Collegia will stop it."

The woman stared at Cordus. "You want to destroy my species. You fear us."

"No," he said, "we just want to be free to make our own decisions, to make our own mistakes. We do not want to be drawn into your wars. Your own archives show what happens to your hosts. I do not want that for my people."

"My species cannot survive without hosts," she said, Cariosa whispers echoing her words. "These bodies will soon fail. We need new hosts."

"Your strain is not compatible with humans," Cordus said. "You can survive in them for a while, but their physiology will eventually reject you. Look at what has become of you."

"We need new hosts," the woman repeated. The longing in her voice—the voices of all the Cariosa—chilled Kaeso. They all stared at him, Lucia, and Cordus with ravenous, feral eyes.

Kaeso was impressed with Cordus's poise while arguing with a creature from a nightmare, but he saw the debate as pointless. The Muses and humans wanted diametrically different things: Muses wanted humans to be hosts, but humans didn't want that. Compromise was impossible.

But the conversation was useful so long as it kept the Cariosa busy while the files uploaded, and saved pulse charges for when they needed to blast their way back to *Caduceus*.

Kaeso glanced at the timer counting down the minutes until the data uploaded to *Caduceus*.

Keep them talking five more minutes, kid.

The woman's eyes widened, and she bared her rotting teeth in an inhuman scream. The Cariosa around her screamed, and they resumed their attempts to cross the support beam.

Cac!

"What happened?" Lucia yelled, then fired several pulse shots at the Cariosa on the beam.

Kaeso turned to Cordus, but the boy shook his head. He glanced at the timer on the terminal. Three minutes.

He looked at the infected woman again. She gathered herself up and leaped toward him, along with other Cariosa. But like the others, she fell far short, and her body shattered on the sleeper cribs and Cariosa bodies below. At this rate, Kaeso thought, he wouldn't need to blast his way through the Cariosa to escape. They'd just kill themselves trying that jump.

He was starting to feel better about their chances when he saw flashes from the door a hundred paces behind the Cariosa.

Pulse flashes. The Romans were coming through the door.

Chapter Fifty-Two

Lepidus and Appius crept down the last flight of stairs to a half-open door at the bottom. Through the door, several emaciated people stood motionless and staring off to the right. Each whispered words to one side of a conversation. Lepidus could not hear the other voices clearly, but he determined they came from the right. Beyond them, a vast cavern was alit with flickering lights.

Cariosa. How did they survive the bombardment and irradiation? Have they been living down here for two years? There must be a source of food and water—a meager source, judging by their appearance. It must lie beyond the door in the cavern.

The Consul's voice crackled in his ear. "Lepidus, have you found my son?"

Lepidus flicked his com to silent. Sensors pressed against his throat above his vocal chords, then he whispered, "Not yet, my lord. But I have visual confirmation of Cariosa."

The Consul paused. "That is impossible."

"I see them right now, my lord. They're ragged and starving, but they have the hairless bodies and swollen necks."

The Consul's voice rose an octave and lost its usual serenity. "I was told the planet had been irradiated. That nothing could live, not even that *damned virus!*"

The Consul's uncharacteristic anger surprised Lepidus. After a startled pause, Lepidus said, "I cannot speak to that, my lord. All I can tell you is what I see."

"Lepidus," the Consul growled, "you will find my son within thirty minutes. Because in thirty minutes, I am going to drop half my antimatter bombs on your location. *I* will rid the universe of the Cariosus, because my generals are too incompetent to do it for me."

"My lord—"

"Thirty minutes, Lepidus."

The channel broke, leaving Lepidus confused and frustrated. The Consul's decision made no sense. Why was he so quick to shatter a continent without giving Lepidus a chance to find the boy? If Cordus was a traitor, death was a necessary punishment. But what if he wasn't and Lepidus could not find him in time?

Then it is the will of the gods that he should die, Lepidus told his faithless doubts.

He motioned Appius forward and tightened his grip on his pulse rifle.

When he descended the last stairs, he saw what made the flickering lights. It was a massive holographic globe in the cavern's center with a running video inside. The video's clarity was stunning in its three dimensions and color, and Lepidus marveled at how such a projector could have run unattended so long.

Then an image stopped him.

Ancient Roma burned. He could make out the walls crumbling under the blasts of old gunpowder cannons. Fires raged on the Capitoline Hill. The Senate House and the old Temple of Jupiter Optimus Maximus lay in ruins.

The view swerved to cheering legions, all wearing the bronze-colored armor and helms from the days of Marcus Antonius's ascension. They waved muskets in the air. Lepidus realized he viewed these scenes through the eyes of another person. The person turned his gaze back to Roma and spurred his horse toward the broken gates. Streams of dirty refugees flooded from the burning city, hollow-eyed and fearful, but the man ignored them. While the refugees looked on him in fear, the soldiers along the roadside cheered him. The man waved as he passed.

The perspective shifted, and the man now stood in front of a younger man dressed in the purple and gold robes of the Consul. But Lepidus knew this man was no Consul, and he instantly recognized him as Octavian Caesar. Octavian spoke soundless words to the man whose perspective Lepidus shared, but then the man's hands shot toward Octavian's throat. Octavian struggled against the powerful grip, kicking and beating at the man's arms. His face turned blue, his eyes bulged, his tongue flailed until he was still, his sightless eyes staring past the man who killed him.

It was the historic assassination of Octavian Caesar by Marcus Antonius. Why was this re-enactment playing here? And from the eyes of Marcus Antonius?

More images flashed by from the same perspective. Marcus Antonius performed a strange ritual on what looked like pontiffs dressed in black robes, though Lepidus could not be sure considering they dressed in dark blue now. They were in a candle-lit room with walls covered in Egyptian hieroglyphs, while a pontiff sat in an old wooden chair, his arms and legs strapped down.

It was the same set-up as the room where the Consul interrogated Marcia Licinius Ocella.

Marcus Antonius cut his wrist. Blood spilled into a bronze bowl held by a priest in Egyptian accoutrements. He then dipped the knife in the blood, turned to the pontiff, and plunged the knife into the pontiff's chest. The pontiff gasped, then his eyes glazed and his head slumped down. The images shifted, and Antonius performed the same procedure on another pontiff, and then another. He stabbed nine altogether.

The scene shifted. The nine pontiffs Antonius had stabbed, all alive and wearing the same serene expressions as today's pontiffs, stood in the hieroglyph chamber dipping scrolls into large bowls of blood. After the scrolls were soaked through, they laid the scrolls out flat to dry. The scene shifted again, and the pontiffs wrote on the dark red scrolls with a stylus and white paint.

Now Marcus Antonious and the pontiffs stood in the Forum reading the scrolls. Lepidus recognized the ritual. It was a Reading of a Missive of the Gods. It was how Roma gained the technology and wisdom that made it great. After the Consul and the Collegia Pontificum spent days in prayer, the gods would convey their wisdom on the scrolls, and then the Collegia and the Consul would read the Missives to the people.

But the scrolls only turned red when the gods touched them, and the "ink" was written by the finger of a god.

Not the Consul or the Collegia.

This hologram was some blasphemous re-enactment. Lepidus ground his teeth. Cariosa were insane, but he had no idea they were so depraved they would create a video insinuating the most sacred Roman ritual was a lie.

Lepidus decided he would facilitate the meeting of these Cariosa with the gods. Let the gods punish their souls for this blasphemy.

"We're going in," he whispered in his com to Appius. "You clear the left, I'll clear the right."

"Acknowledged," Appius whispered back.

Lepidus centered his pulse rifle's targeting laser on the nearest Cariosa head and fired. The man's head exploded in a spray of blood and tissue. Lepidus acquired a new target and fired. Other Cariosa fell from Appius's fire. Lepidus charged forward.

He stepped through the door, turned to his right, and faced a screaming Cariosa horde. With a flick of his eyes on his helmet display, he switched his rifle to fragmentation shot, and blasted away at the Cariosa leaping at him. Behind him, Appius's rifle destroyed the Cariosa coming up the stairs from the cavern.

Lepidus never took pleasure in killing. But this time he gave a savage roar as he blew apart the Cariosa. These inhuman savages had defiled Roma's most sacred ritual with their mockery of the Missive. It was the gods who gave Roma her wisdom and guided her people to greatness. These Cariosa *bastards* had no idea what faith was or what it was like to fight for a cause greater than themselves.

Cariosa came at him, one after the other. Lepidus destroyed them all. He mowed them down, his point-blank fragmentation shots cutting them in half. Legless torsos grabbed at him with bloody hands as he advanced, but he gave them savage kicks that sent them off the walkway and into the cavern below. He was an instrument of the gods, like the rifle in his hands. He would kill them all for their blasphemy.

He came to a section of the walkway that had fallen way. There were no more Cariosa in front of him. At least none standing. The walkway was covered in the grisly remains of Cariosa ripped to shreds by his fragmentation shells. He was out of breath, and sweat trickled down his forehead. He only now realized he'd been screaming the whole time.

He whirled around and saw Appius methodically killing Cariosa who continued to rush up the stairs towards them. Only a couple dozen more Cariosa came up in frenzied madness. Beyond them were no more.

Appius can handle the rest, he thought.

Lepidus calmed his racing heart. He felt ashamed. Not at the Cariosa massacre, but at his loss of control. He was surprised that horrible, blasphemous video affected him so. He had not lost control like that in years.

Not since the day he killed his wife.

After he shot her, he had retreated to his quarters and broke down into rage-filled sobs. He had prayed to the gods; asked them why. No answer came that day. It was the closest Lepidus ever got to losing his faith. But after a fitful sleep, Lepidus awoke the next morning at peace. The gods had taken away the pain and left in its place a devotion to them he never had before the battle. He realized he never would have found such faith had the gods not decreed the decimation through their Missive. It was a harsh punishment, but a necessary one, for it enabled Lepidus to do all the things for Roma's glory that he never would have done had he refused the order.

"Drop your weapon, Praetorian."

Lepidus turned slowly toward the broken walkway and the control station twenty paces beyond. He'd been so focused on slaughtering the Cariosa that he never noticed the people in EVA suits crouching behind the control station panels. Each panel was pockmarked from Lepidus's fragmentation blasts. Someone in an EVA suit aimed a pulse rifle aimed at Lepidus. It was *Caduceus's* pilot.

"Appius, get up here," Lepidus whispered, then he smiled and turned his voice to external audio. "Lucia. Is the Consular Heir with you?"

"Drop the weapon or I drop you, Praetorian."

"I think you would have dropped me by know if you really—"

Lucia's rifle flashed. A charge slammed into Lepidus's helmet, knocking his head backward. Lepidus fell into the soft, wet remains of the Cariosa he'd just slaughtered. The shot stunned him. When he regained his senses, he glanced at the streak on his helmet where the charge hit. The armored faceplate held.

Before he could stand, a fragmentation blast hit the control station, and Lucia ducked behind the panels. Appius rushed up to Lepidus and tried to help him up, but Lepidus waved him off, grabbed the pulse rifle he dropped, and stood on his own.

He stooped to one knee and aimed at the control panel, waiting for Lucia or anybody else to dare look around the corner.

"I think it is you who will drop your weapon, Lucia," Lepidus said.

Chapter Fifty-Three

Kaeso blinked away the stinging sweat in his eyes. While crawling along the support girders beneath the walkway, he clenched his teeth to stifle his grunts of effort. He figured he was twenty paces behind Lepidus and his backup. Any closer and they'd hear him climb onto the walkway behind them, but any farther and he risked giving himself away when he approached from behind. And he wouldn't have the energy to attack after the brutal hand-over-hand crawl.

As soon as Lepidus started shooting near the door, Kaeso quickly explained his plan to both Lucia and Cordus. Afterwards, he lowered himself over the side of the walkway and onto the support girders beneath. They were set diagonally every six feet, one end bolted to the cavern wall and the other to the walkway's outer edge above. To get from one girder to the next, Kaeso had to crawl hand over hand along the I-beams beneath the walkway. It was a short hand over hand crawl, and Kaeso avoided looking down at the infectee bodies on the cavern floor. He made the crawl six times before reaching the last support girder. His forearms and hands trembled with the effort.

He was about to climb onto the walkway behind the Praetorians when Lepidus stopped shooting and Lucia issued her ultimatum. As he expected, she shot Lepidus, but also, as he expected, Lepidus's armor easily repelled the shot. Lepidus's man ran across the walkway above Kaeso, firing at the control station. Lucia's pulse rifle had no fragmentation rounds, so she was outgunned by the two Praetorians.

Kaeso took several deep breaths, then pulled himself onto the walkway, struggling to do it quietly in his bulky EVA suit. He swung his right leg up, slipped off the walkway on some infectee blood, then swung it up again and found purchase. He pulled himself onto a pile of glistening infectee bodies and pieces. He was thankful once again that smell did not invade his EVA suit.

Lepidus fired another fragmentation blast into the control panel. Kaeso turned his external audio down to keep the blasts from deafening him. He hoped Lepidus and his man had to do the same.

"Surrender now," Lepidus said.

"You'd kill the Consular Heir?" Lucia called out, keeping Lepidus occupied. "I may have been away from Roma too long, but isn't that blasphemy? By the time they were done with you, you'd beg for crucifixion."

Kaeso crept forward, trying not to make a sound or slip on the blood and tissue.

"It is not blasphemy to kill traitors," Lepidus said. "You have ten seconds to surrender yourselves."

Another ten paces before Kaeso reached Lepidus and his man. He decided to take out the man first. Kaeso didn't know his abilities, so it was better to remove him quickly.

"The Consul and the Collegia are not what you think," Cordus's voice shouted. The boy tried to make his young voice deep with conviction.

"Five seconds," Lepidus said.

"They are using you, Lepidus. They do not want humanity to know the secret they have kept for a thousand years. The Consul, Collegia, and their families are infected with an alien virus called the Muses—"

"Time's up." Lepidus raised his rifle to destroy the control station.

Five paces away. *Now.*

Kaeso charged Lepidus's partner. The man whirled around, but was too late. Kaeso gave him a violent shove. The man's eyes widened as he fell backward, his arms flailing. He tumbled off the walkway and into the chasm below.

Kaeso did not watch the man's landing. He attacked Lepidus. The Praetorian brought his rifle around to Kaeso, but Kaeso knocked it aside with his left forearm. Shots fired into the wall behind Kaeso. He brought his foot up into Lepidus's groin. The Praetorian grunted then fell to one knee. But with a lightning attack, he swept his leg under Kaeso's feet. Kaeso jumped away, but tripped over the body of an infectee and fell on his back.

Lepidus leaped at him, a knife in his right hand, his teeth bared. Kaeso rolled off the infectee corpse, and Lepidus plunged his knife into the body. Kaeso jumped to his feet as Lepidus did the same. They stared at each other, both seeking advantage.

Lepidus feinted to the right. Kaeso dodged, but did not see Lepidus's right leg sweep Kaeso's left foot out from under him. Kaeso stumbled forward, saw Lepidus's pulse rifle to his right and aimed his fall that way. Lepidus jumped over an infectee body and plunged the knife into Kaeso's calf.

Kaeso screamed at the searing pain engulfing his leg. He brought his other leg down on Lepidus's hand and felt, more than heard, the crunch of broken bones. Lepidus cried out, and pulled his hand back. Kaeso scrambled toward the rifle and grabbed it. He aimed at Lepidus and pulled the trigger.

Nothing.

He cursed, knowing why the gun didn't work. Praetorian weapons had biometric safeties.

Lepidus brought up the knife and leaped at Kaeso.

Lucia cursed. She aimed her rifle at Lepidus, but every time she got a clear shot, Kaeso got in the way. She could not kill Lepidus in his armor, but she could at least knock him down or distract him long enough to give Kaeso an advantage.

"I have an idea," Cordus said next to her. He jumped up and tapped on the control panel.

She didn't bother to ask what he was doing. She kept her aim on Lepidus, her finger curling on the trigger, waiting for one clear shot.

"I found it!" Cordus cried. "These archives are amazing. I could spend years just—"

"What do you have?" Lucia asked.

"Lepidus."

Cordus tapped a few keys. The holographic projector went blank, and then blurry images materialized. They were wavy and insubstantial for a moment, but soon became clear.

Lucia stared at the video.

Kaeso brought the rifle up and blocked Lepidus's strike. He fell onto his back, Lepidus on top of him. He pushed against Lepidus with the rifle, but his arms still shook from the climb along the bottom of the walkway. All he could manage was a weak grunt.

Lepidus slammed his knee into Kaeso's stabbed calf. Kaeso screamed, the pain weakening his push against Lepidus. The Praetorian's knife would soon pierce the thin EVA lining around Kaeso's neck, and there was nothing he could do.

Petra, I hope you're waiting for—

"—Please confirm, my lord. You want me to implement *decimation*?"

Lepidus blinked, then turned to the holographic projector. Kaeso's heart thundered in his ears, but he recognized Lepidus's voice coming from the projector.

Kaeso gathered his strength and gave Lepidus a shove with the rifle. The Praetorian fell backward and against the cavern wall. He didn't move, however, only stared at the projector with wide eyes. Kaeso stood, the rifle in his hands, and he pulled it back in a swing to do as much damage to Lepidus as his armor would allow.

"Kaeso, wait!" Cordus called out.

Kaeso held the rifle in a half-swing, his eyes on Lepidus. "Why?"

"Lepidus needs to see this."

Kaeso half-turned to the projector, keeping Lepidus in the corner of his eye. The view in the holographic sphere was through the eyes of someone standing on the command deck of a Roman Eagle looking at a com display showing Lepidus's face. The Praetorian was years younger, dirty, sweat-soaked, and weary. Though he had tired eyes, they were not filled with the zealotry Lepidus now had.

"Correct, Tribune," said the man who stared at Lepidus. "The XVII Legion has dishonored the entire Republic with this humiliating defeat today. It must be punished. It is the will of the gods."

"But...decimation will not—"

"The gods have written a Missive. I received word this hour."

Lepidus paled. He worked his lips, but no sound came from them. Finally, he said, "How many centuries must...must be punished?"

"The entire Legion."

Lepidus's eyes twitched. "We will destroy ten percent of our soldiers when the Kaldethians are still lurking in the Caan Forest. We have no idea how many—"

"Do you question the will of the gods, Tribune?"

"No, my lord, but surely we can delay the punishment until after we've secured the planet."

"The Missive said the punishment must be carried out immediately."

Lepidus stared at the man, his eyes desperate. "Brother."

"I understand how difficult this is for you, Lepidus," the man said in a gentler voice. "That is why I wanted to tell you myself. But it is the will of the gods. Have faith they know what is best for you and the Republic."

Lepidus sagged, then nodded reluctantly. "I will begin immediately."

His face winked out on the com screen. The man turned to another man next to him wearing the dark blue robes of a Pontiff. The second man was old and frail, and Kaeso recognized Savix IX, the Pontifex Maximus from the days of the Kaldethian rebellion.

"We will need to create a Missive to validate what you just told your brother, Avitus," Savix said with a frown.

"It was necessary, your grace. He would not have carried out the decimation without one. I know my brother. He is sentimental when it comes to his soldiers."

"You don't think he would have carried out the order if he knew it came directly from the Consul and not the gods?"

Avitus paused. "My brother is a patriot. But I don't think he would understand that our new Consul had to demonstrate his resolve to the Kaldethians. I apologize if the lie bothered you."

Savix shook his head. "No, no, the lie does not bother me. It is just that Missives are so damned hard to create. I did not bring scrolls or pig's blood."

"I doubt Lepidus will ask to see the Missive. It would demonstrate a lack of faith on his part, and he is the most faithful man I know."

Savix put his spotted hands into the folds of his robes. "Good. My hands are not as nimble with calligraphy as they once wore."

Lepidus groaned behind Kaeso. "It's not possible...how could they have known my exact words...my brother's exact words..."

"Because it's not an act," Kaeso said. "Your brother was infected with an alien virus. The Muses. That thing records every event every Muse in the universe sees. If your brother is infected, then his memories will show up here."

Lepidus closed his eyes. "It's not true..."

"It is true," Cordus said from behind Kaeso. He turned to see Cordus jumping off the support beam onto the walkway. Lucia was in front of him, her rifle aimed at Lepidus. "They lied to you, Lepidus. Just as they have lied to humanity for a thousand years."

Lepidus opened his eyes again. He had the look of a man who'd lost everything. Kaeso tightened his grip on the rifle. A man who lost everything might be harmless, or he might be even more dangerous.

"No," Lepidus said. "The gods are challenging my faith again. You can't break me with—"

The holographic images shifted again. The view was still through the eyes of Lepidus's brother, but this time he regarded Lepidus in person on a grassland at night. Lepidus stood before a funeral pyre staring at it with vacant eyes.

"Triaria is in Elysium now, brother," the man said. "She died with valor. The gods will reward her."

Lepidus continued to stare at the pyre. "I shot her myself, Avitus." He said this as if explaining how he shaved that morning.

"I heard. And the gods saw. Your faith will be rewarded a hundredfold."

"Rewards," Lepidus said. "I serve the gods because it is the right thing to do. For the Republic and for humanity."

Avitus put a hand on Lepidus's shoulder.

"I would like to see the Missive, brother," Lepidus said. "It would give me solace."

"Of course. You can see it when you return to the flagship next week."

Lepidus nodded.

The image blurred and then faded. The holographic globe became a swirling mass of colors.

Lepidus stared at the globe for many moments, his face slack. Kaeso was about to nudge him to see if he still lived, but Lepidus said, "My brother and I were the only ones there. Nobody knew of our conversation. I never did see that Missive. He kept delaying it. And then I just stopped asking."

Cordus walked closer to Lepidus. Kaeso grabbed the boy's arm, but Cordus waved him off. "It is all right."

Kaeso let him go. Cordus knelt on one knee next to Lepidus. "You served Roma for many years, doing things you thought were right and good. But you were lied to. The Muses use loyal people like you to further their own agenda. They are using humanity to continue a war they have fought amongst themselves for millions of years. You did not know. You could not have known."

"The gods don't exist?" Lepidus whispered. "Triaria..."

"Lepidus, hear me," Cordus said. Cordus waited until Lepidus turned his head to face him. Cordus was too close to Lepidus for Kaeso's comfort. He inched forward with the rifle held back, ready to smash it against the Praetorian.

"The gods do not speak through the Consul or the Collegia," Cordus said, "but that does *not* mean they don't exist."

Lepidus stared at Cordus for a long time. The Praetorian did not blink, did not move. The only way Kaeso could tell he breathed was from the hum of the air scrubbers on his back.

Finally he closed his mouth, set his jaw, and said, "My lord."

Lepidus glanced at Kaeso, then at the rifle. "I'm getting up now, Liberti. Please do not hit me."

Before Kaeso could respond, Lepidus slowly stood, wincing as he held his left hand close to his body. Cordus backed away behind Kaeso, and Kaeso kept the rifle at a half-swing. Once Lepidus stood, he turned his back on them and walked toward the door.

"Where are you going?" Kaeso asked.

"To my shuttle and then off this planet," Lepidus said without turning. "I suggest you do the same. You have fifteen minutes before the Consul glasses this entire continent."

Chapter Fifty-Four

Kaeso wasn't sure whether to stop Lepidus or let him go. Cordus answered the question for him. The boy ran back to the support beam and made his way to the control station.

"What are you doing?" Kaeso called out.

"I need to make sure the right files have uploaded."

Kaeso glanced at Lucia, who asked, "You think Lepidus was serious?"

"About the Consul bombing us?" He paused. "We have to assume he is."

"The Consul would kill Cordus? His own son?"

Kaeso shook his head. "These are the Muses. If the Consul believes Cordus is lost, I'm sure he'd rather kill the boy than let him escape."

Lucia scowled, then turned back to Cordus. The boy was already tapping keys on the control station. "How much longer?" Lucia yelled.

Cordus just frowned.

"Cordus?" Kaeso said.

"Twenty minutes."

"You said fifteen minutes before," Kaeso growled. "And that was fifteen minutes ago."

"There are more files I did not see before. They are important, too."

Kaeso shifted his weight accidentally to his wounded leg. He gasped and then yelled out, "You have five minutes, and then we leave."

"It will not be enough," Cordus shot back. "If we do not get it all, we will not convince people—"

"If we don't get off this planet before your father bombs us, we won't convince anybody. Five minutes."

The boy sighed, then turned back to the control panel and began choosing files.

Kaeso hobbled over to the wall and leaned against it. He activated his com. "Nestor, have Daryush fire up the engines. We leave as soon as we get back."

"Understood, Centuriae, but the way line engines aren't working yet."

"I don't care. We have to get off the planet now."

Kaeso said to Lucia, "I want you to go ahead and make sure our way back to *Caduceus* is clear of infectees. Lepidus probably got them all, but I don't want any surprises."

Lucia shook her head. "You can barely walk. You'll need my help getting up those stairs."

"*Cac*, Lucia, just follow my orders."

"Bring me up on charges before the Merchant's Guild, but I am not leaving you behind, Kaeso."

Kaeso glared at her. For the first time he could remember, she used his name rather than "Centuriae" or "sir." She returned his stare, her eyes showing him the depth of her feelings. *Damn, woman, this is no time to make things awkward.*

He frowned and then nodded. He turned to Cordus. "Three minutes!"

Cordus shook his head. "It will not be enough."

"It'll have to be."

Kaeso then turned to the projector, which resumed showing random videos from Muse history. Colorful centipede-like species performed a ritual that included mating and pipe smoking. More images showed dozens of humans in wide-brimmed hats hoeing a large, flat field. Above them, in the cloudless blue sky, hovered a ringed gas giant with yellow and orange swirling bands.

Kaeso wondered what images belonged to which Muse strain. How had the Cariosus strain gathered all these memories? How many species had the Liberti Muses infected before they found humans? How many had they destroyed? Cordus was right: these archives were a priceless source of information that could help humanity defeat the Muses.

Kaeso glanced at the time on his helmet display. They would have to defeat the Muses with that they got.

"Time's up, Cordus! Let's go, now!"

Cordus sighed. "Please, just another—"

"Your father," Kaeso said, "is he or is he not a man who will bomb this planet when he says he will? You tell me."

Cordus looked at Kaeso, and his face fell. He tapped a few keys on the console, then ran to the support beam. "I selected one last file," he said when he reached the walkway. "It will be uploaded by the time we leave the planet."

Nestor's voice crackled over the com. "Centuriae, what's your status?"

"We're on our way."

"Good," Nestor said. "The Roman flagship just launched half its payload of missiles at us. If they stay on their current heading, they will arrive in ten minutes."

Chapter Fifty-Five

No sooner had Lepidus reached his shuttle than his systems detected missile launches from the Consul's flagship.
Right on time. At least there is some *honesty in the man.*

He sat in the pilot's seat, not bothering to remove his armored EVA suit. He'd only removed his helmet so he could see the controls better. He powered up the shuttle and set a course for the Roman flagship. It would take three hours to reach the flagship, and he would safely pass the missiles minutes before they impacted the planet's surface.

It was three hours to think.

He did not feel the way he thought a man with a destroyed faith would feel. He mind was detached, as if he watched his limbs perform tasks he did not remember directing them to do. He had killed his wife based on the tantrum of a young Consul who did not get the easy victory he had wanted. His own brother had lied to him. And yet he did not feel any emotion knowing all this, certainly nothing like he felt hours after the decimations. Should he not feel something? Anger? Resentment?

The only feeling he could identify was that something had broken in him. He wondered if his mind and soul would ever heal.

Perhaps these Muses are creatures of the gods, the faithful part of his mind pleaded. *They* are the true conduits. They are blessings given by the gods to the Consul and the Collegia.

The faithless part of his mind ignored these excuses. The Consul and the Collegia lied to him. They did not hear the gods.

The gods do not speak through the Consul or the Collegia. But that does not mean they don't exist.

The com chimed. It was the flagship. He tapped the receive key on his console. The Consul's face materialized on the screen.

"Did you rescue my son?"

"No, my lord. The Liberti overcame me and my apprentice. Appius is dead. The Liberti will likely escape to their ship before the antimatter bombs hit."

The Consul nodded. "Unfortunate." Lepidus didn't know if the Consul referred to the death of his son, to Appius, or to the mission's failure. "No matter. Our missiles will destroy any lies the Menotans created to sow doubt in the Republic."

"Yes, my lord."

The Consul stared at him. "What did you find there, Lepidus? I see...confusion in your eyes."

"This is the first mission I've failed in a long time, my lord. I regret not rescuing the Consular Heir. And I was fond of my apprentice."

The Consul regarded him several more heartbeats, then smiled. "Your service to me and to the Republic is invaluable. You did well in finding my son. Do not be troubled that you could not save him."

"Yes, my lord. And the Liberti fleet?"

The Consul's face twitched, and his eyes took on a savage glint. "We have them on the run, Lepidus. Once you dock, we will continue to pursue them all the way back to their homeworld."

"How many ships do we have for the pursuit, my lord?"

"Only the flagship is unscathed," the Consul said. "We have more than enough firepower to crush the remnants of their fleet."

Lepidus paused. *One flagship assaulting the rest of the Liberti fleet?* Even their "remnants" would have no trouble fending off a single flagship, especially after it had sent half its missiles into Menota. Lepidus searched the Consul's eyes and confirmed that everything Cordus said was true. The Muses inside the Consul could not let the Liberti strain live, even if such an attack was suicidal. The Consul's madness would take Lepidus with him.

Calculations and emotions sped through Lepidus's mind in an instant, and he arrived at a decision he hoped would bring him peace.

"My lord, I saw the lies the Menotans created. They would be convincing to people whose faith was not strong."

The Consul waved his hand. "Yes, the people can be weak. Our missiles will destroy those lies in five minutes. Then we will destroy the Liberti fleet."

"It's just that the Liberti...and your son...were at a control station before they escaped. I believe they were uploading those lies to their ship. If the lies should spread..."

Lepidus watched the Consul's face go from an eagerness for the hunt to a slack blankness, as if he were in a trance. Then he blinked, and his eyes turned cold and calculating.

"We will follow the Liberti fleet and intercept them before they reach the way line," the Consul said. "Then we will wait for *Caduceus* and destroy them when they leave the planet. I have it on good authority that their magical new way line engines were damaged during their trip here. They will not leave the system anytime soon."

"Yes, my lord. But I overheard the Liberti saying they'd hide in Menota's rings. It could take days to find them, which would give them time to repair their engines. If you wish to stop them now, you must do so as soon as they leave the atmosphere."

"If the Liberti fleet escapes—"

"Forgive me for interrupting, my lord," Lepidus said. The Consul's eyes hardened. "If your son gets away with the lies he has gathered from Menota, he will sow doubt among our people. Not all Romans would believe, but enough will that we might have another Kaldethian-style rebellion. Perhaps on Terra this time."

The Consul's face went slack again, the look of a slave receiving orders from his master. Contempt for this man roiled in Lepidus, and it took all his will to keep calm and subservient.

Finally the Consul said, "We are setting a course to intercept my son. Dock with the flagship when you catch up."

The Consul's face winked out on the display. Lepidus set a course for the flagship.

Chapter Fifty-Six

Kaeso limped most of the way up the stairs and through the vaults, and even made it to the theater lobby before his leg gave out in a blast of pain that almost made him vomit in his helmet. From the lobby on, Lucia and Cordus helped him walk and stumble to *Caduceus*.

Nestor had already lowered the cargo ramp, and Daryush had started the ion engines. The ship was ready for takeoff when Kaeso, Lucia, and Cordus shuffled into Cargo One. As soon as they were in, Nestor closed the cargo hold's door ramp. Lucia shed her EVA suit as she rushed through the hold on her way up to the command deck.

Nestor and Blaesus helped Kaeso to a nearby bench, where he sagged against the wall. "Did you get it all?" he asked.

Both nodded.

Blaesus said, "I'd think it an epic myth worthy of Homer if I didn't know it was real."

Nestor turned to Cordus. "Was it everything?"

"Not even close," Cordus said, removing his EVA helmet, sweat drenching his dark hair. He frowned at Kaeso, but Kaeso ignored him.

"It'll have to be enough," Kaeso said through gritted teeth as he unfastened his EVA suit. "Engine status?"

"Daryush is still making last second repairs," Blaesus said. "Gaia is helping him."

Kaeso looked at Blaesus, and the old Senator shrugged. "The woman is rather unique for a patrician. I've yet to find any topic of which she doesn't have at least a passing knowledge. Including magical way line engines, it seems."

"Lucky us," Kaeso said. He sucked in a breath when he pulled his EVA pants over his stabbed calf. Nestor bent down with a med kit and studied the wound. He rubbed the prong of his blood scanner near the wound, set it aside, then washed away the bright red blood on Kaeso's leg with a wet towel. He applied a spray-on sealant and then injected a painkiller into Kaeso's calf. The pain washed away in a cool numbness that engulfed Kaeso's entire leg.

"No radiation poisoning or Cariosus," Nestor said, reading his blood scanner. "Fortuna was with you there. The sealant on your wound will hold for another hour or two, but you will need stitches and surgery to repair the muscle damage. And be gentle with it or you'll—"

"After we leave Menota," Kaeso said. He stood and fast limped out of the hold toward the command deck. "Get to your delta couches. We're jumping as soon as the way line engines are online."

While climbing the ladder, Kaeso fought through the ship's jerking motions and momentary vertigo when the artificial grav kicked in. Up top, the view out the windows was gray and brown as Lucia ascended through the dusty atmosphere.

He strapped himself into his command couch and brought up his tabulari displays. Sixty Roman antimatter missiles streaked toward Menota. They were less than a minute away.

The Praetorian was right. This would be close.

Kaeso tapped his collar com. "All crew to your couches. The missiles will impact in forty seconds."

Kaeso heard Nestor jump into his delta control couch and then he checked the indicators for the other couches. Eight crew, eight couches occupied. Kaeso hoped the old ship would hold up to the antimatter blast that would leave a crater the size of Terra's European continent.

Kaeso glanced at Lucia as she piloted the ship. She had the same expression she always had while concentrating—teeth set, eyebrows furrowed.

"Thank you for getting me out of that damned city," he said.

She gave a quick nod without looking at him.

Kaeso watched the countdown on his display. As soon as they topped the planet's lower dust clouds and entered the sunlit upper atmosphere, brilliant white lights from behind drove the window filters up to their highest levels. The light overcame the filters and Kaeso had to close his eyes.

Kaeso's stomach lurched. He opened his eyes to see dark blue sky fill the command window. An alarm wailed from Lucia's pilot's console.

"Blast wave knocked out steering," she said through gritted teeth. "Backups not responding."

The ship felt like it dropped a hundred feet, and the view outside the command window began to spin.

"Inertia cancelers are weakened, but holding," Lucia said. "We're in a spin."

Kaeso tapped his collar com. "Daryush, the steering—"

Gaia interrupted, "Primary steering is blown. We're fixing the backups."

Kaeso averted his eyes from the command window, for the spinning made him nauseous. The inertia cancelers kept the worst of the spin from affecting the crew, but vertigo still tugged at the corner of his eyes.

"Backup steering systems online," Lucia and Gaia announced at the same time.

The spinning outside the window gradually slowed and then stopped altogether. Lucia set a course toward the dark blue sky, and the ship rocketed through the upper atmosphere. Once the ship cleared the atmosphere, the tremors from the blast wave and atmospheric turbulence stopped and the ride smoothed.

Threat alarms blared when they reached space. Kaeso glanced at his displays and cursed. The Roman flagship waited for them.

"Four antimatter missiles chasing us," Lucia yelled.

Kaeso checked his display. Five minutes to impact.

He tapped his collar com. "Gaia, Daryush, where are we on the way line engines?"

"Ready," Gaia said. "I've selected coordinates to a Saturnist world where Cordus should be safe for the time being. At least until we figure out another place for him. However..."

"What, Gaia?"

"It was all we could do to simply repair the engines. They should work...but we couldn't fix the automated systems."

"What are you saying?"

"It means the ship won't engage the engines while we're in delta sleep. Someone will have to stay awake to make the jump manually."

Kaeso exhaled.

"I know," Gaia said. "But if someone doesn't do it..."

"We all die," Kaeso finished. "Fine. I'll do it. Transfer way line controls to my console."

Lucia said, "Damn, Centuriae, I knew you'd—!"

"Lucia, this isn't a debate. Prepare for way line jump."

She stared at him, emotion warring in her eyes. "Kaeso..." she whispered.

I know the feelings you have for me, he wanted to say. *But I cannot return them. I doubt I can ever give them to another woman again.*

Instead, he simply said, "I know. I *know*."

He reached over and put his hand on her hand. She looked at it, blinked, and then pulled her hand away.

"Centuriae," Nestor said behind him, "there is an old theory among Saturnists that way line travel without delta sleep can kill the Muses."

Kaeso turned around. "Kills humans, too."

"Yes, but—and this is just a theory—the Muses protect the human mind during a way line jump in order to protect themselves. But the mental turbulence during the jump is too much for them and they die once they reach the other side."

"I'm not a Vessel."

"But you have a Muse implant. I don't know the exact mechanics of the implant, but it might be enough."

"I appreciate the encouragement. I suppose we'll see if you're right."

Nestor nodded. "I thought I'd mention it."

Kaeso turned his couch back around, then an idea came to him. "How valid is this theory?"

"It's old," Nestor said. "I'm not aware of any testing. It's floated around Saturnist cells for generations. I thought it might give you...well, hope."

Kaeso nodded. Nestor's 'hope' might save the only family he had left.

"When you start delta sleep for the crew...make sure Ocella is still awake."

Nestor's eyes widened, and he opened his mouth to protest, but Kaeso cut him off. "It's either this, or she lives her life enslaved. Either way, she'll be trapped in a body she can't control."

"What about Cordus? We can use his blood to—"

"What do we do with Ocella until then?" Kaeso asked. "She can communicate her position wherever we go. And if we leave her on some rock of a planet, they'll pick her up and we'd never get her back." Kaeso sighed. "I don't like this either, but she's my wife's sister. The only family I can... We have to try."

Nestor frowned, but said nothing more. He returned to his console and Kaeso swiveled his couch back around.

Two minutes until impact.

Kaeso tapped his collar com. "Ocella, if you can hear me, we're going to try something that might free you."

"She cannot hear you, Centuriae," Ocella's voice said calmly. "There is nothing you can do to bring her back."

"Ocella," Kaeso said, ignoring the Muses, "we're going to keep you awake during the way line jump. We're not positive, but it might kill the Muses."

"If you keep her awake during the jump, you will kill her."

"I'll stay awake with you, Ocella. The automated way line systems aren't working, so someone has to engage the engines manually. I could use some company."

"You will be a murderer, Centuriae," Ocella said, an edge creeping into her voice. "You would murder the only member of your family who knows who you really are?"

Lucia said, "One minute to impact. Sir, if we're doing this..."

"Ocella," Kaeso said, "I won't abandon you. I will keep this line open while we go through."

"You cannot do this!" Ocella's voice screamed.

Kaeso turned his couch to Nestor. "Engage delta sleep for the crew."

Nestor gave him a long look and nodded slowly.

Kaeso turned his couch around and then glanced at Lucia. She stared at him through glistening eyes. "You'd better come through this, Centuriae. You'd better..."

Kaeso gave her a reassuring grin that didn't seem to reassure her. Then her eyes closed, her face relaxed, and her body settled into the couch.

"Delta sleep engaged for the crew, Centuriae," Nestor said. "Transferring delta controls to your console. May the gods be with you, Kaeso Aemilius Rulus."

Kaeso didn't say anything. The delta monitors on his console said the entire crew was asleep except for him and Ocella. His proximity displays showed the missiles would reach them in thirty seconds.

"You are going to kill her!" Ocella's voice raged.

"Ocella, I pray you can hear me. Be ready to come back." *If this works...*

"Kaeso, please, don't do it, it's me. It's Ocella. Oh gods, they let me go. I don't want to die or go mad! Please, Kaeso! Turn on my delta sleep!"

His finger hovered over the way line engagement controls on his console, a sudden paralyzing fear coming over him. He had never feared death, but the loss of his mind terrified him. He knew men whose delta couches had malfunctioned. He had seen their vacant stares, the saliva dribbling from their mouths, the sanatoriums where the "way liners" on Libertus lived out their mind-dead lives. There were times when he thought the Roman practice of euthanizing way liners was more humane than the Liberti custom of keeping them alive.

Alarms blared from his console. The missiles would impact in ten seconds.

"Kaeso, please!" Ocella screamed.

Sweat trickled down his forehead and his heart pounded. Kaeso waited until the countdown had ticked down to the last second, and then slammed his thumb on the console to engage the way line engines.

What are they waiting for? Lepidus wondered. *The missiles are less than—*

Four white spheres appeared on his display indicating clouds of antimatter plasma hotter than the core of a star expanding near the speed of light. The cloud would have destroyed a continent and would certainly have vaporized *Caduceus*.

Had she been there less than a second before.

Why did they wait so long?

Lepidus's com chimed, and he tapped the receive button. The Consul appeared on screen.

"Our missiles detonated," the Consul said. "*Caduceus's* beacon no longer transmits, but interference from the rings prevents us from confirming their destruction. Your shuttle had a better line of sight above the plane of the rings. Can you confirm the ship was destroyed, Lepidus?"

The Consul stared at Lepidus with hard eyes that bored into his mind even from a screen. Did the Consul already know the truth? Was he testing Lepidus's loyalty? If Lepidus answered yes, but the Consul knew the ship had jumped, then Lepidus's punishment would be death.

At least I will be with you again, Triaria, my love. If you can forgive me.

"They are gone, my lord," Lepidus said, his voice steady. "The missiles destroyed them."

The Consul stared at him a moment longer, then smiled. It was the same smile the Consul gave worshipful crowds—perfect white teeth beneath dead eyes.

"Congratulations, Lepidus," the Consul said. "Once again your faith and loyalty has saved the Republic. You will be rewarded for your wise suggestion to chase *Caduceus*."

"Rewards," Lepidus said, his heart breaking that he would live. "Serving Roma and the gods is its own reward, my lord."

Chapter Fifty-Seven

Kaeso had braced himself when he tapped the jump button, but no sensation whatsoever came when the ship entered the way line. No acceleration or deceleration. Kaeso checked his console. The Roman ships were gone. The missiles were gone. Menota was gone. Only space and stars showed outside the command window. They had jumped, but to where?

Lucia was asleep, her chest rising and falling with each deep breath. He swiveled his couch around. Nestor also slept. The medicus console said the whole crew slept besides Kaeso and Ocella. He brought up the delta sleep controls and tapped the keys to release the crew from their sleep.

Lucia and Nestor did not stir.

Kaeso tapped the delta controls again. The crew's delta readouts showed no change. Kaeso clicked his teeth together and reached for the delta release again.

Ocella's screams from one deck below were animalistic. They could not have come from a human throat. She shrieked in Latin, then Germanic, then an Atlantium language Kaeso did not know. Her shrieks turned to hoots and whistles he remembered from the projector room in the vaults. The language of a dead alien race the Muses had destroyed.

Kaeso threw off his couch belts, slid down the command deck ladder to the crew deck; his calf wound a distant throbbing. Ocella's screams echoed from the last hatch down the hall. Kaeso rushed to the open hatch and stopped.

Ocella writhed and kicked against the straps holding her in the couch. Blood flew from her mouth and nose in stringy mucous with each scream and thrash. Sweat drenched her hair. The stench of feces hung in the air. Ocella had the eyes of an animal frightened beyond madness.

Kaeso rushed in and held Ocella's shoulders to keep her still. "Ocella, fight them!"

His words had no impact, or if they did, Ocella's mind could not get past the fear and madness of the Muses. His muscles strained against her terrified strength. The straps from the couch bit into her clothes. Bloody streaks formed beneath the yellow prison tunic near her shoulders and trousers where the straps met the buckle between her thighs.

Kaeso stood above Ocella, holding her. "I won't leave you, Ocella," he yelled over the screams. "I won't leave you."

It took Ocella—or the Muses controlling her—almost a half hour to exhaust Ocella's body to the point where she could no longer scream or move. Once she fell into a fitful sleep, Kaeso went to Nestor's medical hatch and grabbed towels, bandages, antiseptic, and wound sealer. He brought the supplies back to Ocella's bunk. Blood no longer streamed from her nose and mouth, but began caking around her cheeks and chin. Kaeso used the wet towels to gently wash her head and neck.

Once he finished, he considered unbuckling the couch straps. He had to get at the wounds on her shoulders and thighs. After thinking on it, he decided he didn't want her leaving the couch if she woke up, so he loosened the straps only enough to get at the wounded areas. Ocella did not stir, not even when Kaeso cut open her shirt and trousers to clean, seal, and bandage her wounds. Once he finished, he wrapped the towels around the straps so they wouldn't cut so severely if she woke up again in the same terrified state.

He hobbled into Nestor's medical lab and pulled up the trouser leg over his wounded calf. He frowned at the swollen, enflamed wound. The last thing he needed was of infection to set in. He searched Nestor's med supplies and found an antibiotic injector. He injected the medicine into his calf, then grabbed another pain killer and injected it in the same place. The sharp throbbing went away.

On his way back to the deck ladder, he looked in on Blaesus. The Senator's chest rose and fell in a steady pattern. Kaeso inspected the readouts on Blaesus's couch, which showed normal delta sleep patterns.

He went down to the engine deck and checked Daryush, Gaia, and Cordus, all three with the same normal delta sleep patterns as Blaesus.

Kaeso climbed all the way up to the command deck and checked the patterns on both Lucia and Nestor's couches. Both normal. He sat in his own couch and stared at his console.

Time ticked by on the chronometer. According to the display, it was an hour since they jumped away from Menota.

He brought up his nav system readouts again. Just as before, there were no ships in the vicinity. He checked the navigations charts and told the tabulari to calculate the ship's location. The tabulari came back with "unknown." This was not unusual, since travel along a new way line could dump a ship in any corner of the universe. But Kaeso had set a specific course to the Saturnist planet Gaia assured him would exist. Kaeso's instruments said there wasn't a planet within the ship's limited scopes. There wasn't even a star nearby.

"Fine," Kaeso muttered to the tabulari, "then where's the nearest star?" He tapped a few keys and then waited for the response.

The console blinked. *Nearest star system: None.*

Kaeso looked out the window. "I can *see* the godsdamned stars," he growled.

If they were between galaxies, he would've seen only blackness out the window. But the view showed a multitude of stars as if he were in the middle of a galaxy. The tabulari should have picked up at least one star.

He entered the instructions again. *None.*

Kaeso routed piloting controls from Lucia's console to his and tried engaging the ship's ion engines.

No response. Not even an error warning. The engines simply did not fire when he moved the acceleration sliders on his console.

He tried other systems—com, grav control, inertia cancellers, life support—but none responded to his commands. He ran diagnostic after diagnostic, and each one said the systems ran normally.

So he got up from his command couch and ran the same diagnostics from Lucia's console, standing over her sleeping form as he did so.

Still no response.

He descended the ladder to the engine room, stood over Daryush, and ran the diagnostics. All returned normal, yet none of the systems responded to his commands.

Kaeso walked back to the ladder, climbed up to the command deck, and sat down on his command couch. He stared at his console, wondering what to do.

Three hours after the jump, Kaeso considered waking his crew without using the delta system. It was dangerous. One possibility was the sleeper wouldn't wake up. Another was the sleeper *would* wake up, but his higher brain functions would still be shut down. The person would be in a coma for the rest of his life.

Madness was another danger.

Like any starship centuriae, Kaeso knew the worst-case scenarios for delta sleep failure. But after working at his console for hours, he realized he'd need more minds to think their way out of this limbo.

He ground his teeth, stood up from his command couch, and descended the ladder to the crew deck. He walked down the corridor and turned into Blaesus's quarters. The former Senator still slept soundly in his couch. Kaeso stared at him several minutes, gathering the will to doom one of his best friends to a life of madness. Centuriae logic dictated he start with the most expendable crewmember. He needed Lucia, Daryush, and Gaia to run the ship. He needed Nestor in case of medical emergencies. Cordus was obviously too important. And he would not sacrifice Ocella, his only family.

"Forgive me, Gaius Octavius Blaesus."

Kaeso swallowed once, then reached down and gently shook Blaesus.

"Wake up, Blaesus," he said in a loud voice.

The old Senator did not stir.

"Blaesus!"

No movement.

Kaeso shook Blaesus harder, but he still didn't wake up. Kaeso unstrapped Blaesus from the delta couch and pulled him over his shoulder. He carried the old man to the bunk behind his delta couch, and lay him down. Kaeso shook Blaesus again.

"Blaesus, wake up! Wake up, old man!"

Blaesus continued to sleep. Kaeso pinched his arms, fingers, and toes. He slapped the Senator across the face.

Blaesus didn't stir.

Kaeso exhaled sharply. He lifted Blaesus back on his shoulders, carried him to the delta couch, and strapped him back in. The old man slept through the whole experience.

Kaeso tried the same methods with the rest of the crew, going from Gaia to Nestor to Daryush to Lucia. He finally tried waking Ocella, but she didn't even whimper.

After Ocella, Kaeso paced the corridor outside the crew quarters. At least one of them should have awakened, even if into a coma.

Kaeso stopped pacing. Or what if they were already in a coma? Gaia had said the way line engine's automated systems were not fully repaired. Perhaps the delta sleep system was also broken and they simply missed it? Maybe his entire crew was in a delta induced coma from which they would not awaken unless he repaired the delta system.

Like any good centuriae, he hired people who did their jobs well. Kaeso was no expert on the delta system. That was why he hired Nestor.

Kaeso climbed the ladder to the command deck. He sat back in his command couch, tapped a few keys on his tabulari, and brought up the schematics for the ship's delta system.

※※※ ※※※

Kaeso saw the first *numen* one day after the jump.

His 'repairs' on the delta system were not going well. Every diagnostic he ran told him the systems worked normally. Not trusting the diagnostics, he proceeded to take apart every component on the main delta circuits and boards, and inspect each one. Kaeso lay on the floor next to Nestor's delta couch, the delta panel beneath Nestor's console open and components littering the floor. He was running a diagnostic on a bio-crystal when motion at the command window caught his eye.

A face stared at him from outside the ship. He blinked and it was gone. He stared at the empty window, his heart pounding.

When nothing appeared, he put down the delta component and rubbed his eyes. He'd slept only two hours since the jump, and he'd been working on the delta systems the rest of the time, besides brief interruptions to eat or use the latrine. He was surprised it took this long before he started jumping at shadows.

He glanced at Nestor sleeping soundly in his couch. Kaeso never thought he'd envy someone so much for being able to sleep. Even considering his previous work and the guilt he bore over abandoning his daughter, he never had trouble sleeping. This night had been different. It took him over an hour to fall asleep, and then he awoke with his heart and mind racing. He lay in his bunk for another half hour before giving up and returning to work on the delta system. But throughout the day his body was exhausted while his mind refused to rest.

Kaeso looked from Nestor to Lucia, wondered what they were dreaming, then shook his head. If they were in delta sleep, they weren't dreaming at all—besides the most basic life support, their brains were shut down.

Kaeso then wondered how he'd give them water or food. If he could not repair the delta system, his crew could die of thirst long before they starved. Nestor had intravenous solutions in his medical hatch, but not enough for everyone.

Kaeso stood up, stretched, and then turned to the ladder to see the back of somebody's head drop down the ladder and out of sight. He froze, a cold wave exploding through his body. He regained his ability to move, then leaped toward the ladder and looked down.

Nothing.

He slid down the ladder to the crew deck and hurried to each one of the crew quarters. He searched each bunk while staying mindful of the corridor in case the stowaway rushed past.

Besides Ocella and Blaesus, there was nobody on the crew deck. Kaeso hurried over to the ladder and went down to the cargo/engine deck. He searched the engine room where Daryush, Gaia, and Cordus slept, and then checked both cargo bays. Dariya was still frozen in her sleeper crib.

He found no one else.

He stood in the corridor between the two cargo bays and listened to the sounds of his ship. A slight hum came from the engine room. Air flowed through the cylindrical vents in the corner where the walls met the ceiling. He detected no other sound except the thumping in his ears.

"I saw you," Kaeso said to the empty corridor. "It wasn't my tired eyes, was it?"

Only silence in the ship.

"Who are you?" Kaeso yelled.

Did one of the infectees get on the ship? A Praetorian? Kaeso glanced at Cargo One to his right. Lucia's pulse rifle lay on the floor next to a plastic drum. He went into the bay, picked up the rifle, and ensured it was charged. He strode back into the corridor, resolved to inspect every corner of the ship.

Kaeso went from cabin to cabin, then closed and locked each door after he'd finished searching them. When he finished a deck, he closed and sealed the pressure hatches between decks. The hatches could only open with his voice authorization. If anyone was on the ship, the stowaway would be trapped between decks.

So unless the stowaway knew a hiding place even Kaeso didn't know, his search revealed a secure ship.

Kaeso knew what he saw. Head, shoulders, and hands disappearing down the ladder. Long black hair, diminutive shoulders, and slender hands. Kaeso thought of the stowaway as a "she" because of this. She wore a tan vest with long, white sleeves. He ruled out an infectee since she did not have the hairless, gray skin, and dirty, torn clothing of the infectees in the vaults. That left either a Praetorian...or his imagination.

Sweat ran down his brow after he completed his final search, his mouth and throat dry. The painkillers had worn off and his entire calf ached. He limped to Nestor's medical closet and injected more painkillers into the swollen calf. Then he went to the galley, took a *kaffa*-stained cup from the dish drawer and filled it with water from the tap. He downed the water in three gulps, then ran the cup under the tap again.

A noise behind him. He dropped the cup, swung the rifle around and aimed at the door. He gasped, staggered back against the sink, the rifle falling from his hands.

His dead wife Petra stared at him from the doorway.

The realization came crashing down that he was mad. This whole time he had thought the ship was lost, the delta system didn't work, or the ship wouldn't respond to his commands because it was damaged. Was his mind a prisoner in his own body? Was he really now in some sanatorium for "way liners," staring at the wall while drool streamed down his chin?

"You're not mad," Petra said. Her voice had the same ethnic Indian lilt that overwhelmed Kaeso with sweet memories of her singing to an infant Claudia.

"I think I am," he whispered. "You're dead."

"Yes," she said, walking into the galley. "But I'm also here, with you. I always have been. I always will."

Kaeso squeezed his eyes shut, then opened them again.

She was gone.

He slid down the wall and landed hard on his bottom. He pulled his knees up to his chest and stared at the empty corridor.

※※※

Recognizing his own madness proved liberating to Kaeso. Now that he knew this wasn't real, he was free from any responsibility for his crew. He would not have to feed them or force water down their throats to keep them hydrated. He stopped worrying about the delta system—after all, the system was not really broken, and he was not really here. He didn't even attempt to inspect the way line engines. What was the point if he were sitting in a sanatorium somewhere?

His calf, however, would not heal, though it did not worsen either. He changed the bandages twice a day, and injected painkiller after painkiller, but nothing seemed to reduce the infection around the wound. Perhaps madness would eventually take care of the calf as well.

More *numina* came after Petra. One *numen*, the first face he saw outside his command window, appeared again when Kaeso went back to the command deck and sat in his couch to think. He recognized the Roman Senator he assassinated almost ten years ago. She had been his first. The Senator wanted to push through a law to ban Liberti goods from Roman vassal worlds. Liberti goods were already banned from Terra in a symbolic, rather than effective, embargo. But a ban on vassal worlds would have devastated the economy of Libertus. So Umbra ordered Kaeso to take care of the problem. Kaeso administered a subtle poison that made it appear the Senator died of a heart attack.

Now the Senator stared at Kaeso through the command deck window with accusing eyes.

"I'm not going to apologize, if that's what you want," Kaeso told the floating face. The face stared at him, then disappeared moments later.

He saw more *numina* of the people he killed. In mirrors, reflected off the cargo hold's glass walls, on tabulari displays. He ignored them all, knowing full well his madness was dredging up guilty feelings he never had after he killed them.

He didn't see Petra again until three days later.

Kaeso was taking a shower for the first time in four days. Even in his madness, he could still smell his own body odor. He had just cleaned the soap off of his head when he noticed the outline of a figure outside the shower. He opened the door and saw Petra standing before him. She was naked—goose bumps covering her olive skin, erect nipples on delicate breasts. By this time, Kaeso had grown comfortable with his madness. The sight of Petra did not shock him, only created a longing he hadn't felt since her death. A longing mirrored in her brown eyes. He held his hand out to her and she took it.

The first time they made love was in a shower in a resort hotel in the Liberti capital city, Avita. It had been passionate, sweet, and filled with shy giggles. This time, on a starship beyond the known universe—or a dark corner of his insane mind—was every bit as passionate, sweet, and full of giggles.

Afterwards they wrapped each other in thick towels and Kaeso guided her to his bunk where they made love again. She responded to his touch and kisses with the quickened breath and goose flesh he remembered, responses that multiplied his own excitement.

He had missed Petra beyond all reasoning.

When they finished, they lay on the bunk, both exhausted with a sheen of sweat covering their bodies. Kaeso held Petra's warm naked body tightly to his, afraid he would lose her again.

Afraid sanity would return.

"I'm still dead, you know."

Petra's chin rested on Kaeso's chest. Her brown eyes were bright and she wore the same dreamy grin she always had after they made love.

"And I'm mad," he said. "What a pair we make."

"You're not mad."

"I'm either mad or dead. Am I dead?"

"No."

"Ergo..."

She sighed. "You really don't understand what's happening, do you?"

"I understand I'm in a sanatorium staring at a crack in the wall." He gave her a squeeze. "I'll take this kind of madness any day."

She didn't smile. "You can't stay here forever."

"Seems I don't have a choice in the matter."

"You do have a choice," she said. "You've always had a choice. You just never had the courage to make it."

"Insulting my honor now, are we?"

"I'm being honest," she said. "Like always."

"Do we have to talk about his? Can't we just..." He ran his fingers gently down her soft back and smooth thigh. She sighed contentedly, but continued regarding him with sad eyes.

"If that's your choice," she said.

When Kaeso awoke, Petra was gone. He sat up straight in his bunk, the crushing weight of loss descending on him like the day he watched her ship explode.

He hurried to the open hatch.

"Petra!"

He charged down the corridor and then skidded to a stop in front of the galley. Petra sat at the table eating a freeze-dried meal. She wore one of Kaeso's merchant jumpsuits, the sleeves rolled up to her forearms. A strand of dark hair hung over her left eye, and she pulled it back behind her ear when she looked up at him.

"I can't believe you have red curry chicken in freeze-dried," she said. She took another bite and sighed. "Not like the real thing, but it's still nectar from the gods."

"I thought you left me," he said.

"I'm not going anywhere. Unless you want me to."

"No!"

She frowned and then turned back to her food. She acted as if he'd said something wrong, and he was about to ask when she laughed. "Aren't you cold?"

He realized he was naked. He grinned, then went back to his quarters and put on a merchant jump suit. When he returned,

Petra was scooping out the last bit of curry gravy from the plastic tray. She licked her spoon clean and then placed it in the dish. Kaeso watched her, marveling at the detail of his madness. Her idiosyncrasies—from her soft moans when they made love to her eating habits, things Kaeso had not realized he'd forgotten—were on display. His love for her blanketed him in a warmth he had not felt since the day she died.

She smiled. "You haven't stopped grinning since our shower."

"I missed you."

"I could tell." She stared at him a moment longer, then asked, "Why am I here?"

He shrugged. "I'm either mad or dead."

"You're neither."

"Then what am I? Because I know you're dead. I watched your ship die. I heard your screams on the com."

She licked her lips. "Yes, you heard the dying screams of Petra on that ship ten years ago. The Sodalicium's bombs were quite thorough."

"You say it like you're talking about a different person."

"Because I am. I'm not *your* Petra."

Kaeso smiled. "You sure look and sound like her to me." He reached across the table and held her soft, warm hands. "You feel like my Petra."

She took his hands in hers and kissed them, but she wore the same expression as before, as if he had said the wrong thing. He knew she was trying to tell him something important, but he ignored it. She was all he wanted. To stare into her brown eyes, to feel her warm skin next to his, to take in her natural scent. He wanted to hear her voice, to feel her heart beating when he laid his head on her chest.

He knew she wanted to tell him something important. Something that might bring him out of his madness.

He just didn't care.

⋙ ⋘

"When was the last time you checked on your crew?" Petra asked him.

They lay on his bunk in the darkness, the lights from the corridor illuminating the room in a soft yellow glow. They held each other beneath the blankets; Petra's warm naked skin pressed against his bare chest and legs.

"They're fine."

"When?"

"I don't know. Two days ago."

"Aren't you worried about them?"

"No."

"Why not?"

"Because they're not real. How many times are you going to ask me this?"

She put her chin on his chest, looking at him. "They are very much real. And they need you."

He sighed. She had not said much about the crew or the reason she was here in days, so Kaeso hoped she had given up trying to "save" him. They made love, played games on the ship's tabulari, talked about old times, ate more freeze-dried foods. It had been this way when they first married—complete focus on each other. He wanted it to go on forever.

"How can I help them?" he asked. "Even if what you say is true, and I'm not mad and I'm not dead—which I still think I'm one or the other—then what am I supposed to do? I've already tried waking them up. I've tried engaging the way line engines. I've tried the com systems on all channels. Nothing works. Unless Mercury picks us up, we're stuck here for eternity. We might as well get comfortable."

She shook her head. "The Kaeso I remember would not have given up this easy."

"*Kaeso* didn't exist when you knew me."

"How is your calf?"

"Bandaged and numb."

"But no better? Don't you think it odd you've had that wound over two weeks, but it's never gotten worse or better?"

Before Kaeso could respond, she asked, "Aren't you wondering why I haven't asked about Claudia?"

Kaeso stiffened.

"We've been together almost a week," she continued. "Why haven't we once talked about our only child?"

"We...we were distracted."

"We never talk about her because you don't want to," she said gently. "Because you are ashamed of how you treated her after I died."

He got up and started putting on his jump suit.

"Have you noticed we only discuss the things you want?"

He grunted. "If that's true than why are we having this conversation?"

"Because you know you *need* it. Even though you don't *want* it."

He zipped up his jump suit. "I don't *need* to be reminded I was a bad father."

Kaeso left the quarters. His calf was throbbing again.

⁂

Petra was gone when Kaeso returned to his bunk. He'd been gone ten minutes; long enough to inject more painkillers in his calf and go to the galley to make some *kaffa*.

The blankets were rumpled and empty. He searched the crew quarters but did not find her. He ran up and down each deck, but she was gone.

After searching the entire ship multiple times, he went back to his bunk, sat down, and pulled the blankets up to his face, taking in her scent.

"Petra," he said, a sob breaking through. "Petra..."

⁂

Kaeso stared at the two week's worth of beard in his bathroom mirror. He briefly considered shaving, but didn't see the point.

"Ready to talk?"

He whirled around and saw Petra standing in his quarters. She wore the white robes and tan vest of the Prosecutorium where she once tried cases in Avita's criminal court. Her long dark hair was pulled back into looping braids that hung down her back. She looked exactly the same as the day she died.

"Why did you leave?" he asked. It had been two days since she disappeared from his bed. He spent those two days either sleeping or talking to his unconscious crew.

"Because you wanted me to."

"I never—"

"You didn't want to discuss why you're here."

Kaeso looked away.

"You can only stay here for so long before your way back is closed. Then you *will* be mad. And it certainly won't be like this."

"So where are we?"

"You stayed awake during the way line jump. This is how your mind perceives the way line."

"Who are you?"

She smiled. "I'm glad you finally asked." She put her hands in the folds of her sleeves. "Your Petra is dead. I'm simply the memory you retain of her. You created the image that stands before you."

Kaeso walked out of the bathroom and into his room. He stood before her, studying her. She returned his stare with a patient one. "Those memories should have been wiped out when I got my Umbra implant. How is it I remember you so vividly?"

"The implant does not wipe out memories. It only diminishes them so you may devote your full attention to Umbra."

"So if you're a memory, how do you know all this?"

"I'm not just a memory. I am the vessel through which the Muses in your implant are talking to you."

Kaeso scratched his beard. "The Muses in my implant aren't alive."

"They are alive. They just don't infect your body. How do you think you communicated with Libertus from Roma?"

Kaeso was suddenly angry. "So you plucked an image of Petra from my mind to manipulate me."

"No," Petra said. "The Muses cannot read minds. No strain can. *You* created this image."

"Nestor said staying awake during a way line jump would kill the Muses. Is that true?"

Petra nodded. "Ocella will control her body when she wakes up. The reason I am here is because your implant protected the Muses within it, to some extent, and the Muses within the implant protected your mind."

"To some extent?"

"To protect your mind, they had to create a shelter for it. They do not have the strength to bring you out. Now you've turned that shelter into a prison."

Kaeso glanced around. "Looks like my ship to me."

"Like me, this prison is something you created," Petra said. "If you're honest with yourself, you'll admit that's the only way you've ever seen this ship."

"A starship is freedom, not a prison. It means I can go wherever I want, whenever I want."

"A starship is responsibility," Petra said. "Responsibility has always been a prison for you."

Kaeso scowled at this "constructed image" of his beloved Petra. He did not see *Caduceus* as a prison. He bought the ship for the reasons he just told her. A starship was freedom. All he'd ever wanted since he was a child was to wander the way lines, see all the star systems colonized by humanity, and maybe discover an unknown way line terminus. Before Petra was murdered by the Sodalicium, a Liberti criminal syndicate angry at her prosecutions of its members, he'd commanded a small police cruiser in the Liberti system. But he'd always viewed the system-bound cruiser as a stepping-stone to an interstellar command. One that would give him his childhood dream of exploring the universe.

But even a small lictor cruiser showed him that running a ship was not the same as exploring. Command meant responsibility for the ship and the crew, minutiae that prevented Kaeso from doing what he really wanted. When Petra's ship exploded while his lictor cruiser escorted it, he realized that responsibility was too overwhelming.

So when Umbra recruited him because his genetic makeup matched the requirements for the Umbra implant, he jumped at their offer like a drowning man reaching for a lifeline. He abandoned his command with the Liberti System Patrol. He abandoned his aging parents. He abandoned his only child. All because responsibility was a prison in which he could not bear to spend one more moment.

In Umbra he found what he always wanted: The freedom to explore without a team for which he was responsible. Umbra Ancilia worked alone. He performed his missions without worrying his mistakes would kill someone he cared about. If he made a mistake, only he would suffer the consequences. That was freedom.

That freedom ended when he was blacklisted from Umbra. He tried to gain back a measure of it by buying *Caduceus*. He was thrilled he'd finally have his own ship to explore the universe as he'd always wanted, but he ignored the dread in his heart over the prospect of another command. That he would be responsible for the lives of its crew.

When Umbra came calling again with their mission to Terra, he jumped at it. Like a drowning man. Because of his attempts to escape responsibility, he'd lost two crewmembers and was about to kill the rest.

Petra stared at him, a smile pulling at the corners of her mouth. "You see it now, don't you?"

Kaeso sat in his bunk, his shoulders slumped and his head in his hands. Selfish. That's what he'd been. His whole life he'd only wanted things for himself, and had viewed the most important people in his life as obstacles to getting what he wanted. For himself.

"Why didn't you tell me this before?" he asked.

"You didn't want to know. Before you can change, you have to want to change."

"What do I do?" he asked.

Petra smiled. "You need to leave the prison."

※ ※

Kaeso and Petra stood in front of the Cargo Two door ramp.

"You're kidding," he said.

"You need to leave the prison you created for yourself. It is the only way you will wake up."

"Can't I just snap my fingers? Say "I want to wake up"?"

Petra shook her head. "The way out is difficult. The Muses had to construct a strong shelter for your mind against the way line's effects. You made it stronger. They have already removed the barriers they created. Now you have to remove yours."

"But spacing myself..."

Petra put a hand on his arm. "As I said, the way out is difficult. You must prove to yourself that you want to leave. It requires great effort to climb the walls you've created."

"Why should I trust you? My ship carries a weapon that can defeat you. Maybe you just want to kill me."

"What would that solve?" Petra asked. "You already initiated the way line jump. Your friends are safe. The Muses have nothing to gain from your death."

"And nothing to lose."

Petra paused. "What I say comes from the Muses. They want you to know they are much like humans. Each strain has its own culture, ambitions, needs. Like humans, they also make mistakes. They don't expect you to believe this, but the Liberti strain does have the greatest regard for mankind. They may do things you don't understand, but they do them because they do not want to repeat the mistakes they've made in the past with other hosts. You cannot deny that without them, Libertus would have fallen to the Romans or the Zhonguo or some other tyrant long ago. They have done this by learning from past mistakes and avoiding direct confrontation with rival strains."

"I suppose killing Galeo is in that bucket of "things I don't understand." Or sending Ocella to assassinate Cordus."

"I just told you they make mistakes. Galeo died because he *refused* to give you the answers you wanted, whereas the Muses *wanted* to answer your questions."

"What? Why would he do that?"

Petra sighed. "Sometimes even Liberti Vessels begin to worship the Muses as gods. And they begin to think they know how to protect the Muses better than the Muses do. Galeo thought that giving you answers would enable you to destroy the Muses."

Kaeso shook his head. "I thought Galeo was my friend."

Petra put a hand on Kaeso's arm. "He was. But his...faith always came first."

"As for Cordus," Petra continued, "they assumed he could never be extracted from Roma, so the only way to keep the Terran strain from discovering his skills was to kill him. They never dreamed the boy *wanted* to leave. Now that he has, however, you are free to take him to the Saturnists."

"Just like that," Kaeso said. "We're free to go. Free to reveal the Menota archives. Umbra won't hunt us down?"

"They won't."

"And Ocella?" he asked. "The Muses will let her go, too?"

Petra exhaled. "Ocella is a problem. Not only did she destroy Umbra on Terra, but she also gave the Romans technology enabling them to block Umbra and Muse communications. That is why it has taken Umbra so long to strike back at the Roman siege fleet. The damage she did to Umbra will take years to overcome, if it can be. There are many Ancilia who would kill her on sight." Petra paused. "But no such order will come from the Muses. Just be sure she stays away from Libertus."

"It's too easy. Why are they just letting us go?"

Petra turned and regarded the stars beyond the porthole on the Cargo Two door ramp. "There are other strains in the universe. Strains a thousand-fold more vile and manipulative than the Terran strain. They lay beyond the way line termini you saw on Menota. Many started out as idealistic and protective of their hosts. They changed over time..." Petra turned back to Kaeso. "The Liberti strain wants you to keep Cordus because they do not trust themselves to do the right thing with him. They believe only humans will know what to do. Humans who do not trust *any* strains. In time, they hope this...concession will engender trust between the Liberti strain and humanity. And, in time, perhaps a path to coexistence."

Kaeso wasn't sure how to respond. How could he trust the Muses if they couldn't even trust themselves?

"Gaia and Nestor's Saturnists will need your help when you wake up," she said. "Libertus is still under siege. Umbra ships are gathering and will attempt to break the siege, but that will mean a long, brutal war."

Kaeso frowned. "All I can promise is that I will fight for Libertus."

Petra smiled. "That's all they ask."

He looked back at the Cargo Two door ramp. "Why do I keep wondering if this is some trick to get me to open those doors and kill everyone on this ship?"

"How does your calf feel?" Petra asked patiently.

For the first time in weeks, there was no pain. Kaeso pulled up his pant leg and removed the bandage. There was no wound, or even a scar.

The wound had been there this morning.

"*Cac*," he breathed.

She wrapped her arms around his neck and embraced him tightly. He smelled the perfume in her hair, and he held her tighter. This wasn't his Petra, but for this moment she was.

"It is time, Kaeso Aemilius Rulus," she said, pulling away.

Kaeso nodded slowly. "Will I remember you?"

"The important parts."

Her eyes went from the hold's door ramp and back to Kaeso. He took a deep breath and strode over to the ramp controls next to the door. He brought up the release controls and disabled the safety locks. His finger hovered over the opening button. He looked back at Petra.

"Thank you for bringing her back to me," he said.

She smiled, the dimples in her cheeks showing. *Gods, grant the memory of that smile is one of the "important parts."*

Kaeso pressed the open button.

A siren wailed and red lights flashed. The door ramp slowly opened and a loud rush of wind pulled Kaeso toward the expanding opening. He grabbed part of the grating on the ramp in a reflexive move to avoid getting sucked out into space. He caught a glimpse of Petra. She stood in the maelstrom, her prosecutorial robes unmoving. She watched him with an encouraging expression, as if giving him the will to let go. He didn't know if he could. His instincts screamed not to kill himself. He knew what would happen once he entered the vacuum of space. He'd seen "spaced" bodies when he was with the Liberti System Patrol and in Umbra. It was a terrible way to die.

This isn't real. Let go. I'm not going to die. Let go!

He let go. The gale wind was a soft hammer that pounded him through the cargo opening and into space. The cold was agonizing. He clawed at his throat, desperate to bring air into his lungs. His eyes bulged; his tongue flapped. The last thing he saw before his eyes froze was Petra watching him.

He fell through space, blind and praying to all the gods to end this agony and kill him now. But he only fell and fell and fell...

Chapter Fifty-Eight

Kaeso gasped. He strained against the straps holding him down. He could not think, could not conceive of where he was.

Hands held him down and voices cried out to him. He looked up and realized it was Lucia and Nestor trying to calm him.

"Nestor, is he...?"

"I'm not mad," Kaeso croaked, taking in deep breaths and settling back into his couch.

Nestor leaned over, held Kaeso's head, and studied his eyes. "I'd say he's still with us." He laughed. "Congratulations, Centuriae. You're the first person to make a way line jump awake and come out sane."

Kaeso checked his implant, but felt nothing from it—no low-level buzz from the interference around Libertus, no concealment protocols. It was as if he never had the implant.

"Centuriae," Nestor said, staring at him. "What was it like?"

Memories came back to Kaeso in flashes, mostly emotions. He remembered being worried, then afraid, then lonely.

Petra.

He took in a deep breath as the memories of her came back. He remembered her soft, warm skin beneath his fingertips. He remembered the scent of her body, her hair, her perfume. Her dimpled smile. It all came to him in images and feelings. The memories made him ache for her like he hadn't done since she died.

"Centuriae," Lucia said, putting a hand on his arm. "Are you all right?"

Kaeso blinked several times, realized tears were running down his face. He wiped them away with his sleeve.

"I'm fine," he said. Then he looked to Nestor. "I'll tell you about it another time." He glanced out the command window. The ship orbited a gas giant with swirling red, pink, and orange clouds. "Where are we?"

"If Gaia's coordinates are correct," Lucia said, "this is the Saturnist colony. The moon with their base is on the other side of the planet."

Kaeso nodded. "Ocella?"

Nestor shook his head. "We just woke up. My console says everyone's awake, but I haven't had a chance to—"

Kaeso unlatched his straps and jumped from the command couch. He hurried down the ladder to the crew quarters, and then to Ocella's bunk. Her eyes were open and she stared at the ceiling. When Kaeso entered, she looked at him, tears brimming.

"They're gone," she said.

Kaeso watched her a moment, then asked, "What was the name of the stray dog you and Petra adopted when you were children?"

Ocella regarded him blankly, and then understanding entered her eyes. She smiled and said, "His name was Kaeso. And he wasn't a dog. He was a cat. An orange tom cat who had chased away two dogs trying to steal his mouse on our olive plantation outside Avita."

Kaeso smiled, then unbuckled Ocella's restraints.

"Welcome back," he said.

Chapter Fifty-Nine

Lepidus stared at himself in the full-length mirror. His barber had done a fine job evening out his hair and scraping away two weeks of facial stubble. The barber had also scrubbed and trimmed his finger and toe nails, making them gleam. Lepidus checked the folds on his white toga, made sure they wrapped securely around his shoulders and left arm in the traditional fashion of Roman men for over a thousand years. Even his sandals were made of aged leather, soft as silk but durable as Praetorian combat uniforms.

It felt good to look like a nobleman again.

Lepidus strode through the atrium in the center of his quiet house. He had allowed his slaves to join the Ascension revelry. Silus had already left, so Lepidus could not say good-bye. The boy would be sitting with his friends in the Coliseum Magnus box seats Lepidus had promised to use with him. But Lepidus would be in the Consular suite, far across the arena from his son.

Lepidus paused at the entryway. He stared at the wax bust of his dead wife several moments, and then he walked out the front door.

He entered the courtyard where the Consular flyer awaited him. The golem pilot stepped forward and opened the passenger side door for Lepidus. He climbed in without a word to the pilot and secured himself in the plush seat. Chilled wine awaited him in an ice bin next to his seat, but he ignored it. The pilot started the flyer and it rose. They floated above his Ostia neighborhood, the blue waters of the Mediterranean gleaming under the sun, then the flyer shot off to the east.

Roma bustled at all times, but today it was particularly crowded. Today was the millennial anniversary of the Antonii Ascension, the day Marcus Antonius liberated Roma and became Consul of the Republic. People from all over Terra—indeed, all human space—streamed into Roma to take part in the celebrations and games. On the ground, the roads were clogged with cars, and the railways jammed with backed-up trains. The skies buzzed with hundreds of flyers, shuttles, and various other air traffic. As Lepidus's flyer approached the Seven Hills, crowds materialized in the streets as each neighborhood seemed to hold its own parties and games.

The death of the Consular Heir and an ongoing war with Libertus had not dampened the celebratory spirits of the Roman people. The Consul and the Collegia Pontificis had issued a Missive saying the gods had raised Cordus to godhood upon his martyr's death by Liberti agents. The Consular Family proudly unveiled a bronze statue of Cordus in the center of the Capitoline just outside the Temple of Jupiter Optimus Maximus. The dead Consular Heir stood at the right hand of a similar statue of Marcus Antonius. It was an amazing work considering Cordus had ascended to Elysium only two weeks before.

Lepidus wondered what really happened to Cordus.

The flyer glided over the Tiber River to the secure lot near the Coliseum Magnus just outside the Forum Borum. Other flyers were landing or had landed, each containing guests of the Consular Family that would sit with them during the Ascension games. Senators, pontiffs, and wealthy equestrians and their families filed up the marble stairs to the Consular terrace. Lepidus joined the line, exchanging arm clasps and pleasantries with those he knew, none knowing exactly what role he played in the hunt for Cordus. He was a simple Praetorian whom the ignorant politicians and noblemen assumed was important to the Consul, but none knew why. So to be safe, they treated him as if he had been given a triumph.

Lepidus approached a security station where the line of Consular guests strolled through a sensor arch. Even the Consul's most trusted friends needed to be swept for weapons. Lepidus walked through when it was his turn, exchanging nods with the Praetorians manning the station. The younger Praetorians saluted him with a fist over their chests. Lepidus returned the salutes. Over the last few days, he had reviewed the security the Praetorians set up on the terrace—showing them where to sweep for weapons or listening devices, pointing out possible sniper positions in the Coliseum Magnus, setting up checkpoints throughout the Coliseum. The commanders appreciated his advice. While Lepidus never received public recognition, he knew his service to the Republic was at least respected among the Praetorian Guard.

Lepidus emerged from the security station and onto the terrace overlooking the Coliseum Magnus. The open terrace had raised rows of plush chairs for the Consul, pontiffs, and various patricians to view the games below. The Coliseum Magnus itself was spectacular. It held up to 200,000 spectators in a bowl-shaped arena that was the largest in the entire Republic. Lepidus sat down in his assigned seat and stared at the throngs below. Caretakers finished spraying water on the arena's dirt field to give it better footing for the gladiators. The drums and trumpets of martial music filled the arena from hidden speakers. The sky was clear and blue, and the air was warm, but not hot. A comfortable breeze rolled across the terrace.

Just before noon, the seven members of the Collegia Pontificis—Vibius Laelius had died during the battle of Menota—and their families took their seats on the raised podium behind the high-backed chairs reserved for the Consular Family.

At the noon hour, a crier approached the back of the terrace and bellowed to the assembled guests, "Pontiffs, Senators, Citizens, rise for Pontifex Maximus Decimus Atius Avitus!" His amplified voice echoed throughout the Coliseum Magnus.

The guests on the terrace stopped talking, stood, and turned around, as did the throngs below. Lepidus watched the entryway as the Pontifex Maximus of the Roman Republic entered the terrace, along with his wife and three sons. The Pontifex wore the blue robes with gold trim of his office, and his wife was beautifully dressed in a traditional white gown with her long black hair pinned up and braided. The Pontifex's sons ranged in age from seventeen to five years old, all well-dressed in embroidered togas and groomed as befitting young men of their station. The Pontifex strode onto the terrace, his chin held high. When he noticed Lepidus, he gave him a slight nod, his eyes softening. Lepidus returned the nod. The Pontifex and his family sat with the other Collegia Pontiffs behind the Consular Family's seats.

The crier bellowed again, "Pontiffs, Senators, Citizens, raise your voices for Marcus Antonius Publius, Consul of the Roman Republic, the Light of Humanity, and the Guardian of Divine Wisdom."

The terrace guests and the crowds below erupted in cheers as the Consul, his wife, and their four remaining children appeared at the entryway. Six Praetorian Guardsmen, all wearing blood-red cloaks under gold breastplates embossed with a scorpion insignia, escorted the Consular Family. The entire Family had the same preternatural air, and Lepidus had the urge to scream his loyalty and love with the noble guests and the throngs of citizens in the Coliseum Magnus below. The Family glided down the center of the terrace and took their seats in the high-backed chairs on the raised podium in the center. The nobles and the crowds continued cheering until the Consul raised his hands. The terrace guests and the citizens below all bowed their heads to receive the Consul's blessing.

"Citizens and honored guests, I bless you in the name of all the Pantheon Gods, and I bless these games..."

Lepidus bowed his head like everyone else. But while the others took in the blessing with adoration, Lepidus reached under his seat and retrieved the two items he'd stored there during his security sweep yesterday. He hid the items in the folds of his white toga.

Once the Consul finished blessing the attendants, he declared the games open. A deafening cheer arose from the crowd as the first round of gladiator golems marched onto the arena. They used the same formations as Marcus Antonius's legions when he liberated Roma from the pretender Octavian. On the other side of the arena, Octavian's forces arranged themselves before a makeshift wall that symbolized Roma's walls a thousand years ago.

Antonius's "legions" wielded the muskets they used to roll through Italia and then Roma. They lined up in their formations, the first line dropping to one knee and firing. The front line of Octavian's legions went down in sprays of blood as the musket balls took out heads, entered chests, and shattered arm and leg bones. Musket balls pinged off the bulletproof shields protecting spectators behind Octavian's forces.

The wounded golems in Octavian's legions screamed, while the unhurt golems decided to charge the line of Antonius's musket legions rather than wait for a musket ball to find them. And like a thousand years ago, the legions of Antonius mowed them down.

As the games proceeded below, Lepidus joined the line of nobles who filed past the Consul's seat. As tradition allowed, the Consul granted his guests a few brief moments to give them his personal blessings and gods-granted wisdom. At least a hundred guests filled the terrace, the most powerful senators, pontiffs, and wealthy equestrians in the Republic. They had many blessings for which to ask.

By the time it was Lepidus's turn, the battle for Roma had ended, and the arena caretakers were cleaning up the golem bodies and readying the field for the old-fashioned chariot races. Lepidus stepped up to the podium and stood before the Consul.

He dropped to one knee. "My lord Consul."

"Rise, Quintus Atius Lepidus," the Consul said. "You are a friend of Roma and a loyal servant of the gods."

"Thank you, my lord," Lepidus said, standing. "My only desire is to serve the gods and the Republic."

"And what blessing or wisdom do you seek from your Consul?" the Consul asked, finishing the ritualistic words.

Lepidus faced both the Consul and the Pontifex Maximus directly behind him. Both men gazed at the chariot races in the arena below, as did their families.

"I have but one question, my lord. May I see the Missive that ordered decimation after the Battle of Caan?"

The Consul's eyes darted to Lepidus. "All Missives of the Gods can be seen in the Temple of Jupiter Optimus Maximus."

"I do not wish to view a copy of the text, my lord. I wish to view the actual Missive written by the fingers of the gods."

Lepidus saw wariness in the Consul's eyes. He felt an instant desire to worship the Consul, to bow low and beg for the Consul's pardon. Only two weeks ago he would have welcomed those feelings as confirmation of the gods instilling the desire to serve the Consul, their Holy Vessel. But he fought the feelings, for they clouded his mind and made him shrink back from doing what he came here to do.

"How would viewing a Missive of the Gods enhance your ability to serve?" the Consul asked.

Lepidus glanced at his brother, who now frowned and looked from the Consul to Lepidus. *The* Pontifex Maximus. *I keep forgetting he is not my brother.*

"It would give me peace to view the divine order that told me to kill a tenth of my soldiers...including my wife."

The Consul's eyes narrowed. "No one sees a Missive of the Gods besides myself and the Collegia Pontificis. That is the law. Your request is denied." Then the Consul leaned forward. "It seems to me that peace is not what you need, Quintus Atius. It seems to me you need faith."

Lepidus smiled. "Consul, you have no idea what I need."

"Brother," the Pontifex Maximus growled, "you are treading close to blasphemy."

Lepidus turned to him. "I am not your brother, *Pontifex*."

Lepidus was aware the petitioners and sycophants behind him had grown quiet. He also noticed the Praetorians near the Consul stiffen and watch him with confusion. Lepidus had trained many of the Consul's own bodyguards, so they were likely conflicted between their duty to the Consul and their loyalty to him. Lepidus had counted on that.

He drew the pistol that he'd secured beneath his seat and fired point-blank shots into three of the Guards. They fell before they could reach their weapons. The fourth Guard drew his pistol, but Lepidus dropped him with a shot to the heart. The Guard—a promising young man named Fidelias—stared at Lepidus in shock and anger before the life drained from his eyes.

Just as Lepidus hoped, the guests on the terrace panicked. As one, they rose up and fled toward the exits, many screaming and trampling others. Several Guards from outside the terrace tried making their way through the hysterical crowds, but the stampede blocked them.

Lepidus aimed at the Consul, who stared at him with amusement. The Pontifex Maximus looked disappointed. The families of both men, and the seven Pontiffs behind them, all Vessels, regarded Lepidus with detached interest.

"What do you hope to accomplish with this childish display, Quintus Atius?" the Consul asked.

"I told you, Consul. I want to know it was the gods that ordered me to kill my wife after the Battle of Caan."

"Who else would give such an order?"

Lepidus shrugged. "The virus in your brain perhaps?"

The Consul arched an eyebrow, while the Pontifex Maximus clenched his teeth.

"Where did you get such a—?" Then the Consul nodded. "My son. He was a very disturbed boy and had strange notions of aliens living in his brain, whispering to him stories that the Collegia and I were also infected. That *is* what he told you, correct?"

Lepidus eyed the exits, which were still packed with panicked patricians. The Praetorians were almost through and would soon have a clear shot.

"Fine," the Consul said. "Before you die, you may know the gods are not real. They never were. But you and all of Roma have worshiped beings far greater than mythical gods. Beings that are just as immortal and just as capable of the wondrous miracles that legends attribute to the divine. These beings have infinite wisdom, and it was from their wisdom that came the order to punish your legions after the Battle of Caan. Did it not work? Did we not inspire our host to take Kaldeth and bring it back to the Roman fold?"

"Brother," the Pontifex said. "Make your peace with this knowledge and put down your weapon. You are a Hero of Roma. Evocatus of the Praetorian Guard, one of four that has existed in the Guard's entire history. Do not die a blasphemous traitor. Think of what such an end will do to your son. He will be stripped of his titles and assets. He will be exiled at best. At worst, he will be interrogated..."

The urge to prostrate himself and beg forgiveness enflamed every nerve in Lepidus's body. He had to concentrate just to continue standing.

"I did not want this to be true," Lepidus grunted.

Kneel before your gods!

No!

The Consul leaned forward, his deep blue eyes trying to bring out the worship Lepidus once gave him. He spoke in a whisper, barely audible above the screams now coming from the crowds below. "If you shoot me, this body may die, but *we* will live until another body is found for us."

Worship them!

No!

Sweat streamed down Lepidus's face. At the exits, the Praetorians were getting closer.

They deserve your devotion, your love—

NO! NOT MY LOVE! THEY TOOK MY ONLY LOVE!

He lowered his pistol.

"Tell me," Lepidus gasped, "only you, your family, and the Collegia know these beings?"

A smile curled the Consul's mouth. "Only the powerful are so worthy."

Lepidus nodded. "You're all here, then."

He dropped his pistol and then took from his toga the other item he had hidden beneath his seat. The Consul's smile vanished.

Yes. He knows an antimatter grenade when he sees it. He knows it will vaporize everything within fifty feet.

Lepidus looked from the Consul to the Pontifex, both men showing fear for the first time. The Pontiffs jumped from their seats and tried to flee, as did their families. As did the children of the Consul and the Pontifex Maximus.

"Triaria," Lepidus whispered.

The Praetorians broke through the crowd and raise their pulse rifles.

Too late.

Lepidus activated the grenade and let the fire of the gods purge him of his sins.

Chapter Sixty

Claudia stood on a stage in an amphitheater with over 15,000 people, singing a hit song she recorded five years ago. It was about rising from the ashes, maintaining hope when all seemed lost, and trusting the gods and one's family to overcome trying times. With the sudden end of the Roman siege of Libertus, she thought it an appropriate choice to finish her show.

When she sang, the world melted away until all she could feel were the notes rising from her chest, passing her throat, and then beyond her lips in a way she always thought miraculous. She knew her voice was a gift from the gods. This was not vanity. Her voice had given her so many things in life, and she thanked the gods every day for blessing her with a gift that brought her such joy and prosperity.

As always when she finished a song, she felt as if she were leaving a vision of Elysium. She blinked at the erupting applause and remembered where she was. She bowed to the audience, her smile genuine and grateful. While she did not sing for the applause, she was pleased when she did well enough to earn her audience's praise. It meant she had given them a glimpse of the place she dwelled while she sang.

She exited the stage to the continued cheering. Backstage, a crowd of well-wishers complimented her. She exchanged pleasantries with friends, colleagues, and producers, then saw Abram standing behind them. He wore a proud grin as he clapped, a bouquet of sky blue flowers in the crook of his arms. She excused herself from the well-wishers and made her way to Abram. As always after a show, he handed her the bouquet with a bow of his head.

"My lady."

"Sky roses," Claudia said. "How did you know they're my favorite?"

Abram shrugged. "You might have mentioned it. Once or twice."

She laughed, then set the flowers down on a nearby table and hugged her husband. He returned the embrace and then said into her ear, "You were beautiful tonight. It was your best performance."

"You say that after every show."

"I know." He glanced at the stage behind her. "You hit a nerve. They're still cheering."

Claudia nodded, half-turning to the lit stage past the curtains. "It's been a hard month."

The Roman fleet besieging Libertus abruptly left three days after the deaths of the Roman Consul and the entire Collegia Pontificis in a mysterious explosion. There was already talk of the Kaldethians rebelling again, along with several other worlds, not to mention native populations on Terra itself. Like any Liberti, Claudia found herself conflicted. She hated the Romans for what they did to Agricola and Dives, along with the horrible fear to which they had subjected her world. But she empathized with the average Roman who would suffer greatly before stability returned.

"Where's Pullus?" she asked.

Their three-year-old son loved watching his mother's performances, but refused to go backstage with Abram due to all the frenetic activity.

"He's with my mother in the box," Abram said. "Probably still clapping."

Claudia smiled, thinking of her little boy. When she took the stage, she had glanced up at the family box above the main theater. She could not see much due to the stage lights shining in her eyes, but she knew Pullus was there and could feel his love.

Claudia was about to ask Abram to bring Pullus to her dressing room when she noticed a tall man staring at her from the stairwell exit. He wore the dark green dress uniform of the Liberti System Patrol; a centuriae if she remembered the rank stripes correctly. When he captured her gaze, he took off his ceremonial *pileus* and walked toward her. His head was clean-shaved, which made it difficult to tell his age, but judging by the lines on his face, Claudia guessed him to be in his upper forties. A thin scar ran across his forehead above deep-set, light blue eyes.

"Lady Claudia Abiff?" the man said.

Abram turned and regarded the man curiously.

Claudia nodded to the man. "Yes?" He seemed familiar, especially his eyes, though she could not remember where she may have met him.

The man paused, then said, "My name is Kaeso Aemilius. I served with your father in the LSP over ten years ago. I was with him the day he died."

"My father," Claudia repeated. She took a sudden breath, and Abram put an arm around her shoulders. She leaned into him. She thought of her parents now and then, especially when with Abram's family. How could she not be around her husband's parents without remembering the tragic deaths of hers?

"My apologies, Lady Abiff," the man said hurriedly. "I did not wish to upset you. I should go." Aemilius blinked and turned around.

"Wait," Claudia said, hurrying to catch up. Aemilius stopped. His eyes held inexplicable fear, and he would not meet her gaze.

"You knew my father," Claudia said.

Aemilius nodded once, his jaw clenching and unclenching.

"What did you want to tell me, Centuriae?"

He finally looked at her. "He made me promise to tell you some things. He wanted you to know he was sorry. He knew he'd been...distracted after your mother's murder, that he had not given you the support you needed. He knew you suffered just as he did, yet he didn't have the strength to get past his own suffering to comfort you. He felt like a failure at the end. But he made me promise that I would find you and tell you that he loved you more than he could ever convey in words or deeds."

Claudia realized tears were streaming down her cheeks when she tasted their saltiness on her lips. Abram held her tighter as she wiped the tears with her sleeves.

The last day she'd spoken to her father before he died in a raid on the Sodalicium was, in many ways, the worst day of her life. Even worse than the day her mother was killed. At least she had told her mother she loved her that morning. Claudia's final moments with her father were spent in a screaming argument over something as ridiculous as the clothes she wanted to wear to a friend's birthday party. The last words she'd spoken to her father were *I hate you* before she stormed out of the house. She never forgave herself for those words, and that day had been an open wound on her soul ever since. She felt she had somehow cursed her father; that she was the reason he died. It took her many years to find peace, to have faith that both her parents had found joy in the light of the gods in Elysium.

"I apologize for upsetting you, Lady Abiff. I shouldn't have—"

"If you apologize one more time, Centuriae, I *will* get upset," Claudia said. She put a hand on his arm. "I'm glad you told me these things. They do bring me peace."

Those familiar eyes glistened. "I regret I was unable to come sooner. The life of an LSP officer is rather busy."

"I understand," Claudia said.

There was a pause in the conversation, and Aemilius glanced at Abram.

Claudia gasped. "Where are my manners? This is my husband, Abram Abiff."

Abram held out his hand to the officer, and Aemilius clasped it with a smile. "I'm very happy to meet you, sir."

Abram nodded. "Thank you for telling Claudia about her father."

Aemilius looked from Abram to Claudia with a satisfied smile, as if he had just finished an LSP mission he had feared for a long time. He seemed to stand straighter, and there were fewer lines on his forehead.

He put his *pileus* back on. "I must be going."

"Would you..." Claudia stammered. "Would you like to come with us? My family and I always have dinner after my shows."

Intense longing crossed Aemilius's face, his mouth opened as if to say something, but then he closed it again.

Then he said, "Thank you, Lady Abiff, but I need to catch a shuttle. My departure orders are strict."

"Perhaps another time," Claudia said.

"Perhaps." Aemilius said it in a way that felt to Claudia she would never see him again. It saddened her, but she didn't know how else to convince this mysterious man to tell her everything he knew about her father.

Aemilius turned toward the exit, stopped and then said, "You sing beautifully. He would have been proud."

Claudia smiled as she wiped away more brimming tears.

Aemilius strode out the softly lit theater exit.

Abram gave her a squeeze. "Are you all right?"

She nodded, staring after Aemilius. "This may sound awful, but it comforts me to know he bore the same guilt I had. It means he forgave me for what I said. It means he never stopped loving me."

"You were his daughter. Of course he never stopped loving you."

"I know that," Claudia said. "Now. But not before I had a child of my own. Before Pullus I thought it *was* possible for parents to stop loving their children."

"Let's go see our boy." Abram guided her toward the elevators near the exit.

When they reached the observation box, Claudia heard her son's laughter from the hall. She entered the box to the standing applause of Abram's family. Her family. Pullus ran up to her and threw his arms around her legs. She stooped to one knee and hugged him just as tight.

He pulled away and said, "What's for dinner?"

She laughed, though he wore no smile, and his light blue eyes were entirely serious—

His light blue eyes.

Aemilius's light blue eyes, his tone of voice, the way he stood...

Gods.

Kaeso saw the tension on Ocella's face through the window of the ground car in which she waited for him, and then relief when she noticed him jogging toward the car. He opened the passenger side door and was barely in the seat when Ocella pulled into traffic on the street in front of the amphitheater.

"In a hurry?" Kaeso asked.

"This was a bad idea. They know who Claudia is. They know you might try to contact her. And that old uniform won't fool them." She focused on the road, navigating through the post-show traffic. Throngs of people spilled out of the amphitheater and mingled with the ground cars leaving the theater's parking areas.

"So you've said. Many times."

"I'll keep saying it until we leave Libertus."

"Relax," Kaeso said. "We have a deal, remember?"

Ocella snorted. "I'm sorry if I don't trust some memory of Petra who claims to be speaking for the Muses. You were awake during a way line jump."

"In other words, I'm mad." He turned to her and smiled until she rolled her eyes.

"I'm not saying you're mad. Even if it were the Liberti Muses talking through Petra, I still wouldn't trust their promises as far as I can— Gods, how many people were at this concert?" She lay on the car's horn. People in front of the car returned annoyed glares, yet they moved out of the way.

"Claudia's popular," Kaeso said, still smiling.

"And you need to stop that. It scares me."

"Stop what?"

"Smiling. You've barely stopped since we escaped Menota."

"Why would my smiling scare you?"

"Because you never did it in your pre-Umbra days and it makes me wonder if that way line jump *did* scramble your brains."

Kaeso chuckled. "You'd be surprised how easy life is when you stop trying to be someone you're not, and accept who you are. You should try it sometime."

Ocella grunted, then laid on her horn again.

She finally calmed down once they escaped the theater and entered the expressway. After several minutes of silence, Ocella asked, "What was she like?"

Kaeso considered his words. *How can I explain how beautiful, kind, talented, and wise my daughter has become? How proud I am? How much it broke my heart to turn down her dinner offer, a chance to spend just a few more hours with Claudia and her family?*

Kaeso stared at the amphitheater in the car's side mirrors as it receded into the background. "I didn't want to leave," he said.

Ocella put a hand on his leg, and Kaeso put his hand on top of hers.

"You can always tell her the truth," Ocella said. "If you believe your vision of Petra, then you're no longer bound by the concealment protocols. Umbra has no hold on you."

Kaeso shook his head. "She's made peace with my 'death.' I won't disrupt that. Besides, our fight with the Muses has only started. I don't want to put her through my death again."

"Finally, the pessimistic man I once knew."

A half hour later they arrived at the temporary ship yards where starships capable of atmospheric travel landed while the Liberti Way Station was repaired. The Way Station was not completely destroyed during the Roman attack, but large chunks of it were. It would take years before the Way Station was rebuilt to its former glory. In the meantime, some atmo starships were allowed to land outside Avita, the badly needed commerce taxing the planetary traffic control systems to their breaking point.

Ocella drove the car to the rental lot, turned it in, and both she and Kaeso jumped on a shuttle bus that drove them to *Caduceus*.

Other starship crews rode the bus, and it stopped many times to deposit everyone at their parked ships. *Caduceus* sat near the end of the lot.

It's Vacuna *now*, Kaeso reminded himself. He chose to keep the name the Praetorian had given the ship because he thought it fitting that a ship with a new mission have a new name.

That and he didn't want to risk frying his expensive com systems by trying to change the beacon again. His crew may have their freedom, but they still had money problems. Even the small grant Gaia Julius gave them was only enough to make repairs on the ship and pay for the Avita parking fee.

Kaeso and Ocella strode up the open Cargo One ramp and into *Vacuna*. Inside, Dariya and Daryush were examining a rack of way line plasma canisters. Dariya's eyes flitted to Kaeso and then back to the canisters and the tabulari pad she held.

"Two more minutes, and we were going to leave without you," she said.

"'Welcome back, Centuriae.' 'Glad you weren't captured, Centuriae.'"

She grunted and returned to the canisters. Daryush grinned from behind her. Kaeso was happy to see her strength—and attitude—returning to normal. Even Daryush looked healthier and content. The large Persian was no longer hollow-eyed with worry, and he stood straighter with his sister around.

With the knowledge of Cordus's Muses—and the boy's own blood—Gaia's Saturnist medicus team created an antidote that helped Dariya's body defeat the Cariosus. However, the antidote itself was not enough. It only weakened the Cariosus. To eradicate it, Dariya had to endure a way line jump while awake, just like Ocella. She claimed she didn't remember much about the jump, but Kaeso saw it had changed her, just as it had changed him. She was calmer now, less abrasive with the rest of the crew, especially Lucia. Kaeso believed it was a change for the better, but he knew it bothered Lucia. She missed sparring with Dariya.

Blaesus strode into Cargo One as Kaeso closed the ramp door. "Centuriae, your daughter was breathtaking! I watched her concert on the bands. She has a voice that would make Apollo weep. How she came from your loins, I shall never know."

"You've never heard me sing," Kaeso said. "I could be very good."

"Centuriae, you have many talents, but I doubt singing is one of them."

"Get enough wine in me, and I'll prove you wrong."

"Deal! We shall test your voice in the most expensive tavern at the next way station we dock!" Blaesus clapped Kaeso on the back, then left Cargo One.

Kaeso and Ocella entered the corridor and then climbed the ladder up to the command deck. Lucia sat in the pilot's couch making pre-flight checks on her tabulari. She nodded to Kaeso.

"Centuriae," she said, then returned to her checklist.

Things had been awkward between them since he came back from the way line jump. She only spoke to him when she had to, and even those times involved the ship or crew. They left many things unsaid just before the jump. It seemed Lucia wanted to forget those things, but her silence told him she couldn't. Kaeso knew he'd have to face this sooner rather than later.

Kaeso strapped himself into the command couch, while Ocella took Nestor's place in the delta couch. Nestor was with a Saturnist team searching the Menota system for the way line termini Kaeso saw in the Pomona vaults. So far they had not found any, but they were there. He could still see the way line map in his mind. If what Petra said was true, they had to be found. Humanity could ill afford a surprise Muse invasion from way lines they never knew existed.

Especially now that humanity was in a struggle for survival against itself. Roma was in chaos, with dozens of subject worlds rebelling. Civil war was breaking out amongst the Legions themselves in the fight over succession. The Zhonguo had annexed several Roman systems and made threatening moves toward some of the Lost Worlds. Libertus would take years to rebuild after the siege and was in no shape to resist attacks on its Lost World allies. Humanity had not been this fractured since the days of Marcus Antonius Primus.

"Avita flight control has cleared us for take off," Lucia announced.

"Ion engines online," Dariya said over the com. "Wayline engines spooled and ready once we reach orbit."

From the delta couch behind Kaeso, Ocella said, "Delta systems ready for way line jump."

Kaeso checked his delta couch readouts and saw that his crew was safely fastened in. "Take us up, Lucia."

Caduceus rose above the ships in the Avita yards, hovered two hundred feet above the ground a few moments to wait for another freighter to launch, then shot toward the upper atmosphere. Kaeso watched the rear cameras on his tabulari. The lights of Avita grew smaller until they became a tiny point on the horseshoe continent of Taura.

He was still watching Avita when he engaged delta sleep.

Read MUSES OF TERRA, book two in the Codex Antonius series.

Afterword

Thanks for giving *Muses of Roma* a read. If you enjoyed it and have the time, please leave a review, I'd appreciate it.

If you're ready for more adventures in the Codex Antonius universe, continue with the next novel, *Muses of Terra*.

Check my website (https://robsteinerauthor.com) for a full list of my novels.

If you'd like a quick note when I release something new, please sign up for my newsletter on my website. For social media fans, you can find me on Twitter, Facebook, Goodreads, and BookBub.

Acknowledgments

Thanks to Chris Hooker for setting me straight on my Latin and space battle physics. Time for another Ruth's Chris steak, my friend.

Thanks to my editor, David Drazul (dedzone.net), whose keen eyes catch the typos that I and numerous others missed. And a special thanks for putting up with my ellipses....

Thanks to my design team at 100covers.com for the fantastic cover.

And as always, thank you Sarah and Amelia. I'm a lucky man to be able to return home from my dreamed-up worlds to a family that's a dream-come-true.

Printed in Great Britain
by Amazon